THE CRIMSON TAPESTRY

1
TWILIGHT OF THE GODS

THE CRIMSON TAPESTRY

MICHAEL R. JOENS

F
JOE

MOODY PRESS
CHICAGO

ISBN: 0-8024-1693-4

1 3 5 7 9 10 8 6 4 2

Printed in the United States of America

To my beloved wife, Cathleen,
who patiently endured

CONTENTS

ACKNOWLEDGMENTS

Many thanks to those who contributed their valuable time and insight to the making of this book, among whom are the following:

To Cathleen again, my faithful sounding board and most honest critic and supporter. And to Brandon, Shannon, and Stephanie, our children; as always my three orbiting lights of inspiration.

To my brother Patrick, whose knowledge and love for the hunt and longbow was a source of inspiration for the character Terryll.

To my partner in crime Ken Johnson, for giving me his keen editorial insight, whether he wanted to give it or not.

To my literary agent, Ron Haynes, for believing in me and opening the door. Thank you, Ron.

And thanks to Jim Bell and to the many kind folks at Moody Press for letting me in; and to Ella Lindvall, my editor, for not kicking me out.

And finally, to the Lord Jesus Christ, without whom life is so much chasing after the wind.

GRAMPIANS

THE MAP
of
BRITAIN
CIRCA A.D. 450

River Tweed

River Nith

River Annon

IRELAND

Loch na Huric

Caer Luhl

Bowness

Whitley Castle

Solway Firth

KILWYNEDEN

River Eden

River Cree

BRIGANTES

PARISI

NORTH SEA

IRISH SEA

Pennine Chain

River Ouse

Cambrians

CORITANI

Glenrych

River Trent

Badonsward

River Severn

River Avon

Cotswolds

TRINOVANTES

Aquaesulis

Stonehenge

Sarum

River Thames

Londinium

DUMNONI

CANTII

THE CHANNEL

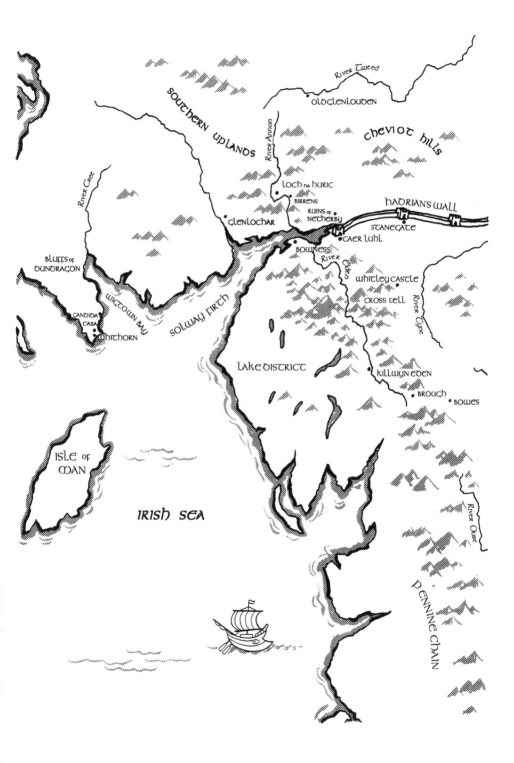

PART ONE
THE BEGGAR BOY

1
A BEGGAR NAMED WORM

The lone howl of a wolf, or something like a wolf, sounded over the verdant sward of foothills, and then there was quiet. An eerie, dead kind of quiet. A quiet such as might attend a neglected plot of gravestones.

Moments later they came. Silhouetted in a spectrum of grays and blacks against a pewter sky, the horsemen filed long out of the fortress of Badonsward, riding soundlessly into the dank and gloomy predawn mists that swirled upon the moors of the lowlands. Their serpentine profile, like that of a great reptile slowly waking from its watery slumber, came undulating and flexing sullenly from some wretched lair, and the lights filtering through the mist glinted dully off battle accoutrements and violent eyes.

The line of riders paused, grunted throatily, then broke off into smaller files, each setting its course on one of several points of the northern landscape, each casting an ominous pall of dread upon the distant and gray horizons of the Pennine Chain, a mountain range extending the length of the island, known as "the backbone of Britain."

The lead file took the westernmost route, following the meandering path of the great River Trent toward its headwaters in the mountains through towering marsh grasses, peat moss, and sedges, taking them past the Celtic village of Glenryth, last of the British civitates to surrender its arms to the brutal dominion of the Saxon conquerors.

The howl of another wolf pierced the foggy veil over Glenryth, finding the inner ear of the slumbering beggar boy. His eyes opened with a start.

Immediately the diffused light of daybreak flooded him with the reality and comfort that it had been but a dream. The boy breathed a sigh of relief. He lay on his mat for several moments, blinking the sleep from his eyes. Staring up into a vault of wet haze, he searched the gray shapes around him for a point to focus his eyes.

And then he heard it again. The wolf. Its baleful cry carried over the village, echoing up and down the streets and alleys, finding his quickened heart, pounding. There was a sinister, almost malefic quality to the voice that sent a shudder up the boy's spine. It was no dream. But his mind quickly reasoned with him: It is a wolf—it is only a wolf. And he shrugged it off.

The boy crawled out from under an old tarp and climbed groggily to his feet. It had rained during the night, so his head was soaked, his demeanor noticeably soured. His eyes suddenly jerked open, and he began shaking his leg furiously, muttering something to no one apparent. A roach fell free from his trousers and scurried across the washed stones before the boy could flatten it.

He scowled at the thing, then let out a loud yawn as he massaged his fingers across his wet scalp, raking the long matted thatch of flaxen hair from his face. Not that he was concerned about his appearance necessarily—it just made his world easier to see, bleak though it lay beneath this inordinately dismal spring morning. He reached his arms skyward through another yawn, arching his back the while. Then grabbing two handfuls of air, he stretched the soreness from his muscles, the attendant kinks up his spine, and saluted his routine with a short, flatulent reveille, signaling the start of another day.

The boy grunted, ostensibly at the world, as he scratched his belly. He was tall for his age, large-boned and lean-muscled, and his wide, deep-set hazel eyes looked out onto his world with the wariness of a wild animal.

Taking a survey of the morning, he looked up and down the familiar alley—his home—an uneven strip of cobblestones that separated a broken array of shops and dwellings on either side, with a cement trough winding through its middle for drainage and sewage. Not much had changed since yesterday. Nothing actually; the fog gave it a different cast though. But he had seen it before. It was quiet. Hushed. The village still lay sleeping beneath the misty quilt, save for the intermittent caw of a jay and the muffled dialogue between two distant dogs.

The boy slowly shogged his way along the backside of buildings— some built of stone, some of wattle and daub—driven by survival's gnaw in his stomach, not desire. Today, he decided, he would try his luck on the north end for food. Yesterday's take on the south side had been miserly.

Soon the beggar was rooting through the decaying stench of several refuse heaps, barefoot and covered with a filth that stained beneath the skin to the marrow of soul, hoping to find enough scraps of edibles to boast a meal. But he found nothing. Undaunted, he turned his attention to another pile. Again, nothing. Not even a pea. Some birds had gotten there ahead of him and made off with the best offerings. A bunch of them were perched on a rock pile twenty yards away, tearing something apart. He picked up a stone and winged it at them, but they just sneered. He hated the birds.

Somewhere a man yelled something, followed by a woman's crying. Or was it a child? No matter. The boy looked up anyway, more out of reflex than of any concern, but things quieted down.

Then without warning he was showered with a bucketful of swill, tossed from a second-story window. His clothes, mere rags he had scrounged or stolen that did little to comfort his body, were now drenched with refuse.

The day was shaping up poorly.

Just like yesterday.

And the day before.

The thick mantle of fog finally began to lift, draping around dark hills like shawls of cottony white, letting in shafts of sunlight that poured jealously over the tiny village and warmed its wet and puddled streets. Mist crept over the cobblestones and snaked up alleys. Cats hunted rodents in the haze.

And now the town bustled with a throng of people, mostly middle-aged, elderly, and small children, who were each attending to the miserable chores of the day, bending abjectly to the Curse.

A stoop-shouldered woman in her mid-to-late thirties, with a line of children in tow, stopped for a moment on her way to buy some bread and lifted her face to bathe in the rejuvenating rays of the sun. But her respite was interrupted by a cry of alarm.

"Stop him! Somebody stop that little thief!" wheezed a fat man, as he panted out of his shop into the busy market street. "That worthless beggar stole a loaf of my bread!"

"Catch me if you can, old fool!" challenged the youth, as he zigzagged through the swarm of startled villagers. The boy had played this game many times before, however, and with each play he varied his tactics. Today he bumped into some and jostled the baskets of others until he created an initial disturbance. Then he cried out alarming tales, fomenting bedlam in the growing whorl of confusion.

"Herds of wild boars stampeding on the east side of the village!" he cried out to some. "Picts! Picts! Dozens of 'em!—attacking women and children on the north side!" he called out to others.

The dizzy crowd's confusion fast became a panicked rout.

Mothers, terrified at the thought of savage Picts, ran screaming after their children, who had vanished in gleeful pursuit of imagined wild pigs. The men gathered into nervous little groups and wondered out loud what to do about the matter. Two or three of them had military training and began to argue among themselves who should take the position of leadership to subdue the disorder. But when no one could agree, insults were exchanged, then shoves, followed by the inevitable trading of blows.

Within seconds there was a brawl in the street. Further adding to the row, several women jumped into the fray, screaming and clawing at their husbands, trying desperately to remove them from the melee. Some of these were soon caught up in the broil and were scratching and pulling one another's hair like cats in season. Some small children stood on the sidelines, crying at the sight of their fathers getting beaten up, some at the sight of their mothers doing the beating. However, most of the children had made a game of it all and were running to and fro, laughing and squealing and playing "Catch the Pict on the wild pig."

The boy ran into an alley to catch his breath. He quickly stuffed several hunks of bread into his mouth while peeking around a corner at the unruly scene he had created. *A masterpiece,* he thought. He ran his grubby fingers through the tangled mess of straw-colored hair to comb it out of his face, ripping off another chunk of bread with his teeth as he did so.

Orphaned at six, Worm had been forced to beg on the streets of Glenryth these past many years, finding comforts for body in squalid hovels and refuse heaps, and companionship for soul with the likes of street trash and other spurious sorts. Like himself. He had fared better in the earlier days, however, managing to draw upon the sympathies of those who would take pity on a small boy and his misfortunes. But as the years grew darker and more oppressive under the yoke of Saxon tyranny, food became the scarcer and with it the milk of human kindness.

The beggar became a thief.

Worm watched with impish gratification as the fat man, a respectable baker named Moeldryth, stood in the midst of the brawl, chest huffing and heaving, trying desperately to calm everyone down.

"Citizens! Citizens of Glenryth! Stop this fighting, I beg you!" he shouted over the din. "'Twere that worthless beggar boy who stole a loaf of my bread! *He* is the one responsible for creating this panic, not wild pigs and barbarians!"

The man nearest him looked up, wearing a heroic sneer as he released the head of another man, who seemed possessed of unbounded relief to have it back.

"No doubt the scalawag is laughing at us this very minute as he makes good an escape!" Moeldryth rasped in a high-pitched voice, pinched as it was by an abundance of fatty tissue around his vocal cords.

18

Slowly a tranquil hush blanketed the storm as reason was given ground. Tempers cooled, anger dissipated like mist, order was restored. One by one, the men and women extricated themselves from the tangle of flailing limbs and body parts, and soon an attentive, if disheveled, gaggle of red-faced and black-eyed villagers had rallied around the exasperated baker.

"That's better!" Moeldryth exclaimed, collecting his wind. He patted his perspiring brow with a bread cloth, sending tiny puffs of flour into the air. "Look around you, now. Do you see any wild pigs running about? Do you see any Picts? I ask you."

The villagers looked up and down the street, gaping stupidly at one another, shaking their heads and shrugging. And when no one could produce either a wild pig or a savage Pict, they all agreed that they'd been the victims of a clever juvenile prank.

Worm was beside himself. What fools! He was hidden from view in the shadows of the alley, but he was laughing so hard that he nearly gave his position away. He bit off another chunk of bread and peeked around the corner again to see how things were shaping up.

Moeldryth was wagging a corpulent arm at the crowd, carrying on as before, only he was now pointing vaguely in Worm's direction. Worm let out a sardonic grunt. It was time he made himself scarce for a while, at least until the dictates of his stomach told him otherwise. He was about to leave, when he heard a sound that riveted his heart to his throat—a sound that made his skin crawl. Horse hooves!

The clap of iron against stone echoed up and down the streets and pierced through the renewed clamor like an arrow into flesh. Instantly the crowd choked to silence. Abject terror enveloped each person, young and old alike. Mothers quickly gathered their children and hurried them out of the street. Men began hedging their way to the curb, trying to blend in with one another as much as possible, no one daring to stand out. The time for bravado had passed as the crowd quickly dissolved into an anonymous mass along one side of the street.

Even the fat baker angled hastily to the side, his swollen visage contorted into a mask of terror, almost comical in its distortions. Suddenly a stolen loaf of bread was no longer of consequence. An airless, anxious curse spilled over his lips as he stumbled onto the curb in front of his bakery.

"There would have to be a patrol riding by just now," he muttered. "They'll want an explanation. They'll want it from me." The baker cursed again, almost in tears.

Moeldryth was also the village magistrate, appointed by the Saxons to keep the peace, *ordered* to keep the peace. He had not asked for the job. He didn't want it. He only wanted to sell his bread and pastries and to live out his dull years in quiet anonymity with his wife, bouncing a string of grandchildren on his knees and instructing them of better times.

It did not matter that his cause was just. There was a disturbance in the town, and men had been killed for less.

Besides, justice was a privilege that belonged to the generation past, during the *Pax Romana* when the Romans dwelt on the island. But when Emperor Honorius withdrew his legions in A.D. 410, bloody conflict was quick to fill the void that the once-ruling "Peace of Rome" had left in its wake. The Picts and Scotti, unruly barbarians who lived in the unconquered lands north of Hadrian's Wall, spilled over the borders in droves and roamed about the countryside freely, raiding unprotected British villages, killing their inhabitants, carrying off women and children to be their slaves or sacrifices for their gods.

German mercenaries were soon hired by the British king Vortigern to aid in fighting the northern raiders. This helped for a season, but only for a season, for the Germans themselves were quick to seize a good opportunity. Although the land was not always choice for farming, it was plentiful nonetheless, with cattle and sheep dotting the landscape in abundance and minerals and other natural resources there for the taking. So they took them. It seemed, in retrospect, that Vortigern was not only a weak king but a foolish one as well, for he had let the proverbial fox into the chicken coop. Because of it a bitter war ensued.

Under the leadership of the brothers Hengist and Horsa, the Saxons quickly conquered many of the British tribes in the southlands, driving resistance ever north and westward into the mountains, meting out "justice" with a bloody mace to guilty and innocent alike. Terrible things were afoot in the land of Britain, the land called Albion, of Gaelic lore.

Terrible things indeed.

As the horsemen galloped into the square, an old man hobbling across the street was too slow to move out of their way and was bowled over deliberately by one of the horsemen. He fell sprawling into the street and cracked his head against the curb.

This drew a chorus of throaty chortles from the Saxons who witnessed the act.

None of the townspeople came to the old man's aid—none dared but his wife—and he lay in a swelling pool of blood before a crowd of horrified faces.

And suddenly it was no longer a game. It had all been in good fun, a lark, but no one was supposed to have gotten hurt. Peering around the corner, his mouth slightly agape, Worm stared wide-eyed at the old man lying on the ground and then at the crowd of onlookers pressed against one another, gazing stupidly at the man like sheep.

Worm felt a pang of conscience, a stranger to his mind. Then anger. *Why doesn't anyone help the man?* he wondered, and his face contorted into an imprecating scowl. The cowards, their heads all lowered in obeisance. How he loathed them.

He began to fume like a judge. Indictments against each person in the crowd were recalled, each transgression brought to light and condemned. The names of deities were suddenly invoked and advised, the little gods of his fashioning. And then a thought ambushed him, a terrible thought: why didn't *he* go to the old man's aid? He looked again, saw the crumpled form bleeding. He felt pity for the man but had no courage in it.

Worm stood in the umbrage of the alley, wrestling with the assailing thought in the half-light of his mind, questioning it. The answer was discovered slithering in the murky hollows of his stomach, a dark malignant thing that uncoiled craftily within him, whispering, *It is you, Worm. Think of it—you. You must be careful. You must protect, preserve, guard yourself. Be reasonable. You must . . .*

The boy let out a sigh as he acknowledged the truth. It was fear that riveted his feet to the stones—cold, debilitating, white-knuckling fear. He too, it seemed, like those whom he loathed, was nothing more than a frightened dumb sheep, nothing more than a coward. In his eyes he was a detestable thing. A curse died in his throat.

He scanned the long line of Saxon horsemen, not fifty yards away. Their column boasted twenty men in number, two packhorses fully laden with provisions, and eight boarhounds on leashes. Something was afoot, the boy thought. Normally a patrol numbered no more than eight horsemen, with one or two dogs and a day's rations. Curiosity sidled into his thoughts, edging fear to one side.

To a man, the horsemen were clad in heavy chain mail that glistened with a dull black sheen in the now hazy sun. Draped all about them were hideous animal skins and furs that gave each rider an appearance of something half man, half beast. Each carried a long broadsword or battle-ax at his side, a short stout bow strapped across his back, and bore a shield with the crest of his Saxon lord emblazoned on it—a crimson wolf's head arched against a field of black.

Their helmets and primitive armor were covered with all manner of strange and curious design, most honoring the German gods: Woden, Tiu, Frig, among a pantheon of others. Adorning their crowns were colored plumes, stag horns, and curved metal plates that took the winged shapes of both bird and bat. A fierce-looking lot, with insatiable eyes. And their restless truculent shapes seemed bent on violence.

Worm looked on in wonder as the commander reined his mount before the others and deliberately surveyed the crowd. He was a man of magnificent stature, of terrible countenance, and the boy realized for the first time that his legs and arms were trembling. His conscience now stricken dumb, instincts and fear commanded him to flee the alley as fast as he could run. However, juvenile curiosity and awe compelled him to stay and watch. After a bitter struggle, his instincts finally gave ground to his youth.

It would prove to be a grave mistake.

The commander was a powerfully built man. He had heavy, muscled limbs and a massive chest and torso that fit neatly into armor more splendidly arrayed with furs and engravings than the others'. No one in the crowd dared counter his fell gaze for fear of offering him a face as a focus for his wrath, for fear of being singled out of anonymity.

"*Was ist der*—" the man said and then caught himself. "What is the meaning of this disorder?" he continued in a broken British tongue. His tone was strangely calm, almost paternal, though it was edged with a most chilling tyranny.

There was no response. The man waited a few moments, then, turning nonchalantly in his saddle to a burly red-headed warrior, he pointed to a small, stoop-shouldered woman at one edge of the crowd, the one with a clutch of children clinging to her dress, whimpering.

"Kill that woman over there," he ordered calmly.

"*Ja, Olaf!*" The warrior grunted, and without hesitating he spurred his horse toward the woman and raised his battle-ax.

The soldiers and boarhounds howled at the scent of blood. The crowd gasped in unison. The woman and her children shrieked.

"Stop!" a man's voice cried out from the midst.

"*Halt!*" the leader bellowed.

The burly warrior pulled up sharp in front of the terrified woman and her children, looking down at them with a hellish grin. Before turning away, he snarled, then spat at her feet.

The fright was more than the woman could bear, and she collapsed into the arms of a man standing next to her, who, not wishing to be identified with her, let her fall as he stepped to one side. Her children crumpled onto the wet cobblestones beside her and wailed.

But the crowd's attention quickly turned from these to the leader.

"Who said that?" he demanded. "Who cried, 'Stop'?"

"I . . . I did," came a timorous reply from somewhere at the rear of the crowd. It was Moeldryth, the baker.

Olaf's eyes narrowed as he peered over the throng at the trembling form of the fat man. *The magistrate no less*, he mused. His lips compressed into a humorless smile.

Olaf was second in command to the underlord Norduk, and commander of all Saxons, Angles, and Jutish warriors that rode under the

22

banner of the Crimson Wolf. He had a flowing blond mane that framed his chiseled features, and a thick, ropelike mustache that fell several inches below his jawline, which he often pulled in thought. An iron helm sat upon his leathery brow—eagle wings rose a full eighteen inches from his temples—and was fit with a bridge-plate that hung between his fierce blue eyes to protect his nose from sword blade. A rose-colored scar jagged down the length of his face from the corner of his eye, past his taut mouth to the edge of his jutting chin—a scar that was his glory and pride. Unlike the others in his command, Olaf was a Norseman—a Viking—and the sight of him stirred both awe and terror. He was not a man to face in battle.

"Come over here," he ordered the baker, making an impatient gesture.

Moeldryth threaded his way haltingly through the press of frightened villagers to the Saxon commander, stubbing his toe twice along the way. "Yes, my lord," he said obsequiously. "How may I serve you?"

Olaf grunted. "You know the penalty for rioting," he said flatly. "As magistrate, you are responsible."

"There . . . there has b-b-been no riot, my lord," Moeldryth stuttered. He mopped his perspiring brow with his bread cloth, leaving little white flour splotches caked to his skin. "A b-beggar boy stole a loaf of my bread is all. He incited a small disturbance in the town—nothing of consequence, mind you," he was quick to add, trailing it with a nervous giggle. He gestured to the ordered gathering behind him and said, "You see, my lord. We have matters well in hand."

A contemptuous sneer curled across the Norseman's brow. "You are telling me that a *beggar boy* is responsible for this disturbance?"

"Yes, my lord." Moeldryth chuckled. "Just a little flea. A flea is all. Heh, heh, heh. Nothing to concern my lords with."

Olaf threw his head back and laughed drunkenly. "Did you hear that, men? There is a little flea hopping about that makes cowards of British dogs!" The Saxons broke out into malevolent laughter.

Moeldryth joined in tenuously, as did a few others in the crowd.

Then Olaf lowered his eyes on the baker.

It was a cold, expressionless face that Moeldryth beheld, a face void of humor—savage, piercing, terrible, and without mercy or kindness. And Moeldryth knew, as he stood trembling before the Norseman, that he was staring into the face of Death. A shiver shuddered the length of his body.

"I think that you are lying to me, magistrate," Olaf said coolly. "I think that you are plotting sedition."

"No, no, no, no, no," the baker squeaked, quickly kneading more flour into the thin crust of dough on his forehead. "It's just a boy, I tell you. A worthless beggar boy that we would be pleased to be rid of."

"Then where is this *bug* that I might squash him and save you mongrels from his sting?"

Moeldryth struggled momentarily with a ghost of his manhood, hesitating. Too long. A broad swath of silvery light cleft the air with a terrible rush of wind, and the cold edge of the Norseman's broadsword was laid smartly against his throat, pressing deep into his corpulent flesh.

"Do not toy with me, fat man," Olaf threatened. "Tell me where this thief is, or my sword will drink the blood of your blubbery British neck."

Moeldryth stuttered something incoherent as he gestured up the street in the boy's direction.

The Norseman followed his point.

Worm jerked away from the corner and flattened himself against the wall of a two-story building. His eyes bugged white with fear as he stared at the opposing wall in a cold trance. Immediately the blood drained from his head, and bile collected in the pit of his stomach and mouth. He felt nauseous; his breathing was shallow, fast.

The whispers of fear were now shouting. Thieving was a capital offense under the martial rule of the Saxon conquerors. Mercy was a concept unknown to these men. There was no doubt in his mind that, if he were caught, he would be executed on the spot. He fiddled anxiously with the small bronze medallion that he wore around his neck, as if by holding it the thing might bring him good luck or comfort. The boy looked down the alley for a route of escape.

"Here he is! The little worm is hiding over here!" a voice cried out from somewhere.

But where? The lad whirled around panic-stricken, looking for the Judas voice. Who? Why? Looking up, he saw an old woman in a second-story window, frantically waving her arms and screaming, stabbing her finger at him. He threw what was left of the bread at the woman, cursed her, then darted down the winding narrow alley, running for his life.

"Loose the boarhounds!" Olaf ordered, jerking his steed toward the boy. The dog handlers obeyed at once, and in moments the rabid fury of eight boarhounds and twenty battle horses was thundering up the street amid scattering townspeople, in pursuit of the fleeing beggar boy.

Seeing their tails, Moeldryth and the others exhaled a sigh of relief. For now, the baker mused, he and the villagers had escaped the wrath of these mounted villains. But at what cost? The life of an orphan boy—*that* orphan boy—and the pride of having been Britons, a once-noble breed of men.

He hung his head in shame as he slowly turned toward the bakery. *Oh, the day*, he thought, *when there were men in Glenryth who would have stood their ground against such devils.* But such a day lay buried in the slopes and fields along the River Trent, nevermore to raise voice or sword in protest. Moeldryth envied the singleness of their fate; for those who had surrendered, such as him, those who had yielded to "reason" and the prudent way, had been dying a slow, miserable death each day ever since. *We have already begun our sojourn in hell,* he reflected. *The grave will be but a minor interruption.*

He raised his head before entering his shop and gazed across the market square. Frightened men were quickly gathering their women and children and hurrying them off to the safety of their farms and cottages. Each was consumed with his own business, each entertaining his own dialogue with fear, each without thought for those around him, either in whole or in part. An old woman sat huddled abjectly beside her fallen husband, wailing, a solitary shape twisting in anguish and seen through a lattice of running legs. The baker let out a disconsolate sigh.

"Like rabbits," Moeldryth thought aloud. "Like scared little rabbits." The baker sighed again, unaware of the crust of bread flaking on his brow, unaware that a single tear had left a pasty streak alongside his cheek, marking his own private passage of torment. He entered his shop and closed the door.

Worm ducked into a narrow street, hoping to shake the boarhounds in the labyrinth of alleys just ahead, but they were right on his heels. Gaining. And speed was not his gift. The boy was large-boned, gangly, at an awkward stage of growth where everything seemed to get in the way of his huge feet. He would have to rely on his cunning if he were to survive. His mind was keenly focused on the terrible sounds of snapping teeth closing on his heels. A gruesome image bit into his mind, and he struggled to cast it off.

Suddenly he brightened.

Ahead on the left was a long, narrow court that dead-ended into a small yard with a tavern and a few shops. He turned into it at once and raced toward the tavern. Seconds later the pandemonium of yelping hounds and warhorses turned into the court behind him. A roar shot over the boy's head like a blast of furies, then resounded off the buildings to create deafening confusion.

But the boy's focus was pristine, his mind clear. The streets had taught him well, and he ran. Reaching the tavern, Worm yanked the heavy wooden door open and ran inside, leaving it agape behind him.

Inside the tavern were several tables, where a few men waited impatiently at board for the taverner to bring them fresh tankards of mead and ale. Worm ran through the room yelling, hurdling benches, stools, and wine barrels with amazing agility for a boy at the clumsy time of life.

Confused men turned to look. The man nearest the door wheeled about and bit his lip, then hurled a curse into the air.

Without missing a step, the boy leaped from a bench to the top of a long table and dashed across its surface through several plates of mutton and boiled cabbage and half-filled tankards. Food and ale flew in all directions, much of which landed on the startled faces and bellies of irate patrons. Scrambling men shouted and threatened violence. The heavyset taverner scurried from the kitchen in time to witness eight snarling boarhounds bounding through the door right at him.

"My!" he gasped quietly, then, squealing like a stuck pig, dove for cover under a table.

Worm jumped off the table and hit the floor running, scant yards ahead of the snapping dogs, then raced toward an open window. Climbing onto the sill, the boy grabbed the heavy wooden shutter and slammed it shut as he vaulted to the ground outside. A moment later the boarhounds slammed into the wall behind him, sending shock waves under his feet from their violent crush of weight.

The dogs were trapped. They pounded and scratched against the wall and floor, howling and yelping in crazed, angry blood-lust, as they tried to get through the wall to the boy. But to no avail. It seemed for the moment that Worm's plan had worked. It would take the dog handlers some time to gain control of the frenzied animals and put them onto his trail—enough time for him to make good an escape.

But his moment of triumph was short-lived. As he sped down an alley toward the edge of town, one of the horsemen spotted him.

"Over here!" the man cried.

And in moments the soldiers were hard upon him.

The boy ran toward the edge of the village, cleared a low stone wall in a single bound, and made his way across a sloping meadow as fast as his legs would carry him. Beyond the meadow were the thickets, and beyond them the woods. The woods!

"Got to make the thicket . . . got to!" Worm panted. "Lose the horses in there . . . then the woods!"

But the rushing clatter of horse hooves quickly dashed his hopes. Shooting a glance over his shoulder, he saw the Viking's horse clear the stone wall.

"There he is!" Olaf barked. "It'll be your miserable hides if he escapes!"

The other horsemen cleared the wall en masse and spurred their mounts toward the boy.

Then the lad tripped on a stone and stumbled for a few terrifying feet. Everything moved in slow motion—or so it seemed—as he tried desperately to keep from falling headlong into the dirt that came at him rushing. His legs were leaden and felt as though they were refusing his commands to save his life. *Such treason!* he thought, then hit the ground with a jarring thud and rolled. He could feel the earth trembling beneath him from the punishment of the horses. He sprang up, gasping for air, and scrambled to catch his stride.

"Shoot him!" howled the Norseman's voice over the confusion. "Shoot him now!"

A buzzing noise rifled over Worm's head, and with a muffled thud the shaft of an arrow hit the ground a few yards in front of him. Another shaft whistled past his ear. *Zip!* And then two more passed him on either side. *Zip! Zip!* All around his feet and in front of him—*Zip! Zip! Zip!*— the boy could see arrows thudding into the ground.

The horsemen were fast closing the gap.

Panting desperately for air, he raced for the thicket with a despotic command of will. It was now but twenty yards in front of him. "Got to make the thicket! Got to make the thicket!" he chanted. "Got to!"

The pain in his body was excruciating, now screaming at him. The ground was a shuddering terror beneath his feet. Only a few more yards to go. "Got to make the thicket!" His lungs felt as if they were sucking fire rather than air, and his sides ached as though skewered with knives. Feathered shafts rifled all around him and marked his course as they stabbed the earth in anger. Just a few more feet to go. "Got to make . . ." Every joint and limb in his body burned from the torturous pace. Then, mercifully, the thicket enveloped him.

Ha! Ha!

The horsemen pulled up their mounts just a few feet behind him.

"After him!" Olaf shouted as he sprang from his horse.

Quickly the riders flew off their mounts and scrambled into the undergrowth after the lad. But with their heavy mail and bulky forms, they were no match for the youth's size and agility.

Worm quickly gained a vantage point on a small knoll about fifty yards from the edge of the copse. It was surrounded by low gnarly shrubs and trees in front and behind, which concealed him from sight and yet afforded him a clear view of the horsemen.

It was a suitable place to catch his wind and to let his aching sides and muscles recuperate before moving on. He could see the riders awkwardly hacking their way through the thorny tangle of bramble with their useless broadswords. Obscenities were hurled rhythmically. Worm grinned as he thought how clumsy and puny they looked separated from their horses, and he wondered how these Saxon oafs could ever instill such fear.

"I think I hit him," he heard one of them say.

Ha! The boy laughed to himself. *What fools!*

27

And then he noticed that a pain in his left shoulder had not subsided. As he began to rub it, he was shocked to find that his shoulder was wet.

I'm wounded!

For a moment he just stared at his gleaming red hand as though the thing didn't belong to him. It seemed to him a curious apparition. Then horror struck. *I'm wounded!* He gasped incredulously, as though realizing it for the first time.

Coming to his senses, he wiped his hand across his breast, then quickly inspected his shoulder to determine the severity of the wound. Craning his neck, he could just see the wicked little feathers and black shaft of an arrow protruding from behind the shoulder. A sharp pain shot through his body, and he reeled like a drunkard. *Can't give in to the pain,* he thought.

He glanced down and let out another gasp. His left flank was covered with blood, and he grimaced as another bolt of pain stabbed his shoulder. He thought he might faint.

"I did hit him!" he heard one of them gloat. "Here's his blood trail, all right!"

The others quickly mustered around the spot, dancing like large apes about the spoor, and began to screech fiercely, throwing big arms into the air, brandishing swords and axes.

Got to get away, the boy said to himself. *I'll die here.* He tried to move, but pain overwhelmed him, and he fell face-first into the dirt. *Got to get . . .*

Lying in his spilling life, his cheek pressed against the dirt, he could feel consciousness slowly ebbing. A cold numbness enveloped his body, and the pain quieted because of it. Mercifully. The air was thick and still, with not a hint of stirring. A black ant tottered past his eye, trundling a tiny leaf. Now he could hear the frenetic hacking of the horsemen's swords and axes, drawing ever nearer in the thicket, only yards away, and their hideous shrieks and cries as the blood spoor drew them inexorably. *It won't be long now,* the lad thought, as he sank further into the cool and peaceful darkness. *Can't be. So this is what it's like to die.*

Finally he heard booted footsteps approaching along his right flank, and the boy prepared himself mentally for the final blow that was sure to fall. It had been a short life. He sighed, clutching the bronze medallion with his right hand. Many regrets. As the last waves of consciousness receded from his pallid form, he felt a pair of strong hands grab him by his tattered jerkin, felt himself being lifted from the earth, and the young beggar named Worm quietly surrendered to the blackness.

2
ENCOUNTER
IN THE CAVE

The great bear paused amid the ancient yews—those stalwart sentinels of a more ancient land—and turned his gaze to the rocky trail below. His wet, coal-like eyes stared intently down the blunted mountain for the betrayal of movement, anything out of the ordinary that marked the presence of the stranger, the intruder into his domain, something that had culled his scent from the air and was tracking him.

A soft breeze whispered through the trees above him, rustling shimmering leaves. The fiery yellow orb, now cresting the eastern rim, was dappling the forest bed with mutable patterns of light, and small creatures roused from their slumber and frolicked in them.

Lifting his heavy bulk up onto his hind legs, the bear sniffed the air. The golden tips of his thick, reddish-brown fur glistened as they caught the early morning rays of the sun. A low growl rattled in his throat. He shook his massive head and lowered himself to the ground, blowing out a snort of contempt as he landed. He paused, blinking. Then the magnificent beast turned and lumbered quickly up the trail that led through the forested hillside, his grizzled withers bristling with smoldering rage.

Slowly, the veil of darkness lifted from Worm's mind. At the first hint of cogent light, in that twilight world between consciousness and unconsciousness where reality's focus is blurred by an ethereal fog, a collage of distorted images swirled through the synapses of his brain like a maelstrom: people screaming . . . fighting . . . running in mindless, frantic circles like summer swarms of gnats . . . squealing children on the backs of squealing wild pigs. The sounds, at once distant, compressed, supernal, were yet resonating against the walls of his vision with a terrible presence.

What is that smell? The thought flashed, short-circuiting the scene with an explosion of colors. At once Worm was running from a street teeming with people, their faces contorting into grotesque pig snouts and beady, little piggy jet eyes, their angry howls punctuated by maniacal piggish snorts. *It smells awful,* the thought reiterated, now dissolving the pig people into old hags, ghoulish crones who were screaming like banshees from second-story windows that encompassed him like a circle of mirrors.

As is indigenous to the terrain of nightmares, the boy was again running with unnatural segue from one plane to the next, now through a street littered with bloodied old men, now through a gauntlet of disembodied arms, each wagging corpulent rolls of flesh at him, each stabbing at him, accusing him, condemning him to death.

And then there was the hissing, the roaring venomous hissing from a host of Cheshire smiles as delirium or death took his mind.

The hulking bear splashed through a small creek for about a mile, then cut upward along a winding grade through some dense foliage, keeping his gait at a slow, rolling lope. Once again, as he came to a small clearing in the trees, he paused obediently. Instinct commanded it. He sniffed for scent as he looked around the glade, slowly taking in all the sights and sounds.

A small gust of wind raised some fallen leaves and scattered them about his large feet. There were splashes of color along the periphery of the clearing, where the exposed sunlight gave life to a myriad wild flowers and the purplish, pinkish hues of ubiquitous heather. The lazy drone of bees floated on the warming air as they collected nectar, and from somewhere in the canopy of tree boughs came the lone, obnoxious caw of a jay as he heralded the borders of his territory.

But these did not interest the bear. These did not hunt, did not kill. He looked down the mountain at his back trail.

The demons came at him, snarling with the faces of rabid hounds, wearing a gruesome panoply of furs, plumage, burnished armor, and winged helmets, and brandishing other devilish accoutrements. They rode a legion of fiery-eyed demon horses that undulated atop a boiling thunderhead of lesser devils. A torrential thundering rolled before them, and flashes of lightning sparked from their flinted hooves, setting to light a great conflagration over the dream-scape that was all consuming.

Hell.

This must be hell! The thought stabbed his mind. *It is so hot!* Suddenly it began to rain. At first cool, then warm, then hot, then searing hot, stabbing the ground at his feet with a hail of sulfurous firebrands. *What is that strange odor?* The fiery hail dissolved into sticks—at the outset a few, but then a torrent were falling all around him, hitting him, hurting. He tried to run from the falling sticks, but his feet refused his commands. His legs grew tired, heavy as though laden with sucking mud. *Where is the thicket?* The forest. The womb. Falling, the sticks kept falling. The pain! And now he was falling. *If I land on my shoulder I'll be dead. It is so hot! Boiling. What is that awful smell? I've got to get out of here, but it is so wet! So hot. My shoulder . . . the thicket . . . my shoulder . . . the thicket . . . the pain!*

The boy screamed and sat bolt upright in a cold sweat, panting for breath. "Easy, easy," a voice commanded. "Your fever is finally breaking."

The boy's eyes labored open, blinked slowly, rolled painfully, then closed. He lay back down onto a soft bed of leafy fronds. It took a few moments before the maelstrom of demonic images cleared from his mind, allowing shafts of wondrous light to penetrate the dark mists that lingered there.

I'm alive? This whole thing has been a bad dream. And then another jolt of pain from his shoulder fully awakened him to a kind of reality. The boy winced in agony and grabbed his shoulder.

"It's a bad wound," the voice continued. "But it'll heal if you give it rest."

Worm felt his head being lifted by someone's hand, then felt the sensual comfort of a warm vapor enveloping his face.

"Here, drink some of this broth," the voice commanded gently. Tendrils of vapor curled up into the boy's nostrils. Immediately his eyes jerked open. "What is that stuff?" he cried out. "It smells awful!"

"It'll help," the stranger retorted, feeding a spoonful of the warm liquid into Worm's mouth.

Worm choked and coughed, causing him again to grimace in pain from the violent movement. Clutching his shoulder, the boy reopened his eyes and let his vision clear to another kind of reality. Then, blinking once or twice, he noticed that his shoulder had been tightly bandaged with strips of clean white linen. He studied the bandages skeptically, as one eyeing an unsolicited gift in the post. "You do this?"

"You were losing a lot of blood," the stranger replied, as he dipped the wooden spoon into the bowl. "Didn't think you were going to make it for a while there. You still need proper tending, though—better than what I can give you here. Shouldn't move you—leastwise, not till you've gained a little more strength." He raised the spoon to Worm's lips. "Here, drink this."

"Who are you?" Worm asked, after taking the fluid. "Why're you doing this?"

But the stranger did not respond. Perhaps he hadn't heard him. The thought struck Worm that he might have lapsed back into the fever and had only dreamed the question. But that didn't make any sense. He could *see* the stranger, now clearly. He could *smell* the awful broth vapors. He could *feel* the pain in his shoulder. The pain, certainly. He was awake. Alive. Why?

Worm almost repeated his question, but instead he eyed the stranger suspiciously as he choked down another spoonful of broth. As best he could determine, the stranger was a youth of about the same age as he was. He had neat, jet-colored hair that fell to just above his shoulders. And deeply set into gregarious features were blue eyes, so blue, so piercing, they were hard to gaze into without turning away. He was a fair-looking fellow, Worm supposed, but he considered himself a poor judge on matters of aesthetics.

The stranger fed him another spoonful of broth. "That ought to do for a while," he said. "Now get some rest." He set the bowl down, then covered Worm with a woolen blanket. "My name is Terryll," he said, finally answering Worm's question. Then standing, he smiled a broad, infectious smile. "You needed help, is all."

Worm forged a wooden smile in return and, glancing furtively at the other's stature, noted that the stranger had about the same build as his own, though it was certainly more developed. His arms and shoulders were well-muscled. The muscles seemed to leap and pop about his limbs in a continual celebration of movement. And his legs were thick and rippled beneath his trousers as though he had spent much time walking or running great distances. Worm marveled at his physique the way boys in their growing years are wont to do—with a tension between admiration and envy.

Of all the men and boys that Worm had known from his village, none had what would be considered a muscled physique, except maybe the blacksmith. But even he had an ample paunch from too much ale. Most of the others were either fat men with bloated cheeks—or skinny men who were like sacks of bones, all pasty-faced and drawn and dead looking—or men just so mousy or weasely-appearing as to go without notice. He loathed the thought of them. Cowards, every one.

The only valiant men that he had known in his life, it seemed, were reverently buried in his mind and imagination and long forgotten in time. And there were only a handful of them at that—men who had perished gallantly during their lonely stand against the Saxons ten years earlier on the fated Hill of Badon.

His father had been one of them.

As a small boy, Worm had often resurrected their memories. Each night as he lay beneath the vault of stars in some wretched corner of Glenryth, he would dream of these men, adding to their stories his own inventions of valiant exploits until they had reached fabled proportions in his mind. And in every dream, without exception, his father and the British warriors would drive the Saxons back into the sea from whence they had come.

But after a time, as the need to survive stripped away the whimsy of his youth, and as a daily appraisal of the human race refined in him a profound cynicism, their courageous deeds, their glorious victories, grew dim in his mind. And when he could no longer conjure up the sweet image of his father's face, or cared to, he put such fantasies away. Until now.

The stranger walked away toward a cooking fire in the center of what appeared to be a large cave. Worm continued to study him as he carefully laid pieces of wood on the blaze. There was an economy in his movements, every one of which was deliberate and without waste. He took note that, every few minutes, the young stranger would glance over to the entrance of the cave as though he was expecting someone.

There was an unusual presence about him that Worm had not seen in men before, let alone teenagers. He seemed to exude a confidence that one would expect to find perhaps in a military leader, and yet it was attended by a quiet spirit. The coexistence of the two seemed paradoxical, if not contradictory. Worm was intrigued by the stranger, and the coals of Worm's past were somehow fanned by his presence—coals that time and bitter struggle had long since covered over with sand.

The boy Terryll turned his gaze from the cave's entrance and caught Worm staring at him. The young stranger smiled broadly again.

But Worm flushed with embarrassment. Then, attempting a pathetic smile, he looked away. He glanced around the cave and took stock of his surroundings, though there wasn't much stock to consider. As far as the boy could see beyond the periphery of the fire glow, there were no furnishings in the place. The thatch of leafy fronds that he lay on, the smooth stones encircling the fire, the little wooden bowl and spoon, and a large flat rock placed near it were about the sum of them. Then he noticed a quiver of arrows set against a longbow in a small recess of the cave's wall.

Perhaps he is a warrior, Worm mused, then looked back at the boy squatting next to the fire.

"My name is Worm," he offered.

Terryll looked over at him and nodded. "Pleased to meet you," he said, placing another piece of wood on the fire.

"You saved my life."

"You're not out of the woods just yet," Terryll replied.

"How'd you get me away from the Saxons?" Worm asked. "It seemed like they were right on top of me." Then he suddenly realized the magnitude of his question. Even though Terryll looked as if he could take

33

care of himself, there had been at least twenty men and eight boarhounds that were hard upon him. And he was, after all, still a boy.

"There'll be time for explanations later," Terryll said. "For now, you're safe here. Now get some rest." Then he added cryptically, "You're going to need it."

Worm was tired and feverish, and his shoulder ached, and he wanted nothing more than to sleep. But there would be plenty of time for sleep. He could tell by the tone of Terryll's voice that the presence of danger hung in the air, and that alone would keep his mind piqued. Sleep, even if he wanted it, would be far from his grasp.

"Where is 'here'?" he asked.

Terryll looked up and smiled again. Obviously his wounded charge wasn't going to take his advice. "It's a cave that I use when I hunt in these mountains. We're about ten miles south of Bainbridge."

"Bainbridge!" Worm exclaimed incredulously. "Why, that puts us about twenty miles north of Glenryth!"

"As the crow flies, maybe," Terryll responded dryly.

"How'd you carry me here?"

"We've had a long day and night."

"Day and *night?*"

"You've been unconscious for twenty-four hours."

"Twenty-four—" Worm looked straight ahead, stunned.

Terryll sprang up without a sound and moved to the entrance of the cave. Standing in the pool of sunlight that spilled into the opening, the young hunter scanned the wooded slope for several minutes. Then, just as quickly, he moved back to the fire, sat down upon the flat stone, and nursed the coals with a stick. After a few moments, a queer expression crossed his face, and he looked over at Worm.

"Is . . . uh . . . 'Worm' your given name?"

"Huh?" Worm had been pondering his missing day.

" 'Worm' . . . is that your given name?" Terryll repeated.

Worm chuckled sardonically. "No. It's just the name that everybody calls me."

"Seems like a strange name. It doesn't bother you?"

"I don't mind." Worm grunted. "I guess I've gotten used to it. You can get used to most anything, you know—most anything that doesn't kill you."

"I suppose," Terryll mused, not sure what he meant. "Then, what is your given name?" he pressed. "I mean, your Christian name?"

"I doubt if I'm a Christian," Worm said flatly. "Or anything else, for that matter."

There was a bitterness in his voice, and Terryll did not pressure further. Instead he asked, "What do your parents call you?"

34

"My parents both died when I was little," Worm replied. "I really never knew them."

"I'm sorry to hear that."

"No need to be." Worm fumbled reflectively with the bronze medallion around his neck, then added, haltingly, "My mother died in childbirth. And I don't remember much of my father at all, except that he was killed in battle." He looked over at Terryll. "I grew up begging on the streets of a village that he died protecting, and everyone there just called me 'Worm.' It's the only name I can remember." He cursed.

"Many valiant Britons were killed at the Battle of Glenryth," Terryll countered. "Because of their bravery, the Saxons were forced to abandon their campaign against the north. Songs are sung in halls all over the highlands about the heroes that fell on the slopes of Badon." Terryll paused. "No doubt your father was one of them. What was his name?"

"I don't know." Worm sighed wistfully. "I can't remember that either."

Terryll looked into the little jumping flames and shook his head. "It's a great loss. Still, you should be proud. I'm sure that he fought well." After saying these things he looked over to the mouth of the cave.

Worm pondered his words for a few moments, allowing them to breathe over the coals in his mind. Then a pang in his shoulder quenched the thoughts, and he dismissed them. He followed Terryll's eyes to the cave's entrance and asked, "Are you waiting for someone?"

"Yes. For a friend."

"Who?"

Suddenly Terryll jumped to his feet. "Ah! Finally!" he exclaimed, then bolted toward the opening without a word.

"Finally what?" Worm said, startled by Terryll's sudden action. "I didn't hear a thing."

As Terryll ran outside, he called out, "There you are, Hauwka, my friend! What has kept you?"

But Worm heard no response. A span of silence passed. A gentle breeze rolled into the cave and played with the wisps of smoke from the fire. Worm studied the play of smoke and flame and was soon mesmerized by their wild dance. A hazy image of a blacksmith's furnace ignited his memory, striking it with a resonant peal of nostalgia. At once his mind was overwhelmed with the smells of burning coke and the sweet sweat of men working amid a smothering heat; the happy, singing cadence of their hammers clanging against molten metal, beating it, shaping it, conforming it to their resolute wills; sparks flying everywhere in exultant arcs like tiny shooting stars; and the sound of white-hot metal screaming as it was plunged into great water vats.

It was a wonderful image, powerful, rugged, a glowing aura full of mannish vigor. But as Worm tried to peer into the fiery haze to capture substance from the shades, all at once the image was gone, just like a wisp of smoke and steam. Worm marveled at the dream. From whence had it come? Was it a lingering child of the fever? Or was there once form to this apparition?

As his head cleared, he remembered that the stranger had left to meet someone outside the cave. But how long ago? How long had he been in the vision of the blacksmith's furnace? Worm was stricken with a little panic. Had he been deserted? Was he really dead after all and the cave really some sort of anteroom of Hades? He shuddered at the thought, then realized that his brow had beaded with perspiration. It was the fever, nothing more. He was relieved.

Presently Terryll ran into the cave and rushed over to Worm. "We have to leave at once!" he said, with a look of grave concern.

"Leave? What's going on?" Worm asked. "You said we were safe here!"

"We're in danger."

"Who said?"

In that instant a great form suddenly filled the cave mouth, momentarily blocking out all outside light. And there was no way that the boy could be prepared for the sight that was to follow. For as the large shape passed through the entrance into the cave, sunlight streamed back into the room, and immediately Worm's eyes widened in horror.

Before him was a great beast the likes of which he had never seen, one that lumbered over to him and put his large wet nose up to his face.

He gasped. "It's a *bear!*"

"It is Hauwka."

"And he's your . . . your friend?" Worm cried.

The monstrous bear sniffed his bandages, snorted once, then let out a low, empathetic moan. Not at all comfortable with the friendliness of the hairy behemoth, Worm kept his bulging eyes riveted on the probing wet snout, fully expecting to be eaten alive at any moment.

"Are . . . are . . . are you sure it's friendly?" he asked nervously. "I can't believe how big he is! Bears don't get that big. Do they?"

Then he realized that he had no idea how large bears got, for he'd never really seen a bear up close before—or far away for that matter. He quickly sifted through his memory for bear-sightings but came up empty-handed. Once, when he was a small boy, he thought he had seen a bear lurking among some trees outside his village. But, as it turned out, it was only a man carrying over his shoulders a deer that he had killed in the mountains. Even so, Worm had suffered a week of bear dreams because of it. Then the thought struck him: how did he know that this huge creature was a bear?

Before he could answer the question, he felt the bear's presence again, felt the wet, coal-like eyes boring through him with a wild intensity.

Worm started fidgeting with his medallion and darted a look at Terryll. "Why is he looking at me that way?" he asked, petrified.

"He likes you!" Terryll said, then added, smiling, "You're fortunate. He doesn't like too many people! Now, come—we have to go."

Terryll quickly moved behind Worm and placed his hands under the boy's arms, then began to lift him up.

Worm did not take his eyes off the bear for a moment, not even once.

"We can't delay," Terryll added. "The boarhounds are onto our scent."

"Just because I stole a loaf of moldy bread?" Worm asked. "It doesn't make sense!"

"I had to dispatch one of them," Terryll said. "A huge brute, with flaming red hair and a bushy beard—one who was just about to separate your head from your shoulders with a rather large battle-ax, I might add."

"You killed a Saxon horse soldier!?"

"No, I knocked him out with a stone," Terryll retorted. "But Saxons don't take very kindly to that either. I'm surprised that they've followed us this far into the mountains, though. This Saxon commander is a bold one. It troubles me." The latter sentence was said more to himself—or to the bear. Worm couldn't tell which.

Worm slowly toiled to his feet. He winced as another bolt of pain shot through his shoulder.

"I'm sorry," Terryll said. "But it can't be helped. Here now—see if you can climb up onto Hauwka's back."

Worm froze. "You mean—you mean, get on top of the bear?" He gasped, not believing his ears.

"How do you think you got here?"

Worm looked up at the massive span across the bear's shoulders and back and almost cried. A little squeak escaped. He choked down a large lump in his throat and glanced sideways at Terryll to see if he was really serious. He was. Then slowly, as he put his trembling hands onto the bear's girth, he resigned himself to his fate. Hauwka lowered himself as best he could, but even so there was still a great height to scale.

Terryll grabbed him by his ankle and made ready to hoist him up. "Are you ready?"

"Uh . . . I don't know." A horrible thought blinked into Worm's mind: that this whole business was nothing more than an elaborate ruse to feed the bear. "Does he bite?" he asked timorously.

"Oh, yes," came the quick reply. "Often."

Terryll smiled wryly, then boosted Worm onto the bear's back, the warm, furry place that was to be his home and bed for the next several hours.

Worm let out a scream as he landed. However, Terryll didn't know if it was because of the pain in his shoulder or because of his terror of the bear. Worm knew!

3
FLIGHT THROUGH THE FOREST

The boarhounds, driven into a wild frenzy from the blood scent, razed the deserted cave. Howling and gnashing their teeth, they scratched and dug furiously at the bed of leafy fronds and tore strips of bandages to shreds as they searched for their prey. Finding nothing, they turned on each other in fury.

The largest hound in the pack attacked the dog nearest him, grabbing the exposed nape, and sank his teeth deep into the animal's muscles. The smitten dog howled and immediately fell under the weight of his attacker. The rest of the pack sensed his fatal weakness and flew at him with mindless abandon, quickly finishing the kill.

They were a ferocious breed with powerful jaws that could easily rip apart heavy limbs and crush the bones of man or beast. The pointed ears that stood erect from the tops of their squared heads gave them an almost demonic appearance and would send fear into the stoutest of hearts in battle. Standing waist high at the withers to a normal man, the dogs were bred to track down and kill three-hundred-fifty-pound wild boars—and men.

The horsemen reined their mounts in the narrow clearing outside the cave's entrance, persuaded by the row inside that the chase was over. Olaf, several riders, and the two dog handlers flew off their horses and entered the cave. However, upon viewing the grisly carnage, the Viking cursed.

"Separate them!" he ordered the dog handlers. "Then get them back onto the scent at once!"

The dog handlers were usually large men of great strength—they had to be—who covered themselves with thick leather padding on their arms, legs, and torsos. Each wore a heavy leather collar around his neck and a small steel helm with leather flanks to protect his head and ears. It was not uncommon for boarhounds to turn on their handlers. Each carried a long wooden staff, having a leather noose on one end and a steel prod on the other, for separating the dogs from one another or for just keeping them at bay.

The dog handlers set to the task with dispassionate professionalism. Adroitly slipping nooses over the more aggressive dogs' necks, they yanked them free of the pack, while prodding the others into submission. Within moments the animals were separated and attentive, waiting obediently for their masters to command them.

Meanwhile, the other Saxons were rummaging through the scant debris of the abandoned cave, looking for anything that might aid in their pursuit. One held up a strip of bloodied linen and the arrow taken from Worm's shoulder, as though he had discovered gold.

"They will be moving slowly, Olaf!" he exclaimed, grinning.

"Give me that," one of the dog handlers growled, snatching the strip from his hand. At once he and the other handler led their hounds outside to hunt for blood spoor.

The men were glad to be rid of the hounds from such close confines, not trusting the ferocious blood-cast in their eyes, and continued their rummaging.

"The fire still glows with coals," another warrior called out as he prodded the embers with his sword. "We cannot be far behind them."

Olaf stooped to examine the embers and grunted.

Somewhere outside, the hounds had fallen upon the scent and were raising a tumult. Without a word the Norseman stood up and strode out of the cave.

Immediately a Saxon with fiery-colored hair and bushy beard moved into the entrance, blocking it, and faced the men. His hand rested on the handle of his battle-ax. "The young Briton who hit me with the stone is mine!" he declared forcefully. "By Woden, he is mine!"

He waited a moment for protest, but there was none. None dared. So he released them with a churlish grunt, and each man exited the cavern toward his horse.

Outside, Olaf was conferring with the dog handlers. The latter, their bodies jerking violently under the leash-pull of yapping hounds, pointed away to the northeast.

"Are we to continue our pursuit, Olaf?" one of the handlers asked. "It seems as though they are fleeing along our very course."

"It is good sport!" the other added.

"Loose the hounds!" Olaf commanded the handlers as he mounted his horse.

The boarhounds, howling and yelping, took off across the forested mountainside in hot pursuit of the two boys and the mammoth bear, provoked to lust by the fresh scent of blood, which, though invisible to the retarded senses of man, marked a trail of rubescent brilliance in the feral minds of the boarhounds.

Immediately Olaf spurred his mount and was into the trees after the hounds, whose savage cries were quickly fading into muted snarls. The warriors galloping behind him added their bestial cries to the hounds', also provoked to lust by the sporting chase.

The sun was at its zenith overhead. Rays of warm sunlight streamed through a canopy of sycamores, poplars, and yews, and painted marbled patterns of shade and light across the canvas of the cool, wooded floor. The thick forest air teemed with a variety of bird song and multi-colored butterflies that floated on the swirling air currents. Squirrels scurried overhead in the tree limbs, chittering noisily back and forth, totally unconcerned with the plight of the wounded boy and the mammoth bear below them.

Hauwka found a suitable place and forded the River Ouse. It was the spring of the year, so the water was deep and the current strong from the snow melt. But these proved little obstacle to the size and strength of the great beast, and he made the crossing with little effort. He then veered off the river and followed one of its small tributary streams along its serpentine course, upward through the forest toward its headwaters in the highlands.

In a series of small cascades that marked its ascent, the stream splashed over its rocky bed and formed deep restless pools of dark water at the base of each waterfall. In these, native brown and rainbow trout thrived on tadpoles and mosquito and mayfly hatches and were wary of the strange, rippled forms slanting above them.

Worm tried desperately to stay awake. His life depended on it as far as he was concerned. Terryll had left him hours before to lay false trails, so it was just the bear and Worm now, and he was sure that the bear wanted to eat him. He knew that the bruin was just biding his time until he fell asleep, and then, while he was unable to defend himself, the monster would make his move. It would all be over in short order.

Worm envisioned what it would be like to be torn limb from limb —the rending of flesh, the crunching of bones, the final, pitiful gasp of life. But the imagery was too gruesome to contemplate, so he tried to shut it out of his mind. He would not give the bear such satisfaction; he would stay awake if it killed him.

As they padded along the stream's stony banks, Worm could hear the irregular, rhythmic *plop, ker-ploink, splash*, as frogs and terrapins hopped off logs and rocks into the water. He focused on these noises to keep his mind alert, awake, alive. But added to such rhythms was the drone of dragonflies and bees as they buzzed around his ears on lazy sine curves, the sapping warmth of the sun, and the easy, rolling gait of the bear.

Slowly the boy was lulled into a head-nodding doze by the woodland music. Occasionally he would jerk his head up in stark terror, fully expecting to see a mouthful of teeth closing around him. But he would see only the back of the great bear's massive head, rocking back and forth like a hairy metronome. Once, he caught the bear looking back at him, *smiling* —or so it seemed. He was waiting. The boy tortured himself so for two or three hours, but he was fully resolved to outlast him. He would stay awake.

Meanwhile, Terryll busied himself by laying several false trails behind them for the hounds to follow, hoping that the Saxons had discovered the bloody strip he had left behind in the cave, hoping they hadn't guessed the purpose of his "negligence." But he doubted it. How could they know that he was a hunter? How could they know that he was fluent in the language of the wild? They couldn't. Most men were stupid when it came to such things. And so he would simply write a clear set of directions upon the forest floor for the hounds to follow and hopefully lead their masters on a wild and merry goose chase.

First he dragged several strips of bloodied linen from Worm's shoulder along the ground to decoy their scent along a game trail leading to the northeast. Then he shinnied up several trees and fastened portions of the strips to limbs out of sight. Another strip he stuffed in the cleft of a rock (accessible only through a tangle of briars). Yet another he tied around a boulder and pushed it down the mountainside, where it would bounce and roll for a thousand yards or so.

Each of these, he prayed, would lead the hounds to a dead end and would keep them confused precious minutes, perhaps even hours, before the horsemen would arrive and discover the ruse. The young hunter knew that without such diversions there would be no way for them to elude the Saxons.

Satisfied that he had done all that he could to gain them some time, Terryll ran swiftly through the forest toward the place of rendezvous with Hauwka and Worm, several miles to the northwest. His hunting instincts kept his path on rocks and fallen trees, through rivers and streams, and along hard surfaces in order to bury or obscure his scent. He had fled trouble before but never while nursing one so wounded and never from twenty or more horsemen and boarhounds. At best, he could only delay the inevitable—he knew it. At worst—well, he would deal with that when the time came.

Worm screamed, snapping upright out of a dead sleep. He was panting for breath as his mind reeled through a disorienting fog. Terror crawled all over him. He blinked it away heavily, thinking, *Where am I? What's wrong? The world is different, darker now, colder,* and he resigned himself calmly to it. *I'm dead. It's over.* A thought jolted him: *The bear!*

He swung his head around, and his eyes darted about in a new panic, looking for the beast that had been chasing him. *Where'd he go! He was right on top of me, his big fangs closing over my face!*

And then it struck him, beginning with a needle prick at the base of his neck. As he turned slowly back around, his eyes filling with the dreaded image, waves of chills prickled up his spine and burst upon his scalp with a rush of cold terror. *The bear!*

Hauwka glanced back, his wet eyes twinkling in the bright gloaming. Then, letting out a terrific snort, he swung his massive head back toward the trail and continued to pad along.

The boy stared mystified at the back of the bear's head. It was another dream, he thought. Another stupid dream. He was filled with a sudden disgust at himself. *If this bear doesn't kill me, my dreams will.*

Worm held his aching shoulder and gazed about at the unfamiliar terrain. But his eyes kept a surreptitious watch on the back of that big furry head.

Dusk had overtaken them like a thief during his sleep. They were passing through a dark wood now, heavy with the boughs of old trees hanging low, and wet with gray moss. The limbs were festooned with dark green vines that draped here and about like hanks of yarn before screwing down around the black tree trunks and smothering great boulders, then spilling carelessly onto the path. A quiet eeriness pervaded the thick, unattended foliage, giving the boy the feeling that they were intruding into some ancient bailiwick gone to seed.

A continual dripping reached his ears from some distance, and his eyes moved warily about in the umbrage, then back to the head, always back to the massive head of the bear. An owl hooted inquiringly somewhere overhead, following their progress up the thread of trail. *Who are you?* it seemed to ask. *What are you doing here? This is no place for a boy.*

Worm screwed his eyes up at it, couldn't see it, looked back on his path, at the arching trees gathering darkness into their great limbs, kept looking back, for he had the feeling that there was something just inside the shadows that was watching him, a spectral thing stealthily pursuing him, clicking just behind his ear.

Shuddering, he looked ahead. The horizon, brighter now and sharp with forests, rose into view as the boy and the bear finally crested the mountain. It had been a long and arduous ascent. But now, in the cool of the evening, with a steady breeze blowing in their faces and his path gently sloping away from him, the bear quickened his pace. There was a wild scent in the air.

Worm scanned the forest for signs of movement. He could see, falling behind the bear's steady progress, the dark, almost black, silhouettes of trees and shrubbery, standing out in sharp, pristine relief against the glow of crimson, gold, and purple-to-blue hues of a beautiful mountain sunset. And though the situation they were in was serious, if not desperate, it did not diminish such a glorious view.

A pair of mourning doves flew overhead on their way to roost for the night. Moments later, the erratic flight of several bats caught his eye, as they flapped and swooped along some invisible course, searching for insects, fruit, or the blood of small nocturnal rodents.

Worm could see the shimmering reflection of the sunset in a large mountain lake nestled in the forest below them about two miles ahead. In the distance he saw the glassy shapes of several smaller lakes, like so many mirrors, bearing witness to the heavens. It was a beautiful sight, and the concerted anthem of sights, sounds, and smells caused Worm's spirit to swell with exhilaration.

The great bear turned his head and looked over his shoulder at him. Worm looked down at the bear's face, studied the watery eyes that seemed to be looking through him, the large snout that concealed the deadly teeth. The bear seemed to be smiling at him again, sizing him up, as it were. A shiver trembled through his limbs. *But bears don't smile, do they?* his mind reasoned. *Then again, what do I know about bears?* Suddenly he had a desperate urge to jump off the brute and flee.

Terryll removed the spit from the small, smokeless flame. Again he had obeyed his instincts as a hunter and built the fire beneath an overhang of rocks, jutting out from a stand of yews and hawthorns. Whatever smoke there might be would be filtered through the colander of leaves above him and dissipate into the breeze downwind of the mountain. There would be no danger of scent.

He tasted the rabbit to see if it was done. *A few more minutes,* he thought. Then he placed the spit back over the fire and stood up to scan the mountainside for movement. He was careful to keep his profile obscured by the trunk of a yew, for the silhouette of a man could be seen for miles in the evening twilight.

"Ah, there you are, Hauwka, my friend," he said with a smile. "Right on time."

With his keen night vision, Terryll made out the form of the bear threading his way along the trail parallel to the lake, a few hundred yards away—just a black speck moving with an easy, plodding gait, and a much tinier speck on top. Terryll smiled.

The two boys picked the bones clean of meat and refreshed themselves with cold water from the lake below them. Hauwka had quickly devoured the rabbit that Terryll had left uncooked and was busy rooting through some raspberries he had found nearby. Terryll covered the fire with dirt, scattered leaves over the area, then slung his quiver of arrows around his chest and made ready to depart.

"We must leave at once," he said, grabbing his longbow.

"Where are we going?" Worm asked, glad to have the young hunter's company again.

"To the village of Killwyn Eden."

"Killwyn Eden?" Worm was astonished at the prospect of it. "Why, that's—"

"Another twenty miles through the mountains," Terryll retorted. "We should be there by noon on the morrow, God willing, if we can keep ahead of these Saxons." And then he added, "And assuming we don't run into any Picts along the way."

"*Picts?*" Worm shuddered.

He had never seen a Pict but had heard horror stories about them, mostly sung by traveling bards who came through his village during the summer and winter solstices. He had heard tell how they carved and painted strange designs all over their bodies and screamed hideously as they went into battle—and how they displayed the skulls of their fallen enemies all over their houses as trophies.

The bards told also through their songs how the Pictish warriors raped women and killed children, just for the sport of it, and that those who might be spared were either taken into slavery or sacrificed to their gods on altars of stone.

Worm remembered being so scared after the bards left that horrible nightmares attended his sleep for weeks. The distant whispers of fear once again echoed in his mind.

At Terryll's insistence and with his aid, Worm climbed up onto Hauwka's back again, cautiously—still fearing the worst—and with each movement, grimacing with pain. Once in place, he looked curiously down at the bear. Again, Hauwka seemed to be smiling back at him. The boy dismissed his thoughts and turned to Terryll, who had struck a quick pace for them.

Seeing the young hunter looking this way and that for danger suddenly triggered the reality of what Terryll had done, and was doing, for him. As far back as Worm could remember, he had always taken what he wanted. No one had ever offered him anything, let alone risked his life for him. The thought was too foreign and lofty to comprehend. It overwhelmed him.

"You risked your neck for me," Worm said at last, searching for the unfamiliar words to express his meaning. "I don't understand. I—"

"You needed help," Terryll cut in. "I'm sure that you would've done the same for me."

Worm remained silent. *No, I wouldn't have,* he thought. *I would've gotten away from there as fast as I could.* His thoughts troubled him. *Why? Why would I have run? Am I a coward? Or am I just smarter?* He looked down at this curious stranger and tried to balance his thoughts.

Terryll was unlike anyone that he had ever met. He seemed genuinely to care about Worm's well-being. Why? Perhaps he was just a fool. *That's it,* he deduced. No one would risk his life for a complete stranger. Or perhaps he wanted something from him. But what? Worm had nothing to give. He must be a fool. *That's it. He is nothing more than a fool.*

And with that, Worm tried to satisfy himself with his deduction. But strangely, the thought bit his conscience. So the boy continued to wrestle with the dilemma, uncomfortable with any of his answers, uncomfortable with everything about this stranger, and especially uncomfortable with this strange bear.

The moon rose full over the jagged horizon, casting long fingery shadows over the silvery landscape. The rugged mountain terrain, stacked high with a variety of conifers—fir, pine, spruce, and yews—gradually gave way to rolling hills that were congested with the broadleaf trees.

The two boys and the large bear continued downward on a winding course through the forest that eventually opened into a large meadow about a mile in width. They would have to skirt around its periphery to avoid detection out in the open.

But as they were circling the far side of the mead, a glint of light toward its center caught Terryll's eye.

Worm turned to follow his gaze and caught the back-lit shapes of a magnificent stag and several does trailing behind him. The stag paused and looked directly at the odd trio to see if they were cause for alarm. Worm could see the moonlight gleaming off his antlers as his head turned on his thick powerful neck. He followed the thin slivers of light as they arced and curved across each of their graceful outlines. *What beautiful creatures,* the boy thought. Suddenly the stag and does took off with a start and bounded away toward the tree line.

Hauwka froze and looked back on their trail. A low growl rumbled in his throat.

"I hear them too, my friend," Terryll said.

"Hear what?" Worm asked, not having heard a thing.

"Boarhounds," Terryll answered. "My diversions did not gain us enough time." The young hunter reacted at once. "Hauwka, you must go home. Home, boy—home!" Terryll looked intently into the bear's eyes.

46

Hauwka whimpered mournfully and turned reluctantly away from his friend.

The young hunter quickly fit an arrow onto his bowstring. "God be with you . . . er . . . Worm," he added, then ran toward the oncoming boarhounds.

Looking over his shoulder, Hauwka watched Terryll's sinewy form disappear into the blackness of the forest and whimpered again.

"What's going on?" Worm called out to Terryll, straining his eyes into the darkness. "Where are you going? I don't hear any boarhounds! What's—"

Hauwka took off down the slope like a shot.

Worm cried out in shock, grabbing hold of the bear's fur with both hands to keep from falling off his back. A knife of pain ripped through his shoulder from the sudden jolt of the animal's movement, and the boy gritted his teeth, biting back a cry.

He desperately clung to the bear's hide, like it or not, for it seemed as though they were flying. In fact, they were going so fast that the boy's eyes watered from the cold night wind that rushed past his face.

Even so, Worm felt the strangest sensation. Though his body was chilled from the cold blast upon it, his shoulder was actually getting warmer. He looked down at it and, to his horror, saw that his wound had reopened and that he was once again losing blood. He felt sick to his stomach. Never before had the boy felt so utterly helpless.

4
INTO THE FIRE

The iron broadhead ripped into the throat of the lead boarhound. The dog let out a muffled yelp and crumpled headlong to the earth with such force that Terryll could feel the ground shake. The young hunter loosed another arrow and hit the second dog square in his chest, killing him instantly. Then fitting a third arrow to his bow, he spun around and ran through the trees, leaping over boulders and fallen limbs toward higher ground. Hit-and-run tactics would be his only means of escape.

Sensing the gap closing between the dogs and him, Terryll turned and loosed his arrow at the foremost hound. But the dog, wary, leaped to the side in time for the shaft to miss him, and the arrow skittered harmlessly across the ground. Terryll raced down the trail as the hounds pressed their attack.

Terryll's path took him to the foot of the mountain where the sloping terrain was nothing more than a spill of rocks and boulders. He scrambled up the incline and quickly gained a vantage point from which to shoot. Again he loosed an arrow.

This time, however, the lead hound reacted too slowly and was hit high in its left shoulder. The dog let out a yelp and rolled several times before coming to a halt in the middle of the narrow path. The three dogs behind him, barking, foaming, and flinging bloody slaver into the air, hurdled him without breaking stride.

Terryll released two more arrows within heartbeats of each other. The first shaft took the lead hound in the heart, killing him, and the second struck the following hound in its hindquarters. The third hound shied in his tracks and retreated to lower ground to reevaluate his tactics.

Terryll continued to scale the face of the rocky mountainside, putting more distance between him and the horsemen, and the moribund wailings of dogs fell behind. This was precious time gained, but before he could stop to catch his wind, he heard the sickening thunder of horses crashing through the trees toward his position. Since he was on foot, the terrain was working to his advantage, but he was still well within range of bowshot.

The horsemen reined their mounts at the base of the slope amid the stricken boarhounds. The dogs that could walk quickly hobbled to the side to get out of the way of the horses, howling plaintively. Those that couldn't move were trampled underfoot.

"What madness is this?" Olaf yelled, looking down at the feathered shafts sticking out of the hounds.

"Are we chasing after a demon?" a man behind him added, awed by the carnage.

Some of the men nodded to one another. They had heard tales that strange unearthly creatures inhabited these dark British hills—devilish creatures that preyed on the souls of men.

Olaf snorted. "Are you becoming women at the sight of dead dogs?"

He wasn't concerned that men held religious beliefs or even superstitions. *Let them believe what they will,* he thought, *so long as it aids them in battle.* But he despised weakness in any man, friend or foe, choosing rather to witness the death of a Saxon coward than the death of a brave enemy. It was the way of Odin, the Norse god of warriors and heroes. It was also the way of the Viking. Olaf stood in his stirrups and strained his eyes into the darkness.

"Where is this *demon?*" he mocked.

"There he is, Olaf!" shouted one of the riders. "Moving along the face of the rocks!"

Following the man's point, Olaf found the moonlit shape of the young hunter, picking his way along the mountainside. His visage narrowed into a pitiless smile as he surveyed the boy's position, then ordered three of his bowmen to strike him down.

The men quickly drew their bows, aimed, and loosed their arrows, but their shafts fell short of their mark.

"You fools!" Olaf snapped, grabbing one of their bows. "You've aimed too low." He loosed an arrow at the boy, but it too fell yards short. He cursed aloud.

The youth had climbed out of their range.

Sensing his advantage, Terryll turned and set his feet. And then, with one fluid, instinctive motion, the young hunter drew the length of his arrow along the bow to the neck of its razor-sharp broadhead, and, pressing his thumb and draw fingers lightly against the anchor point of his cheek, he took aim.

There was a shuddering twang of bowstring, and the arrow was loosed at its distant mark. It had taken three seconds. The arrow rifled through the air—a perfect cast—and hit a man in the shoulder, piercing his chain mail with a sickening thunk, knocking him from his mount. The Saxons looked down at the wounded man writhing in the dirt and were amazed.

"What manner of bowman is this fiend?" one of the men thought aloud, as he and the others reined their horses backward. They knew that they were well within range of the boy's longbow. It was a range that Terryll needed to keep between them if he was going to survive.

"Get after him, you cowards!" The Viking scowled. "He is but flesh and blood. I'll have his miserable hide hanging from a pike, or I'll have yours!"

Olaf ordered several men to pursue the young Briton up the mountainside on foot. The men obeyed immediately and hurried up the path, their bows at the ready. He ordered several others to swing their horses around the lower slopes in order to outflank the boy, thereby heading off any attempts he might make to flee into the trees below. Finally, he commanded the rest of his men to follow him along an alternate trail leading to the crest, in an effort to cut off any upward route of escape.

Being on horseback, they would easily outdistance the boy to the summit. Once there, Olaf hoped that the lad—like a fox before the beaters—would be driven into the nets of the waiting hunters. It was a good battle tactic, and the horsemen spurred their mounts to the task.

Terryll looked over his shoulder and read their plan immediately. The half-dozen men on foot behind him kept their distance and moved from boulder to rock, providing the young archer with little target. It would be a foolish waste of arrows at this distance, Terryll thought. He could do nothing but press forward and hope against hope that somehow he would elude their trap.

His thoughts paused on Hauwka and the wounded boy, Worm. *A strange name,* he thought. *A strange boy.* He liked him though, strangely, and there weren't many boys in his village that he did like. He was comforted to know that for every mile that these Saxons pursued him, his friends would be another mile closer to Killwyn Eden, closer to the safety and comfort that his parents would provide. He said a hurried prayer for God's mercy on their behalf.

Running.

It had been several hours since the wounded boy slumped into unconsciousness. Worm's condition was now critical. He had already lost too much blood from his wound, most of which had poured onto the bear's left flank, matting his thick fur. Without treatment soon, it wasn't likely that the boy would see midday.

The bear looked up from the trail at the gray light breaking on the horizon. It was at least an hour before sunrise. Hauwka, following some

50

internal compass, knew that there was yet another valley to descend and another ridge to climb before the mountain terrain would fall away into the broad, fertile expanse of the Eden Valley, the "home" of Terryll's command.

Worm suddenly let out a loud moan. And soon after, the boy—delirious again from fever—started shouting and cursing at whatever demons or memories there were that were tormenting his mind.

Hauwka quickened his pace, even though the great bear was long spent from the night's hard journey.

The arrow shot through the side of his shirt and ricocheted off the rocks in front of the boy. Terryll gasped in shock. One of the horsemen had managed to gain a position behind him without his notice and was able to get off a bowshot. The gap had closed. Terryll swung around and returned the attack, sending the broadhead of his arrow deep into his enemy's chest. With a look of stunned disbelief frozen on his face, the man jolted upright from behind his cover, then fell hard to the ground in a seated position. Slowly he slumped over onto his side into the dirt.

"God have mercy on his soul!" Terryll cried out, as he gaped at the man's crumpled body.

The other men ducked behind rocks to avoid the young archer's aim, and Terryll, fighting an overwhelming feeling of nausea, raced ahead to reclaim his lead. The instinct for survival commanded it. Day would soon break. He had hoped to elude his pursuers under the cover of darkness, for there would be little chance of it in the light.

The trap was closing.

Slowly the roll of the earth dipped the horizon below the rising sun, and the blanket of darkness was uncovered with golden fingers of radiant light—light that reached through a crimson pane of glass over the eastern rim of hills. The crow of a distant rooster sounded amid bird song of myriad variety; each in its own way heralding the conquering light in obedience to the Creator's decree.

The bear reached the final summit and paused to catch his breath. At last. The demons of the fever had ceased to torment Worm's mind, and for the time being he slept quietly. Hauwka looked back on his trail for a moment to the rugged mountains of the night, then turned his massive head to gaze at the radiant landscape that framed the new day.

Stretching out before the bear were miles of the gently rolling and fertile Eden Valley, which sloped down from the northern hump of the Pennines to the Solway Firth sixty miles farther north. Tilled in rows against rows by the farmer's plow, it gave the vast landscape the appearance of an immense, quilted blanket. Separating the farmlands from one another were neatly trimmed hedgerows, stands of various shade trees, and low stone walls. Many of the stones had been quarried from the roads and ruins of the Roman predecessors.

Small stone and wooden farmhouses with roofs of thatched straw dotted the countryside in little clumps to provide community and protection. At first there were a few of these clumps, then a few more. At long last, the clumps of houses and farms met together in the center of the horizon, surrounded by woodlands, rivers, and lakes, to present the familiar profile of Terryll's village—Killwyn Eden of the highlands.

Once a Roman garrison called Braboniacum, Killwyn Eden—encircled by a berm of dirt and stone with wooden palisades surmounting it—was one of many military outposts built to defend Roman Britain against the barbarous raids of the Picts to the north. Roman-built ballistae and catapults still stood behind the berm, having effectively served over the generations in the village's defense.

But with the departure of the Romans and their legionaries, the outpost became a village, among others in the highlands, that had to stand on its own against whatever threat arose. Since the *Pax Romana* was no longer in effect, valiant and noble Britons such as Terryll's father, Allyndaar, were lifted onto their shields and proclaimed chieftains of their civitates. These men became the *Pax Brittania*, the peacemakers and defenders of their villages and farmlands, whose defense of such was measured solely by their courage and their prowess with longbow and broadsword.

Hauwka's great heart swelled against his cavernous breast. If animals experienced emotions kindred at all to those of the human spirit, then he was possessed of a little joy. For this was Terryll's village, this was his home. He took off down the slope in a loping gait.

Terryll watched the small line of horsemen thread its way through the trees at the foot of the mountain below. In the early morning light he could see the sun glinting off their armor and weapons, the crimson wolf's head on their shields cutting through the various green hues of the forest like blood spatters. Their eyes, glistening murderously, would be trained on the young hunter's position.

Turning his gaze upward, he scanned the summit of the rocky mountainside. He knew that the trail would open up into a bleak, flat, and treeless span of wind-blasted sandstone, providing him with not a stick of cover. He also knew that others would be waiting to greet him there with a volley of arrows. He had little choice but to move ahead and face them.

He knew that his time was short, and thoughts of his family filled his mind—each cherished face, like a sparkling jewel in a whirling setting of chronological events, smiling, crying, laughing, conversing, praying, and finally bidding him farewell.

Terryll let out a deep sigh, and as he rounded a bend in the slope—still given to a bittersweet reverie—four Saxons were suddenly upon him.

One of them was Ruddbane, the large burly man with red hair and bushy beard. Immediately the man knocked him against the wall of the mountain with his fist, taking his wind. Terryll fell in a sprawling heap.

"Get up, boy!" Ruddbane scowled savagely. "You are mine now!"

Still stunned, Terryll scrambled to his feet, but Ruddbane smashed him to the ground again. The boy lay in the dirt, dazed, furious, fumbling for his bow. Then a large net was thrown over his head by two others, rendering him powerless to defend himself. He was caught and now at the mercy of these merciless men.

Ruddbane grabbed Terryll's neck through the net and yanked him to his feet. Then he drew his battle-ax and raised it over the boy's head. "You should have killed me when you had the chance, boy. You robbed me of a kill back at Glenryth, so now I'll take your head as payment."

"Halt!" Olaf boomed.

Ruddbane jerked his head up the rocky path to the familiar winged silhouette standing at the crest of the slope.

"Bring the young Briton to me," Olaf commanded.

Ruddbane did not move. Instead he held his battle-ax still poised, his eyes burning with hate. "By rights he is my kill, Olaf. This is our law!"

"I said, bring the Briton to me!"

The horseman nearest Ruddbane quickly grabbed his arm. "Don't be a fool, Ruddbane."

The burly Saxon looked into the man's eyes and growled, "But he's not even one of us. He's a filthy Dane."

"He is Norduk's right arm," the man countered. "And you know that the Wolf will not tolerate disobedience. Even to the Dane."

"This is not right," the red-haired man snarled under his breath. "The Briton is my kill." Grudgingly he lowered his ax and glared down at the boy. "Do not think that you will escape the edge of my blade, Briton!" Then, shoving the boy to the ground, the Saxon dragged him, still in the net, up the stony path and threw him at the feet of the large Viking, making no attempt to conceal his disgust.

"Take the net off him," Olaf commanded two of his men. "I would like to see what manner of hellion has given us such pleasant sport."

The men removed the net and relieved the boy of his weapons, handing the longbow to the commander.

When Olaf saw how young his adversary was, he shook his head and laughed. "We have caught ourselves a suckling pig!"

Terryll rose to his feet and stood untrammeled before his captors. Peering at the Norseman, he said, "You have caught nothing but grief, Saxon."

"*Wie bitte?*" Olaf said, suddenly intrigued by the boy. "I see you understand our tongue."

"*Ich spreche etwas,*" Terryll retorted. Then added, "*Du bist einen Saxoner Schweine!*"

"Silence, whelp!" Ruddbane yelled, then blind-sided Terryll with his fist.

Terryll recoiled from the blow and glared into Ruddbane's eyes. "Even a woman can strike a man when he is not looking."

Ruddbane raised his fist again. "You little—"

"Leave him be!" Olaf interrupted. "I will handle the interrogation of the young Briton alone."

Ruddbane bristled. "As you wish . . . Commander." He backed away a few paces to the line of men that encircled Olaf and the boy. His eyes narrowed hatefully on the Norseman's head.

Olaf turned his gaze to Terryll with a look so piercing, like a steel edge, that it was difficult for the boy to endure it. The man was easily a head taller than the lad and twice his breadth. Bronze wings extended a foot and a half beyond the Norseman's helmet. Terryll felt as though he were looking up at a giant.

Then the man walked around the boy slowly, pulling on his mustache as he looked him over from head to toe. He made a full rotation without a word.

Terryll felt his hot scrutiny piercing his skin, probing his insides for weakness. If the truth were known, the boy's bravado was a desperate feint of courage, for inside he was terrified, and he knew without question that this fierce-looking Viking was not fooled for a minute. Death had caught him, was now taunting him, playing with him as a cat would a mouse. He knew that, as with cats, this Viking would soon tire of the game, and that would be the end of it. He prayed it would come quickly. Mercifully.

"What is your name, boy?" Olaf asked in the Latin tongue. Terryll's surprise registered around his eyes. He studied the man warily as one would a coiled snake.

"You are surprised that I speak Latin, boy? I speak Gaelic also," the Norseman boasted. "Though I consider it a barbaric language." Olaf examined the boy's longbow, hefting its weight. He appreciated fine craftsmanship. Testing the pull, he asked, "Where did you get this weapon, Briton?"

No response.

Olaf grunted. "Who is your father? Is he a British warrior?" he pressed.

No response.

"Did your father teach you to shoot the bow?"

"No. My mother did," Terryll replied, surprised that the words had come out of his mouth. "And she's the worst archer in my village."

Olaf stared at the boy as his mind translated the humor, then he threw his head back and laughed. "Perhaps she might teach a few of my men then," he chortled. "Most of them shoot no better than old women." Olaf admired the courage and wit of the boy. He would have made a good Viking, he mused. He will die well. "Are all Britons as scrawny as you?" he said in German for the benefit of his men. "Perhaps we will throw you to the dogs."

"I don't think there's enough of him to feed to the dogs," a man chortled.

"Perhaps not," another said. "But I'm sure they wouldn't mind having a little sport with him."

The horsemen elbowed one another and laughed.

"You wouldn't be speaking of those dogs below, would you?" the boy asked.

Olaf narrowed his eyes and smiled. "Where are you from, boy? You've got a lot of sand."

"Where I am from is of no concern to you," Terryll answered. "And where I am going is in God's hands alone!"

"Is that right? And which of the gods is that?" Olaf asked.

"I serve only one."

"Then perhaps that is why you are in such a bad way," the Viking mocked. He drove his thick finger into Terryll's chest. "You are in my hands, Briton. Tell your one god that as you prepare to meet him!"

Terryll stared at the man and held his peace.

Olaf grunted. Then, weary of the banter, he shouldered Terryll's longbow and strode to his horse, leaving Terryll standing alone, surrounded by the circle of violent horsemen and their murderous stares, narrowing on the boy's lonely form. A form that had stiffened perceptibly. A thought entered his mind to flee, but it quickly left.

"Kill him," Olaf ordered calmly.

Ruddbane stepped forward, a wicked sneer forming on his mouth as he took hold of his battle-ax.

Terryll looked heavenward, and a prayer winged from his lips.

Olaf paused by his horse and glanced back. "I've changed my mind," he said just as calmly. "Tie him up instead, Ruddbane! We will have a little sport with him later!"

"Tie him? You mean we are not going to kill him?" Ruddbane protested.

"When and where we kill him is my business, not yours!" Olaf countered. "Now do as I say."

Again the red-haired man glowered at his leader and fingered the haft of his battle-ax. The crest of the hill was suddenly very tense.

Olaf turned and faced him before mounting. "Do you have something else to say?"

Ruddbane grunted and fell away from his stare, then walked over to the boy, grumbling obscenities under his breath.

"What of the wounded thief?" asked another. "He cannot be far from here."

"Forget him!" Olaf snapped. "He is a flea—a dead flea by now!" The Norseman reined his horse to the northeast, digging his heels into its flanks. Ruddbane grabbed Terryll's hands and jerked them behind his back, causing a jolt of pain to shoot through his shoulders. But the boy did not cry out. Instead he stood straight and held his head up. The burly Saxon tied his hands tightly together with leather thongs, taking sadistic pleasure in cutting into his wrists, cursing him with every breath. Finishing his task, he leaned in close to the boy until the coarse bristles of his beard chafed against the back of Terryll's neck.

"You are mine, Briton," he promised. The stench of his breath was nauseating. "I'll not let any other rob me of my rightful kill. Do you understand? You are mine."

Ruddbane made a noose out of rope and slipped it over the boy's head, pulling it snug to his neck. Then the Saxon mounted his horse and tied the other end of the rope to his saddle.

Terryll screwed his head slightly as the coarse fibers of the rope scratched against his skin, but there was no relief from it.

"Now, you best keep up with me, boy," Ruddbane chortled, looking down at him over his black shield.

He spurred his horse, and the rope jerked taut against the back of the boy's neck with a biting slap of pain. The other horsemen laughed as Terryll stumbled forward and nearly lost his balance.

"If you don't," Ruddbane snarled, "you might fall down and get dragged from here to everlasting!" The burly Saxon let out a loud guffaw and clucked his horse forward.

Then the column filed sullenly off the barren hill into the trees below, heading on a bearing of north-by-northeast into the heat of the day.

Terryll wondered, as he struggled to keep his footing, where the day would take him.

A light wind stirred and then died.

5
THE BOWYER OF KILLWYN EDEN

The bowyer's heavy, calloused hands deftly held both ends of the draw knife as he skillfully pulled it along the bronze-colored stave of yew toward himself, carefully shaping its once-crude length into the graceful belly of a longbow. He smoothed his right hand over its surface to clean it of dust. Then, with eyes honed from years of experience, he examined every inch of curve, back and forth across his work.

He turned the stave in the wooden vise and tightened it gently. Again he drew the blade, following the straight lines of the yew's dark grain. He shifted his feet to view the bow from a different angle, looking for any imperfections in his cuts. What his eyes might not detect, his sensitive fingertips certainly would as they slowly stroked the limbs.

Flecks of wood dust fell into the pool of morning light at his feet as he, again, shifted his weight. Time and again the meticulous craftsman worked the wood, repeating the sequence like a choreography of dance until he was satisfied that he had finished the task to his liking.

He loosened the handle on the vise and removed the bow from its grip, blew minuscule wood particles from its surface, then hefted its weight. It was deceptively light for its six-foot length. He then grabbed its center with his left hand and held it away from his body to test its balance. Good. The longbow felt as though it were an extension of his very arm. It was a feeling of connection with the wood that only an archer could understand.

Holding it up to the light, the bowyer peered down its length and slowly spiraled its shape with his fingers. He studied the ivory-colored flat of its back and the delicate curve of its belly with his unforgiving eyes. It was as perfect as any man could make it.

His steel-blue eyes narrowed as he admired his work, forcing the lines of his weathered face to push deeply past his temples into his salted black hair. A hint of a smile played on the corners of his mouth. He was satisfied.

"The yew is God's gift to the bowman!" he exclaimed for the thousandth time. "Thank You, Lord, for the gift."

Allyndaar turned from his workbench and placed the longbow alongside several others in a grooved wall rack adjacent to him. He would add the leather grips, arrow shelves, and string nocks to these bows at a later time. For now he would select another stave from among those in a small room off the workshop, which had been drying for two years.

He walked across the oaken floor of his shop, a large airy room filled with bows of varying lengths and in various stages of completion, which was attached to his spacious red-tiled villa. Hanging about the plastered walls on wooden dowels were balls of twine and animal sinews used for making bowstrings and attaching different kinds of arrowheads (fowling tips, target points, and the broadheads for hunting and warfare) to the soft-wood shafts of the arrow.

Off to one side stood a small table used for making arrows. On it was a little wooden clamp that the bowyer used to secure the shafts, mostly fashioned out of spruce, and several small piles of bird feathers from both cocks and hens, used for the fletching. His wood rasps, mallets, chisels, drawknives, and sanding blocks were kept within reach on his heavy, time-worn workbench, where the bowyer had spent the better part of his life. There was a smell of wood and linseed oil in the place. A fine, masculine smell.

He paused for a moment and looked out the small, rounded arch that commanded a view of the courtyard below. In the center was a three-tiered water fountain set upon a patio tiled with flagstones. Encircling the fountain were a half-dozen granite benches having colorful mosaics cemented into them, and several wooden trellises resplendent with a variety of flowers. These were arrayed to take the best advantage of the beautiful aquatic focal point. An ivy-covered stone and plastered wall, tiles surmounting it, surrounded the sizable estate and enclosed the vegetable gardens, orchards, animal pens, horse stables, and well-watered grounds of field and shade trees. Such was Latin culture on the outposts of the Roman Empire.

The Romans had built a few more of these villa estates in Killwyn Eden (though on a smaller scale) and throughout Roman Britain, leaving them to the care of British chieftains, gentry, and clergy when the Empire waned in power. Many had fallen into ruin by this time, particularly in the south, where the invading Saxons and Angles (used to living in crude wooden huts) were unimpressed with such architecture and culture. They razed them or left them to decay in the elements.

The bowyer raised his eyes from the courtyard and scanned the verdant highlands that surrounded his village. He, too, was unimpressed with his lavish surroundings. He pondered the landscape before him and sighed. He was a hunter, a warrior, a Briton with Celtic blood flowing through his veins. He felt the most alive and free when wandering over the forests and wolds of the Pennines. Give him a bed of fir needles under a canopy of stars, a skin of apple cider, and his longbow, and the man had all the comforts of home that he needed. Indeed, it would be a continual feast.

But alas, Helena was of Roman parentage, of aristocratic stock that traced its origins to the first triumvirate of Rome, and he doubted whether she would appreciate keeping house in the forest with the squirrels and such.

He would wait until his son returned from his hunting trip, then take off into the hills and refresh his soul in God's wilderness. It was a shame, though, he mused, that Terryll and he couldn't hunt more together. But with the constant pressure from the Picts up north and now the Saxons southward, it would be unwise to leave Helena and Dagmere alone without a man in the house to defend them. Of course, Helena didn't like the notion of Terryll's being out in the hills on his own either.

"After all," she would argue with her husband each time the young hunter prepared to leave, "Terryll is still a boy!"

"He's seventeen," Allyndaar would counter. "Nearly a man."

"He's only sixteen, and he's still a boy," Helena would correct him.

"Well, he's almost seventeen." And so it would go.

But the boy had a wisdom and knowledge of the mountains and could track game and shoot the longbow like no other man he knew. Helena always worried about her boy being all over hill and dale with such savagery afoot. But Allyndaar knew well the heart that beat within his son, and to corral it, he argued, would do greater harm than to set it free.

Every time the argument arose, Helena capitulated—grudgingly— and off into the hills Terryll would go. And every time Allyndaar stood by his window, watching his boy climb the slopes outside their village until his form was embraced by the forest beyond. And every time, taking with him a piece of his own heart.

The bowyer let out another sigh.

The sound of an arrow thumping into a bale of straw pierced his thoughts. He looked over to the broad expanse of field off to the side of the house, where Dagmere had begun her morning archery practice.

Much to her mother's chagrin, Dagmere spent more time with her bow than she did with her studies in Latin, mathematics, and Scripture reading. Helena already had two hopeless bowmen in the family; she didn't need a third—especially her only daughter.

Dagmere's second arrow shot wide of the mark by a few inches, prompting Allyndaar to call out, "Don't pluck the string, Dag. Release it! Release it!"

"I know, Papa. I know," she answered. "I was careless."

She was a beautiful, slender girl of fifteen, with the soft curves and graceful limbs that begin to appear through the adolescent years of a young woman. Her long, auburn hair was pulled back loosely and fell to the small of her back in a single braid of three heavy cords, tied at the end with a leather thong. She had large blue eyes, thick lashes that curved outward with a delicate sweep, and a thin line of freckles spanning the bridge of her nose that faded softly into the roses of her cheeks.

Most of the boys in the village made stammering fools of themselves whenever they tried to win her affection. But she wasn't interested in them. They were all so immature, she thought. Right now, she was interested in perfecting her skills with the bow; there would be time for social amenities later on.

She fit another arrow onto her bow, then slowly drew her fingers back to her right cheek, keeping her eye riveted on the mark, not the tip. Then she arced the tip of her target-head downward until it fell just below her mark, all the while taking in a steady, shallow breath. She held it a short pause to steady her aim, and loosed the arrow.

Zwiiipp . . . thump! Dead center. She looked up at the window to see if her father was still watching. He was.

"Didn't miss the mark *that* time, Papa!" she bragged with a cocky smile.

"In battle, Dag, if you miss the mark once, you may be dead before you can try for it again!" he said, feigning a stern countenance.

"Oh, Papa!" she teased. "I'm as good as Terryll."

Her father just looked at her with that look of his.

"Well . . . almost."

"Don't compare yourself with your brother, Dagmere," he chided. "Compare yourself with the mark! It will teach you humility."

"Oh, Papa!"

Allyndaar smiled broadly as Dagmere turned and fetched another arrow from her quiver. She wore the quiver snug to her thigh and fastened to her hip by a leather strap that was slung around her waist. This was more ladylike, she thought and knew that it would help to appease her mother's objections.

As Allyndaar turned from the window, he bellowed out his final command: "Release the arrow! Release the arrow!"

The bowyer walked over to the small drying room. As he entered, he heard the muffled thump of Dagmere's arrow smacking the target. Dagmere was indeed very good with the bow, he mused. At one hundred yards, there were only a few in the village who could best her. At two hundred yards, she was better than all her peers. But this still didn't impress her mother a lick.

If it were not for the constant threat from the Picts, he would side more with Helena concerning Dagmere's upbringing. It troubled him, though, that she did not agree with him on this point. Helena insisted that mathematics and reading (especially the reading of Scriptures) were the most important foundations in a child's education. Allyndaar agreed. But he had seen too many times what the ruthless Picts could do to women and children who were taken in battle. His little girl would know how to defend herself if need be.

The bowyer selected a long stave of yew from the shelves, one that had a good balance of heartwood and sapwood. The heartwood was bronze in color, out of which the curved belly of the bow would be shaped. From the heartwood the longbow received its tremendous power. The sapwood was ivory, or light beige, from which the flat back of the bow would be planed. The softer sapwood gave the limbs of the longbow its springiness, its snap that would loose an arrow quickly from the bowstring.

It never ceased to amaze the bowyer that the very two kinds of wood needed to make the perfect longbow were placed in one tree—the gnarly little yew. Allyndaar shook his head at the thought.

The bowyer walked over to his workbench and placed the stave into the wooden vise and tightened it snugly. This one was to be for the chieftain of Bowness—a large, heavyset, bear of a man named Belfourt, who had a bushy red-brown beard and applelike cheeks.

The Celt was good-natured and broad-spoken, with a hearty laugh, but in battle he was as fierce as a sow bear protecting her cubs. He and Allyndaar were the best of friends. The two had spent many nights together in the halls of Killwyn Eden and Bowness over mugs of ale, talking of past battles, the valiant exploits of fallen heroes, and religion.

Belfourt's beliefs lay in the Celtic traditional deities (Belenos, Toutatis, Taranis, among a pantheon of others). He could not fathom the Christian notion of a single God, nor was he able to grasp the most salient point of the Christian faith: that God, incarnate in Jesus Christ, had suffered humiliation and death upon a Roman cross—a point that was a major stumbling block to him. However, he immensely enjoyed sparring with Allyndaar over the issue, more out of good fun than of any serious pursuit of truth. The chieftain of Bowness had lost many of his village and family to the Picts. Because his hamlet was the northernmost civitas in Britain—situated as it was on the Solway Firth—it was often raided by those warlike painted men, who swarmed over Hadrian's Wall, inflicting death and destruction upon the Britons. His people had seen much bloodshed at the hands of these northern invaders, and bitter hatred toward them formed the bedrock of their culture and lore. The thought of a God who could love such brutish people was beyond Belfort's sensibilities.

But Allyndaar was patient; he understood his friend's heart. They would talk again.

A clap of thunder brought the bowyer's mind back to his work. The morning sunlight that had shone into the workshop was gradually eclipsed by a cool umbrage that inched its way down the wall opposite the window, pulling its darkness, like an evening shade, across the floor to Allyndaar's feet, enveloping the room. A bolt of lightning ripped diagonally through the sky, followed a moment later by a second, louder clap of thunder, much louder.

Allyndaar glanced out the window at a black wall of thunderheads cresting the southern mountains. They took on a menacing form and countenance as they descended like a huge breaker of black water, rolling down into the Eden Valley toward the village. The air before it was charged with a bright and quiet expectancy.

"Looks like we're in for a storm," he said redundantly, then turned his gaze back to his longbow. As he reached for his drawknife, he heard the familiar thump of Dagmere's arrow hitting the target—and then the unexpected.

"Papa! Papa! Come quickly!" Dagmere cried out. "It's the bear! It's the bear coming down from the hills!"

Allyndaar leaped up from his bench and rushed to the window.

"And it looks like someone's lying on his back!" Dagmere caught his gaze, then turned and pointed to the hills behind their village. "Look, Papa! It's Hauwka!"

Allyndaar strained his eyes to pick up the movement of the bear. He spotted him then, on the western slope, lumbering slowly toward them with his head low and heavy. He saw the quiet form astraddle his back and knew at once. "Something's wrong!"

Obviously hearing the commotion outside, Helena hurried out of the house to her daughter. "What are you shouting about, Dagmere?"

"It's the bear, Mama!" the girl cried, pointing excitedly to the hills. "Hauwka is coming, and someone is lying on top of him! It looks like he's hurt!"

Helena looked up at the hill, and, finding the uncertain shape, her eyes stared in horror. "Terryll!" she gasped. "O God, have mercy!" Then she cried up to her husband's workroom for help. "Allyn! Come quickly! It's Terryll!"

But the bowyer was already on his way.

He raced past Helena over the broad steading with its many trees bending now before the storm, their leaves flickering silvery. Then he ran through the villa's gates and headed for the gateway of the village. Dagmere took after her father, leaving her mother trailing behind.

Lifting her dress away from her legs to avoid tripping, Helena cried again, "O God, have mercy! Have mercy on my son!"

Allyndaar could tell even from a distance that it wasn't Terryll on Hauwka's back. He reached the bear within minutes. Dagmere arrived seconds later. The bear paused and let out a loud moan, then turned his head toward the wounded boy who lay deathly still.

"Easy, boy . . . easy," Allyndaar said, calming the bear. "We'll take care of him now." Then he wiped the hair out of the boy's face to check for signs of life.

"Is he . . . is he *dead*, Papa?" Dagmere asked, stricken by the appalling sight.

Allyndaar checked the pulse on the boy's neck. "Not yet." Then he looked at the wound in his shoulder. "But he's hurt bad, real bad. His breathing is very shallow. Come on, big fella."

The bear looked from the boy to Allyndaar. Again, he let out a moan.

"I know, Hauwka," Allyndaar said. "You've done well in bringing him to us." He looked at the boy again and added, "I just hope that you're in time. Come. We must get him to the house quickly."

Helena met them on the hill, wild-eyed and panting, and, seeing the boy's long, sand-colored hair, she burst into tears. It wasn't Terryll. "Thank You, God! Thank You!" she cried aloud. But her relief was immediately eclipsed by the horror of what filled her eyes. "Oh, merciful heaven! The dear boy."

Blood from the boy's wound had dried on his tattered clothes and left arm, which hung limp over the bear's flank, a single scab of sickening reddish-brown. Much of Hauwka's fur was also matted with the boy's blood, blood that fused the two of them together with a grisly bond.

Helena could not believe that the lad was still alive. As she walked alongside him, compassion for the young stranger swelled in her breast— the tender mercies of motherhood fiercely edging away the revulsion— and taking hold of his quiet hand, she gently patted it, gently caressed his face, and smoothed the long tangles of hair from his brow.

"Oh, Allyn. How could such a thing have happened to him?" she wondered. "His clothes are such tatters. Who could he be? Do you suppose that he is a friend of Terryll's?"

"I don't know, Helena."

"Why has God brought such a one into our hands?"

Allyndaar did not answer. Instead, he glanced back at the boy's gray face and shook his head.

"Papa, where is Terryll?" Dagmere asked. "Do you think that he's in trouble?"

The question had already been asked thoughtfully in each of her parents' hearts.

Allyndaar turned his gaze to the storm-shrouded mountains in the distance, then over to Helena. She looked up to him and met his eyes, and for an instant he was struck by her beauty—a strange interruption, given the circumstances.

His eyes quickly swept along her thick brown tresses, which trapped the remaining highlights of darkened light and cascaded down over her graceful womanly shape. She kept her hair pulled away from her face with an ivory comb, revealing her refined classical features. He could read the questions of a mother's heart in her beautiful brown eyes, her intelligent, inquisitive eyes, eyes moist with concern for their son.

Helena had brought such gentle strength to him during the many hardships of their married years, and now, with life's uncertainty again looming dark overhead, he felt a longing for the comfort of her touch.

Allyndaar smiled warmly to reassure her that everything was going to be fine, but he knew in his heart that something was desperately wrong. So did she.

He turned his attention to his daughter's unanswered question. "I'm sure that Terryll is well, Dag," he said. "No one knows the mountains like your brother." Then he patted her head gently and added with a smile, "And there is no one in all the land who can match his skill with the longbow—not Picts, not Saxons—not even little sisters!"

His intention was not lost on the young archer.

"Oh, Papa."

A jagged sword of brilliant light stabbed into the darkness, followed immediately by the deafening report of the thunderclap. The bowyer's family quickened their pace to the village gates, in hopes of outdistancing the oncoming sheets of rain. The mind of each was burdened with questions about the wounded young stranger and the welfare of Terryll. But before they could reach shelter, the storm overtook them, instantly deluging them in a fierce torrent of rain that drew across the landscape's stage like some monstrous curtain of water.

The great bear paused for a moment before entering the gates. A sudden surge of wind blew through the wet blades of field grass at his feet. He looked over his shoulder toward the cold, drenched mountains to the south and let out a long mournful cry that echoed up the Eden Valley and beyond into the lonesome forests of the highlands.

6
THE RAGING
STORM

Hauwka stood to his full height and placed his front paws on the outside ledge of the small, rounded arch that was the window of the
master bedroom. It was pouring rain. The storm released its full fury
against the village of Killwyn Eden, but the bear seemed ignorant of its
wrath. He peered through the opening, drenched to his skin, and
watched as Allyndaar lowered the boy onto a bed against the wall, laying
him on his right side to expose the back of his left shoulder.

Helena sat down on the bed next to the boy and immediately began to cut away the clothes from his shoulder with a pair of shears, revealing bloodied bandages beneath. As she felt the texture of the woolen
fabric, she let out a little gasp.

"Allyn, these bandages were made from one of Terryll's tunics!"

"Are you certain?"

She turned her eyes to one of the ties of a knot. Stretching the
fabric between her thumbs, she examined it closely. "Yes! The weave in
these bandages is mine!" she said excitedly. "I always triple-stitch the
end of a sleeve to keep it from unraveling. See here," she said, pointing
out the stitching. "Terryll must have bandaged this boy!" She looked up
at Allyndaar and asked hopefully, "Our boy is safe, isn't he, Allyn?"

"I'm sure he is," Allyndaar assured her. But the confident smile
on his face belied a darkening concern.

Dagmere came into the room carrying a basin of water and set it on
a small stool next to the bed.

Helena quickly dipped a towel into the water, then gently dabbed
the bandaged area around the wound. She did this several times, allowing
the water to thoroughly soak through the blood-hardened fabric so that
she could pull the bandages free of the wound without reopening it.
Slowly she stripped away the layers of cloth and tossed them to the side.

Dagmere sat at the boy's head and combed several strands of matted hair away from his eyes with her fingers. Then, with a cool, moist
towel, she gently wiped away the beads of perspiration. Watching her

hands move across his brow, she noticed how ghostly pale his skin was beneath hers, as though she were attending to the needs of a corpse. She shuddered at the thought.

Allyndaar checked the boy's pulse and grunted. It was weak, and his breathing was still shallow and labored.

"Is he going to be all right, Papa?"

Allyndaar shook his head. "It is too early to tell." Then he left to prepare an herbal poultice.

Helena carefully tugged on the last strip of bandage, but it was stuck fast on the clot of blood. "This poor boy," she said aloud, easing her pull. As she squeezed more water on it, her heart swelled with concern for Terryll. Where was he? What was he doing? Was he safe?

"Who do you think he is, Mama?"

"I don't know, Dagmere, but I know that in some way this boy's path has crossed Terryll's."

Dagmere looked at the bear, who was keeping a silent vigil from the window. "*You* know, don't you, Hauwka?" she asked wistfully.

The bear opened his mouth and let out a low moan.

Helena smiled as she looked over at Hauwka. His glistening black eyes were looking directly at hers. With his big rain-soaked head and paws hanging over the sill, craning his neck as though to see how the boy was doing, the bear was indeed an unusual sight.

Ordinarily Helena would have been terrified at the thought of a wild bear anywhere near their home, let alone hanging through their bedroom window during a thunderstorm. Especially this bear! He was the largest bear that anyone in the village had ever seen—not at all like the smaller black bears that were indigenous to the area. Hauwka was indeed an aberration—one of the anakim of his species.

He was also fierce-looking. With a mouth full of sharp teeth, finger-length claws, and huge, powerful limbs, he could tear any man or beast to shreds in seconds, if he so desired. And yet there was a sweet, gentle spirit about him, a kindness in his eyes that belayed any fear of him. Hauwka was truly a mystery. A wonder.

Helena dabbed more water onto the wound, gave another gentle tug at the bandage, and . . . "There," she said, as the cloth pulled free, revealing a cruel, crimson tear in the boy's skin.

Fear gripped Helena's heart as she gaped at the wicked rend of flesh. *Oh, God*, she thought, *how could this have happened? The dear, dear boy.*

Dagmere winced at the ugly sight, and once again Hauwka let out a mournful cry.

Quickly Helena moistened her towel and began to cleanse the area around the wound. Apart from a slow ooze of blood at one corner, it hadn't reopened. This was good, for it showed that the wound had begun to seal itself from within.

Allyndaar entered, carrying several strips of clean linen and a small wooden bowl. "Here is the poultice," he said, offering the bowl to Helena.

"Look at the wound, Allyn," she said. "Isn't it an—"

"Arrow wound," he interrupted, as he studied the familiar shape. A dark cast swept over his brow.

"Who do you think shot him?" Helena asked, her eyes betraying an umbral shift in her thinking. As she pressed the poultice onto the wound, she noted that her fingers were trembling.

"Could've been anybody," Allyndaar said, veiling his suspicions. "There's no way to tell, not knowing where he is from."

"But Terryll said he was going to hunt more to the south this time, didn't he?" Helena said anxiously. "He probably found this boy somewhere down—" She broke off. A thought suddenly occurred to her, a terrible thought, and she struggled to hold back a deluge of emotions. As she continued, her voice grew noticeably agitated, thin, accelerating in tempo. "There are horrible men in the south, Allyn. Saxons. Men who are cruel and uncivilized—men who murder women and children. Why would Terryll want to hunt anywhere near them? Why did we ever let him go? I knew we shouldn't have allowed—"

"Now is not the time, Helena!" Allyndaar interrupted, too harshly.

She looked at him as though he had just slapped her, then she buried her face in her hands and wept.

Allyndaar shook his head and blew out a desperate sigh.

"He'll be all right, Mama," Dagmere offered, suddenly feeling very awkward and confused. She reached her arm over her mother's shoulders and patted her gently. "Terryll can take care of himself. He'll be all right. You'll see."

Helena sat upright and pulled herself together with strong Latin resolve. Then, smiling at her daughter, she took her hand and said, "I know, Dag. I know."

"I'm sorry, Helena," her husband offered. "I didn't mean to speak so harshly."

"It's not your fault, Allyn. I'm just all jangled up inside, that's all. It'll pass. I'll be fine. Now, let's take care of this boy."

Allyndaar helped her wrap the lengths of cloth firmly around Worm's shoulder, then carefully rolled the boy over onto his back. Finishing his task, the man stood up with a determined look on his face.

"I'm going now to look for Terryll," he said. "I can do nothing more here for this boy, but I can at least try to find our son."

"But, Allyn, the storm," she said. "Do you really think you can find him now?"

"Hauwka knows where he is. He'll lead me to him, or at least to the place where Terryll dressed this boy's wounds."

Allyndaar was about to leave when Dagmere called out, "But Papa! The bear's gone!"

"What!"

Allyndaar raced to the window and looked around the courtyard below. There was no sign of the bear. He quickly scanned the hills in the direction from which the bear had come. A flash of lightning lit up the terrain for a flickering moment, but still there was no sign of the bear—just the steady, black downpour that was sure to wash away any sign of his tracks.

"But he was looking through the window just a minute ago," Helena protested.

"Well, he's gone now!" Allyndaar yelled, then he slammed his fist hard against the windowsill and cursed.

Dagmere's eyes bugged open.

Helena reeled in shock. *"Allyn!"*

Not hearing the rebuke that followed, Allyndaar ran out into the great room, grabbed his longbow and quiver, then bolted from the house into the storm. He ran first to the place outside the window where the bear had been standing. But there was only a small lake of rain-pelted water that totally obliterated any sign of the bear's presence.

The man spun around and ran to the village gates, then onto the hill, frantically looking for any tracks that might still be intact. Nothing. Nothing but a confluence of a thousand little rivers rushing down the slope, meeting at each of his footfalls. He cursed again.

A blast of brilliant light rent the sky, illuminating the trees and hills and rocks with a ghostly pallor, and everything flickered surrealistically for a second in black and white contrasts. Immediately a deafening clap of thunder cracked a retort, and the ground shuddered.

Slowly, a rage born out of helplessness began to rise within the man like a fever. Bracing himself against the slanting downpour, he ran panting up the watery hillside into the dark-gray tree line, soaked to the skin. Reaching the crest, he searched vainly through rocks and mud for any sign of the bear. He prayed desperately for God's mercy, while out of the same breath he cursed the rain and the bear and his own foolhardiness for letting the beast out of his sight. Without the bear he could not hope to find his son.

Where was that bear?

Driven by a paternal madness, Allyndaar ran through the trees over fallen limbs and rocks, half-blinded by the driving rain and the slapping of soggy leaves and branches against his face that whipped him with cruel mockery. Still the bear was nowhere in sight.

He stopped. The wind howled angrily about him and tore tree limbs and leaves violently from their moorings, flinging them mindlessly about. He squinted through the downpour into the forest, looking every direction, eyes glaring, blurred and wild, often mistaking the black boles of trees for the bear. He would run each time, fighting the trees and elements to investigate. He had to—the madness was driving him now.

And each time, nothing. With each disappointment the panic grew, the desperation quickened. He looked. Peered into the black wash. A movement caught his eye. What was that? Running, his foot caught a jutting rock, and he fell headlong into a trough of mud. It was the final insult to his plight and dignity.

He lay sprawled in the mire in humiliating silence for several moments, soaked to his skin with rain and mud and sweat, while his rage built to a violent crescendo. Then, unable to contain his fury any longer, he jumped to his feet, screamed at the heavens, and flung his quiver of arrows into the trees—a futile, mannish demonstration of puny defiance against the overwhelming storm.

The storm answered with a blast of light and an ear-splitting peal of raw power.

Angered to a blood-rage, Allyndaar grabbed his longbow by one end, hurled it into the nearest tree with all of his strength, and split the thing in two with a mournful crack.

"Terryllll!" he cried plaintively to the wretched skies, then collapsed onto his knees in the muck, spent of his human reserves, a man beaten and broken like his longbow, and he wept bitterly.

In time the black thunderheads passed by overhead, leaving behind steady but gentle rains that spattered noisily on the leaves and earth. Like so, the dark and violent rage in Allyndaar's spirit abated, leaving in its wake a cold, hollow, and despondent void.

But voids are not long empty. Slowly, with a singular clarity in his soul, Allyndaar looked up to the heavens and blinked away the rain and tears. Then, altogether finished with himself, he raised himself out of the mud, full of contrition, and surrendered his boy to God's mercy. There was nothing more that he could do. And with that he was filled with a sweet Presence.

Helena had done all that she could do for the wounded boy and stood next to the bed, looking down at him thoughtfully. Hopefully the continual application of cool towels to his brow and limbs would lower his body temperature and aid his healing, a task for which Dagmere had gladly offered her services.

The girl dipped the towel into the basin and gingerly wiped the beads of sweat from around his temples. He was so young, she thought, not much older than she—perhaps a year or so. Presently the weary voice of her father sounded from across the bedroom.

"I'm back."

Helena and Dagmere both looked up as Allyndaar now stood slump-shouldered, rain-soaked, and muddied, in the doorway.

"What happened, Allyn?" Helena asked. "You look terrible! Are you all right?"

"I feel like a fool," he replied.

"You couldn't find the bear, Papa?" Dagmere asked.

"No, I couldn't find the bear." Strangely, he chuckled. "There's nothing more we can do, except to give Terryll over to God's providence."

Helena hurried over to her husband. "Come. Let me get you out of these wet clothes, before I have two sick men to take care of." Then looking back to her daughter she said, "We'll be right back, Dagmere. Call if you need help."

"I will, Mama."

As Helena left the room with her husband, her heart swelled again for her son. She wondered if somewhere, out in the storm, he too was warm and dry . . . and safe.

Dagmere watched them leave, feeling the weight of their concern. She looked out the window. In the distance the dark clouds flickered with lightning, followed by a low, almost friendly rumbling. And the rain fell gently from the sky and made a hissing sound. She took a deep breath and let it out in a sigh.

Then, turning to the boy, she focused her attention on his needs. She wiped the young stranger's brow and pondered within her heart who he might be.

In the aloneness of the room, she noticed his features for the first time. There was an eerie familiarity about him that struck a distant chord in her mind. But the note was fleeting and disappeared as quickly as she gave ear to it.

A foolish thought, she mused.

7
THE CREST

Twenty minutes later, Dagmere's parents entered the room and walked over to the bed. Allyndaar, markedly fresher looking in a change of clothes, pressed his fingers lightly against the boy's carotid artery.

"His pulse and breathing are more steady," he said.

"That's good," Helena offered, as she cupped his warm cheek in her hand. "We've done all that we can do for him." She turned to Dagmere. "Has he stirred any?"

"Not a bit," she replied, rinsing her towel. "He's been quiet, actually." She applied the cool cloth to his cheek. "He isn't going to die, is he, Mama?"

"I think he's weathered the worst of it," Helena answered. "All we can do now is hope that his fever breaks soon. Do you want me to take over? You look tired."

"No, I'm fine. I enjoy it, really."

Helena smiled. She grabbed the shears and began to cut away the rest of the boy's tattered shirt. But when she tried to pull his right arm free of the sleeve, she noticed that he was clutching tightly something tied around his neck. She struggled to pry the object out of his fingers, but the boy held onto it with a deathlike grip.

"Help me please, Allyn," she said. "He doesn't want to let go of this thing."

"It looks like a medallion," offered Dagmere, who could see a part of it shining through his fingers. She hadn't noticed it before.

Allyndaar loosened the boy's fingers and slipped the medallion over his head. "You're right," he said, glancing at it casually. "It has some sort of engraving on it."

Suddenly the engraving caught his attention. His eyes narrowed with interest as he studied the piece more closely. Then, slowly, his expression was eclipsed by a look of amazement.

Observing the shift in his features, Dagmere asked, "What is it, Papa?"

Helena detected the change as well. "Is there something wrong, Allyn?" she asked. "What is it?"

Allyndaar looked down at the boy's face and scrutinized his features. "A crest," he answered slowly. "A family crest." After a few moments he glanced over at Helena with a look of incredulity. "I believe I know who this boy is."

"Who?"

"Yes—who, Papa?"

"It's astounding," Allyndaar said, gazing at the medallion.

"What?" Helena wanted to know.

"Yes—what, Papa?"

Allyndaar looked at his wife. "Do you remember many years ago, when the metalsmith from Glenryth came here to trade for some longbows?"

"Vaguely," Helena responded. "But what has that to do with this boy?"

"The Saxons were marshaling their forces against the southland," Allyndaar replied absently, as he looked across the bedroom.

There was a large wooden chest beneath the wall table.

"Yes, I remember, Allyn," Helena said, growing frustrated. "And the boy . . ."

But Allyndaar had walked over to the wall table, lost in a whirl of questions, and had not heard her query. He pulled the chest from under the table and removed the blankets covering it, then unstrapped the two leather belts that secured the top. Slowly he raised the heavy lid.

Immediately a musty smell wafted up into his face, the kind of heavy smell that is born of time and dust and men. But it was a pleasant smell, aromatic, like the heady bouquet of a fine, aged wine or the greeting of a good friend after many years of absence. Allyndaar drank it in.

Helena's eyes shot open. "Can you see what he's doing, Dag? He hasn't opened that old trunk, has he?"

"I think so, Mama."

"Oh, don't, Allyn," Helena pleaded. "It'll smell up the whole room."

"*Huh?*" He heard that. Then he grunted with holy contempt.

"It'll take a week to air the room out," she added.

"Phew, Papa," Dagmere agreed. "Mama's right. It does smell awful."

Allyndaar frowned and mumbled, "Women," under his breath as he rummaged eagerly through the box's contents, ignoring further comments, which were legion.

This was Allyndaar's war chest, his private place. It hadn't been disturbed in years. Helena had her house, her imported furniture, porcelains, scrolls, and sundry knickknacks, but Allyndaar had only this chest, this beat-up bastion of manliness that he guarded jealously. Had he not opened it today, it would have remained undisturbed for many more years, aging to some indescribable fineness.

In it were tendered the treasures that find their way into a man's life—an ill-fitting suit of mail that he had worn as a young man when he fought against the Picts along the Wall; a dented helm with a broken side-horn that was taken from a Norseman who had departed suddenly to the halls of Odin and had no further need of it; and an old cloak, made from several wolf furs that he took from a dead Frisian, twenty-five years past, in his first battle. This piece alone was responsible for most of the aroma emanating from the trunk. He had managed to rescue it time and again from Helena's clandestine attempts to toss it, but now it lay secure inside his war chest, safe from female nostrils and extradition.

As he rummaged through these and other such treasures, he added to his explanation. "Do you remember the little boy the metalsmith brought with him? He would have been about five—maybe six years old then. Wait!" He brightened. Moving aside an old wineskin, given to him by Belfourt to commemorate their lasting friendship, he raised a long slender object out of the bottom of the chest. "Ah! Here it is!"

"Here is *what?*" Helena asked, growing impatient, craning her neck to see around his back. "And please shut that trunk."

Allyndaar did. He had what he was looking for in his hands. Carefully he unwrapped its leather covering, as Helena and Dagmere looked on, suffering.

"I'd forgotten how beautiful it was!" he exclaimed, beholding the exquisite workmanship of the sword. He turned the blade in his hands and examined its hilt. Helena was not the least impressed. "Allyndaar. Will you please tell me what that old sword has to do with this boy's identity?"

Allyndaar's face brightened again as he scrutinized the engraving on the hilt. "The little boy who came with the metalsmith is this boy here," he said, walking back to the bed.

Helena's interest was suddenly piqued. "How do you know?"

"Yes, Papa, how do you know?"

Allyndaar held the medallion in front of Helena's eyes. "Do you see the crest that is on his medallion?"

Helena took the medallion from Allyndaar and studied it for several moments. Her eyes first fell on a laurel wreath that encircled the head of a bear. It was beautifully engraved. With delicate chisel-cuts made in the bronze oval, the image of the wreath and bear was raised above a background of stippling, and with such fine detail it was obviously the work of a master craftsman.

Then she noticed two letters on either side of the bear's head: the Greek letters Chi and Rho—X and P. She immediately recognized their meaning.

"The chi-rho," she said, without taking her eyes off the medallion. "It is a symbol for Christ. And the laurel wreath represents His victory over death."

Dagmere angled her head to see.

"Now look at the crest that is engraved on the hilt," Allyndaar said, lifting it.

Helena looked at the crest on the sword, then again at the one on the medallion. "They are the same! But surely there are other crests with the chi-rho and laurel wreath."

"Yes, but not with the head of the bear in its center," he countered. "This crest belonged to the family of the metalsmith alone. He told me so." Allyndaar looked over at the sleeping boy. "His father was the leader of the Britons who fought at the Battle of Glenryth. His name is sung in halls all over Britain."

"Why, Papa?"

"Because he was a great man," her father replied. "Why, with only a handful of men he halted the Saxon invasion—routed their army." He chortled. "Sent them running back to Londinium with their tails between their legs."

"But weren't all the Britons killed in the battle?" Helena asked.

"Yes. But because of their great courage. Yes—" the chieftain broke off for a moment's reflection "—we of the northlands have enjoyed a time of peace because of the metalsmith from Glenryth. And this boy is his son—the son of Caelryck."

"Caelryck?" Helena gasped. It was a name that had grown into legend. "Are you sure, Allyn?"

"As sure as I know that this is the crest of Caelryck," he said, turning his eyes to the engraving on the sword. "The boy's name is Aeryck!"

"*Aeryck!*" Dagmere perked up. A chord of memory was struck at the sound of his name, then joined by a symphony of notes. "It *is* Aeryck! I knew there was something familiar about his face. Hey . . ." She trailed the last syllable as her symphony was interrupted by a discordant note. "Wait a minute! I remember that I didn't like that boy." She looked down at his face and scowled. "He used to make faces at me, and he called me a funny name."

Without thinking, Dagmere covered her nose with her hand, then, catching herself, quickly pulled it away.

"You can remember something that long ago, Dagmere?" Helena asked. "You were only about four or five at the time."

"I remember," she said, giving the boy a sour look. "Vividly!"

"Really, Dag?" her father teased. "What did he call you?"

"Never mind."

"You know that little boys always tease the ones they like." He chuckled.

Dagmere frowned. "Oh, Papa."

But as she looked down at the boy, he grimaced with pain and groaned a little, and she softened with compassion. She wiped the water from his brow with her towel and combed the hair away from his wet temples. "But that was many years ago," she said, changing her tone. "And I'm sure that he's changed by now."

Suddenly the boy moaned and turned his head back and forth on the pillow, as if struggling with his dreams. "Get away from me . . .no . . . don't eat me!" he mumbled, then grew silent and exhaled a deep sigh.

Dagmere and Helena exchanged looks, shrugged their shoulders. Helena opened her hand to look again at the small bronze medallion. She studied the images carefully. "Do you think that he is of the Christian faith, Allyn?" she asked.

"I know that his father was. We discussed his faith at length when he gave me this sword." Allyndaar gently stroked his thumb over the relief of the crest, adding, "But whether or not young Aeryck is, I cannot say."

Helena stood next to her husband and looked down at the sleeping youth. He was at peace. She looked at her husband and was surprised to see deep lines of concern drawn across his brow. "What is it, Allyn?"

"It puzzles me that the son of Caelryck would be dressed in such rags," he said, as he scrutinized the artistry of the bear's detail. He considered the thought for several moments but could only find more questions.

Allyndaar moved to the window and gazed dully across the drizzled panorama of the highlands, pondering the well-being of his son. His concern grew darker with each thought collected. He could see lightning flashing in the north and hear the tympany of thunder rolling away into the distance, trailing off into echoes. The storm had hit sudden and hard; its passing was just as it came.

But the British chieftain felt the rumblings of another front approaching over the horizon, like a runner heralding ill tidings from a distant battle. There was nothing concrete that he could point to, save the wound in the boy's shoulder. It was more a feeling of dread that had begun to worm its way into his mind, one that he couldn't shake. It worked on him like a spell. The air grew still and heavy, almost oppressively so. He felt a shiver race along his spine, but he attributed it to his earlier drenching.

Then a cool touch to his hand broke the spell. It was Helena. She embraced him warmly and laid her head lightly against his shoulder. Neither spoke a word as they stood staring out the window for several moments, each drawing upon the other's strength.

"I think he's waking up, Mama," Dagmere interrupted.

The boy stirred and let out several incoherent moans.

Helena moved to the boy's side and felt his face; it was cool, diaphoretic. Then water began to pour out of him profusely. The fever had broken. Again he stirred and groaned a few more unintelligible phrases about moldy bread and something wanting to eat him.

Dagmere looked at her mother. "What should we do, Mama? Should we feed him or something?"

"No, not yet," Helena answered. She smiled down at the boy. "Let's let him sleep for now. He's going to be just fine."

"Can I stay with him, Mama? He might need someone here when he wakes up."

"All right, Dagmere," her mother answered. "But call us as soon as he does."

"I will, Mama."

Helena picked up the dirty bandages next to the bedside and left the room with Allyndaar—she holding the small medallion and he the sword of Caelryck.

Dagmere was alone with the boy. The room was quiet save for the soft rhythm of his breathing and an occasional panicked utterance from his dreams. She looked down at his sleeping face and gently caressed his brow with the cool towel and smiled.

He breathed a quiet sigh and rolled his head so that his face looked directly up at hers.

Dagmere studied the face thoughtfully. He was handsome, she noticed, as she cupped his cheek in her hand. *Maybe a little coarse around the edges from his circumstances, but through the rags and grime he is still pleasant to look at. I wonder what color his eyes are. Blue. They have to be blue. Brown would be nice too, though.*

She was drawn to the boy and rolled his name around in her mind. *Aeryck . . . Aeryck, son of Caelryck.*

She liked the sound of his name.

8
A RUMOR
OF WAR

Terryll had walked several grueling miles behind the horses in the blistering white heat of the day, without rest or nourishment. At first he was led across desolate moors in the thick, humid aftermath of the storm. Then he toiled up and down mountainous terrain, fording rivers and creeks and skirting wide of villages and farms, all the while with a scratchy rope noosed over his head. The line slapped against his nape in tempo with the gait of the horse. If the boy slowed his pace, it would grow taut and jerk against the back of his neck, pulling him forward and off balance. This kept him in a constant and exhausting struggle to maintain a slack bight in the lead. But even the slackened rope chafed against his neck like sandpaper, leaving a raw and painful burn.

To make his grim situation worse, the horsemen made cruel sport with the boy. They nudged and brushed their horses against him so that he would lose his balance and fall. One rider in particular vented his cruelty on the young Briton—Druell, a ruddy-complexioned Jute with a thick neck and heavy sloping shoulders, one of which had been bandaged from a recent wound. Druell was the one who had been knocked from his mount by Terryll's arrow.

His cruelty was manifested in a dozen ways. At the last, Druell brushed his mount against the boy, knocking him forward. Terryll scrambled to maintain his erect attitude. However, he caught his toe on a tree root and stumbled headlong. With nothing to break his fall but bone and flesh, he fell hard. The violent jolt sent a flash of lights exploding in his brain before pain wracked his body.

Immediately the rope yanked taut against his neck, and its coarse fibers cut deep into his flesh, causing him to bleed and gasp for air as his dead weight was pulled along the ground. His face quickly swelled to a sickening purplish hue. Terryll was dragged for several feet before the horseman realized it and reined to a stop.

Druell and several others laughed as the tortured boy thrashed his legs furiously to put a slack in the rope.

"Look at him kick!" Druell mocked. Then he made a crude jest. The men laughed loudly.

Ruddbane had long since tired of Terryll's pulling against his horse and had given the rope to a man named Manfreyd, a stout Frisian with long, curly blond hair and beard. The man looked down behind his mount at the spent boy in the dirt. "I don't think he's going much farther today, Olaf," he called ahead to the Norseman.

"Then drag the miserable wretch till he's hanged!" Druell snapped. "Or better yet, let us find a good limb that he can dance from."

Several other men fell in line behind Druell and chanted ghoulishly that the young Briton be hanged. It had been an arduous trek through the mountains, and the sullen mood of the soldiers quickly turned ugly. A little sport with their prisoner would be just the thing to enliven their spirits.

"No!" Ruddbane shouted, breaking the murderous cast in the air. He angled his horse between Druell and the fallen boy, threatening the man with his battle-ax. "He is my kill. I will not be robbed by a lynching."

Druell glared, measuring his threat, a sure one by the violence in Ruddbane's eyes. Certainly the men around him sensed a fight and reined their horses to give them room. The Jute showed no fear in his visage, only contempt. However, he must have known that with the wound in his shoulder he would be giving Ruddbane a decisive advantage in single combat. And against Ruddbane, one could little spare such generosity. He jerked his horse away with a curse.

Then Ruddbane narrowed his gaze on the other men, who, likewise, wanted no part of him.

Olaf angled his mount over to the group. He glanced down at the exhausted young Briton, then turned to Ruddbane. "What is this?"

"Nothing. The whelp has just stumbled is all."

Olaf looked down at the boy again.

Terryll had raised himself up onto his knees and was taking the opportunity to rest. His face and body were bruised and covered with abrasions from being dragged. He was bleeding from just about every part of his exposed body. His clothes were torn and soaked through with perspiration. Beads of dirty sweat trickled down his brow from his tangled hair and were caught by the corners of his eyes, causing them to burn. A gnat buzzed into his ear, torturing him. With effort the boy struggled to his feet and stared up at the large Viking defiantly, blinking away the stinging salt from his eyes.

Olaf studied him for a few moments, then glanced at the sun. "Take the rope off him," he commanded. "We'll make camp here for the night."

"But there is yet another hour before the sun sets," Ruddbane protested.

"We will make camp here!"

The sun fell below the layers of purple-to-gray mountains and sent a fiery blaze of color spilling back across the western sky. The trees and hills and rocks at once glowed brilliantly for several seconds, as the ancient guardian of the day sent up its grand finale. But then, just as suddenly, like the wake of a passing review, it was gone. The evening, with its still, full moon and host of stars, quickly fell in step behind the sun to continue the procession into the night.

The Saxon camp was a broad expanse of gentle sloping earth, thirty yards wide by at least fifty yards in length, that opened into a moon-washed blaze amid a forest of yews and other conifers.

Olaf quickly assigned four men to take the first watch: one as a picket to guard the tethered horses, and the others (two of whom were dog handlers) to patrol the periphery of the campsite with the remaining boarhounds.

Terryll noted their positions. Several other men in the group, scattered about the camp, were inconsequential to the boy—inconsequential because they neither rose above nor fell below a median profile in the herd. They were the common soldiers, the faceless, nameless entities that filled the rank and file of any army, men who were fit only to obey whatever charge or menial task commanded them. These sat in a large circle around a bonfire, on fallen limbs and stones that they had dragged into the center of the camp.

The boy sat to the edge of the group, just outside the glow of the fire, under the canopy of a yew tree, and studied the men as they ate their rations. He looked for weaknesses, made mental notes of them. The better part of them were taller and more lank in stature and fairer of skin and hair color than the Britons. But they were uncultured and fiercely warlike —a proud people who were his hated enemies.

Even so, and perhaps because of it, they fascinated him. He had seen Saxon warriors before and just as close. Usually if he happened upon a group of them during his travels or hunts to the south, he sneaked up on them and spied out their activity. He made a game of it to see how close he could stalk them without being detected and would listen in on their conversations (sometimes from no more than a foot or two away) as he hid in a bush or even in a tree whose limbs hung low over their campsite.

He could pick out most of their tongue, having learned it from the Gaulish traders who came through their village during the spring and autumn to buy and sell goods. It was a harsh, staccatolike language, guttural and full of consonants, that was hard on the palate and even harder on the ears.

But Terryll would listen and glean what information he could—mostly useless soldier palaver—and inform his father about it. He also collected various articles of clothing and weapons—even a lyre on one occasion—as trophies, or "spoils of war," as he called them. And he was sure that some confusion, if not swordplay, broke out among them because of his little raids.

Manfreyd, who was now assigned to guard the boy, sat in front of Terryll to his right in the circle, and Olaf sat to the right of him, but slightly back and apart from the rest of the men. Manfreyd did not interest the boy. He was one of the inconsequentials, so his eyes glanced over him and fell upon the big Viking.

Not being a Saxon, Olaf had little in common with these men other than their shared military purpose, so he was aloof in his demeanor. Terryll studied him for some time, wondering what manner of man he was. Where was he from? Why hadn't he killed him earlier? And then a thought struck him: perhaps he was being saved for the after-meal entertainment. His mind busied itself with escape.

Olaf was looking away from the fire into the shadows of the trees, mindlessly stroking the length of his mustache, seemingly unconcerned with the petty events of the camp. From his brooding posture, it was clear to Terryll that he was thinking over some matter of importance.

Olaf removed his helmet briefly and ran his thick fingers through the blond mass of hair on his head and scratched his scalp. Replacing the helm, he leaned over to Manfreyd, spoke a few words, then stood up and walked into the woods.

The young hunter scanned the circle of men before him. Most of the horsemen were finishing their meals and had begun to break up into smaller groups for some evening banter and gambling. Others walked about the camp clanking their broadswords and shields as they cleaned and polished them, calling out to each other as though they hadn't a care in the world. None seemed the least concerned with Terryll's presence.

Except one. Across the circle, Terryll found the shaded eyes of Ruddbane staring at him through a gap in the men. The boy countered his gaze for several seconds. How long the man had been gazing at him, Terryll didn't know, but he did know that the red-bearded Saxon was a man that sooner or later he would have to reckon with.

Terryll looked up from the burly Saxon to the stars to determine a bearing. The hunting wasn't good in these parts, so he was unfamiliar with the area. Even so, he dead reckoned that they were somewhere in the foothills northeast of Bainbridge.

All day long they had meandered along trails that took them close to several important British villages, pausing to clandestinely observe each one, he presumed—to take stock of strengths, weaknesses, fortifications, manpower, and so on, before continuing on their journey. Earlier, as they approached Catterick, they had actually stopped and observed the goings-on inside the village for the better part of an hour, while Olaf and a few of his men conferred quietly.

Although Terryll appreciated the respites, it troubled him. What were they up to? They had to be a reconnaissance patrol of some kind. Why else would they be traipsing around the countryside so far north of their hill fort? They were acting unusually bold. Questions pelted his mind. Yes, it troubled him.

Terryll turned his attention back to the horsemen and listened in on the ebb and flow of their conversations. As would be expected, the men told stories of past victories in battle, their prowess with women, and off-color jokes to pass the evening around the fire. After each tale of valor or sexual conquest—mostly told with obvious embellishment of the truth —the men nodded and made asides to one another, as if they could somehow identify with the particulars of the story.

And following each joke, they laughed heartily, especially one smaller, weaselly-looking man named Snelling, who sat off to the boy's left. The man had a nose that was too long for his face, who—instead of laughing—would let out long, wheezing guffaws, then back snort several times through his nose as he took in air. Terryll wondered that he didn't hurt himself.

The man wheezed and snorted at anything that was said, funny or not. It was an irritation not only to the boy but apparently to Druell as well, who sat to Snelling's left. He told him to shut up every so often and gave him sharp jabs to the ribs with his elbow each time. Even such rebukes caused the little man to laugh uproariously.

Finally, Druell had his fill and stood up. "You stupid idiot!" He scowled. "You don't got the brains of a toad's wart." Then he walked over and joined a noisy group of men who had a fast game going.

Snelling must have thought about Druell's words for some time, wondering whether or not a toad's wart had any brains to speak of. He was dragging his sleeve through the rheumy discharge under his nose, when suddenly his eyes brightened, and he let out a loud howl. Apparently it had just occurred to the man that toad's warts didn't have any brains at all, and that Druell was just having a little fun with him. The whole notion of it set him off, appreciative as he was of any small atten-. tion. The little man wheezed and snorted and bobbed all to himself for a solid minute before he finally gave it up and commenced picking his cavernous nose.

The other men—oblivious to Snelling's little world—were as raucous as a banquet hall. They laughed and howled and swore at each other with gusto, all the while throwing little painted stones and money onto a blanket, as if there were actually some understandable purpose or method to it all.

Terryll had been watching the game with some interest, trying to figure out the rules, but eventually he gave it up and turned away. He looked back at Snelling.

Apparently feeling himself being watched, the little man quickly looked over at the boy. He became indignant. "What're you lookin' at?" he demanded.

"A misunderstood man," the boy answered in the man's tongue, struggling to translate a fitting nuance of flattery.

"Yeah?" The man brightened, then quickly furrowed his sloping brow and asked suspiciously, "What you mean by that?"

"Oh, nothing really. Other than that you strike me as an intelligent man is all."

Snelling pondered the thought for several moments before retorting. "Oh, yeah? Well, mind your own business."

"It was just an observation," Terryll added.

The confused man turned away and stared into the fire, mired in new thoughts.

An outburst of swearing caught Terryll's attention, and he looked over at the men gambling. Two of them had gotten into a heated argument concerning the rules of the game and nearly went to blows. One stood up in a cursing rage and drew his sword on the other man but was quickly blindsided by a short jab from Ruddbane's ax handle with a force that sent him staggering.

"If you two want to kill each other, it's fine with me," Ruddbane growled. "But you'll not do it in my camp."

As he was Olaf's second in command, no one dared challenge either his authority or his skill with a battle-ax. A few had tried before, but they were no longer among the living. The stricken gambler picked himself up, rubbing his skull, and mumbled a few obscenities under his breath.

It was clear to Terryll as he studied their behavior that these men weren't particularly concerned about concealing their presence. He couldn't tell, however, if it was because of ignorance or because of a haughty Saxon confidence that somehow the Britons in these parts wouldn't dare strike against them.

Olaf returned and spoke a few more words to Manfreyd, while gesturing over at the boy. Manfreyd immediately got up and untied Terryll's hands.

Surprised, the boy rubbed his numbed and swollen wrists to move the circulation of blood through them, then flexed the aches and soreness out of his arms and shoulders. He looked around the camp warily. *Maybe this is when the sport begins,* he mused.

"Here, Briton," Manfreyd said, handing him a small chunk of salt pork that someone had tossed in the dirt, and a mug of water to wash it down. "A little sustenance to fill the ache in your belly."

Terryll looked up at the man, truly surprised at the kindness. "Thank you," he replied, taking the food.

"Don't thank me. I had nothing to do with it."

Terryll looked over at Olaf's expressionless face and made brief eye contact before the Viking turned and headed toward the horses. The boy watched until the night shadows enveloped the man's form, then, looking down at the meager offering before him, he brushed the dirt off the meat and set into it with relish. It was as tough as cowhide to chew, but to the half-starved boy it was a feast, for which he was grateful.

After he had finished his meal, Manfreyd hog-tied Terryll's hands and feet but this time, mercifully, in front of him.

Terryll slowly scanned the camp and noticed that most of the men had collected around the game, which had picked up again. Likely feeling his charge secure, Manfreyd slowly drifted over to look on.

The boy was watching the play, still intrigued by the apparent nonsense of the rules, when he felt someone's eyes upon him. He turned and was startled to find Snelling, sitting by himself, staring at him. Terryll smiled at the man and nodded his head. Everyone in the camp was fixed on the game except this one little man with the mind of an idiot.

Snelling stared blankly at the boy for a full two minutes before he got up and moved over to him. He stood in front of Terryll, looking down at him for several more moments, sniffing and wiping his nose.

"You . . . uh . . . you think I'm smart?" he asked finally, feigning aloofness, poor attempt that it was.

"I know that you're probably smarter than I am," Terryll responded, fully convincing.

"How's that?"

"Well, for instance, for the longest time I've been trying to figure out the rules of that game the men are playing, but I just can't seem to catch them."

"What ya mean?" Snelling asked, arching his brow.

"The game. What game are the men playing over there?"

Snelling looked briefly over at the men gambling. His brow cleared abruptly, then he turned back at Terryll, chuckling through his nose. "They're playing scuts. It's easy."

"Really? Well, there you have it," the boy said earnestly. "It may be easy for you, but not for me. Do you think that you could teach me how to play?"

"Why should I?" Snelling retorted with surly bravado, all the while digging a hole in his left ear.

"Well . . . if you really don't know the rules, I suppose you couldn't—"

"I *know* the rules!" the man snapped. "I even got my own scut stones." At this point Snelling reached into a pocket and pulled out five irregularly shaped rocks that bore scant resemblance to the smooth black-and-white-painted stones that the men were using. "See?"

"I apologize," Terryll offered, eyeing the pathetic-looking rocks in his palm. "Then what's the problem?"

Snelling glanced cautiously around the camp, working on his other ear now. "It's just that I don't know if I should."

"What could it hurt?" the boy asked. "The other men are all playing." Terryll paused and leaned forward. Then in a hushed voice, he added, "I'll bet that they don't let you play with them, do they?" He let the thought take root in the little man's mind. Then he said, "They probably think that you're just too smart for them and don't want to lose all their money to you."

Snelling stood gazing at the men across the camp, nodding his head absent-mindedly for several moments.

Terryll had never observed anyone strain so hard at thinking, and he had a fleeting fear that the man's mind would snap under the pressure, thereby unhinging his escape plans. He was relieved when the little man quickly spun around and knelt down beside him.

"The first thing you need is a blanket to throw the scut stones on," Snelling said. He looked around the immediate area, taxing his faculties to locate anything that resembled a blanket. Finding nothing, he dropped his rocks on the ground and tore off a sizable portion from his woolen sleeve. "Well, we don't need no blanket anyways," he said, spreading the sleeve out on the dirt with great care. "This'll work even better!"

As Snelling looked around for his rocks, Terryll offered, "I see. And I'll bet that you have to shake the stones and then throw them down onto the blanket . . . right?"

"Right. But we don't got a real blanket, so we'll throw them onto the—hey!" Snelling recoiled, frowning. "I thought you didn't know the rules!"

"It was just a guess."

"Hmm . . ." The man furrowed his brow thoughtfully. "You're pretty smart too."

Terryll glanced at the men, then over to Manfreyd. They all had their eyes on their game, and enthusiasm was growing. He turned to Snelling and gestured at his wrists. "It'll be difficult for me to throw the stones with my hands tied, though, won't it?" he asked.

Snelling looked down at the boy's wrists and went back to digging in his right ear. "Hmm . . . I never played with no one with tied-up hands before." He looked over his shoulder to see if anyone was looking, then back at the boy. He furrowed his brow again, then spoke sternly. "I'm gonna untie your hands, but not your feet so you can't run away. And I'm gonna keep a sharp eye on you, so don't you try no tricks on me."

Terryll lifted his wrists up to Snelling, and the man started to untie the leather thongs.

"Are you sure you won't get into trouble?" Terryll asked.

Snelling guffawed, then hissed through his nostrils as he fumbled with the knots. His whole body shook up and down as he did so, then he capped it off with a trail of snorts. "I'll have you know that next to Olaf and Ruddbane, I'm just about in charge around here. Why as a matter of fact—"

Suddenly a large stone bounced off the side of Snelling's head with a hollow thunk. He thudded face-first in the dirt next to Terryll and groaned.

Ruddbane strode up, wielding his large battle-ax. He knelt down beside the boy and pressed the edge of the blade next to his throat.

"Nice try, Briton. I was wondering just how long it would take you to get this dolt to untie you." He backhanded Terryll across his face, then stood up. "I'm looking forward to peeling the flesh off your pretty face an ugly little inch at a time." Then he screamed at Manfreyd for neglecting his duty. "If the whelp escapes, I'll cut *your* throat instead!" As he walked away, the man gave Snelling a hard kick, sending him sprawling into a disheveled heap.

Snelling let out a loud moan and rolled back onto his stomach with his face and nose buried in the dirt, blasting little puffs of dust into the air with his huge nostrils.

The exhausted boy sighed deeply, looking first at the prostrate Snelling, then over to Manfreyd, who stood glaring at him with his hand on the pommel of his sword. He knew that from now on escape would be more difficult, if not impossible. But somehow it no longer mattered. For as the deprivation of his body slowly eclipsed his mind and will, he lay down against the yew tree on a bed of soft needles, and soon, as the obstreperous noises of the camp narrowed to a distant point in his mind, he fell hard asleep.

Terryll was awakened from a dead sleep by Snelling's obnoxious laugh.

Someone yelled across the camp for him to shut up, trailing off with several curses.

The boy opened and closed his eyes several times, blinking the sleep from his mind. The cool of the night caressed his face, gently stirring him from a kindlier place. He narrowed his eyes to a squint and carefully scanned the camp without moving his head. Everything was different, yet everything was the same, though quieted now to an almost reverent stillness. A haunting stillness. Surreal. The moon had swung low to the opposite end of the sky and seemed snagged in the treetops. Several hours had obviously passed. The fire had died down to glowing embers, and, from what he could tell by the unearthly stentorian sounds blowing through the camp, most of the men had fallen asleep. Manfreyd, too, was asleep, apparently relieved of his vigil by roving sentries, whom Terryll could hear vaguely in the trees behind him. A twig snap here, a muffled cough there. He found Olaf's shape reclining against a tree about fifteen feet away. But whether he was asleep or not, he couldn't tell, for the man's face was hidden. To Olaf's left, about six feet from his head, he could make out the silhouettes of three men huddled in hushed conversation. They looked eerie as the reddish glow from the dying fire front-lighted their hunkered-over shapes and collided against the cool sheen of the full moon that highlighted their backs. The scene conjured up a strange apparition of a microcosmic war between the powers of light and darkness, forces that were embattled upon their brutish forms, acting out their timeless drama upon so unlikely and base a stage.

Snelling's long, hooked nose cut an unmistakable profile against the skirmish line of shifting lights, and the other two men—the ones that had been assigned the first watch—were large, shapeless lumps. These two were engaged in conversation. The little man occasionally cut in with his own meaningless contributions.

Terryll's position was downwind of the men, and every so often a cool conspiratorial breeze stirred and carried the sound of their voices to his ears. But because there wasn't a steady air current, he could make out a only a few words at a time. From these, the boy tried to piece together their conversation.

Again, most of the banter that he collected concerned one woman or another, or a tract of land that they might earn, upon which to graze a few sheep or cattle once they were freed of the military, or it consisted of a word or phrase whose translation was either nonsensical or unattainable with his broken language skills. The fireside palaver was also punctuated with an occasional wheeze and snort from Snelling, which seemed a constant dripping irritation to his fire mates.

Terryll tested the thongs around his wrists but found little room to move his hands. There would be no way for him to work them loose without drawing attention to himself. Escape did not look likely—at least not tonight. He thought about another day dragging behind the horses, the brunt of exquisite cruelties, and he groaned in his spirit. *Have mercy, God. Have mercy.*

Again the wind stirred, and he caught the phrase "Horsa's army will . . ." before the breeze settled to the earth and buried the rest of the sentence.

Terryll's interest was immediately piqued. *Horsa's army?* What about Horsa's army? He strained to hear the rest, but the wind refused him. Frustrated, he was tempted to roll closer to the men so that he could eavesdrop more easily, when he heard one of them say, "Coming with . . . sev . . . to Badonsward . . . to . . . the Wolf . . . maybe then . . . army . . . push the filthy Britons . . . the sea . . ."

After this, the conversation wandered back into talk of money, land, more women, and crass jokes. Snelling covered his mouth with his hands and blew out muffled chortles and snorts through them. The two men who had been on guard stood up, snickered, and disgustedly shook their heads. They'd had enough of the little man. They left him to himself and his own entertainment to find sleep on the far side of the camp—as far from his chuckling and snorting and other effluences of wind as possible.

The cool breeze rustled through the yew needles around Terryll's head but brought him only the confidences of the night—crickets chirping, a dozen or so frogs bleating out their cares to the moon, the distant hoot of an owl, and the garrulous recitations of other nocturnal goings-on.

Snelling, rubbing the knot on his head, looked over at the boy, cursed him gruffly, and spit contemptuously in his direction. Then the little man settled down into a lonely, prosaic pose, chuckled a few times, wiped his nose, and stared at the dying embers, deep in whatever little paradise he found comforting.

Terryll closed his eyes and mulled over the words in his mind. He constructed several different conversations with the fragments of sentences that he had heard, turning them first one way, then another, scrambling them, adding different word possibilities in the gaps between the phrases.

He realized that all he had heard were bits and pieces of conversation between three soldiers of little consequence around a campfire—the kind of dialogue, no doubt freighted with hearsay and veiled prospects, that trickles down through the rank and file through a filter of innuendos, oblique allegations of truth, and rumor—the stuff of soldier's talk. Scuttlebutt.

The ramifications could be enormous, he mused—or meaningless babble that he had completely misconstrued. Whichever, the words weighed heavily on his mind for the next hour or so before Terryll finally fell back into a fitful sleep that tormented him with wild dreams.

Suddenly he was awake! His heart was pounding in his chest as if trying to escape its prison. His eyes opened wide with alarm, his instincts screaming that something was dreadfully wrong! But what? And then he heard the noise. Gone were the voices of the night—no crickets, frogs, not even a hint of the wind, nothing except a strange gurgling coming from a point nearby.

He was looking around to locate its source, when, to his bafflement, he saw Snelling lying at his feet, the moon glinting dully on his open eyes and a black feathered shaft sticking out of his throat. Strangely, the image escaped his comprehension.

At once the air over the camp was rife with irrelevant noises that further astonished the boy. The buzzing, muffled thumpings hitting all about the campsite evaded his unpracticed mind. However, the death cries of men and the screaming yelps of boarhounds rushed him with an assault of knowing terror.

The Picts had fallen upon the bewildered Saxons, killing several with arrows and battle-axes in seconds, wreaking amazing havoc and mayhem. Many of those who weren't killed in the initial attack were hewn down as they struggled to their feet from a dead sleep. Men cried out senseless reproaches at the black line of man-shapes—no more than painted ghouls—that came rushing, closing upon them with furious unheeding gestures. Frenzied glints of metal played over the mutable black shapes, as the roaring pitch of battle at once resounded with an overburdened fortissimo.

Manfreyd and Olaf managed to get into the confused fray, as did Ruddbane, Druell, and a few others who had not been sleeping in the center of the camp. They turned on their attackers, hurling themselves against the Picts' superior numbers with a terrific crash.

Seizing the moment to escape, Terryll furiously worked at the thongs on his wrists, keeping one eye fixed on the fight and the other on the task at hand, using his teeth to tear the knots loose. The din encompassing him was an ovation of deadly thunder, a roaring paean to the gods of war that numbed his senses.

And at last having freed his hands, he quickly untied the thongs around his ankles, then scrambled to his feet and turned to flee the battle.

But whether because of the odd movement seen from the corner of his eye or because of the glimmer flickering toward him, his instincts compelled him to spin and duck. Immediately a flash of blinding light exploded in his brain as the flat side of a thrown battle-ax cracked hard against his skull. He staggered to the ground, stunned almost senseless, and struggled on his hands and knees to maintain consciousness. Had he not ducked, the ax blade would have split his skull in two.

Olaf was quick to recoil from the shock of the attack and quickly drove the length of his broadsword through the ribs of the Pict warrior he had been fighting. The man turned to him with a bewildered, plaintive look, as though there had been some kind of terrible, redeemable mistake. He was young and had made a fatal error. He had been distracted from Olaf's gaze. Another warrior to his side turned to look down at his fallen comrade, making a similar transgression, and was instantly felled by the Viking's sword thrust.

A sudden rush of cold wind blew through the trees, carrying the din of battle into the waning night sky. Battle-axes and swords rang out a bloody clarion call to eternity, as iron clashed against iron with flashes of sparks and light, cutting hard into bone and flesh. Death was everywhere, greedy, searching for blood-sate, devouring the souls of hapless men whose time had come, coming now to claim the boy.

As he groped about on the ground, a wave of nausea overwhelmed Terryll, and he vomited what little food there was in his stomach. The Pictish warrior who had struck him with his ax now rushed over to retrieve it and finish him off.

But as the Pict grabbed the haft, a monstrous, blurred form took shape out of the night, and something raked across his chest. The warrior stood erect with a confused grimace on his face, dropped his battle-ax, then fell headlong onto the ground beside Terryll. He was stone dead.

The huge, blacker-than-the-night shape swiftly moved across a splash of moonlight and tore into several Picts who were fighting on the nearest flank of battle. They let out screams of terror as the thing raised itself a full fourteen feet above the earth, its fiery eyes glowing in the night, its flared nostrils blasting contempt upon these puny men. The Picts thought it a demon and cried out for the mercy of Dagda to save them. The Saxons cried out to Woden and Tiu.

But the demon, or thing, or black beast of the night cared little for their gods and fell upon them with indiscriminate rage. It let out a fierce roar that eclipsed the clamor of the battle, shaking the ground with a violent thundering.

The rest of the men reeled about, mouths agape, stunned as they were by the suddenness of the giant's entrance and outrage. Those who were unfortunate enough to be nearby were slain before they knew what had happened. Terror filled the heart of Pict and Saxon alike, melding them together into an unlikely shared purpose, as the thing scythed a swath through their midst, crushing men beneath the weight of its trunk-like limbs and claws as it continued to vent unbridled fury upon them.

Taking the advantage of surprise away from the startled Picts, the black shape drove the warriors to the far side of the battleground, where they massed into little knotted clumps of reckless and ineffectual fighting. The monster then turned its rage back across the clearing toward the stricken boy.

Terryll had managed to get to his feet and was rubbing the throbbing bump on his forehead as the menacing beast reached his side. Looking up, his eyes opened incredulously.

"Hauwka! God be praised!" the boy exclaimed. "Am I glad to see you!"

The bear turned to the hinder battle and let out another thunderous roar, warning the men to keep their place. Then he lowered a shoulder to the boy.

Terryll grabbed hold, and he and the great bear disappeared like shades into the womb of the forest without looking back, leaving the pitied souls of men to be sucked into the voracious maw of hell behind them.

The men resumed killing each other as the battle returned to the smaller human drama, now fast approaching the end. A wall of Picts moved against, and quickly engulfed, two of the remaining Saxons. Manfreyd was one of them and was felled as a Pict buried his ax into his back. Not sure what had befallen him, the stout Frisian made a dutiful attempt to swing his broadsword against the man facing him, but his limbs refused the final commands from his brain, and he crumpled to the ground.

Then, like a frenzy of jackals, the swarm of Picts converged on the other man and slaughtered him. Laughing, howling, and shrieking drunkenly, they cut off gruesome trophies from the dead men's armor and bodies.

This opened a break in the battle near the tree line opposite, as the Picts around the fallen Manfreyd focused their attention on their grisly spoils, thinking the battle won. Ruddbane and Druell, who were fighting alongside the Viking, seized the opportunity to flee through the break before the distracted Picts realized their error and turned on them.

The three remaining Saxons easily cut a path through the Pict warriors barring their way to the horses. Ruddbane paused momentarily to guard the rear of their escape, as a group of four Picts rushed them. The burly Saxon hurled his battle-ax at the lead man. Then Ruddbane drew his broadsword and ran after Olaf and Druell into the trees.

The other Picts paused for an instant as they reached their slain comrade, gaping curiously at the corpse as though to ascertain the deadness of it. Then, howling, they took up their pursuit of the Saxons. The rest of the Pict warriors—two dozen or so—quickly fell in behind them and rushed into the trees, screaming savagely.

The Saxons sped through the forest toward their horses, having the slight advantage of surprise and distance.

The Pictish warriors loosed several volleys of arrows at them, though the trees took the brunt of the missiles.

Ruddbane, however, was struck in the back of his right thigh. He winced but continued on his course without breaking stride, for he knew that to do so would mean certain death.

Olaf and Druell reached their whickering horses and mounted, followed moments later by the hobbling Ruddbane. Finding their reins and a gray corridor of light, the three raced into the cover of the forest, scant seconds before enemy warriors arrived on the abandoned scene.

The Picts loosed another volley of arrows at the fleeing men, hitting Ruddbane in his left forearm and grazing the shoulder of Olaf. Druell alone, came through the battle unscathed.

The dull, dreary, and filtered morning sky found the bent silhouettes of the three horsemen cutting a soundless path against the grain of the earth's eastern roll, through a veil of thick mist that blanketed the gloomy forests of the Pennines, leaving behind them the bodies of their fallen comrades to be dishonored by their enemies and consumed by bird and beast. Slowly, and without a word between them, the men reined their horses to a course that would take them to the hill-fort of Badonsward in two days.

Olaf pondered the fate of his men and the young Briton he saw fall in battle behind them. The Viking had survived the bloodletting once again, cheating the bone-swollen earth of his dust. Death was the warrior's seductive mistress, and though he had danced with her many times before, she had not yet stopped the music.

Such was life's bitter and seemingly cruel logic—to take the young while sparing the old. It was an unsearchable mystery that would grant to one a swift and final judgment, and to another the mercy of yet another day in which to find grace.

9
THE TAPESTRY

N o! Don't eat me!"
Worm's eyes jerked open full of cold terror. His heart raced with the news of a thousand hawking voices. He blinked several times at the ceiling, gasping for breath, trying to make sense of his screaming thoughts. But nothing made sense. Everything was a muddled blur, a swirl of confusion. His head felt heavy and groggy after waking from a deep sleep, so his eyes took several long moments to find a focus. He could tell by the cool, slightly damp smell in the air, and by the way the light hit the ceiling, that it was morning and not some other time of day. It was the first rational thought that was cleared through his mind.

That he was alive was the second.

The uncomfortable pressure in his shoulder goaded a recollection of his recent ordeal, shaking him rudely to the present tense, of Terryll, the flight from the Saxon horse-soldiers—the bear. His pulse quickened. Where was the bear? *Where am I?* Did Terryll manage to get away from the Saxons? He hoped so. Still, the boy was a fool for risking his neck like that, especially for someone he didn't even know.

Worm quickly rehearsed the events that led him from Glenryth to the point where he must have lost consciousness on the back of the bear. His thoughts, like dispassionate analysts, quickly positioned themselves to observe his reclined being, his immediate surroundings, his recent history, probing his mind and context for usable data.

But the images received were mostly a blur. And as to where he was now, the boy had no familiar points of reference. He assumed that the giant bear had brought him to this place, and that it was perhaps Terryll's home in Killwyn Eden. But there was no way for him to know for certain.

Worm looked over at his shoulder and noted that his dressings were fresh. He wondered who it was that had changed them. *What happened to my shirt?*

He glanced around the large room to familiarize himself with his new surroundings, allowing his eyes to move freely about the chamber without any force of direction.

The bedroom was amply furnished—opulent would better describe it. There was a heavy wooden table, with pomegranates and grape clusters engraved along its edges and legs, set against the wall opposite him, and two wicker chairs on either side facing outward. Set upon the table to one side were several rolled-up parchments neatly arranged in stacks, a wooden cross that commanded the focal point of the room, and two bronze lampstands, one on either side of it. He studied the cross for a moment, blinked dully, then his eyes were drawn to a large chest beneath the table. A blanket was folded neatly on top. Worm studied the chest for a while, wondering what it contained.

Other furnishings and decorations betrayed the woman's touch: a vase of fresh flowers sat on a small table next to the bed, a full-length bronze mirror stood in the corner to his left, a spinning wheel and loom sat in a corner to his right, with a basket full of colored yarn next to it, and a large tapestry that hung from the wall adjacent to the table.

Not the decor that would interest a man, but to the boy, who was only accustomed to the streets and hovels of Glenryth, it was a wonderful place, full of warmth, that gave him a queer feeling of security, of belonging—something quite new to the boy. Something strangely unsettling. It made him wonder about the people who lived here. Were they indeed Terryll's family? If so, how would they receive someone such as he? No matter. He wouldn't be here long.

After taking a brief inventory of the furnishings, Worm's eyes were drawn back to the tapestry on the wall. He was immediately struck by the intricacy of detail that was woven into the fabric. He had not seen many tapestries, but those that he had seen were of scenes more simple in technique and composition, or of family crests, or names of people or shops—nothing that approached the artistry of this one.

The tapestry depicted a lush garden, filled with all manner of colorful fruit trees, splashes of flowers and shrubbery. The scene looked so lifelike that it was startling.

In the center of the garden was a white lamb with a bloody slash across its throat, standing upon the neck of a vile-looking serpent. It was an unnatural, strange, even grotesque image that drew the boy's mind to inquiry. How could a mere lamb conquer such a fierce-looking serpent, he thought, let alone one whose throat had been mortally wounded? *It must have been a terrible fight,* he mused. The image so unsettled him that he quickly averted his eyes to other parts of the cloth.

To the right of the lamb and serpent were a man and a woman—both naked—who appeared to be fleeing in terror from either the serpent or the lamb. Worm couldn't decide which one. He thought about it for some time, imagining both possibilities, but still couldn't resolve in his mind which was the source of their terror.

Then, curiously, he began to picture himself in the tapestry, running at first from the serpent as it slithered after him to devour him, then fleeing from the bloody lamb, who, Worm decided after much reflection, was really the more frightening of the two. He kept turning his eyes away from the tapestry to other objects in the room, but each time he was immediately drawn back into the midst of it. Never in his life had he seen anything so wonderful and yet so haunting, so beautiful and compelling, yet so evocative of awe and terror. Worm wished that he had never laid eyes upon it.

Footsteps to his left startled him, and he spun his head to the doorway to see who it was. It was a girl. She was looking down at a wooden basin in her hands as though trying to keep from spilling its contents, so she hadn't seen that he was awake. For reasons of his own, Worm instantly shut his eyes and pretended to still be asleep.

Her footsteps whispered across the floor and stopped once they reached the bed. Then, for what seemed an inordinate span of time, there was not a sound.

What is she doing? he wondered. He guessed that she was looking down at him, studying him. Why? Had she guessed his ruse? Of course she had. With each passing moment of silence, the weight of her presence grew exponentially, pressing him deeper into the discomfiture of his charade. He sensed the heat from her eyes piercing through the sham of his eyelids to his crime, accusing him, mocking him. He was struck with such a panic that he was about to sit bolt upright and confess his guilt.

Then the girl sat down next to him on the bed, and the nearness of her presence enveloped him completely, terrifying him. And immediately the cool touch of her hand was against his face, cupping his cheek gently, soaking up his transgression, absolving him, anointing him with peace. Such soft fingers. After several seconds she took her hand from his face, then applied a warm, moist towel to his brow, gently wiping away the dried perspiration.

Worm was filled with a tingling sensation that started from the point of her touch, traveled the length of his body to his toes, and then shivered back up again. It felt as good as anything he ever remembered or imagined, and he almost giggled from the sheer ecstasy of it. It struck him that it was the first time in his life that a girl had ever been so close to him, ever touched him. Never had he dreamed . . .

Suddenly a woman's voice spoke to the girl from across the room, shattering the mood into a thousand laughing pieces.

"How is he doing, Dagmere?" the voice asked. "Has he woken up yet?"

"Not yet, Mama. But his face is cool."

"That's good."

Dagmere. What a pretty name, the boy thought. *Dagmere . . . Dagmere . . .* At once the name took on deific eminence as he rolled the delicious syllables around in his mind. He had seen but a glimpse of the girl's form when she entered the room, and he wondered what manner of face might be attached to such a name. Was it a pretty one? Was it homely? Without suitable references in his past from which to draw, the boy could only search the wasteland of his imagination. Then after a few moments he determined—by juvenile fiat—that she had to be beautiful.

"Have you been up all night?" the woman asked.

"It hasn't been a bother," the girl answered. "Really, Mama."

The girl—Dagmere—has been taking care of me all night long, he mused. He had to get a better look at her. But still, he didn't want to be discovered. How long he would keep up the ruse, Worm didn't know.

He could tell by the sound of her voice that she was looking away from him toward her mother. He chanced a look. Slowly he opened his right eye to a squint.

The girl obstructed his view of her mother, who was standing just inside the doorway. That was good; he didn't have to concern himself with the intruder. Then he opened both his eyes fully so that he could see the girl in better perspective.

"I want you to get some rest in a little while, Dagmere," the woman said.

"Mother, honestly, I'm fine. If he doesn't wake up within the hour, I promise I'll get some rest."

Looking up at the side of her face, he was struck by the soft feminine underline of her jaw when she spoke and the feminine lilt in her voice—the way her words fell and rose in pitch during a sentence as though they were skipping playfully up and down a series of hills and valleys.

He followed the thick, auburn braid of her hair as it fell onto her shoulders and around to her front, leading his eyes to her delicately shaped hands, to the exquisite, porcelain design of her fingers that held the water basin in her lap so prettily—hands that had touched his face, kissed it with her fingertips. His imagination had failed him miserably; she was more beautiful by a hundredfold than the shamed goddess withering on the pedestal in his mind!

"Still no sign of Terryll?" she asked her mother.

There was a long pause.

"No, nothing yet."

The verdict was in: this was indeed Terryll's home. And also, the young hunter—the fool—had possibly paid for Worm's escape with his life. The truth was, he had no idea how Terryll had fared. He presumed him dead. Who wouldn't? If the boarhounds hadn't caught him and torn him to shreds, certainly the Saxons would have run him down with their horses and killed him. But he realized that these were only speculations.

Enough of Terryll. Worm studied the girl's slender fingers as they fidgeted apprehensively along the edge of the basin, dancing to the siren of some distant pipes. He heard the woman's footsteps walking away. Finally. Dagmere looked after her for several moments, then glanced down into the basin of water. She began to turn the towel between her hands slowly, gazing thoughtfully at it, giving Worm a moment to study her face in greater detail.

As he looked, he noticed a tear forming in one corner of her eye, alongside her slightly turned-up nose. It swelled to a drop, paused for a second, then rolled down the side of her face and fell into the basin. It was obvious that she was deeply troubled, and Worm was ambushed by an ache in his heart for her pain—an ache that accused him with fiery scrutiny, telling him that he was the author of her grief.

Then the girl seemed to check her mood. She straightened her back and focused on the task before her. She began to turn toward the boy, and he immediately shut his eyes. Gently she caressed his brow and the side of his face with the warm towel, banishing the interlopers of conscience from his mind.

Soon she began singing softly to herself with a voice so clear, with a melody so fragrant with loveliness, that it caused Worm's emotions to rage within his mind. She paused in her song to pull a vagrant strand of hair from his brow, then, once again, picked up the melody.

The sensory exhilaration was almost more than the boy could bear. He loved the touch of her cool fingers upon his face. His mind now recalled vividly their sculpted beauty, but he missed the beauty of her face, her hair, her beautiful eyes. To have the one was to lose the others. And now to hear the lilting melody of her song spilling into his ears, he was vanquished. Her touch surrendered to the glory of her visage.

The boy stirred upon the bed and let out a low, rather forced-sounding moan. He rolled his head back and forth on the pillow several times, letting out several more groans as he feigned—not very convincingly—that he was rousing from unconsciousness.

But the girl was obviously none the wiser and quickly withdrew her hand from him. She darted a look at the doorway, then back to the boy.

His eyes slowly opened and immediately fixed upon her stare. "Hello," he said rather woodenly. "My name is Worm. What's yours?" His mind rebuked him sharply. *Idiot! That sounded awful!*

Dagmere's eyes opened wide as she stared at the boy's face. "Mama!" she cried. But only a hoarse whisper came out of her throat, barely audible. Her face instantly flushed a burning red, then just as quickly it drained from her. Panicking, she jumped up from her chair, spilling the basin of water, and ran through the doorway, calling for her parents. "Mama! Papa! He's awake! The boy's awake!"

Worm just lay there, looking at the empty doorway, dumbfounded. His plan had worked brilliantly. Now he had neither her touch nor the beauty of her eyes to choose from. He had made a slight miscalculation. Girls were not boys. All he had now was the sound of her voice trailing off into the recesses of the house—and the thought of what a fool he had just made of himself.

Several minutes passed before Worm heard the sound of approaching footsteps. He felt like shutting his eyes and pretending that he had never opened them, but he knew that would never do. He was in for it. All he could do was wait now for the constables to come and collect him and drag him to the inquest.

Dagmere and her mother entered the bedroom and paused just inside the door.

"See, Mama?" Dagmere said, pointing to him. "I think he said his name was . . . Worm."

"Worm?" Helena remarked, scrunching her nose.

Then her face brightened as she looked at the boy's tentative eyes peering from across the room. She walked over to the bed and sat down on the chair beside him.

Dagmere followed her but knelt down to mop up the spilled water, glancing back and forth curiously from the floor to his face.

"How do you feel?" Helena asked, laying her palm against his brow.

"Fine, I . . . I suppose," he stammered, shrugging his shoulders. As he did so, pain shot to his left shoulder, causing him to wince.

"Now, you must lie still and let your body rest," Helena said. "You have lost a lot of blood."

Worm felt embarrassed and averted his eyes from hers. He looked over to Dagmere, who was looking directly at him. But caught in a blush of panic, she quickly turned away and riveted her attention to the floor. *This isn't going very well*, he thought.

Allyndaar entered the room, carrying a bowl of hot broth and some bread, and handed them to Helena. Worm looked up at him and was immediately awed by his appearance. Petrified was more like it.

The man was of medium height but built powerfully, with thick sinewy arms and a barrel chest and blue eyes so piercing that they seemed to look right through him. But there was something about the man's face that was somehow familiar, a resurrected shade that peered at him now through the haze of his catacombed past. *Perhaps the man had been to his village on business*, he thought.

"How are you feeling, son?" the shade asked.

Worm had to turn his eyes away from his steely gaze. He looked over at the tapestry on the wall but found it equally uncomfortable to look at, so he turned his eyes to the girl on the floor.

"Uh . . . I feel fine."

"That's good."

Helena, sensing his discomfort, offered him a spoonful of broth. "Here. It is . . . Worm . . . correct?" she asked, as though certain that there had been some mistake.

The boy turned to her and nodded his head.

Helena looked up at Allyndaar, who shrugged his shoulders. Turning back to the boy, she raised the spoon to his mouth.

"Here . . . Worm . . . er . . . son," she stammered. "Drink some of this broth. It will help to strengthen your body."

Tendrils of broth vapor wafted up into his nose, causing him to recoil slightly from the smell. *These are Terryll's parents all right. They use the same recipe for poison.* But despite the foul taste, it was warm and soothing once it passed over his taste buds into his throat. He quickly drained the bowl and devoured the bread.

Helena seemed pleased with his appetite.

Allyndaar glanced down at Helena, who had been growing noticeably anxious during the boy's meal. "Are you well enough to talk?" he asked.

"Er . . . yes," Worm replied hesitantly, daring a look at the man. "What about?"

"You are fortunate that you came to us no later than you did," Allyndaar said. "We were concerned that you might not pull through the night."

Worm nodded but felt no purpose in adding comment. He suspected where this was leading and did not want to go there.

"That is a nasty wound in your shoulder," the man continued. "An arrow wound, if I'm not mistaken."

Worm looked over at his shoulder. "This? It's nothing. Really," he said, chuckling. "It doesn't hurt—" He had started to shrug again, but the pain in his shoulder scolded him for the careless movement. His eyes, unable to endure Allyndaar's scrutiny, quickly fled to Helena's. "It was a good broth," he said, diverting the subject.

Helena smiled politely and fumbled nervously with the empty bowl as she studied his face. She looked up at her husband and nudged him with a look.

"You were brought here by a bear," Allyndaar continued. "Do you remember?"

"Who could forget him?" Worm forced a laugh. "I've never seen a bear as big as him."

Allyndaar and Helena smiled at one another unconvincingly.

"Is he a pet or something?" Worm asked.

"His name is Hauwka," Dagmere offered, rising to her feet. She moved to the bed next to her father.

Worm followed her studiously. He found an advocate in her eyes. "I know."

Helena brightened. "You do?"

Worm realized at once that he had incriminated himself. The girl had distracted him. "Yes . . . er . . . isn't that the bear's name?"

Allyndaar exchanged another glance with his wife. "Yes, it is. Did our son, Terryll, tell you this?"

"Your son?"

"What can you tell us of his whereabouts?" Helena added quickly. Her gaze was fixed on the boy's eyes, searching them for any glimmer of hope, any twinkle of assurance that she might find in them to belay her fears.

"Surely Terryll was the one who bandaged your shoulder. Wasn't he?" Dagmere put in.

"Terryll?"

Worm's eyes were quick and criminal. He was caught in the uncertain light of an unfolding drama, and he couldn't move to escape the stage. The fat baker, Moeldryth, had pursued him to this place and had cornered him at last, caught him, trapped him with the treachery of his own cursed mouth. And now standing before him were his judges, those of his myriad victims who were staring down at him, waiting for him to give a pitiful account of himself, of the least of his misdemeanors.

He had stolen a paltry loaf of bread but at the cost of a human life.

Worm let out a despondent sigh. He wished that they would just go away and leave him alone. Alone, he could then curl up into a ball and retreat into some dark, fantasy womb—a happy place born in the ruined hovels of Glenryth, where he had learned to perfect his desperate circumstances into friends, playmates who would come at his cry and tend to his needs, deliver him from the banal wretchedness of his existence. But under the light of present judgment, his friends scurried away like imps into the shadowlands. He had no choice now but to confess to these people— these strangers who were kin to the boy stranger, the fool who had saved his miserable life—the news they did not wish to hear. They, too, must be fools.

99

Worm took a deep breath. Then, letting his eyes address the sympathetic gallery of lampstands and chairs and darkened corners of the room, he began to relate every detail of his story as best he could—from the moment he first met Terryll in the cave, to his encounter with the bear and news of the boarhounds, to the point where Terryll led the horse-soldiers away as a diversion so that he and the bear could make an escape.

He had stammered at that part, as the volume of his crime assailed him, and embellished the truth to soften his part in it. Quickly he ended his confession, withholding the first cause that had given wing to the terrible flight, and dutifully awaited his penance. However, the pained visages that stared down at him were more than his soul could bear.

Helena buried her head in her hands and sobbed. Allyndaar caught her limp form and enveloped her with strong arms to console her, but it was to little avail.

"Terryll will be all right, Helena," he said. "He knows those hills like no other. We must trust in Christ."

Dagmere sat down on the bed with her back to the boy, staring entranced at the floor. She began to cry softly.

Worm felt shame—not for himself, not for anyone else, just shame. He wished that he could run far away from this place. His heart felt as though it were encased in wax and would soon stop beating from the gripping pressure. His mind swirled from so many first-time emotions that he feared he too would begin to cry.

He looked over at the tapestry and stared numbly at the naked man and woman, whose eyes were filled with such terror, whose frightened animal eyes bore a familial resemblance to the scores of miserable wretches he had known in his few years.

He blinked heavily several times and soon was unable to hold a focus any longer—his mind so wearied from the hour's toil. He was exhausted and wanted only to fall into the protective arms of sleep.

Out of the corner of his eye, Worm could see Allyndaar leading the mother toward the doorway. Dagmere followed along, sniffling. It seemed to him a little funeral cortege had passed from his side.

The beggar boy from Glenryth was troubled by this family—this ring of fools—for they had unmasked him, exposed him, made him look at his ugly nakedness. They had touched him in places that ought not to be touched. Danger haunted their smiles, their deceptive touches of kindness, the siren lilt in their lovely melodies. Their generosities rendered him altogether undone.

And as if this were not enough, this happy band had unearthed in him a dangerous administration—the luster of Eden's Tree now bore unimpeachable witness to himself in the fruit of conscience. The Transgression camped upon his brow, gazing into his mind—his soul—with sentient scrutiny, ruling his thoughts like a spectral despot.

Worm sighed heavily and closed his eyes as they began to brim with tears. But there was no absolution in these, and he turned his head to the unforgiving wall. The shadowy veil of sleep drew over his mind.

The hazy sun arced long and high overhead and played tag with a sky full of fleecy clouds that scudded across the lovely British landscape, chased northward by an unusual wind from the south. Clumps of lichen-crowned rocks and boulders jutted up into the sloping thread of trail, making passage through the thick mountain forest difficult.

But even so—and in spite of their lack of decent food or sleep for more than two days now—Terryll and the bear made good progress. He was certain of their escape but felt a growing uneasiness in the air, as though some imminent danger loomed just ahead or behind them.

They came to a fork in the trail, the right tine leading northeast toward Greta Bridge, and the left tine northwest to Killwyn Eden. They veered left without stopping and plodded upward through the trees until they reached the summit, where Terryll paused for a moment to catch his breath before beginning the descent. The intermittent rays of the sun warmed his face and pulled a colorful harvest of wild flowers from the chalky, gray earth around his feet.

Ahead of them were two more ridges to ascend, with long valleys in between in which Terryll hoped to find berries, other fruit, and water. Beyond the second ridge was a narrow cut of earth two miles wide, which fell away into the broad, fertile skirt of the Eden Valley. Here the village of Killwyn Eden was nestled along the River Eden, and with Godspeed they should arrive there just after first light on the morrow.

Just minutes after Terryll and the bear began their descent onto the other side of the ridge, a column of twenty heavily armored horsemen heading south (each carrying a shield emblazoned with a crimson wolf's head against a field of black), came to the same fork in the trail and paused. They had been scouting the area around Greta Bridge for the past few days to observe the strengths and weaknesses of the Britons in those parts and were returning with news of their findings. Their horses had smelled Hauwka's scent, and they stamped and snorted in fear.

Instinct commanded the Saxon leader to look up at the trail leading northwestward to Killwyn Eden and scan the trees for any sign of danger. There wasn't any.

"It must be a wolf lurking nearby," he said.

"It seems they are everywhere," another remarked.

"Yes, indeed."

Then, satisfied, the leader of the column raised his heavy arm and signaled for his men to continue southerly on their course—one that would eventually take them to the hill-fort of Badonsward.

_10_
BAPA

The morning sun shot through the arched window next to the bed and drenched the room with radiant light. Gone was the thunderstorm, clear were the azure skies above the busy village of Killwyn Eden—an unusual phenomenon in northern Britain.

Worm opened his eyes and cursed the first thoughts that entered his mind. It hadn't been a bad dream after all. And to make matters worse, his legs were soaked through—he had wet the bed during the night. Never before had he done such a thing. But of course, never before had he ever been unconscious and bedridden for two days either.

He cursed again and sank into a sullen mood, a mood that grew darker and more oppressive each minute. A full half-hour passed as he stewed over his situation before he came to a resolve in his mind.

"Enough of this foul-smelling bed." He scowled, lifting the covers from his body. "I've got to get away from this place."

Determined to steal away, the boy looked around the room for an avenue of escape. The door leading from the bedroom wouldn't do, because someone might be up and about by this hour and see him as he made his way through the house. The window to his left was the only possible exit.

He swung his legs around slowly and sat up with his feet dangling to the floor. But immediately the blood rushed from his head, leaving him light-headed, and for a moment he thought he might pass out. Then pain shot into his left shoulder, causing him to grimace, reminding him of his sentence. But it was tolerable, so he tried standing up slowly. His legs were wobbly and refused to support him for more than a few moments. He cursed the slackers and sat down hard on the bed.

"I'll try again in a minute," he muttered.

Then he noticed that it was missing. His medallion—it was gone. He clutched at the empty space around his neck, then searched vainly through the blankets for it. For years he had felt the weight of it sounding against his chest like a tiny clapper. But yesterday he had been too distracted by the whirlwind of events to notice its silence. Suddenly he felt a profound loss.

Just then, Helena poked her head into the room. "Are you awake?" she asked. "I thought I heard someone talking."

He cursed in his mind. *How can I get out of here now?* "It was just me," he grumbled.

"I see that you're sitting up. You must be feeling better." She walked into the room and stood about six feet from the boy.

"I feel . . . er . . . all right," he stuttered.

Worm hoped that she wouldn't come any closer to him and discover that the bed was wet.

"Are you hungry?" she asked. But before he could answer, she spun around and headed for the door. "What kind of a question is that? Of course you are! Let me have Dagmere bring you something to eat right away."

"No!" he shouted, stopping her at the doorway. Then catching himself, he added, "I'm not hungry . . . really."

Helena smiled. "You're just being shy. Dag—"

"I wet the bed!"

The words blurted out of his mouth before he could stop them. The blood rushed back into his head, and he now wished that he had passed out earlier.

"You what?" she asked, turning back into the room.

Worm was red-faced. "I said, I wet the bed."

Helena understood now his odd behavior. She paused for a moment and looked into the boy's eyes. They were dark, painful eyes that betrayed a life of hardship and misery, looking much too old to belong to one so young.

She at once pitied and feared him. After all, she had nothing but his own testimony as to who he was. And for that matter, he had said that his name was "Worm" not "Aeryck." The medallion that he wore might prove that he *was* the son of Caelryck, if Caelryck had given it to him. But for all she knew, he might have stolen it. His shabby clothes and unkempt appearance indicated that he was at least a beggar, if not a thief.

But something inside her refused to believe such a judgment. She could see in his eyes a loneliness, a desperate cry for help, a cry of which, perhaps, even the boy was unaware. Terryll had seen some merit in him, if nothing more than that he needed help and he was there. For now that was sufficient for her to hold onto, unless this young stranger showed her otherwise. She quickly gathered up the soiled blankets.

"Do not worry about the bed, Worm . . . er . . . son," she said, relaxing into a smile. "You've been sick." She found it awkward calling him by such a name, and from that moment on she refused to do so anymore. "We'll let this be our secret, though. All right?"

Worm nodded guardedly.

"How about if I bring you a clean change of clothes, and then we have some breakfast?"

"All right."

Helena smiled and gave him a pat on the cheek. "Good!" she exclaimed. Then, as she turned to leave the room, she gestured to a bronze thing on the floor and added, "And by the way, the chamber pot is next to the bed, if you should need it in the future."

"Oh . . . right," Worm said, eyeing the strange-looking vessel.

He looked after her for several moments, thinking how warm and good she made him feel inside, and decided that he would stay there a while longer—at least until he was well enough to make his own way. After all, free food and shelter made convincing arguments for survival, and right now that was his only concern.

Worm hadn't read her fear of him. The thought of someone's fearing him would have been ludicrous to Worm. However, he read very clearly her pain. He knew that she had been trying to cover a great ache in her heart for her son the whole time she had been in the room. Even though she had smiled, he could see the thoughts of Terryll behind her eyes and on the corners of her mouth.

He had never really been around any mothers before, at least not this close, and certainly not in a house. The only mothers he had known were ones he had encountered on the street. They were the ones who scowled at him, pronounced him unclean, commanded their children not to go near him when he was begging for money or food lest they contract some foul disease.

He thought about Helena for some time and came to the conclusion that she had to be the exception to the rule when it came to womenfolk.

The next hour brought him a bath and a haircut (his first proper ones in many years, on both counts), a change of clothes, a hearty breakfast, and several more tries on his legs. He was feeling much stronger. Soon he would take a walk around the house. He had been resting on the bed observing the fixtured room—the chairs, the lampstands, parchments, the tapestry, lazily contemplating his foreign life with detached interest, when Allyndaar entered the room carrying the sword and his bronze medallion.

"Here, son. I believe this belongs to you," he said, handing the medallion to the boy.

"My bear wreath!" Worm exclaimed. "Where did you find it?"

"We took it from your neck when we changed your bandages," Allyndaar answered. "Is that what you call it—a bear wreath?"

Worm felt a little embarrassed, hearing the name sounded back to him. He stared at the medallion, turning it back and forth thoughtfully in his fingers. He had given it the name as a small child, when he first set his eyes on the bear's image and the olive leaves encircling it. In all the years that he had worn it, no one knew the name but he.

"It's what I've always called it," he said in a low voice.

"The name suits it. Where did you get it?" Allyndaar asked.

"Where did I get it?" Worm looked up at him, not sure of the question. "Why . . . my father gave it to me."

"Really? What is your father's name? Perhaps I might know him."

Worm looked down at the medallion for several moments without answering. He was studying the bear's face. "I don't remember. I always called him . . . Bapa. He gave it to me on the morning he left to fight against the Saxons many years ago. It was the last time I saw him. People told me that he'd been killed."

Suddenly a thought struck the boy. He was in the middle of another inquisition. He shot an angry look at the man. "Why're you asking me this?" he countered defensively. "What concern is it of yours where I got this medallion? I didn't *steal* it, if that's what you're aiming at."

Worm put the medallion around his neck as if to secure its ownership. "The bear wreath is the only thing I've ever owned that I *didn't* steal."

"I haven't accused you of stealing it, son," Allyndaar said. "I need to know that it was your father who gave it to you, not someone else."

"Why?" the boy asked, still defensive. "What difference does it make to you?"

"Because I knew your father . . . Aeryck." He said the name a little tenuously.

The boy's face brightened. "You *did?*"

"Very well."

Worm was astounded. "You knew my *father?*" *This man knew my father,* the thought echoed. Suddenly he was intensely aware of the shade hovering before him. He knew that the man's face looked familiar. But how? Where? Perhaps he had seen him before in Glenryth. *This man knew my father!* He let the news settle in his mind. Suddenly a frown wrinkled his brow. "Wait a minute! Why did you call me Aeryck? My name is Worm."

"No, son. Your name is not Worm." Allyndaar lowered the sword to the boy and directed his eyes to the crest on the hilt. Seeing the crest, the boy's eyes opened in wonder. "The . . . the bear wreath!" he exclaimed. It was as though he had opened a door and found the image of himself gazing back at him, smiling a fraternal salutation. He smoothed his fingers over the familiar relief in the metal several times, as if he doubted the report of his eyes alone. "It's really the bear wreath!"

"Yes. It's the bear wreath."

"How is it possible?"

"Quite simply, son, your father engraved them both."

Worm looked up at the man, awestruck. *Is it true?* he wondered. He searched Allyndaar's face for the telling lines that would guide him back into the murky, forgotten catacombs of his past, hoping in his heart of hearts that this was not some sort of devilish ruse that the gods had decreed to punish him for his crimes.

During the hour that followed, Allyndaar, acting as a midwife of sorts, strove to deliver Worm's forgotten identity into the world—one that had been lost, gestating in the deadened womb of time and memory.

"Your father was a great man," he started. "Britain lost her most valued son when he died."

The chieftain told the boy the legends that surrounded his father's memory, the songs that were sung about him throughout the land, praising his heroic deeds.

The boy listened intently—the dubious lines of astonishment playing on his face—as one being told that his entire life had been nothing but a recitation of lies. He had heard only that his father had been a fool, a liar, a wicked man who had caused death, destruction, and a great burden to fall upon the people of Glenryth, and that he, by the sole accomplishment of his birth, was his wicked son, the devoted believer and disciple and purveyor of the great lie.

The boy's mouth hung slightly agape as the chieftain—the shade that haunted his memory—stripped away his past, a lie at a time.

"The first moment I set eyes on him," Allyndaar went on, "I could tell that he was a good man. And as I got to know him better, he proved my first judgment true."

The bowyer told Worm about Caelryck's great skills with metallurgy—how he had discovered a method of combining certain alloys with iron to make a metal so strong, so hard, that no other weapon made of iron could stand against it.

"As the saying is told by warriors all over the highlands," he said, "'A sword made by Caelryck is the most powerful weapon in the land, but a sword made by Caelryck, held by Caelryck's hand, is the most powerful weapon in the world!' There was none better with the sword than your father, Aeryck."

Worm looked down at the sword and studied every inch of detail that decorated the blade, the hilt, and the pommel of his father's craftsmanship, the delicious little lines and scallops and filigree that breathed into him a forgotten life. As he listened to Allyndaar, he felt a life-nourishing umbilical grow between his father and him, connecting them through the bond of sword, the wonder of metal, the bear wreath, and the lighted words that sounded the depths of his memory.

Then Allyndaar's tone suddenly shifted to a hushed reverence, as though the man were about to lead him into a cloistered holy place. "But I knew a greater weapon which he possessed that many others never beheld."

"What was that?" the boy asked, equally reverent, though his discomfiture with the holy ground was manifest in his trembling fingers.

"His faith," the man replied.

"His *faith?*"

Allyndaar showed the boy the chi-rho on the sword's crest, then told him of Caelryck's deep faith in Jesus Christ, a faith that he spoke not only with his tongue but with his life as well.

Worm studied the chi-rho on the pommel, then referenced the same Greek uncials on his medallion. He had never understood their significance until now.

Hearing Allyndaar speak so reverently about his father made his eyes brim with tears. But tears were strange to the beggar boy, and he quickly wiped them away, embarrassed at his weakness.

The chieftain smiled. He was patient. The birthing process was painful. It had to be, for it was pain that had shut the memories in so secure and impregnable a vault, and only through pain would they be released. Slowly, a glimmer of light at the end of the long, dark, and misty canal shone and moved him closer to new life, to new identity.

Suddenly in the lumen of darkness a face appeared.

Allyndaar's steely blue eyes had penetrated the foggy veil. The shade had not come to Glenryth as Worm had thought. No. It was he, Worm, who had been here, to this place, to this very house. The revelation was staggering. Vague mental pictures of not only his father, but also of his visit with him to Killwyn Eden ten years earlier, gradually came into fuzzy view like returning prodigal shades over the rise, and he ran to embrace them with open arms. They came at him with a rush, shouting, laughing, weeping, each one begging him to hear his recital first.

Worm gave heed to an impression of a man's arm—his father's he presumed—and himself as a vague urchin hedging mischievously at his cuff. He was looking up at the towering bowyer in furtive awe, somewhere in a large, seemingly endless room filled with all manner of bows, arrows, tools, and the sweet, musty smell of wood. In the half-light of this recall stood the rigid, arched shape of a little girl, crying because of something he had either done or said to her. And a vague recollection of a woman sweeping about the home flashed across his mind.

Immediately a table was set before him with a banquet of delectable memories—treasured anecdotes of bygone events—each chair around the table filled with a laughing child. As Allyndaar continued his delivery somewhere outside of him, Worm listened to each tale retold by some facet of his youth, inwardly laughing or crying as each memory took its turn around the table. Deep, wistful soughs marked the passage of each one.

But when his eyes fell upon the chair at the end of the table, the place reserved for his most honored prodigal, he found the chair to be empty. He looked round the table once more, but he could not find the memory of his name.

Aeryck. The name hung lifeless in his mind, threatening stillbirth. He labored hard to find the sound of it in his mind spoken by someone, anyone, even a whisper of it, but the boy could only retrieve the name of Worm. Then, like the swelling of the tide, a lump filled his throat, and a feeling of shame overwhelmed him.

The faces of men and women from Glenryth began to appear all around him in a swirl that grew in velocity and force, becoming a whorl of distorted, nightmarish images, kin to his fevered paroxysms, filled with fierce anger and hatred. He could hear their cries and taunts echoing through his head as they derided him, as they condemned him to a wretched life of shame.

"It is because of your father that we now suffer so under the rod of Saxon tyranny . . . Caelryck would not listen . . . he would not surrender . . . let the memory of his name be cursed forever, and yours with him . . . go away, child of the street . . . leave this place . . . you are no longer welcome here . . .your inheritance is shame, you vile and despicable . . . worm . . . worm . . . Worm . . ."

And then there was a dreadful silence. The faces disappeared, hurrying away to infinite points on a surreal mind-scape. Their maledictions trailed them like a pack of dogs, barking, leaving Worm to stand alone with disturbing thoughts falling about his feet.

At the sound of distant footsteps, the boy turned and beheld the wraithlike image of a large man walking across the years in his mind—across a floor really, now situated in a forgotten place, a home, his home. Each step brought the man into sharper focus, each step incarnated the wondrous apparition of his father, his bapa. He saw an image of the man lowering himself onto one knee and laying his huge, leathery hands gently on his shoulders, his calluses scratching at his little linen tunic. He could see his face, broad and beaming, smiling at him with kind eyes, hazel eyes. His long curls of sand-colored hair, wild and heat blown, and the smell of fire and metal and the smoke of burning coke was all about him like a wreath.

"I have made this medallion for you to have, son," his father said. "Wear it always, for it is the symbol of our family name." He put the bear wreath around the boy's neck and gave him a long hug and kissed his head tenderly.

Then he stood up into the stature of a giant and walked to the door. He paused, turned to his son, and added, "Always remember that your bapa loves you, Aeryck."

And with those words, the ghost of his father faded.

But there they were . . . *Aeryck! Bapa!* The forgotten name, the forgotten love sounded clearly in his mind at last. The seat at the end of the table was filled, and his bapa finally was calling to him from it after so long in the womb and so painful the canal of passage.

The light of his father's face was at first brilliant and glorious, filling Worm's heart with unspeakable joy. But immediately the reality of his identity and his father's death overtook him like a thunderhead. The darkness in his mind through which he had wandered aimlessly about, groping like a blind man for light and course, was now in plain view before his eyes, and on his face he wore the sum of his anguish.

The son of Caelryck could no longer stay the tears, and he wept long and bitterly. "Bapa . . . Bapa . . . Bapa . . ."

He would never forget again.

Allyndaar stood up and left the boy alone to sort out his thoughts. *God have mercy on this boy,* he prayed silently. Then, as thoughts of his own boy poured into his mind, the feeling of helplessness once again swept over his spirit, and he added, *And on my son.*

He walked into the great room, which adjoined the bedroom, and made his way across the large villa toward his workshop. Keeping his hands busy, he thought, would keep his mind from worrying over Terryll.

As he entered the work area he thought back on the day when Caelryck had come to him for help. He pondered the providence of the boy's arrival and, now, the absence of his son. What was God's wisdom in it? Surely it would be revealed in time. Perhaps it wouldn't. He picked up a stave of yew and secured it gently in the wooden vise.

Suddenly shrill cries from his daughter outside pierced the hallowed silence.

"Papa! Papa! Come quickly!" she shouted. "It's Terryll! It really is Terryll!"

Allyndaar ran to the window. On the slope he quickly found the form of his son, wending down the hill with his confident, easy gait, alongside the giant bear.

Then his eyes caught sight of Helena—beautiful, demure Helena —holding her dress away from her legs and running as fast as he had ever seen her move. She was in a footrace. And it appeared to him that she was laughing like a little girl—laughing and running toward their son on the hill like a sprinter, and it was the funniest thing he had ever seen. He laughed rapturously.

Seeing her father at the window, Dagmere again cried out the wonderful news. She was jumping up and down as if she had springs on her feet. "Papa! It's Terryll! It's Terryll! Come quickly!" Then turning, she too was running. "It's really Terryll!"

"I'm coming!" he answered, choking back joyous tears. Then he cried out as he ran to the door, "Thank You, holy Savior! Thank You!"

11
THE PRELUDE TO CELEBRATION

Helena couldn't stop crying. She held her arms around her son and wept, praising God through her tears for His great mercy and kindness.

Dagmere cried too, first for her brother's safe return, then for her mother's joy, then for some indefinable happiness that was budding in her.

Terryll kept reassuring them both that he was all right. Even Hauwka let out several moans to that effect, though his boisterous moans were less than comforting. Once-brave dogs skulked to secret places and whimpered.

After the women had finished weeping all over Terryll, Allyndaar embraced his son in glad arms and welcomed him. Terryll looked up into his father's eyes and saw that they too were moist, prompting his own eyes to brim over. It was good to be home.

Worm watched the scene from the bedroom window, as though from another world.

When he heard Dagmere calling out to her father, he had moved to the window with the promise of hope. He caught sight of Terryll and the giant bear on the slope, and they were to him a vision of resplendent glory—the boy, a timely savior, descending from the terrible mount, redeeming him from the oppressive, unpleasant discourses that thundered in his mind and banishing the sorrowful mood of his crime to desolate islands. It seemed the ranting despot immediately had taken relief in cool fields of green beside stilled waters.

Worm let out an unrehearsed laugh. It was a wonderful joy to see Terryll safe in his family's arms, the ring of fools reconnected, and he none to blame. But then, strangely, and with the swiftness of a falcon in winged pursuit, a cloud of melancholy enshrouded his spirit, snatching tender joy from his heart. The festivity of the moment, especially when he beheld the embrace between Terryll and his father, served to contrast his own bitter loss. The beggar turned from the happy scene with a profound ache, and he mourned again the memory of his father.

Once inside the villa, Helena nursed the abrasions and cuts on Terryll's face, neck, and limbs with furious remedies. It frightened her to think how such wounds might have been inflicted upon her son, but she refrained from asking. Terryll was safe now, a fact that bequeathed to her great peace. She sat him down at the table and, with a vented maternal flurry, began fixing him some food, giggling like a little girl and now and then weeping in private concerts.

The boy was too exhausted from his ordeal to even think about food, let alone labor over the process of eating it. But his mother invoked a feminine scowl that drove away all masculine resistance, and she gave him some bread, goat's cheese, and a mug of fresh cider to wash it down before she let him go to bed. Allyndaar would wait until later to hear the details of his capture.

With all the distractions of the moment, the bear had been overlooked. Because of his size that was a difficult oversight, to be sure, but it had happened. Helena had ushered the boys into Terryll's bedroom, and Allyndaar had left the house to meet with some of the leaders of the village to arrange a celebration in the great hall that evening. Dagmere alone remembered the great beast.

She left the house with a leg of mutton and made her way through a ground cover of lawless chickens that were stabbing the earth with their beaks as though the earth itself were the author of their lowly estate. They clucked excitedly as they opened a path before her, annoyed at the intrusion. Then as soon as she passed, they quickly closed ranks behind her and continued on with their anarchy.

Dagmere was singing a refrain from an earlier melody but with a marked upswing in its tempo. Had Worm been near to hear it, he would have confessed a heartfelt conversion to Morgen, the Celtic goddess of music.

The girl passed by several wattled pens that kept the sheep, sows, and shoats. She had been feeding them when she caught sight of Terryll and the bear coming down the slope, so they were still rooting through the mud and corn husks. Next to them was a smaller pen that kept the boar, a big four-hundred pounder who kept sticking his head through a hole in the wattle and harassing the sows. But mostly they just ignored him, and as Dagmere walked by, the hog caught scent of the mutton and hurried to the other side of the pen. He slogged along beside her, sticking his big snout through several openings that he had made in the wattle, and snorted greedily.

"This isn't for you, my fat friend," Dagmere said. "Anyway, your eating days are over."

The boar looked at her blankly for a few moments as she walked away, mulling over pig thoughts in his head, then turned his attention back to the sows, happy again in his muddy little world. Dagmere rounded the corner of the house and saw the big bear sniffing and snorting through some fallen fruit in their orchard, located on the far side of the estate. "There you are, Hauwka! Did you think that we forgot about you?" she called out. "Here, I have brought you something to eat."

She gave the bear the leg of mutton, which he took gladly in his mouth, then she put her arms around his massive neck and embraced him. "I know that you don't understand what I'm saying, Hauwka, but thank you very much for bringing my brother home safely. You are a very special friend."

The bear let out a quiet moan as Dagmere stepped away from him and looked into his eyes. The bear seemed to be studying her, and she thought for a moment that he actually did understand what she had said. The thought was a little unnerving, but she quickly dismissed it. After all, Hauwka was a bear.

The great shaggy beast lumbered away to find a secluded place to eat and then, finally, after many days of denial, surrender to sleep.

Helena prepared a pallet in Terryll's room for Worm to sleep on while he convalesced. Worm felt much more comfortable with this arrangement. The pallet was harder and more to his liking, and, more important, he knew that he would no longer be depriving Allyndaar and Helena of their bedroom.

He and Terryll spent a few minutes of awkward discourse, covering the events following their separation on the mountain. But as Terryll related the details of his story, his eyelids slowly draped over his eyes—on cue from a less sociable part of his brain—and he lapsed into sleep.

Worm looked at him for several minutes as he slept. He studied the surrogate bruises and cuts along the docile body that Terryll had suffered on his behalf and was struck with a powerful sense of guilt.

It was not an abstract feeling of shame floating about that was inscrutable, but a tactile judgment of conscience that convicted a specific action of his—an action that had caused not only this boy but his entire family much suffering.

Shame was a feeling, a state of mind, of soul, that he had grown up with, but guilt was something entirely new. He was uncomfortable with it. It seemed there was no eluding the censuring despot who had returned with a gavel in its clutches.

His thoughts were interrupted as Helena poked her head into the room to check on the two of them. "How are you doing, Aeryck?" she whispered.

Worm looked over to the doorway and saw her smiling at him. Her face was radiant, and he could tell that her smile now concealed nothing but joy. Hearing his name sounded out loud was strange to him and would take some getting used to.

"I'm fine."

"You need to get some rest as well, Aeryck. Your body needs as much as you will give it."

"I will. I promise."

Helena left the room to begin preparations for the evening meal.

Worm lay down, and, after a few minutes of working through his thoughts, he fell fast asleep.

News of Terryll's safe return quickly spread throughout the village, and soon the iron bell that hung outside the little stone church of Killwyn Eden was ringing out a call for celebration.

The bell had been cast in Auxerre, a city in Gaul, a score of years before and was beautifully engraved with all manner of scenes from Scripture, victory wreaths, and holy writings. It had been presented to Allyndaar and the men of Killwyn Eden as a token of appreciation by a bishop named Germanus.

Germanus had been asked by the Britons to join them in an expedition against the Picts, who had invaded the northern civitates twenty-one years earlier.

Allyndaar offered the one-time military commander the services of his men and helped him secure a great victory along Hadrian's Wall—but not before he had led his men into the waters of Christian baptism. The Bishop of Auxerre would not fight with an army of pagans behind him, so after instructing the men in the Christian faith, he led the British army, as one man, to Christ. The legend is told throughout the land that on the celebration of Eostre's day, these and other Britons, still dripping with baptismal waters, shouted a chorus of "Alleluia!" as they marched into battle, and the Pictish army fled before them in terror. Every time the bell sounded, it was a reminder to the people of Killwyn Eden of that day in which God wrought a great victory through them.

Helena spent the better part of the day singing hymns of praise and thanksgiving as she and Dagmere prepared the evening meal over the stone hearth in their spacious, open-beamed kitchen. Later on that evening there would be a celebration in the great hall, and the whole village would be invited to rejoice with them. This meal would be their own private celebration of Terryll's return. It had to be special. Helena's spirit was overflowing with joy—so much so that she could hardly contain it. She was in her glory.

Dagmere could not remember when she had seen her mother so happy.

The hearth was large enough to accommodate the roasting of sizable portions of meat, as well as having room for several pots and kettles for boiling vegetables or stew at the same time. Having been built to host large gatherings of Roman dignitaries and military leaders, the kitchen facilities were more than ample for their simple needs.

As Helena laced some onions into a chicken stew that was simmering over the fire, one of the militant chickens from outside flew up onto the window sill to the left of the hearth. Not wasting any time, it hopped down onto the countertop and, clucking the while, picked its way through a mess of string beans and tomatoes, jabbing at kernels of grain that lay scattered across the marble slab.

Helena turned her head and scowled. "We already have one volunteer boiling in the pot," she said, wagging a wooden spoon at it. "And unless you would like to join her . . . *shoo!*"

The chicken cackled and squawked as it fled across the counter in terror. Then with a flurry of stubby wings, it flew through the window and landed not far from the house, beating a hasty retreat to safety.

Helena shook her head and returned to her preparations. Dagmere laughed at the sight. She was in a glory of a different kind, and, as it was the spring of the year, laughter was a constant friend.

Off to the other side of the hearth was a brick oven for baking bread, having a flue that drafted up through the same chimney as the fireplace. It had been plastered by the Romans, and much had cracked and fallen away through years of use, exposing the brick beneath it. Allyndaar kept promising that he would replaster it as soon as he found time, but with his duties as chieftain and bowyer, he had little time left for such domestic inconveniences. Or so he said.

If the truth be known, he had little aptitude in such areas and would usually run aground at some point, so he kept a quiverful of excuses at arm's reach. Helena knew that, if it was going to get done, she'd have to learn how to plaster herself. The bricks would wait.

Worm's mind was restless, and he slept poorly. He dreamed that he saw the tapestry on the wall, with each of the images of the lamb, the serpent, and the naked man and woman in their rightful places in the scene. There was such clarity of detail at first. He saw each vertical and horizontal thread of color, woven back and forth, up and down, that composed the warp and woof of the fabric. The colors of the trees and flowers in the garden were more brilliant than any he knew on earth and gave the dreaming boy a feeling of supernal exhilaration.

116

At first the dream focused on the fleeing man and woman. It was interesting to Worm that, even though they kept running, they made no distance in the tapestry. Then after a time, as he considered this perplexing phenomenon, their images suddenly changed into distorted expressions of horror.

The boy followed their stricken gaze to the serpent, who now had—dreams are quick to grant such liberties—its scaly tail coiled around them to suffocate their lives. It would have done so had it not been for the lamb, whose image now buffeted his mind.

The lamb began to stamp fiercely up and down on the serpent's head, wounding it severely. It was a frightening image, which moved the boy's subconscious mind to terror.

But the most frightening image in the dream was the lamb's crimson slash across its throat. The more the lamb stamped on the serpent to wound it, the more the lamb's throat bled. And the more it bled, the fiercer it became. Soon, blood flowed like water from its throat and covered its snowy fleece entirely, so that it was hard to distinguish it as a lamb at all. At once the bloody lamb looked directly at Worm with vengeful intent, petrifying the boy. It was startling to Worm that he had now replaced the man and the woman in the tapestry and was fleeing in fear for his very self. But like the man and woman who made no distance as they fled, neither did he. His legs were leaden, and the surface beneath his feet became as a sucking bog.

Then to his horror, the crimson lamb was running toward him with the speed of a leopard, and he was sure that when the lamb caught him, it would stamp him to pieces as it had the serpent, swiftly and without compassion. The boy tried desperately to cry out for mercy, that it all had been a terrible mistake, but his swollen tongue served only to gag him, to choke him of life and breath.

Worm reeled upright in bed, panting. For a moment, he couldn't tell whether or not he was still asleep, and he shot a look behind him, half expecting to see the bloody lamb on his heels. The realization that it had only been a dream quickly washed that fear from his mind, and he exhaled a sigh of relief. However, the terrible images of the tapestry lingered there, haunting him like a specter of judgment.

It was early evening. The cool shadows fell long across the room, having already made their ascent up the wall opposite him. Worm could tell by the way the objects in the room were bathed in the telltale, reddish-orange glow that it was sunset or soon to be. The day was yielding gracefully to clambering shadows that were pitching a colorless tent over the world.

It was then that he felt the eyes.

Thinking nothing of it at first, Worm looked over at the doorway expecting to see Helena or Allyndaar, but there was no one. Then the boy, as a little prickling began up his spine, slowly followed the lead of his eyes to the window and looked outside.

He jumped, and a little gasp rushed from his throat, for outside the window, sitting on his haunches in the middle of the apple orchard, was the giant bear, looking directly at him—through him it seemed—blinking slowly, studying him with those wet, coal-like eyes, those killer eyes. The bear raised his snout and bawled loudly.

The little prickling whipped a shudder over his body, and Worm decided then and there that he didn't like bears. Not one bit.

Terryll awakened with a groan. Worm looked over at him as the young hunter swung his legs heavily over the bed and sat upright. Terryll stretched his arms into the air, grabbing for his strength, let out a loud, roaring yawn, smacked his lips, and chuckled inexplicably. Then, scratching his tousled black hair with one hand and raking an itch on his side with the other, he looked over at Worm. He wore a sleepy-eyed expression on his face.

"How's it going?" he asked through another yawn.

"Uh, fine," Worm answered, looking back out the window. But the bear had gone. Of course. It was probably lurking outside just below the window where he couldn't see it, waiting to take a lethal swipe at him when he wasn't looking. "Is . . . uh . . . is there anything that strikes you unusual about your bear?" he asked, craning his head over the sill to ratify his thoughts.

"He's not my bear," Terryll replied. "Hauwka belongs to no one but the wilds." Then he narrowed his eyes. "What do you mean—'unusual'?"

Presently Helena walked into the room and interrupted their conversation. She smiled. "I thought I heard talking. Come now, boys, it is time for supper."

Terryll brightened and exclaimed, "Good! I'm half-starved!"

"Me too!" Worm added, forgetting the bear at once.

Helena poured a bucket of water into the large wash basin next to Terryll's bed. "Good!" she said. "Then after supper, we will all go over to the hall for a wonderful celebration."

Terryll's enthusiasm died an agonizing death. "I just love celebrations," he responded dryly. "Don't you?"

Worm looked at him stupidly. He had no idea what Terryll was talking about. To him the idea of a celebration, quite frankly, sounded wonderful, and visions of it immediately chased away his troubling thoughts.

Helena combed her fingers through Terryll's hair gingerly, mindful of his hurts, then kissed him affectionately on his brow. "We don't do this often," she teased. "I know that you'll just have to force yourself to have a good time. Won't you?" Turning to leave the room, she smiled and added, "And by the way, in case you didn't notice, I put some water in the basin. Make sure that some of it ends up on your face!" She looked over at Worm. "And that goes for you as well, Aeryck."

"Why'd my mother call you Aeryck?" Terryll queried, after Helena left the room. "You said your name was Worm."

"It's a long story. I'll tell you about it later."

"Aeryck. Aeryck." Terryll tested the name on his tongue. Then he added, "I think I like Worm better."

"I don't."

The boys readied themselves for supper, sprinkling only as much of the water on their faces as would pass muster.

The boar made a great show of the feast. He would have been proud had he lived to see it. Along with the roast pork, the long oaken table was spread with a leg of roast mutton, a pot of chicken stew, various breads and jams, and an assortment of boiled vegetables and potatoes from the garden. Added to these were several bowls of fruit picked from their orchard. Helena and Dagmere had outdone themselves; it was a table fit for a king. The family had much to be thankful for.

In all his life Worm had never seen so much food in one place, and he felt awkward at the prospect of eating without having first to beg or steal. But the feeling quickly passed, and he was soon grabbing handfuls of food and stuffing them into his face with abandon.

The family watched for a moment in strained silence as the boy, totally oblivious of their stares, continued to eat in blissful ignorance.

"Do you eat like thish every night?" he asked without lifting his eyes from his food.

"Aeryck, it is good to see you in such fine appetite," Allyndaar finally broke in. "But it is our custom to say a blessing of thanksgiving over the food before we eat."

"A blesshing?" Worm coughed through a mouthful of potatoes. "What's a blesshing?"

"A blessing is a kind of prayer, thanking God for His gracious provision of food," Helena replied.

"Ish fine wiff me . . . go right ahead," Worm said, chasing the potatoes with a large bite of mutton.

Allyndaar looked at Helena and shrugged his shoulders, while Dagmere and Terryll exchanged snickers. They bowed their heads as Allyndaar prayed.

"Gracious Father, we thank You for the bountiful table that You have set before us. But above this, we are thankful for returning our son

Terryll to us safely, and for bringing young Aeryck into our home to share in Your storehouse of blessings . . ."

Worm looked up from his cabbage at the mention of his name and glanced around at each of their bowed faces. He had never seen anyone pray before. It seemed to him curious that one should speak so to an unseen deity, but not so curious that his appetite was withheld by it. He reached for a chunk of bread as Allyndaar continued.

"May Your hand be upon his life. In the name of Your holy Son, Jesus the Christ, we joyfully approach You and are grateful for Your rich kindness and mercy. Amen."

The rest of the family added a reverent, "Amen."

Worm belched.

During the meal Terryll related all the events that had happened, from the time he rescued Worm to the night of his escape. Not wanting to frighten his mother and Dagmere unduly, he kept to himself the details of the battle, as well as the business that he had overheard concerning Horsa, his army, and the rest of the purloined fragments of conversation, until he could speak with his father alone later that evening. Terryll knew that he would be particularly interested in the Saxons' observation of the village of Catterick and others along their way to Badonsward.

At several points during the briefing, Worm glanced up from his food and found Dagmere looking at him from across the table. Each time he caught her eye, she quickly looked down at her plate, and a flush of red swept across her face. What she didn't see, however, were the vermillion hues betraying Worm's face as he jerked his eyes back to his own plate.

Later in the meal, Allyndaar cleared his throat while glancing around the table at each member of his family: Helena, opposite him; Dagmere, to his left; and the boys on his right. It was a well-known signal that meant that Allyndaar had something important to say and that he wanted everyone's undivided attention while he said it.

Worm had no idea of any such signal, so he continued to eat with enthusiasm. But after several moments and a short jab to his ribs from Terryll, he looked up from his handful of vegetables.

"Whah? Are you going to blesh the food shummore?"

"No, Aeryck," Allyndaar spoke. "Helena and I have discussed your arrival at some length, and it is our desire to welcome you into our home to stay. Not only until you are fully recovered, but for as long as you would like."

Worm stopped chewing and swallowed hard, nearly choking on the lump of food. He grabbed his mug of cider and, though spilling most of it on his tunic, managed to wash the food down his throat. He looked around the table at each of their faces, the circle of fools, and a wariness edged into his features. "Why?"

Helena leaned forward and smiled warmly. "Because you are without either home or family," she said, "and we would like to provide you with both." She looked down the length of the table at her husband and added, "It is what Christ would have us do."

"How do you know that?" the boy asked, truly surprised. "Did He talk to you?"

"Through the Scriptures, yes," Helena replied. "He tells us to be mindful of widows and orphans."

Worm wiped the food from his hands across his shirt and looked from Helena to Terryll. "Widows and orphans?"

Terryll beamed. "We'll be able to hunt and explore the highlands together, and—"

"Not so fast, Terryll," his mother interrupted. "You've just returned home. I'd like to keep you here at least for a little while."

Worm looked from Terryll's face, over to Helena's, then to Dagmere. She smiled demurely at him and added a little nod of approval. The boy was lost for a moment in the depths of her sparkling blue eyes. Never had he seen such beauty. He awkwardly returned her smile, then turned back to Allyndaar and said, "I don't know what to say."

"Just say yes." Terryll grinned.

"Are we agreed?" Allyndaar asked.

Worm nodded his head, somewhat embarrassed with all of the attention. "I have nowhere else to go."

"Then it is done!" Allyndaar declared, slamming his palm on the table, as was his custom when he concluded a business or family matter.

"Delightful," Helena said.

Terryll let out a yell. Dagmere smiled. And the bell outside the church began to ring, heralding the night of celebration.

In obedience to the clanging herald, the townspeople of Killwyn Eden moved from their homes into the balmy spring night, making their way toward the great hall in the center of the village in amiable groups of twos and threes and little swarms of larger denominations.

These swelled, mostly by means of scampering children full of lark, and escorts of all manner of barking dogs. In the air there hung a joyous respite from the day's toil, and the bell rang out fair warning that the evening held in its ample stores the boon of mirth to one and all.

But not far away, from the darkened cover of the forested brow overshadowing the village, they were being watched.

The light from a waning gibbous moon, slanting slowly across its westerly course, caught the yellowish glow of a pair of eyes, narrowed on the happy scene below and shaded by a scowling brow of fur. The creature sat silent, hunched-shouldered and motionless, save for the subtle shifting of its sinister eyes, resembling a stump of lifeless tree or rock or some other inanimate part of the forest.

Whatever its purpose—dark or otherwise—the ominous sentinel, like some hideous gargoyle perched atop its cathedral promontory, stared through soulless orbs and studied the moonlit forms of the people below as they filed into the great hall. How long it had been there watching or how long it intended to stay was known only to the creature itself. It was certain, however, by its friendless attitude, that the tolling bell brought it little cheer. A tiny whirl of air curled around its clawed feet, then lifted a familiar scent into its black nostrils. Its eyes opened with a start.

Suddenly there was a thunderous roar that seemed to shake the heavens, followed by the sound of pounding feet closing in fast, shuddering the earth. The creature sprang into the safety of the trees just as the massive shape of the intruder lunged for it, narrowly missing its throat with its powerful jaws. The chase lasted but a few whirling moments as the two shadowy shapes crashed menacingly through and around tree limbs, shrubbery, and bramble. They made an unholy racket—the one yelping and howling as it fled, while the other, with bared teeth snapping at the life of its enemy, pressed its attack into the lightless forest. And then, as abruptly as the attack began, it ended, and the ferocious assailant halted his pursuit at the crest of the wooded hill.

Hauwka looked on as the grizzled wolf made its escape into the blackness of the forest, terrified with its sudden brush with death. Then the great bear stood on his hind legs and let out a long, earsplitting roar of defiance—a declaration of intent that pursued the canine beast far into the distant recesses of the highlands. Lowering himself to all fours, he blew out a snort.

While Terryll was en route to the great hall with his family, the sound of Hauwka's great roar pulled him from his trudging step. He looked up yearningly at the jagged black hills flanking either side of his village, and they seemed to him two giant outstretched arms, beckoning him to come hither, to flee quickly the small businesses of men. At once his heart swelled with a bittersweet ache.

He was grateful to be at home safe with his family—there wasn't question of it—but at the same time he longed to run into the hills' wild embrace, again to roam the unfettered forestlands with his hairy friend. The boy couldn't help feeling that he was tragically and irrevocably caught by the citizenry of two countries, a patriot to each in turn, yet traitor to both. He let out a wistful sigh and plodded heavily onward to the hall as one condemned to suffer. Worm, on the other hand, was not troubled in the least with the loyalties of patriots. He was troubled in the most, however, by the rending sound of Hauwka's roar and had quickened his pace to pledge his allegiance to many disquieting thoughts. A shudder of fear crawled up his spine like a skittering of bugs, and he was truly grateful that he was headed toward the peopled confines of the great hall, where he wagered he'd be safe from tooth and nail and large bears that he would swear on oath were devils incarnate.

Fingers of wind whisked the peals of the bell up into the trees, bringing the clangorous, unnatural sounds to Hauwka's attention. The bear looked below at the yellow glow of firelight that lit and warmed the noisy hall in the village and pondered, as a bear might ponder, the lives of the people there for several moments. And as his bear thoughts drifted through the wild mists of his mind, there could be seen in his wet, coal-like eyes the faintest edge of apprehension glinting dully in the pallid light. His instincts warned him that there was danger stirring in the air.

After a time, the powerful bruin turned his massive head toward the southern stretch of the Pennines and sniffed the air for scent. Then, letting out a snort, he slowly lumbered away into the night.

PART TWO
THE SON OF CAELRYCK

12
THE GREAT HALL

The music of harps and flutes mingled with laughter, creating a cacophony of celebration over the village that rose to meet the stars hanging low over the northern nightscape. The great hall of Killwyn Eden was filled to capacity with people from all over the village and its outlying areas, so much so that the excess of people spilled noisily out into the torch-lighted streets.

Inside the hall were four parallel rows of five long tables each, made of heavy oak. Two rows favored one side of the hall's length, and the other two rows favored the opposite side. This arrangement left a large area between them, connected at the far end of the hall by the twenty-foot-long head table.

A stone fireplace, large enough for a man to stand in, sat about ten paces behind it. The hall could accommodate roughly two-hundred-fifty persons, still leaving ample room for standing or sitting on the floor space in the center.

In his recollection, Worm had never been inside a hall before, and he would never have imagined a place of such wonder and awe. The air crackled with an energy that sent his mind reeling with excitement. He was certain that he had entered a most holy place and wondered often, as he gave his eyes permission to explore the hall at will, how Terryll could not find in it the most thrilling of human endeavors. In this place he was certain that stout hearts were forged from lesser flesh, and glorious visions from the downcast eye.

He looked about the hall reverently, taking in the austere tributes of history that gazed down at him from the walls and crossbeams. Adorning these were rows of swords, pikes, shields, and armor that had once belonged to various men of valor from Killwyn Eden, hailed now as heroes for having distinguished themselves in life and death in behalf of their village and country.

The weapons, once gleaming proudly in the clamor of battle, had long since been retired to the hallowed walls with great honor, as trophies and memorials to the men who wielded them. Each had its own story of glory and heroism that was sung or told, time and again, by the bards to wide-eyed children and hearty men flushed with too much wine and ale.

Along the beams and lintels were various scenes that revealed a hybrid of cultures, showing the evolution from Celtic to Roman to Christian occupation of the hall. Across one beam was a scene depicting Jupiter and Juno placing a laurel wreath on Caesar's head in recognition of his own deity. Along another, carvings illustrated both the vernal and autumnal equinoxes, as well as the winter and summer solstices, as the sun and moon gods traveled their annual circuits through each of the four seasons. And finally, on the beam adjoining it, were scenes showing the baptism of Christ, the parable of the Good Shepherd, and the raising of Lazarus. It was a strange amalgamation of cultural artistry and beliefs but certainly one common to the island of Britain at the time.

Worm's eyes arced over the willowy form of a hall maid of fourteen or fifteen years with straight auburn hair, and fell upon a horned helmet made of bronze, having sword dents all over it. As the girl passed in front of him carrying a trayful of empty mugs, she paused for a moment, smiling at him demurely.

But the boy was too absorbed with the details of the helmet to notice her charms. It sat upon a small shelf that jutted out from the pillar near the center of the hall and spoke to him of fantastic battles, of fiery altercations between gods. He later learned that it had been worn by Terryll's grandfather when he was slain in a fierce battle against the Picts years before, and forever after the helmet was a thing of awe.

The boy was seated at the head table—a table reserved for the chieftain and his family—along with several other men of standing in the village.

Allyndaar sat at the center of the table, which afforded him an unobstructed view of the hall. He was wearing a white linen tunic, bound at the waist with a thick leather belt, and twilled woolen trousers woven with the distinctive tartan plaid worn by the clansmen of the Brigantes tribe. Over the tunic he wore a coarse, woolen cloak that was bright scarlet in color, fastened at one shoulder with a silver brooch. Encircling his neck was a torque of twisted bands of silver and gold, having engraved boar heads at each end, which signified his status as chieftain.

Helena and Dagmere sat to his right, each wearing brightly colored, fine linen dresses, gathered at the waist and tied with long silk scarves from the Orient. Helena wore her hair pulled up from her neck and piled onto her head in the fashion of the Roman noblewomen, having secured it with carved ornaments of ivory and jade. Dagmere, on the other hand, wore her hair unbraided and brushed into long, thick tresses sprinkled with an aromatic palette of wildflowers.

They were both beautiful. And many a young and hopeful man in the hall gaped at Dagmere's beauty throughout the evening. But she wasn't the least interested, which is the prerogative of young women in bloom, and she deftly parried every confident stare with steeled aloofness.

Terryll and Worm sat to Allyndaar's left, wearing the outfits they had on earlier in the day—white linen tunics and light woolen trousers cross-laced with leather straps down to their heavy leather boots—with the exception that Terryll now wore an emerald green cloak, befitting his station as the chieftain's son.

Worm's eyes were wide in the wonder of the occasion; Terryll still wore the iron mask of the condemned.

Sitting to Worm's left was a monk by the name of Brother Lucius Aurelius. A Roman. He was an austere-looking man with a heavy sunscorched brow, thick curls of grizzled hair worn in a tonsure, deep-set eyes almost jet in color, and a large aquiline nose that jutted out prominently from his bone-rugged face.

Worm thought him at first some kind of strange warrior, and throughout the evening stole glances at him to satisfy his youthful awe and curiosity. He hadn't seen any monks before, so he had no idea what they were supposed to look like. But if Aurelius was typical of Christian holy men, he mused, then this religion of the Romano-Britons was a fierce one indeed.

Once the man caught his stare, and for a moment Worm thought that he would receive a vitriolic tongue-lashing. But instead, the man smiled at him and greeted him by his given name. Worm was taken aback that such a fellow would know who he was.

During the first hour, the chatter, singing, and laughter of the celebration built to a deafening crescendo. The ale and wine flowed freely, adding to the merriment, flushing faces.

Usually the Britons drank a thick, heady beverage known as mead, made from fermented wild honey, water, malt, and other herbs and spices. Only on special occasions would the amphoras of red and white wines from southern Gaul be brought out. This night was one such occasion.

Terryll was surrounded by a throng of well-wishers to the right of Worm and having a tolerable time of it, while Aurelius was engaged in some theological discussion with several blurry-eyed men to his left, leaving Worm alone between them. This arrangement was fine with him. He didn't want to talk with anyone anyway. He was pleased to just gaze about the hall and take in all of the new sights.

A pretty blonde girl of fifteen passed by with a trayful of flagons, and she too smiled at him.

But his eyes were sweeping upward at the time toward a huge boar's head mounted on the wall to his right, and he missed the ocular tryst. He studied the mounting for several minutes, thinking how it might have been killed. Horrible, bloody images immediately assaulted his mind, for he knew well the tales of these ferocious beasts—how they could tear a man to shreds in seconds with their long tusks. A little shiver raced along his spine, and he was careful to avoid eye contact with the thing for the rest of the evening.

He glanced at Terryll and wondered if he had ever hunted wild boars. Perhaps it was he who had killed this one. The young hunter looked awkward amid the press of townsfolk, like a word out of context. Strangely, Worm felt pity for him. He wished in that moment that he might repay some kindness to him, to excuse him perhaps with a wave of his hand.

And then he felt a rush of pride in his chest, a sudden burst of emotion that took him totally by surprise. It took his breath away, it did. A thing of light was revealed in that instant, an altogether new thing; it was a thing of nobility. And Worm wondered at it, was inspired by it. For to know, or rather to be known by, the chieftain's son who had bravely saved his life was suddenly deemed an honor, and he hoped in that moment the two of them would become friends, true bosom friends —not friends of fancy such as he had known, not companions of convenience who would dissipate under a little driving heat, but friends who were true boon fellows.

Yes, Worm wondered at this new revelation. It seemed also that pride and honor were fertile things in the light, for in these a little seed of love took root.

With a sigh, he turned his gaze from the young hunter and looked about the hall for other wonders to feast his eyes upon.

As he did, a plump girl of thirteen or so, who had two long braids of red hair, dumped a tray of mugs onto the floor in front of him. Her face turned fire red as she stooped to gather them, and Worm, not wanting to add to her embarrassment, looked away as if he didn't notice.

But as he did so his eyes caught the sideways glance of a shapely girl with flashing green eyes and a mass of shiny black hair that fell to the small of her back. She was stunningly beautiful.

She paused in front of his table, straightened the mugs on her tray, then smiled broadly at him before continuing on with her chores. He watched her slowly walk away from him toward a far table, and he could tell by the way she carried her womanly form that she knew his eyes were upon her. At least he suspected that she did.

But he couldn't help himself—nor did he try—and he continued to stare stupidly after her. As she set her tray on the table, she looked back at him and caught his gaze.

He quickly spun his head to the opposite direction, where his eyes were met with those of the girl with the auburn hair, coming toward him from the kitchen.

It was then that he made the connection. The hall maids seemed to be going out of their way to pass in front of the head table in order to deliver an order somewhere in the back of the hall. Each girl, in turn, was making her rounds as conspicuously as she dared. First it was the plump red-haired girl, then the pretty blonde, followed by the tall one with the auburn hair. Finally, the stunning, green-eyed girl with the black, shiny mane passed by, aiming everything at him, after which, the rotation started all over again. Each time, the girls paused in front of him to smile and allure as though they hadn't done it before.

Worm felt his ears burning, and from that moment onward he refused to look at anything in the hall below eye-level. He pondered the situation as he reexamined a crisscross display of swords on a beam overhead, and thought it queer. There were several young men in the hall. Why were the girls looking at him and not at them?

The question was born not of humility but of ignorance, for the boy had seldom opportunity—growing up on the back streets of Glenryth—to view himself in burnished mirrors. To him, his thick flaxen hair, squared masculine stature and features, and wide, deep-set hazel eyes were nothing more than a collection of common things, valueless in any marketplace. But in spite of his ignorance, Worm cut a more handsome figure than he knew.

As he reached for a flagon of cider, a twinge of pain shot through his shoulder, and he winced. For just a moment the noise and revelry in the hall had dulled the memory of his recent ordeal; the jolt of pain served as a rude reminder. As he massaged his wound, a movement at the corner of his eye arrested his attention. Turning, he was startled, for angling through the crowd in his direction was the largest man he had ever seen in his life.

At first glance Worm couldn't believe his eyes, for the man—more a giant—was perhaps close to seven feet tall. He was massive in build, with a barrel-shaped chest and arms that swung like two great battering rams from his hulking shoulders. Each ended with hands twice the size of a normal man's.

One was immediately struck with the thought that this fellow could pick up any man in the hall and snap him in two as though he were nothing more than a twig of kindling. The man was at once a marvelous and fearsome sight to behold—a god, Worm was sure. The boy stared at the man, his eyes bugging slightly, his mouth agape, as the Goliath drew up in front of his table.

"Hello, son," he said. His voice was gruff and imposing, but there was a disarming kindness to it.

Worm continued to gape without answering. His awe of the man's gigantean size got the better of his social graces.

The giant's gray-blue eyes caught the flickering light from the torch fires behind Worm as he angled his head to one side, and they sparkled like small rounded sapphires set deep beneath his thick, bushy brows. He scrutinized Worm's frozen face with an intensity that set the boy on edge.

"Don't you remember me, boy?" the giant boomed.

Worm shook his head and managed to squeak out a barely audible "No."

"You and your father visited me in my shop ten years ago. But you were just a little shaver then, no higher than my knee," he said, indicating the height with his thick hand.

His words somehow rang true in the boy's mind the moment he spoke them. It was no unique phenomenon. Throughout the day, memories had been returning to him like stragglers from a far-away battle, and he welcomed each one with the enthusiasm of a lieutenant mustering a new company.

Worm brightened. At once a scene flashed through his head, filled with smoke and heat and the smell of burning metal. Then out of the fiery plumes the image of his father appeared—hazy at first, as the boy caught glimpses of him speaking with another man. But not just another man. He was a huge bear of a . . .

And then the image was clear. The memory struck his mind like a hammer blow, shooting careering sparks of light out of the darkness.

"I *remember* you!" Worm exclaimed, easing a little. "You're . . . uh . . ."

"Bolstroem, the village blacksmith," the giant finished.

"*Bolstroem!* That's right!" Worm said excitedly. "I can remember my father talking with you about . . . uh . . . uh . . . how to make swords, or metals, or something like that!"

"You do remember!" Bolstroem thundered. "Do you also recall that you started crying the moment you first set eyes on me?"

"I did?" The boy furrowed his brow while he gave that thought. "Yes!" he exclaimed. "And you made a toy to keep me quiet!"

"Uh-huh." The giant smiled broadly, then winked. "But it was really only a block of wood with a nail in it."

"No, it wasn't!" Worm protested. "It was a great ship! Broad of beam and taut of sail. I sailed her across the sea and fought a score of glorious battles against the Saxon infidels! They ran like dogs before my flashing sword!"

"Ha! Ha! It is I who have now forgotten!" Bolstroem pulled on his beard, then raked his fingers through the blast of soot-black hair on his head. "Yes," he mused, "it comes to me now—how your father called you his 'little bear.' He said that some day you would grow up to be a great warrior and a mighty chieftain!"

"He did? Little bear?"

"More than once! He was a proud papa."

"He was?"

And so another page from Worm's history was brought to light. The boy and the enormous blacksmith spent the next hour forging a friendship in the forgotten coals of the past.

During that time, Bolstroem fired the boy's imagination with talk of swords and metals and the smelting of various ores and alloys from which to make them. He told Worm how his father had discovered a way to create a metal that was smelted from iron ore and combined with nickel, carbon, and other alloys, in the intense fire of a coke-fueled forge. It was a metal that was malleable enough to be folded and hammered out, time and again, until a sword blade could be fashioned that was stronger by a hundredfold than any of the more brittle sword blades of iron cast. Forged of this metal, a blade could also be honed and kept to a razor's edge—and polished to a luster that would have tempted the very serpent himself.

"Steel, he called it. 'A metal created in the very forge of heaven itself!'" Bolstroem nodded, then added, "These were your father's words, and they are words of truth."

Worm gazed up at the man and clung to his every word. Before him was a man who not only knew his father but also knew the very heart that gave him life and course. To study the giant Bolstroem was to learn something of his own identity, of his father's.

"You must come and visit me again at my forge, Little Bear," Bolstroem said, smiling. "I will show you many more mysteries that your father taught me."

"I would like that," Worm replied.

With that Bolstroem leaned over and tousled the boy's hair, then left.

As Worm watched the giant return to his table and rejoin the roaring merriment, he decided that he would spend much time in his shop. Perhaps he could even become a smith's apprentice. The thought of it moved him to great inspiration, and he let out a deep and longing sigh.

Abruptly the noise in the hall came to a halt, as though each person were signaled by some unseen cue at the same moment. The silence fell heavy upon the place like a sudden downpour of rain, and it startled the boy. It felt as though something great had just died.

Worm was looking about the hall to see where the magnificent corpse lay, when he noticed that the throng near the main doors was yawning open to allow someone entrance into the hall. When his eyes fell upon the form of the newcomer, he was astonished. Many things astonished him this night. Indeed, it seemed everything he had witnessed thus far astonished him, but there was nothing so astonishing as the creature striding over the threshold that very moment.

Entering the hall was a tall, lanky, almost scarecrowlike man, who was softly plucking the strings of a lyre and calling out in a singsong voice for everyone's attention. He looked like some giant spider. He had long stringy hair, wispy chin hairs that mocked a beard, and a large nose that hung like a blade from the length of his face, the tip of which fell below the line of his mouth. It amazed Worm that the man seemed to be made only of arms and legs, with a short, meatless torso, apparently put there by the Creator almost as an afterthought in order to accommodate his limbs.

Moving with a fluidity of grace and poise that defied the very pull of gravity, the bard reached the center of the hall and stopped. He began to move in a tight circle so that everyone in the room could see him, and, arching his brows, he placed a long, spindly finger to his lips in a gesture that commanded a hush. He paused abruptly in frozen silence, resembling some mannequin awaiting the haberdasher.

Worm attended his every detail with rapt and fastidious scrutiny. For several moments the mannequin waited, until the anticipation of the audience hung in the air an excruciating moment before discomfort. Then, with the instincts of one highly skilled in his craft, he lifted his gaze to the ceiling, breaking the tension in the room, and began to pluck out a haunting melody on the lyre.

At first softly, slowly, hitting one string at a time, then two, then four, then finally, as his fingers danced nimbly across the face of the lyre with quickened pace, he picked an arpeggio that built the lilting course of the melody.

Oohs and aahs emanated from the crowd, now captivated by the music's magic spell. When the bard felt the soul of his audience charged with wonder, he opened his mouth, and with a rich, full baritone voice that seemed too large for his spindly frame, he began to sing a heroic song with a hypnotic chanting cadence.

> "The tale is sung of heroes bold,
>   of battles fought, the widows made;
> From wind-washed cliffs of whitened breast,
>   give their souls to heaven's 'brace.

"The tale is told of Caelryck's bane,
  the Warrior lay in earth's cruel womb;
Ne'er to shine but on that day,
  when trumpet's blast wakes cold slumber."

As the minstrel sang, he walked reverently back and forth the length of the hall. Every person present felt the pain, the sorrow, the agony of the mournful song, as the bard painted each word picture.

Worm had never witnessed anything like it before. His face mirrored the composition of each line, each word. At the mention of his father's name, a tear formed in the corner of his eye, a tiny pool of glistening sadness sprung from deep wells, which hung tenuously at the brink.

Coaxing it, the bard played a musical bridge, or selah, to allow his lyric's import to take root in each mind. Then he continued with quickened tempo.

"Great halls of saints, fear not his tread,
  O hallowed shores, thy bosom's blest;
Fear not the fierceness of his sword,
  his soul is sweet with the reign of Christ.

"For with stout arm and heart and blade,
  the Warrior slew his enemies;
O Caelryck, loose the bloodied bolt,
  and German shores leave fatherless."

Again the minstrel plucked the soulful refrain. He paused, just a beat, then resumed the song, building the tempo to an almost feverish crescendo.

"How will he sing in the Golden Halls,
  the Crimson Stain across his breast?
From cradle long that takes the dust,
  and sends the breath back to His throne.

"For, lo, the seed fell deep in death,
  'neath sod of Albion's misty shades;
The tender shoot pushed hard through rock,
  triumphant fruit of Caelryck's loins.

"The tender shoot in light to shine,
  triumphant fruit of Caelryck's loins!"

Worm didn't know at what point in the song he started to cry, but his face was wet with tears. The words and music had reached down into his soul and moved him deeply, calling forth the hesitant wellspring. Never before had he heard such a beautiful, yet sad, melody. Nor did he understand the exact meaning of the lyrics—only that they paid a kindness to his father.

However, together they carried him to the secret dream places of his childhood. The kinder times he had once lived and forgotten now lived again. They were to him old and cherished friends, the filth of their memories now bathed in light and tears.

As he looked around the hall to see if others were as stirred by the bard's enchantments as he was, it grew upon his mind with a little terror that every eye in the room was fixed on his face. Immediately he was torn from his quiet reflections to ponder a most perplexing scene. Why was everyone looking at him? Had he done something wrong?

He jerked his head over to Terryll to make inquiry. However, Terryll and his family were also looking at him, their eyes moist with tears. Worm's mind reeled at the sight, and he grabbed hold of Terryll's arm to steady himself.

"W-what's going on?" he stuttered. "Why is everybody staring at me?"

"You'll see."

"See what?" It was a question born of a completely baffled state of mind.

Allyndaar stood and raised his right hand in a solemn gesture. "Citizens of Killwyn Eden," he boomed. "Hail!"

Worm looked up at the man as he commanded the attention of everyone in the hall, relieving the boy of their scrutiny, and his thoughts were suddenly captured by the man's regal bearing. In that moment of time, Allyndaar was transfigured before him from Terryll's father, a maker of fine longbows, to Allyndaar the chieftain of Killwyn Eden, shining crown of the Brigantes tribe, a man enwreathed in an aura of power and authority, in whose voice was the command of regiments, the daring of glorious exploits, a vision of magnificence.

Worm marveled at the transformation, so complete had it been, and the once-bewildered boy summarily dismissed the crowd.

"Hail, and well met!" resounded the throng in unison.

The chieftain lowered his hand and began his address. "We are gathered here tonight to thank Christ for His mercy upon our son, Terryll, and to honor the memory of Britain's noblest hero, Caelryck, without whom, I daresay, none of us would enjoy our present liberties."

Several men shouted out Caelryck's name, stirring the people to cry out his name in chanting unison.

The chieftain turned to Aurelius and nodded.

Taking his cue, the monk stood to his feet. He was not a tall man, but as he raised both hands to quiet the people, Worm noticed that his forearms and hands were thick and powerfully built, befitting more the warrior than a holy man.

"Let us pray," he said.

Every head in the room bowed, then the monk raised his eyes to the beams and spoke with a voice that thundered across the hall. "Holy Son of God, we thank You for Your unfathomable grace and mercy toward men who deserve naught but holy vengeance.

"We are here gathered to rejoice in Your most gracious bounty—present peace and liberty, the good fruit of our toils and hardships, the health and well-being of our families and little ones, and for the providential care and protection of two of our favored British sons."

Worm studied the monk as he prayed. He was again awed by the man—his stature, his carriage, the power of his voice—though he didn't hear a word that he spoke. His hands had begun to tremble slightly.

"Thank you, dear Christ, for the life of our son Terryll and for the life of young Aeryck, son of Your servant Caelyrck. May Your divine favor continue to rest upon these and upon Your humble servants of Britain. Amen."

The people responded in unison, "Let it be so."

As Aurelius sat down, the boy quickly looked away to avoid contact with his eyes. In so doing, however, he was caught by the downward glare of the wild boar. Quickly his eyes rebounded onto the crowd but were there met with the eyes of four hundred people. Panic again flushed into his face.

A buzz of anticipation swept across the hall. The time had come. All but one knew it.

Allyndaar turned where he stood and looked down at Worm, who was desperately trying to find a place to rest his eyes.

"People of Killwyn Eden," the chieftain continued, raising his voice in the manner of an introduction. "We are pleased to have with us Aeryck, the son of Caelryck."

Not sure of his hearing or of the chieftain's intentions, Worm looked up at the man and stiffened in his chair. A dull glaze filmed over his eyes. For all appearances it seemed as though he had just died and rigor mortis was advancing rapidly through his limbs, claiming its due.

After a few awkward moments of watching Worm, Terryll jabbed the boy in the ribs. "Stand up," he whispered. "It's time."

To Worm it was the voice of the archangel, and he was resurrected out of his trance. "What? Time for what?"

"You are going to be honored."

Worm was incredulous. "Honored for what? I didn't do anything."

The boy looked up at Allyndaar, who gave him a subtle gesture with his hand, coaxing him to rise. Worm shot a look back to Terryll, who was now sitting with his arms folded and wearing a silly-looking grin. Dagmere was beaming with a look unknown to the boy. Helena smiled in the way a mother would.

Finding no comfort from that quarter, he looked out at the sea of faces, which he deemed immediately to have been a serious mistake. Again he was caught in a drama over which he had no control, no escape. He was doomed, or fated, to flow along some strange and unyielding watercourse with all the command of a wood chip.

Suddenly Worm felt the room moving. Looking down at his legs, he was amazed to see them obeying an order that he didn't give. He rebuked them at once. But they would have none of it, and a sort of mental altercation broke out between Worm and his legs. It was a heated battle, pitched against great odds. In the midst of the fray, Worm nearly passed out once, his legs faltered twice, but when the campaign was over, the boy found himself standing squarely upon his two feet.

He had lost.

"Bring me the sword of Caelryck," the chieftain called out.

A moment later, a young boy of ten or so appeared in front of Allyndaar, holding the gleaming sword of Caelryck outstretched in his hands.

The chieftain took the blade and spoke many words to the people, extolling the memory of the great warrior and hero of the Battle of Glenryth. The crowd punctuated his eulogy with loud paeans and cheers.

After finishing his address, Allyndaar turned and faced Worm. He admonished him to walk in the path of his father and to follow the light of Christ into battle, if need be, and so honor the faith.

Worm, however, stood in a blind daze, not hearing a word spoken to him. Instead, his thoughts were miles away in a secluded niche at one end of a forsaken alleyway, where he lay alone and secure on his mat beneath an old tarp, having only food and sleep on his mind and the occasional howl of a wolf. Somewhere in the disquieting fog, Worm received the exquisite steel sword made by his father. The moment heralded his rite of passage from a despised beggar and thief that pillaged the streets of Glenryth to a beloved son of Killwyn Eden.

The hall burst into an ovation that lasted for several minutes. Taking his cue from the crowd, the spindly bard led the people in several rousing songs. The wine and ale resumed their flow, and the celebration in the great hall continued unabated long into the spring night.

But not everyone reveled in the celebration, at least not outwardly. Worm stood dumbstruck during the ovation and mesmerized by the brilliant luster of his father's sword. He looked up from the blade and found Bolstroem's beaming face above the crowd. Even from across the hall, the boy could see the giant blacksmith shoot him an approving wink.

Then all at once and from everywhere, Worm was swallowed by a swarm of adulatory citizens. He was slapped on the back, jostled back and forth, and pinched on the cheeks all night long by a gaggle of rosy-faced men and heavyset women who loved to hug. The wound in his shoulder barked objections, but there would be no relief from it for many days to come.

And though he would complain to Terryll about the attention, inwardly it served as a balm to quell his anxious soul. For the first time in his life he found himself smiling—not wooden smiles he forced onto his face, but smiles that came easy and often.

Later that evening, when the merry crowd had long since thinned to their homes and cottages, and as they lay in the quiet solitude of each pillow's tender embrace, Dagmere and more than one other girl from Killwyn Eden dreamed of romantic trysts with the handsome, flaxen-haired son of Caelryck, a boy who, three days earlier, had fled for his life a thief and a beggar, with the boon of a moldy loaf of bread.

Later still that evening, as the cool light of the moonset filtered through the small arched windows of the great hall and huddled in the glow of a dying fire, Terryll finally related to his father and several leading men from the village the details of his capture and escape and the pieces of purloined conversation.

They pondered the varied possibilities of such information, each man shaking his head with grave concern. It might mean nothing. It might mean everything. War. Whatever the reason or explanation, the Saxon's bold venture north after so many years of silence did not bode well for the Britons.

13
THE WOLF'S LAIR

Miles away from the sleeping village of Killwyn Eden, the eerie howl of a solitary wolf pierced the moonless night. Soon it was answered by the cry of another wolf, then another, until there was an unbroken chain of howls echoing from the northern ridges and wolds of the Pennines to the rolling plains of the southern lowlands. There had been a subtle, almost imperceptible shift in the atmosphere, an astronomical aberration that the animal world is often keen to sense. The baying of the wolves betrayed it.

Thick, oppressive fog unfurled across the lowlands like a carpet, smothering everything in its path, obscuring the light of stars, woodlands, and villages. It finally rolled over the saddle of a low ridge and poured down into the moors surrounding the hill-fort of Badonsward.

The cries of the wolves carried ahead of the fog and resounded off the fort's high stone walls but were quickly muted as the dense obfuscation swallowed the Saxon stronghold. The night sounds of the countryside lay quiet beneath the blanket, and the howling was muffled to a deceptive hush.

The shadow of a wolf's profile flickered against the stone walls inside a torch-lighted chamber of the hill-fort. The shape of it appeared hunched in brooding silence, waiting, sitting motionless in a large oaken chair, save for the play of light that cast its long shade across the flagstones and up onto the wall. The silhouette of its head lifted slowly as the sound of booted footsteps drew near.

The Viking halted in the aureole of a single torch, his wounded shoulder hanging bloodied. The light caught only one side of his proud form, abandoning the other to the shadows. He struck his breast sharply with his fist and reported, "I have come at your command, my lord."

The wolfish shape sat back in the heavy chair, moving away from the torchlight into its shadowed periphery. In the dim light its appearance was startling. Even the battle-hardened Olaf was uneasy as he gazed into the darkness at its veiled features, waiting like a soldier to be acknowledged by his superior. There was a stench of mildew in the chamber, a clammy wetness pervading the air that clung to the Norseman's skin like a film, reminding him of death, of dead places.

Like a tomb.

The creature had the head of a wolf, yet the form of its body was that of a man. With closer scrutiny it was apparent that it was, in fact, a man wearing the head and skin of a wolf draped over his head and shoulders like some hideous shroud.

His eyes and face were so shaded by the wolf's muzzle that only when he angled his head a certain way would the light catch a glint of his recessed eyes and betray the humanity beneath the skin. The illusion played tricks on the eyes of those speaking with him. Not finding his eyes, they would unconsciously address the unblinking stare of the wolf's head as a focal point. The man beneath received twisted satisfaction from it.

Norduk, or the "Wolf," as he was called by his own soldiers and enemies alike, was the leading Saxon general and underlord, second in command only to the brothers Horsa and Hengist. He had much on his mind this night.

Finally he spoke. "Your shoulder is wounded, Olaf." The voice came in sullen gasps—human, though edged with a bestial timbre.

"We were ambushed by a raiding party of Picts."

"*Picts!*" The underlord let out a low, raspy growl. "There is enough mischief in the air without having those painted devils underfoot." He looked up at the Viking, affixing a paternal gaze upon the man. "I am pleased that you survived, Olaf. You will take care of your shoulder soon?"

"It is nothing."

"Is it nothing that my right arm should bleed to death?"

Olaf considered Norduk's words. "I will tend to it after our briefing, my lord," he conceded.

"See to it. I presume that you and your patrols had a prosperous mission?"

A proud smile curled below Olaf's thick moustache. "I have just met with each of my captains, Wolf," he replied. "The reports they bring confirm my own. They will be pleasing to my lord."

"Go on."

"The Britons have grown fat and careless from feasting long on the carrion of idleness," he gloated. "They hang like a ripened plum, ready to be plucked with ease."

"Horsa will be pleased."

"It is your pleasure that I serve," Olaf said.

"He is the overlord."

141

"He is the overlord, yes, but you are the Wolf, the son of Fenris. I live only to serve your needs."

"I am placing a great weight of responsibility upon your shoulders, Olaf. To obey Horsa is to serve my needs . . . and yours."

"As you wish, my liege," Olaf said, bowing slightly.

Norduk eyed the Viking for several moments. A glint of light caught his eyes beneath the shroud, revealing an ocher sheen. "There is much at stake now, Olaf," he said. "The winds of the gods are sweeping change across this island. Those whose sails are unfurled to their pleasure will move forward to a greater destiny. Those whose are not will be dashed to pieces on the rock. I am the rock. Do you understand?"

"Yes, Wolf."

"Good."

The Norseman peered into the darkness at the wolfish shape. The shadows now forbade its features.

The shape stirred. "Horsa has arrived here at Badonsward, Commander. He will be here soon to brief you on our campaign."

"Have you met with him yet?"

"This morning, with a few of his officers."

"The bitterness between you . . . does it still live, my lord?"

"That is not your concern, Olaf."

As Norduk was speaking, a man's voice, gravelly in tone, bellowed from the entrance of the chamber. "I swear, Norduk, the drafts in this hill-fort of yours could chill the dead."

The Wolf grunted.

Olaf turned his head as a stoutly built, slightly balding man with long brown hair and beard entered the room. His eyes were a colorless gray, busy eyes that took in everything at once and seemed to gaze through things, and they were well buttressed behind heavy eyelids that were like puffy little cushions. He had a wide sensual mouth, a working, expressive mouth that fit well into his thick features.

He was wearing a coat of dull gray chain mail beneath a heavy woolen jerkin, dyed blue, and a pair of darker woolen trousers. Strapped to his flanks were a long broadsword, a small battle-ax, and a jeweled knife, held in place with a thick, brass-studded leather belt.

Norduk did not respond but eyed the man warily as he swaggered across the flagstones.

"I hear that you were met with trouble, Commander," the intruder said to Olaf. "You were overrun?"

Olaf eyed the man guardedly, searching his gray eyes, but saw nothing in them but cold arrogance. In all his battle attire and jeweled finery, the man looked like an incarnation of some Teutonic warrior god, an emboldening inspiration.

But he was not just any warrior god. This was the overlord, Horsa, joint commander-in-chief of the entire Saxon army. And there was in his manner the truculent air of a pugilist, brooding before a fight.

"Yes," Olaf said. "By a large war party of Picts." The Norseman swelled his frame and added, "It was a glorious battle."

Horsa moved to a large table in the center of the chamber, off to the right of Norduk and the Viking. His long woolen cloak swept the air up into Olaf's face as the overlord strode past him. "Glorious, you say," he grunted, as he reached the table. "You lost many men."

"They lost more," the Viking countered flatly. "And our warriors feast now with Odin and Tiu in Valhalla."

"Perhaps," Horsa said, shooting him a quick look. "But the gods have less need of them than we, don't they?"

Olaf narrowed his eyes and raised his bloodied hand to the pommel of his broadsword. "Who can know the needs of the gods?"

"It could have been avoided."

"I did not realize that my lord Horsa was present at the battle."

"That is enough, Commander!" the Wolf snarled. "You are speaking to the overlord."

"And he is speaking to a Norseman," Olaf countered. "He has called me a coward."

Horsa threw his head back and laughed heartily. "No, Commander. I would never accuse you of such a thing! No, never such a thing!" He laughed again as he unrolled a large parchment and spread it across the table. "Come here, my proud Viking. I wish for you to brief me on your reconnaissance."

Olaf looked back at Norduk a little bewildered. He had expected a fight. Horsa was not known for a generous temper.

The Wolf released him with a subtle nod, then warily eyed the overlord. Walking to the table, Olaf thought of how Horsa might have had received his information. Was there an informer in his command? Only Druell and Ruddbane had survived the battle, but could either of them have . . . Certainly not Druell, he thought, but Ruddbane . . . yes, Ruddbane. Who else could it be? He wondered what else the overlord had been told.

The parchment map depicted the island of Britain. It had been confiscated from Gaulish traders who had traveled the island extensively, both overland as well as by ship, along its coasts and up its large rivers, with wagons and ship hulls filled with trade goods from the continent and points east. On the map, both topographical and geographical information (imperative to any military campaign) were drawn: mountains, valleys, rivers, the complete network of Roman roads, as well as the principle villages and civitates of the Britons.

During the hour that followed, Olaf briefed the overlord on his recent findings in the north.

As the Norseman spoke, Horsa transcribed to the map his information of the British fortifications, weaponry, and strength.

"Good," he said, adding the final stroke with a reed pen. "This will be our plan of attack." Looking past Olaf with his colorless eyes, Horsa queried, "You do not care to join us, Underlord?" There was an edge to his voice.

"It is not necessary," Norduk answered. "I am well-versed in our plans."

"It is not necessary, you say? Very well. Let us hope that your verse is more formidable in this campaign than your success was at Glenryth." Horsa grunted and turned his attention to the map.

Norduk looked on from beneath his sinister cowl as the overlord briefed Olaf on the strategy of their northern campaign. A low growl of contempt rattled beneath his breath, and a strange, almost caninelike expression slowly swept over the Wolf's shaded visage.

The bitterness lived.

The purpose of the campaign was motivated more by need for supplies than by need for land. Hengist and Horsa had been waging war against the British king Vortigern in the tribal lands of the Trinovantes over the past several years since their revolt against his power. Due to dwindling supplies in the south, however, the Saxons needed to procure a source of supplies from the north—horses, chariots, weapons, and foodstuffs—to continue their press against the better-supplied British army.

Had Norduk been able to capitalize on his victory at the Battle of Glenryth ten years earlier, the Saxons would have been able to secure the north, build up supplies and reinforcements, then sweep Vortigern and his forces off the island in one major campaign. But alas, Norduk's army was so decimated by the small British force that withstood them that they were unable to do so. Securing a Saxon foothold in the north was all that the Wolf could do. The northern invasion of the island had come to a jolting halt. Hengist and Horsa had not forgotten.

But now the time had come to finally make use of that foothold.

"You will drive a small army of horsemen north with great speed," the overlord commanded Olaf. "You will follow the Dere Street road and cut through the center of the land like a great iron wedge, wreaking much havoc and destruction." Horsa pointed to the long road that bisected the eastern length of the island from Inveresk on the Firth of Forth to the southern coast of Britain. It was one of the major routes built by the Romans during their invasion of the island.

"I trust that you will find this a pleasant task, Commander," Horsa added. He was chortling.

The Viking smiled.

During the briefing, the hostility between them had tempered under the common purposes of war. Olaf was surprised to discover that he was drawn to a man he had hated profoundly only an hour before. The overlord was arrogant, condescending, foul of tongue and spirit, and full of his own grandeur. He was a man easily hated. But always there was an air of the consummate warrior about him—the cold, steely verve and charisma of one who could lead men into the great examinations of battle, into the bloodied crucibles of sod where men's leaden souls are ground and tested by the savage alchemy gods of war, ever in quest of gold. Horsa could win battles, wars, Olaf believed. Yes. The Norseman was drawn to the man.

"The main body of warriors will be divided into two divisions," Horsa continued, "one led by General Norduk and the other by myself and my officers. Our forces will follow behind you, Commander, subduing the Britons on either side of your wake. You will advance to the village of Catterick, Commander. If their defenses are as lax as you say they are, you will take it quickly. Then wait for us to reach you. Is that understood?"

Olaf nodded.

"Good. Then, as a united force," Horsa added, "we will turn westward and strike hard against the village of Greta Bridge and destroy it."

"Why would you not wish to proceed northward, my lord?" Olaf asked. "The Britons there are weak and would fall easily before our broadswords and axes. We would take the port at Wallsend."

"Who needs it?" Horsa grunted. "By then we will have Greta Bridge. And besides, once we have conquered the villages in the west, those villages we pass by will fall without battle."

Olaf pulled thoughtfully on his moustache for several moments, giving pause to Horsa's words. "Yes . . . I see. Their supplies would be cut off, and undoubtedly they would sue for peace without a fight."

"Exactly. In Greta Bridge we will regroup and replenish our supplies before launching the final phase of our campaign. Our army will then continue westward, crushing all resistance, until we reach the very heart of the northern Britons, here, at Killwyn Eden!" He pointed to its location on the map.

Horsa looked up at the towering face of Olaf, whose intense gaze was riveted to the name on the chart.

"Killwyn Eden," the Viking mused aloud. "Their chieftain, Allyndaar, is a great warrior, with many valiant men under his command." He looked over at Horsa. "Their prowess in battle is well-known. Their skill with the longbow is legend. Taking Killwyn Eden will not be a simple task."

"Taking it is imperative!" Horsa scowled, slamming his palm on the table. "Killwyn Eden lies at the junction of all the major supply routes in the north. It is the military seat of power. Its capture will insure our depleted army in the south ample reinforcements. You—"

"You misunderstand my words, Overlord," Olaf interrupted. "The greater my opponent, the greater will be the honor in slaying him."

Horsa grunted. His broad features allowed genial lines. "My apologies, Commander." He raised his heavy frame from the table and faced the Viking. "Have you any questions?"

"We did not reconnoiter the area around Killwyn Eden," Olaf said. "I would like to lead another patrol to—"

"There is no need, Commander," Norduk interjected from his shadowy perch. "I have other scouts who have already briefed me."

Olaf looked at Norduk with a puzzled expression. "Other scouts? But I know of no other—"

"You will lead another patrol into the area, Commander, as soon as your wound is healed," Horsa cut in. "We cannot fail this time. I will not have the spearhead of this campaign going into the heart of battle blind."

Olaf glanced over at the Wolf, but the man's eyes were hidden somewhere in the folds of darkness, narrowed on the stout pugilistic form of the overlord. The implication was clear: the two German brothers were in complete control of the campaign. Norduk would be relegated a minor role.

"So I repeat," Horsa continued. "Do you have any questions, Commander?" The Norseman glanced down at the map and carefully considered the possibilities of the plan. With Horsa's army behind him, he could wreak much destruction with lightning-quick raids, knowing that he could fall back to the safety of the main army to regroup. The strategy of battle was brilliantly simple, one that seemed good to the military mind and goals of Olaf. There would be much glory in it for him.

"No questions," Olaf answered. "It is a good plan."

"If you succeed, Commander, you will be greatly rewarded. But if you fail . . ."

That implication was also clear.

Olaf did not retort. However, the flinty look on his face exuded a confidence that the overlord understood.

"Then it is settled," Horsa concluded. "We must begin preparations immediately. There is much to make ready before next spring."

"We shall fall upon these Britons with the fury of the gods," the Viking gloated.

"Yes, by Woden, we shall."

"By Odin," Olaf corrected, a thin smile curling into his scar. The overlord peered at the man over the little buttresses of flesh, but his face mirrored the humor of the Viking's retort. "Odin or Woden." He grunted. "By whatever name, may he give us victory." Then Horsa dismissed him.

Olaf looked at Norduk, who nodded. The Norseman struck his breast, then turned and strode out of the chamber with many things on his mind.

Horsa watched as Olaf exited the room. "He is a good man, Norduk," he said. "I like him. In my position I am constantly surrounded by sycophants. It is a pleasure to speak with a man who is not afraid to voice his mind—or afraid to die. Such men you can trust." Horsa walked over to Norduk. "I feel that we shall have great success in our campaign."

Norduk noticed the change in Horsa's countenance. The hostility was absent from his heavy-lidded eyes. The arrogance with which he had entered the room was eclipsed by a simple austerity that befitted a military leader. As with Olaf, the briefing had tempered his mood.

"It is no secret that there has been bad blood between us, my old friend," Horsa continued. "There were times when my brother would have removed you from command, but I dissuaded him. I trust that I shall not regret it. Your help in securing a victory for us will restore to you our favor."

"Nothing would please me more," Norduk returned, chafing at the condescending tone.

"Good. Then for now, let us focus our attention on the glorious victory ahead of us."

Horsa placed his left arm behind his back and paced about the chamber, keeping within the circle of torchlight. He gestured broadly with his thick right arm to emphasize a particular point, or accented with a jab of his finger a nuance that might otherwise escape the limitations of words. "There are two phases in our campaign, Norduk."

"Two? I know of only—"

"You know of the second phase," Horsa interrupted. "Hengist and I have devised a plan which must precede the bloodletting. A plan that I am sure you will find amusing."

Norduk angled his form to one side in his chair, cradling the weight of his chin between his thumb and forefinger. He appeared relaxed. However, his calm demeanor belied the shock that Horsa's words had had on his mind, words that stung like salt on an open wound.

He had sought years before to establish a triumvirate of power with Hengist and Horsa, but they had resisted. And now not to be included in every aspect of this campaign's planning was just another indication of his subordinate station. But soon his day would come, and when it did there would be no further need for a triumvirate. The Wolf would bide his time.

"Amusing? What is your plan?" he asked. "I allow myself an amusement from time to time."

"The British chieftains under Vortigern are powerful," Horsa began. "Even with renewed supplies, our army will find them difficult to conquer. Phase one in our campaign will serve to cut off the head of their resistance and thereby weaken their leadership. It will hopefully send their leaders into confusion and a scramble for order. After such a time we shall crush them!" With this he slammed his fist against his palm.

"The head of their resistance? And how do you propose to do that?" So far, Norduk was not amused.

"It has been a difficult campaign in the south for both armies," Horsa continued, walking toward the silhouette of the Wolf. "We gain ground, then lose it. Take it back, then lose it again." From all his violent gesticulations it appeared as though the man was waging a little war—soldiers were falling invisibly all about his feet. Horsa stopped in front of Norduk and fixed his gaze on the wolfskin's lifeless eyes. "We are growing weary with it. Vortigern is as well. We are planning to sue for peace."

Norduk reeled from the words. *"Surrender?"*

"Yes, surrender." The overlord turned and faced the dark recesses of the chamber. A wicked little chortle rattled in his throat, and he rocked confidently on the balls of his feet, allowing his words to sink into Norduk's mind. "We will meet with all of their nobles and chieftains at a peace council, to discuss the terms of surrender."

"But—"

"Let me finish!" Horsa snapped. "Once there, at the appointed time and signal, we will drive our swords into their hearts!" he said, killing the lot of them with a swipe of his arm.

Still not sure of the plan, Norduk queried, "How will you get all of the British leaders assembled in one place to meet with you? Surely they will suspect a trap."

"Not if Vortigern himself calls for the meeting."

"Vortigern?"

"Yes, that's the beauty of it. And here is the amusing part. As you well know, he is married to Hengist's daughter Rowena." Turning back to Norduk, Horsa said this with a little smirk. Then his thick, sensuous lips spread across his face, forming a lascivious smile. "Vortigern believes her loyalties lie in his bed. *Paagh!* The man is a fool! She is first and last a Saxon."

Norduk recoiled as if his mind had been given a lash. Immediately Rowena's splendid form came to his mind in an enticing apparition, stealing his thoughts away to a covert rendezvous. There was no woman in all of Saxony as beautiful as she.

He cared little for the pleasantries of women—actually he found them repulsive—but Rowena was not just any woman. She worked upon his mind as one highly skilled in a secret craft; upon his soul, the prolific mill of her employ that produced in him all manner of desires and forbidden things. Her mystic gaze stalked him in the night watches, haunting him, luring him into little snares of madness. The man groaned as her image ravished his soul. He was not amused.

"Did you say something?" Horsa asked.

"Your words are indeed amusing." Norduk quickly recovered and chased Rowena's teasing image from his mind. "You think the daughter of Hengist will convince her husband that we are sincere with our proposal of peace?"

"She has served us so before." The Saxon laughed wickedly. "The dolt cannot resist her beauty!"

Norduk grunted. The man was disgusting. A pig. "Interesting," he said. "And where will this *peace council* take place?"

Horsa stopped by the table and poured over the map. "That we have not yet decided. It must be in a place neutral to both our armies. But a place favorable to the Britons."

"Yes, of course."

Horsa rolled up the map, saying, "We shall confer later on this matter, Underlord. We are, of course, open to any suggestions from you."

Again the tone, the implication.

"I shall put my thoughts to it, Overlord."

"Do that."

Horsa turned and strode out of the chamber, leaving Norduk sitting behind in the shadows, in the lingering aura of cold, arrogant power that would soon be his and only his.

Norduk was not tall. Neither was he a large man. Rather, his frame was thin and wiry, with sinewy limbs ending in hands that were gnarled from battle. Beneath the wolfskin shroud, he wore a black woolen jerkin with a crimson wolf's head arched across his chest—his crest—the crest emblazoned across two thousand shields of his warriors. He wore a shirt of chain mail that fell to the middle of his bared thighs, and heavy, black leather-soled boots that hit his shins a foot below the knees. He didn't look the part of a mighty Saxon warlord, but he had an irresistible power over men, the kind of absolute power that draws moths to the flame. The earth was littered with the bones of men who had underestimated him, both on and off the trying fields of battle.

Norduk sat in wretched silence, brooding. His wolfish shape was lost somewhere in the frenetic shadows that were flickering in some death dance over the floor and wall. He was beset with terrible inquiries that tore at his mind from some ruined place in his soul, torturing the composition of his body into hideous attitudes. His breath came in low rattles, labored, heaving as though bellowing over some cold hearth, igniting black flames.

No. He was not amused.

Somewhere in the chamber there was a subtle stirring. Immediately the tormentors scurried from Norduk's mind, finding prurient concealments nearby in which to lurk, to await summons.

Norduk shifted his sullen eyes over to a shadowy niche at the far end of the room that served as a landing to the adjoining tower. "I hear you, little man," he spoke into the air. "Come out where I can feast my eyes on your disgusting little shape."

"You are most kind, my liege," a voice replied.

Out of the blackness stepped a small, bandy-legged man with a squat body and bulbous head, who looked more like a large, hairy toad than a human being. His white hair fell over his shoulders, stopping its growth at a length just above the small of his back. The little man raised his hand in a conciliatory gesture. "May the gods favor you, my liege."

Boadix had been waiting in the tiny niche during the briefing, unbeknown to either Olaf or Horsa. As he waddled into the waning pool of light, it caught his features and revealed a large, russet lump of a nose, which stuck out from his fat face like an old potato. The torchlight also revealed that he only had one eye. It bulged out from below a wispy thatch of eyebrow; the other had been gouged out by a Roman soldier before he fled from Gaul years ago. He had filled the empty socket with a glass ball, now flickering with an orangish glow.

"Stop where you are," Norduk commanded. "My eyes have feasted enough."

The little man stopped in the center of the room and bowed slightly. "Perhaps my lord wishes the priest of gods to wear a bag over his head?"

Norduk grunted. He eyed the small man with the contempt of one witnessing a freak of nature. The scorn was directed more at the error than at its victim. "Tell me, druid, what tidings have the stars been revealing to you since our last visit?"

Boadix continued his salutation, taking a step closer to Norduk's chair. "They have been most loquacious, O commander of ten thousands," he said, pointing a stumpy finger into the air. "They reveal that you will live long and be a great ruler—that knowledge pales in the light of your brilliance."

"Stick to your mistletoe clippings and bird entrails, druid," the Wolf chided. "My stomach cannot ingest both your form and your flatteries in one sitting."

Boadix bent slightly forward with suitable obeisance as a grin hid impishly in the shadows of his face. He turned and toddled awkwardly over to the table. It seemed no small feat for the little man, once having labored the distance, to raise up onto his toes and peer over the surface of the table where Horsa's map had been spread out. He let out a little chuckle.

Norduk leaned forward in his chair to observe the druid's curious antics. His features were drawn in humorless lines of scrutiny. "Something amuses you, little man?"

"It is an interesting strategy of war—particularly phase one," Boadix said wryly. "I do love a good deception, don't you?" And then he frowned. "Tsk, tsk. I see a major flaw in it, however—not that I'm a military strategist, mind you. But as I see it, such a plan requires the utmost secrecy in order to succeed. If any part of it were to somehow leak—"

"I would plug it with my sword blade," the Wolf rasped. His fell gaze swept the druid's aberrant form. "To threaten Horsa's campaign is to threaten mine."

Boadix lowered his heels to the floor, then toddled to the window. His squat body swayed furiously to accommodate the chimpish gait. "No, no, no, my liege." He chuckled, fanning the air with his stubby hands. "Surely you misunderstand my intentions. I was merely pointing out the inherent weakness of the plan." He chuckled again. "The little plans of men are of no concern to me. I care only for the will of the gods—and your inestimable success, of course."

"Of course," Norduk responded without enthusiasm. "You were about to reveal to me more details of my 'inestimable success.'"

"Indeed. Indeed."

Immediately the druid began to perform a curious ritual. He lowered his head and plucked the glass orb out of its socket, held it out at arm's length in front of him, then peered through it intently at the heavens with his other eye, all the while mumbling incantations under his breath.

He did this to divine the will of the gods in the positioning of the stars or in the auguries of sticks, stones, spittle, and the entrails of animals and birds. It was his belief that the magnification through the crystalline glass gave the gods a channel of light and power through which to give him clearer discernment of their will. "Canis Major is now rising across the heavens in the south."

"You expect me to believe that you can see the Dog Star through such a fog?"

"Through coats of armor, flesh, and bones, I can see clearly the avarice, murder, and plots of evil that lurk in the darkened recesses of men's hearts," the druid answered. "It is but a small wonder that I can see the brilliance of the stars through a mere veil of fog."

Norduk grunted. "You were saying . . ."

"Your successes are at the command of your visions, my liege. Canis Major is on a most favorable ascent. But—" The druid broke off and lowered the glass eye.

"But what?"

"There is a strange sign that I have observed over the last several days—a star with a long tail that moves slowly across the heavens and is even now passing through Ursa Major."

"The Great Bear?" Norduk was forced to look out the window. "What has this to do with me?"

"I have heard tell of these 'wandering stars,' as they were called by the ancient druids," Boadix continued, "but I have never in my lifetime seen one. That the wandering star passes through Ursa Major is a sign that cannot be ignored. Its sighting portends tidings of good—or evil. Even the wolves have taken notice. Of course, you have heard."

"You know well that I have," Norduk countered.

"And what do they tell you?" Boadix said, with the vaguest of mockery in his tone.

Norduk's look cut him off.

The little druid chuckled. "Very well. The gods have revealed that the wandering star is a good sign, for it moves toward Canis Major." The little man lowered his head and gazed through the orb at the cracks between the flagstones under his feet. He rolled the glass slowly between his fingers, watching the lines squash and stretch in the ball's lustrous center as though he were unaware of Norduk's presence. "But they have placed certain stipulations in your path before their divine favor will be awarded."

A malefic tension immediately stretched taut over the chamber like a drumhead. "I have pledged to restore the ancient religion of the druids," Norduk said. His eyes narrowed on the little man. "What more do the gods demand?"

Boadix raised the skin flap that hung limp over his empty eye socket and neatly rolled the glass orb into place. "There is one other small requirement."

"Out with it!" Norduk snarled.

Boadix turned his head nonchalantly to the window and said, "A sacrifice is required. A blood seal, if you will."

"Human, no doubt."

"You are very perceptive, my liege. The gods have indeed favored you."

152

"Slaughter as many humans as you like, you murderous little dwarf," Norduk fumed. "Throw in some cows and pigs and salamanders as well—draw a river of blood for all I care, if it will grant the gods' favor."

The druid stared out the window as though he had been hailed to a remote event transpiring in the heavens, having left behind his stolid form like a little lump of hardened clay. In his mind he was making minute calculations, working furiously over the last line in the ledger. At last he spoke. "It must be a child—an only son," he said. And then, pausing to quickly reconfirm his totals, he added, "He must be sacrificed on the ancient altar of Stonehenge."

"Stonehenge!" Norduk repeated, not sure of his hearing.

The druid did not respond. Instead, he casually brushed some dirt off his shoulder.

Norduk stiffened in his chair, allowing the torchlight to catch an intemperate ocher glinting in his eyes beneath the wolfskin cowl. "Why not just ask for my head on a platter?" he growled in bestial timbre, rising to his feet.

"These are the terms of the gods," the druid replied perfunctorily. "Accept them, or accept failure." He looked down at his sleeve, slowly shaking his head, and picked at several fallen hairs on his robe. "You need me . . . I need you. It is simple."

He held the hairs out to his side and rolled them between his fingers until they fell free to the floor, all the while inspecting his sleeve further. He had the confident air of a money lender. Chuckling, he added, "The gods are careful to balance the scales."

Norduk flew upon the little man with a sudden rushing violence, knocking him off his feet.

With a shriek of terror pinched from his throat, Boadix fell with such force that his glass eye popped out of its socket and rolled across the floor.

Immediately the wolf shape was hunched upon him like some starved predator, poised to devour a fresh kill. "You lied to me!" the Wolf snarled, glaring at the man through eyes that were cast in a terrible yellow hue, wild and full of animal rage. His gnarled fingers, like steel claws, dug into Boadix's fat neck, and he began to squeeze the life out of the druid's body with inhuman strength. "You swore to me that you would only practice the ancient religion in the north!"

The druid blinked his eyelid nervously over his one bulging red eye. He looked like a large, terrified gecko. It seemed he had made a profound miscalculation, disastrous in its ramifications. The horror of it jumped around his face.

Immediately his lips proceeded to dance a masterful jig. "I s-s-speak only . . . what the g-g-gods tell me, m-my liege . . . wh-why would I lie to you? . . . I c-cannot control the vagaries of the gods, my liege . . . they have changed their minds . . . th-they often do! I s-swear this is not my doing!"

The Wolf searched the twitching, bloated face for deceit, for any look of equivocation hiding in the cast shadows of the torch that might betray him, hoping for it. However, he found only a pathetic visage gaping at him, pleading, the truth unmasked in quivering folds of terror around his eyes, around the whiteness of his busy lips. "There are many altars here that have escaped the Romans!" he rasped. "Why not sacrifice on one of them?"

Boadix wriggled his neck to free a passage of air and coughed out his explanation. "The Celtic gods are angry that they have been ignored for so many years. Only a sacrifice on the chief of the ancient altars will appease them."

Like a skilled mason, feverishly building a wall of bricks against an impending deadline, Boadix paused to let the mortar set the thought securely in Norduk's mind. Beads of perspiration pimpled his brow. The single torchlight cast flickering red and orange hues onto each glistening bead, giving his grim visage the appearance of a little conflagration.

The Wolf scoured his face with a terrible scrutiny. "The gods demand a sacrifice," he hissed. "Perhaps I will give them your wretched little carcass."

Boadix forced a giggle. "Y-you have been chosen by the g-gods to restore the ancient ways, my liege. It is a great honor that you have been given, and with it . . . more p-power than you can imagine. Kill me— and you will have nothing! Nothing but the miserable hide of a dead druid from Gaul."

The final brick was set in place. The druid could see Norduk's mind at work behind his feral eyes, calculating great sums, weighing his words in the balance. His life.

Stonehenge was situated on the southern plains of Britain, about ten miles north of the ringed hill-fort of Sarum. Norduk knew that both Hengist and Horsa worshiped the pantheon of German gods fiercely and despised the druids and their religion as much as the Romans did. He knew that they would take great pleasure in not only killing any druids that they found but also those who followed their religious practices.

To sacrifice a human at Stonehenge would surely incur their wrath if it were discovered—and subvert, if not destroy, his Faustian ambitions. Norduk would have to devise a clever scheme to accomplish such a task, one that would test the boundaries of his intellect. A small thing really, considering the return. He knew that once he had come into the full maturation of his powers, the concern over Hengist and Horsa and their little armies would be a humorous anecdote from the past.

But until then . . .

The Wolf leaned forward and hissed into the one-eyed man's face. "I will agree, druid, but if this is another of your deceptions, I will tear your heart out through your lying throat!"

The druid smiled nervously. "It is a wise decision, my liege." He exhaled slowly with relief. He had laid his words well.

Norduk jumped up from the little man with surprising swiftness and returned to his chair.

After a safe span of time, Boadix got to his feet, dusted himself off, and looked around the floor for his glass eye. He spotted it glimmering in the torchlight, wedged in a gap between flagstones. He hurried over to it, stooped down, picked it up, then checked the ball for any cracks or chips. There were a few small nicks on one side of the sphere where it had apparently first hit the ground, but all in all, it was in decent shape. He let out a little grunt of satisfaction.

Confident that its hidden powers were still intact, Boadix blew the dirt from its surface. After swishing it around in his mouth for a moment or so, he rolled it back into the safety of his eye socket.

"Leave me at once!" Norduk ordered.

"As you wish, my liege."

The little man waddled out of the chamber, pausing once to pick something from his sleeve. He left the impenitent silhouette of the Wolf sitting alone in the darkness, twisting into blasphemous shapes as he yielded to his thoughts.

The cold spring night rolled to its darkest point before the gray light of morning would intrude with its warmth. Hours had passed since the druid had left the room. It was that time before dawn when even the creatures of the night were secured in their burrows and nests, when not even the sounds of the cricket or the bullfrog or the hoot owl were heard to declare life. There was just silence—silence and the muffled gurgling of the great River Trent to the north. It was the time of the night when the air gave vent to great evils.

Slowly the opaque layers of fog hanging over the hill-fort lair of the Wolf began to lift, allowing the trapped air beneath to scurry in every direction through fallen leaves and trees and over the undulating play of the landscape. A rush of wind charged through the small arched window into the chamber and extinguished the dying flickers of the single torch. Instantly the night folded the light's cast shadows into a smothering womb of darkness, leaving naught but faint blue-gray highlights to rim the outline of the room's only window.

Staring out from beneath the muzzle of his grisly shroud, rigid in a ghastly stare, Norduk thought long on the difficult task that lay before him, brooding over the various possibilities that his mind offered him. A plan would not come easily. The echoing howl of a distant wolf found its way through the night and into the quiet, tomblike chamber.

Norduk shifted his eyes toward the sound, paused for several moments giving thought to it. A thin, almost imperceptible smile curled up into the corners of his mouth.

14
THE MONASTERY
OF ST. JOHN'S

The cool days of spring unfolded into weeks following the night of celebration in the great hall, and soon the long hot days of summer were upon them, breathing their languid humors over impregnated arrays of green vales and hills now bursting with color and life. Everywhere the warming persuasion of July lulled the beasts of wing and hoof—each glutted by spring's furious appetite—into happy listlessness.

They were good days, days of healing and regained strength, the buzzing, droning, interminable days that fill a boy's fancy and stir within him powerful inclinations to wander, to try the land and rivers with his youthful ardor and to pit his cunning and strength against their ancient probations.

The euphoria over Worm's arrival had waned somewhat in the village, suiting the boy just fine. He had grown weary of all the backslapping, well-wishing, and smiling, not to mention having to dodge the coy advances of two or three persistent girls.

One in particular, the shapely girl with the mass of shiny black hair and flashing green eyes, seemed fixed upon his affections with the resolute tenacity of a she-badger. Warding off her advances taxed his creative defenses to the point of rudeness. Many a night as Worm lay awake in a sweltering night heat, the thought of her perplexed his mind with strange visions. Dagmere was indeed a beatific vision to behold, and she possessed much of his thought life, but this girl—if she could justly be called such—troubled his constitution in ways he didn't understand.

The boy began to avoid the village altogether except to make furtive visits to the forge, where, at the elbow of the giant Bolstroem, he learned the happy song of the hammer and anvil and the love of burning metal and smoke.

During those roiling days, Terryll and Worm grew in a friendship that was fused in a bond as inseparable as two sides of a single coin. It was the impassioned friendship enjoyed especially by young men before they are encumbered with the responsibilities, family duties, and callings of manhood.

The boys were constantly pitting themselves against each other in youthful combat. Like young bucks testing their mettle against one another in age-old trials, they wrestled, challenged each other in feats of strength (lifting boulders, stacks of logs, and the like), and ran footraces through village and field, fording rivers and streams, hurdling low walls and hedges, and generally troubling the countryside. They had become the stalwart boon fellows of Worm's hopes.

Worm added several pounds of muscle to his frame due to the regularity of meals, the constant physical exercise, and the incessant swinging of the hammer. And it wasn't long before his strength and stature were beyond reach of the slighter, more sinewy build of Terryll. However, when it came to fleetness of foot and nimbleness of limb, there was no peer to the young hunter, and so in time the contests waned through lack of equal venues.

Still, throughout the summer the boys explored and hunted the outlying forests, rivers, and lakes that teemed with all manner of fish and game. Terryll hunted with his longbow, and Worm with the sword of his father slung across his back. The sword served no purpose whatsoever, for usually animals are not favorably disposed to hunters walking up to them and stabbing them with pointy things. But no matter. Worm felt a certain security with it in his hands, not from threat of peril but one of a growing bond with his father's memory. He loved the feel of its weight as he wielded its perfect balance in his hands, staging mock battles with tree limbs and bushes and, of course, scoring glorious victories against imagined Pictish warriors with each awkward slash or thrust of its blade.

Terryll had grown weary with teaching him the art of the bow and soon gave it up as a lost cause. Worm had no aptitude with the instrument whatsoever and was deemed—by the rest of the family and by many of the townsfolk—a hazard to life and limb.

On one occasion early in Worm's tutelage, an unfortunate chicken (who knew well enough to keep out of the way) was struck down by a wild shaft. The creature let out a startled "Cluck-awwk," then ran around the grounds for several minutes, making a terrible row. It finally gave up the ghost and collapsed in a juniper bush next to the water pump, saving Helena the chore of having to catch it later that afternoon for the pot.

Being considered a clumsy oaf—at least in his own mind—cut the boy's self-esteem to the quick, and after several such lessons in humility he vowed never to hold the wretched "stick and string" in his hands again, a vow that he faithfully kept all summer.

It was after the chicken-slaying incident that he picked up the sword, no longer as a thing to be played with like some new toy but as a weapon to be wielded—which it was—sharpening his blunted pride with incessant sword drills. He became a machine of flesh and bone, practicing day and night like a soul obsessed, until the blade became the very extension of his arm.

Worm projected a certain confidence whenever he drew its gleaming length, and by the end of summer the boy who had been the inept archer had blossomed into a picture of agility and dexterity. It was apparent to Allyndaar that the youth possessed the innate skills of his father, albeit raw and untutored. Even Terryll conceded that he was gifted as such, but for the life of him he could not understand how anyone would have preference for a "clumsy slab of metal" over the graceful beauty of the longbow.

One swelteringly humid day in midsummer, the boys took respite from their afternoon chores next to a cool stream not far from the village. Each stretched out in indolent posture amid tall river grasses and flowers with the refreshing lap of water at his bare feet. The odd bee droned nearby, calculating the wealth of pollen. Other woodland creatures chirruped intermittently from green-boughed recesses. And somewhere there was a distant, hollow knocking on wood.

The boys dozed in and out of half-sleep, finding pictures in the scudding clouds. Terryll observed great white stags bounding over mountains, and Worm was the sole witness to battles between colossal giants. Each boy was carried along by powerful fantasies.

"There you are," a girl's voice called out. "I've been looking all over for you two."

The boys looked up from their daydreams, startled at the intrusion, though sluggish to recover from it. Terryll let out a groan once his vision cleared. It was Dagmere.

She found a smooth island stone in the stream, removed her sandals, and eased her feet into the cool waters.

She immediately commanded Worm's rapt attention.

They exchanged hesitant smiles, each flushing when their eyes met. As strange as it seemed, neither of them had exchanged so much as a complete sentence since the night of celebration in the great hall, and each day the silence between them stretched into a profound awkwardness.

"What are you doing here?" Terryll groused as he closed his eyes. Perhaps he could reconstruct his reverie.

"Papa wants to see you in the house," she said, swirling her feet in the water.

Terryll wailed lugubriously as his daydream disintegrated into a million pieces. "What about?"

"How would I know?"

Terryll threw the back of his hand over his brow, as though swooning. The end of the world had come. "He probably found something else that needs picking up or cleaning. Come on, Aeryck." He moaned, struggling to his feet. "We might as well get it over with."

Dagmere raised her feet out of the stream and watched the water drain through her toes. They were pretty feet, Worm noted.

"He didn't ask for Aeryck," she said, glancing at him coyly.

Her brother grunted. "You coming?" he said to Worm. It was more of a statement than a question.

Worm exchanged an uncomfortable look with Dagmere. "Er . . . yeah. I suppose." As he shrugged his feet into his moccasins, his mind whipped him with a thousand fine speeches that would have discharged the tension in the air and won her lasting affections. But his tongue was ever the dumb observer and managed only a queer clicking sound.

The boys left Dagmere sitting on the stone with a frustrated scowl edging into her features. After a time she stood up in the midst of the stream and kicked the water angrily.

The boys stood slump-shouldered before Allyndaar, each wearing the glum look of a condemned prisoner, each for different reasons. "Terryll," his father said, "on the morrow I would like for you and Aeryck to collect some parchments for your mother. Brother Lucius should have them ready for you."

"You mean, go to the monastery?"

Allyndaar smiled. "Yes."

The words came into Terryll's mind like a stay of execution. He looked at Worm with the reprieved face of Pharaoh's chief cupbearer and grinned broadly.

However, Worm's mind was back at the stream, still whipping him. He wore the aspect of the chief baker, condemned to hang in three days.

"Here is payment for the parchments," Allyndaar said, handing Terryll a small purse of coins. "Please be careful—this is a sizable amount of money."

"I will, Father."

The boys left early in the morning before the sun rose, for the monastery was a good ten miles away.

The sun never did rise. At least neither ever saw it rise. It remained obscured by a cloud-oppressed sky that seemed cast in iron, sending neither shadow nor warmth. It just got lighter as the day progressed, confirming to all that it was indeed day.

The shape of the day was of no consequence to the boys, however. They were away from the confines of the village, out on the open road, out on an adventure. And however pedestrian in scope it may have been, it was an adventure nonetheless. They would make the most of it. Worm even warmed up to the idea in time.

En route along the Roman road that stretched northward to Whitley Castle over meadows and through forests, Terryll and Worm talked about a variety of subjects: hunting, fishing, Saxons—even girls, though the subject smoldered from lack of fuel.

Terryll was completely bored with the topic. It wasn't as though he disliked girls. Girls were fine as long as they didn't bother him or act silly whenever he happened to come around. But mostly they did, so he gave them a wide berth whenever possible and steered clear of any discussions about them.

It would be a different matter altogether if girls liked hunting and fishing instead of domestications and such. Then there'd be some promise. But they didn't. At least none that he'd come across. The only girl he knew that fit anywhere close his expectations was Dagmere, and of course she didn't count. Simply stated, Terryll had no interest in girls whatsoever.

Worm did. It was driving him crazy.

He tried to keep the topic alive several times, weaving questions concerning Dagmere in and out of the general discussion as discreetly as he could. Once or twice he mentioned the raven-haired girl with the flashing green eyes, remarking with some reticence on one feature of hers or other. But his efforts were usually met with a shaded eye roll from Terryll, followed by an interlude of embarrassing silence.

Worm finally gave it up altogether. Unsheathing his broadsword, he decided to try an entirely new topic of conversation—religion. Worm's interest in the subject had grown since his arrival at Killwyn Eden, having observed the family's devout practice of it. This seemed as good a time as any to broach the matter.

It started with a question concerning the parchments that they were going to collect. Worm wanted to know what was written on them and why Terryll's parents would spend so much money for them. Terryll told him that today they were picking up the entire gospel of Matthew.

This opened a line of questions concerning the life of Christ. Terryll told him, as best he could, what the Scriptures said about His life and ministry, as well as the Jewish opposition and His subsequent crucifixion, burial, and resurrection.

This was the first time that Worm had ever heard the broad strokes of the account in one stretch, and for the most part he was intrigued with the story. It was compelling. There was one point, however, that Worm struggled with, and, as with the chieftain of Bowness, it was a significant one—Christ's humiliation on the cross.

161

"Why would Jesus let the Roman soldiers crucify Him, if He was truly the Son of God?" he asked, brandishing his sword from side to side.

Terryll explained the substitutionary aspect of Christ's suffering. He was the Lamb of God slain for the sin of the world, through whom sinners might have peace with God.

His answer did little to satisfy Worm's inquiry. "Wait a minute!" he protested. He blocked an imagined sword thrust from an unseen opponent and countered, "First you say that Jesus is a god—"

"I didn't say that He was a god," Terryll objected. "I said that He is God. There's a big difference."

"Whatever." Worm shrugged. "Anyway, first you tell me that He's God, then you say that He's a man as well," he continued, dispatching his first opponent with a broad slash, then side-stepping the jab from a new assailant. "Now you tell me that He is an animal that wanted to die for the world . . ."

"I said that He is the Lamb of God," Terryll again objected. "I didn't say that He was an animal."

Worm pressed his dispute. "If Jesus was really God, then He would have destroyed all of His enemies with His army. And this business about Him being a lamb makes no sense whatsoever. He's a god, a man, and an animal all at the same time?"

"He's not an animal!"

"You said He was a lamb. A lamb is a sheep . . . a sheep is an animal."

"It's just a figure of speech, a symbol. Why is that so hard for you to understand?"

Worm brightened. "I got it! It's kind of like when you really get hungry and you say, 'I'm as hungry as a horse,' right?"

"Er . . . not exactly."

"Why not?"

"Because."

"Because why?"

"Because horses aren't symbols of sacrifice. Lambs are."

"You don't make any sense."

The conversation went back and forth like this for several minutes.

Finally, out of frustration, Terryll shifted his apologetic to a discussion of hell. The picture of a lake burning with fire and brimstone didn't make sense to Worm either. In fact, he got angry about it. He thought it unfair for a god to cast into a lake of fire people who didn't believe in him.

"What right does He have to do that?" Worm argued. "I mean, you said that God loved sinners. If He does, then why does He throw them into a lake of fire? It doesn't make any sense."

Terryll tried to explain the notion of God's holiness and man's sin—and again, the Savior's vicarious sacrifice—but he could see that he was making little headway. "If you really think about it, every one of us deserves to go to hell," he argued. "It's amazing that God saves any of us."

The more he tried to expound on such lofty concepts, though, the angrier Worm became, so Terryll tried shifting his tack to other points of doctrine. But further attempts to redeem the discussion proved fruitless. Worm kept coming back with angry indictments against the notion of a loving God sending sinners to hell.

However, in time Worm grew less heated in the debate and slowed to a stop. He had ceased annihilating the Pictish army. His countenance took on a sullen cast as he stared blankly into the trees, silent, pensive. Inwardly, he was now engaged in a furious dispute with the despot, who had apparently sided with Terryll.

Terryll asked him if he had any more questions about the Christian faith, but Worm only shook his head and looked down at the tip of his sword. It was dug into a joint between two stones in the road.

"I see you've dropped your guard," Terryll jested, trying to put an edge of humor back into the conversation.

Worm sheathed the sword without retort and continued down the road.

"You want to talk about girls?" Terryll called out.

No response.

"It's one of my favorite topics," Terryll continued. "Say, let's talk about girls. How about it? I knew a girl once . . ."

But Worm had fallen to a dark mood. Terryll thought the better of pushing him, so he shrugged his shoulders and followed.

For the next mile or so of the journey, the boys walked together without saying a word. Worm's face was contorted into a troubled expression. He fumbled thoughtfully with the bronze medallion around his neck, stroking his thumb over the relief for a few minutes before he let it fall free.

Terryll cast sideways glances at him every so often, speculating that the business about hell must have set him off.

A sudden gust of wind kicked a few leaves out of an overhanging maple tree. One lighted on Worm's head and perched there like a little cap for a long time before it finally blew to the ground, escaping his notice.

Terryll chuckled at the sight and shook his head, but he didn't say a word. He whistled a tune to keep himself company. A mile later, Worm's brow was furrowed to the point where it must have hurt, immersed as he was in clouded musings. Suddenly the sound of a distant bell rescued him out of his thoughts. He looked up and brightened somewhat, expecting to see the monastery ahead.

But instead, coming toward them on the road was a flock of sheep—about fifty in number—being driven by an old shepherd. The lead sheep had a rather large bell tied around its neck. The rest of the sheep, while bleating out their cares to the world, followed its dull, clanging cadence with mindless surrender.

As the flock approached, the old shepherd called out in a good-humored voice. "Good morning to you, lads!" He beamed at them with an infectious, broad smile. The man had a kind face—one that immediately commanded affection. His cheeks were colored scarlet by time and clime, and his eyes sparkled a generous salutation without the help of voice.

"And to you, sir," responded Terryll in kind.

But Worm remained silent as he passed. The troubled look on his face reappeared, now with more notable distress. Seeing the sheep caused the image of the bloody lamb—the one in the tapestry—to flash into his mind, catching the boy off guard. He quickened his steps.

All summer long he had been careful to avoid the room where it hung. Any thought of it somehow unnerved him. His pace accelerated to a trot. He had seen other sheep during that time. In fact, the family kept several in their pens, none of which evoked the bloody image. It was strange that the sight of these sheep would do so now.

Catching up to him, Terryll called out, "Hey! Where're you off to in such a hurry?"

"What?"

"Why are you running? The monastery isn't going anywhere."

"Running?"

"Yes, running!"

Worm looked down at his legs, and, sure enough, he was running like a sprinter. He pulled up abruptly, studied his feet for a moment as if to question their sudden independence, then looked back. The sheep were cresting a knoll a half mile behind them. The faint sound of the bell and the bleating chorus could still be heard, dipping in and out with the breeze.

Terryll followed Worm's gaze to the sheep, then turned a curious eye on him. "You all right?"

"I'm fine." Worm stepped into a brisk walk. "How much farther to the monastery?"

Terryll stood in the middle of the road and scratched his head in bemused bewilderment as Worm strode away from him. "The turnoff is just ahead about a quarter mile!"

The monastery of St. John's was situated on a low hill ten miles northwest of Killwyn Eden. If a traveler didn't know it was there, it was

164

entirely possible that he would pass right by the turnoff without ever seeing it. It was encircled by a forest of oaks, yews, and various other trees in full leaf, which shielded it from the road's view.

The monastery was an unimpressive gathering of wooden huts thatched with straw, outbuildings and animal pens constructed of wattle, arrayed in a circle around a small stone church—these tended devotedly by the three monks who lived there.

In addition to these tasks, the monks studied the Scriptures, prayed, visited their several flocks, and performed the various farming tasks and maintenances of the church. In order to help with the expenses of the abbey, they also transcribed the Scriptures onto parchments and decorated the margins with paintings of biblical scenes and colorful calligraphy for various patrons. Helena was one of their most faithful contributors.

The abbot was an Italian named Bartholomeo, who ministered to the Christians west of St. John's in the villages of Papcastle, Ambleside, Brougham, and Old Penrith, and was presently away from the abbey serving his circular itinerary.

The two other monks, an Iberian named Guadalupe (called Lupe for short), and Aurelius (having taken the name Lucius upon his ordination), shared responsibilities around the monastery. Lupe served the people of Whitley Castle to the north, and Aurelius the people of Killwyn Eden and Brough southward.

As the boys cleared the forest surrounding the monastery, Terryll spotted Brother Lupe at once—a hefty, gregarious man with a swarthy complexion and a tousled black tonsure—about fifty yards from the church, scratching in the rocky soil of their garden with a mattock.

"Good morning, Brother Lupe!" he called out.

Lupe looked up from his chore. He immediately recognized the son of Allyndaar and broke out into his characteristic toothy smile. "Hail and well met, my sons! Blessings to you! Ho! Ho! How may I serve you boys?"

They angled toward the friar. "We are looking for Brother Lucius," Terryll called. "Is he about?"

"It depends," Lupe said, tossing his mattock to the ground as though releasing a snake. "And who might this lad be?" he said, casting an appraising look at Worm. "Not a Saxon wastrel, I trust. I wouldn't want to send an enemy in to the good friar, now would I?" He let out a satisfied chortle.

"Only if he owed him penance," Terryll countered.

"'Only if he owed him pen—'" Lupe threw his head back and laughed heartily. "Ho! Ho! Clever boy! Clever boy! The lad has wit, doesn't he? . . . er . . . what was your name, my son?" he asked Worm, slapping a big hand on his shoulder.

The boy, disarmed by the friar's familiarity, blurted out, "Worm . . . er . . . I . . . I mean—"

"This is Aeryck," Terryll interrupted.

"Ho! Ho! What have we here?" Lupe chuckled. "A boy who doesn't know if he's a worm or an Aeryck? Perhaps he *is* a Saxon wastrel!" He shot Worm a big wink.

"He is the son of Caelryck," Terryll added.

Lupe stood back, a little surprised. "The son of Caelryck?" He brushed a large calloused palm over the stubbles of his shorn pate. "My, my."

Worm studied the man's tonsure, not realizing that his features were contorting as he did so. This was the second monk that he had met, each having a similar haircut. And though Brother Lupe bore none of the austerity of Aurelius, there was an enigmatic air surrounding both men that intrigued the boy.

The monk leaned toward Worm to get a closer look at him, shifting his voice to a more reverential tone. "Brother Lucius has told me many times about your father. And more recently how, by the providence of God, you have come to Killwyn Eden. I didn't have the opportunity to meet your father years ago, but from what Brother Lucius tells me, you are his very image."

Worm straightened his shoulders, and there was a slight swell to his chest. The dark mood immediately sulked away somewhere into the dirt.

"Have you come seeking spiritual guidance, my son?" Lupe asked like a friar.

"Not exactly," Terryll interjected. "We have come to pick up some parchments that Brother Lucius is transcribing for my parents."

"Parchments!" the friar bellowed. "Well, you've come to the right place! There's no finer scribe in all of Britain!" Then he quickly angled his face to Worm's ear. "But don't you tell Brother Lucius that I said so," he whispered. "We wouldn't want to encourage the sin of pride, now would we?"

"Uh . . . no . . . I suppose not," Worm stammered, looking at the man out of the corner of his eye.

"Ho! Ho! Of course not!" Lupe howled, arching back into a jocund stance. "You will find Brother Lucius at work in his quarters, my sons," he said, pointing a thick finger to a large hut on the hinder side of the church.

The boys left the friar and made their way toward the hut. Worm cast a curious glance over his shoulder.

Brother Lupe chuckled as he watched them walk away. Then, picking up his mattock as if it possessed the sum of his burdens, he broke

166

into a lively hymn and began to pull it once again across the accursed earth.

"What do you think of Brother Lupe?" Terryll asked, once they were out of earshot.

"He sure laughs a lot."

"You should hear him when he visits the great hall with a mug or two of ale in his belly."

"Why do monks shave the tops of their heads that way?" Worm asked. The subject had attended his thoughts on occasion since the night of celebration. "It looks peculiar."

"They shave it so that their hair might resemble the crown of thorns worn by Christ. It is a mark of humility. At least that's what my father told me once."

"I sure wouldn't want to be a monk and have to look like that," Worm said, patting the top of his head as if to insure that his hair was still in place.

The boys rounded the front corner of the church, a small replica of the one in Killwyn Eden, and headed for the hut.

Aurelius was sitting at his desk next to a small window when their knock sounded on his door. He was busy at work, transcribing the last verse of Matthew's gospel from the Latin Vulgate onto a sheet of parchment. "Come in, boys," he said without looking up.

Terryll opened the door, and the boys entered the hut. "How did you know it was us, Brother Lucius?" Terryll asked.

"God gave us eyes with which to see His creation; man gave us windows through which to view it. A concerted endeavor between God and man, wouldn't you agree?" He smiled at the two confused faces. "Come in and make yourselves comfortable, lads. I won't be a minute."

"Comfortable" was an interesting choice of words, Worm thought. He looked around the sizable room and was amazed at the sparsity of furnishings: a wooden cot in the corner opposite the doorway, a small table and lampstand next to it, a chamber pot, and, next to a stone fireplace, the large wooden desk where Aurelius sat. On the floor beside the desk was a wooden bin filled with several parchments, each rolled into its own cubbyhole. Stacked on top of the bin were several shelves that held sheaves of blank parchment yet to be honored with the Scriptures. And lined across the desk were several jars of colored inks and dyes that were used to decorate the pages.

Against one wall were shelves supporting all manner of books and parchments and scrolls that were crammed into every available space. Adjacent to these were more shelves, equally stuffed with the papered depositories of truth and wisdom.

Worm was struck with the realization that he had entered a place of knowledge, an academy of great learning. From every quarter of the room, grand soliloquies of wisdom spoke forth to the attendant student, mocking the dullard and fool. The boy was both in awe and at once intimidated—shamed—for his lack of understanding, for his brutish stupidity. And in that fertile moment of humility, his mind was impregnated by a little seed of enlightenment.

Making a full sweep of the scholarly walls and furnishings, his eyes fell at last upon the rugged features of the Roman monk, the enigmatic caretaker of the place. Curiously, he noted that Aurelius's haircut didn't look so peculiar on him now. If anything, it made him look the more austere, the more learned. "As soon as I finish this last word, you boys may take these home," Aurelius said, adding a cross-stroke to one of the letters.

Worm edged closer to get a better look at what he was doing.

The monk was writing on a piece of parchment about one foot wide by a foot-and-a-half in length. He had already painted a border around the text about two inches in width, using several different colors. Inside the border were pictures that illustrated the text. Decorating the top border was a scene that depicted the resurrected Christ appearing to the women at the tomb. Across the bottom of the page was the scene of Christ giving His disciples the Great Commission. Inside the left border were several angels blowing trumpets, and along the right was a scene showing Roman soldiers receiving money from the Jewish chief priests to keep silent. They were simply but elegantly drawn and painted, displaying remarkable detail for such small images.

Worm's gaze fell on a little table next to the desk, having several finished parchments stacked on it. Each of these sheets as well was illustrated around its border with different scenes from the Scripture text.

Worm was astonished at their artistry. "They're beautiful!" he blurted out.

"Why . . . thank you, Aeryck! I'm pleased that you like them." Aurelius sat back on his stool and examined the last page. "There!" he exclaimed, setting his pen down. "Finished." And then, without announcing it, the monk bowed his head and prayed. "Heavenly Father, I thank You that Your Word shall not return unto You void. May it accomplish that which You please, and may it prosper in the thing whereunto You have sent it. Amen."

"Amen," Terryll added, lifting his head. "They *are* beautiful, Brother Lucius. My parents are going to love them."

"I hope so."

Aurelius stood up and gathered the sheets together, then bound them in a leather valise for Terryll to carry.

Seeing the monk stand to his full height, with his powerfully built arms and ample chest, made a profound impression on Worm—he appeared larger to the boy than on the night of the celebration. Worm's first thought was to marvel that such thick hands could have created the delicate beauty on the parchments. His second thought was one of fear. He felt uncomfortable, as though the room—however sparse in furnishings—had suddenly become too small.

Having taken care of his business with Terryll, Aurelius turned and faced Worm. "I see that you have brought your father's sword with you," he said, smiling. "I wished to look at it closer the night of the celebration, but, as you well know, there were many distractions. Do you mind if I look at it now?"

"Uh . . . not at all." Worm drew the sword from its scabbard with alacrity and handed it to the monk. He was surprised that the monk, being a holy man, would find any interest in it.

Aurelius turned the sword in his hands, carefully scrutinizing the exquisite craftsmanship from hilt to tip. "I've always admired a well-made sword. I have seen many in my lifetime but never one so beautiful. And the blade . . ." The monk paused, searching his mind. "Now, what did Bolstroem say it was made of?"

"Steel," Worm offered, pleased with himself for knowing the answer.

"Steel! That's it! There's nothing like it!" Aurelius tested the sword's balance in his hands. "Your father was a fine metalsmith, Aeryck, one who obviously took great pride in his work. Such skill is a gift from God."

Aurelius's words and tone put the boy at ease, so much so that he was filled with a sudden boldness. "I have been practicing much with it. Ask Terryll."

"Is that right, Terryll?"

"Oh, yes," he said. "Perhaps you could give Brother Lucius a demonstration."

"I don't know . . . I mean . . ." Worm hesitated, turning to Aurelius. "I'm sure that with you being a holy man and all . . . that you wouldn't be interested in such things. Would you?"

"I would love to see a demonstration." He returned the sword to Worm. "Have you been practicing long?"

"All summer."

"You must be quite good by now, then."

"Well . . . *I* think so," Worm said, feigning modesty.

"Go ahead then, show me how you stand with your sword."

"How I *stand?*"

"Yes. Show me your stance, as though you were facing an opponent. Surely that is the first thing you would demonstrate to someone, isn't it?"

"Well, of course. Here, let me show you how I've been practicing my stance." Worm squared himself to the monk, planting both feet firmly on the floor. Then he struck a rigid pose and held the sword out in front of him with a menacing attitude and scowl. "This is how you should look."

"Really? I'm surprised," the monk said, walking behind the boy to examine his footing. "That's not what I would have imagined at all."

"It isn't?"

"Not at all." Aurelius held up his thick index finger as he rounded the boy's flank and turned it backward and forward to let Worm get a good look at it. "In fact, with a stance like that, I doubt very seriously that you could defend yourself against a single finger."

"A what?"

Aurelius placed his finger in the center of Worm's chest. Looking down at it, the confused boy started to ask, "What are you do—"

Aurelius gave his chest a quick shove with the tip of his finger.

Caught by surprise and completely off-balance, Worm stumbled backward a few steps, tripped on his heels, then fell to the floor in a heap. He looked up at Aurelius, dumbfounded.

The monk was still holding out his index finger. "If you cannot stand against a finger, son, how do you expect to stand against a man with a sword in his hand—one who is ready to cut your head off?"

Terryll, who had been watching the demonstration silently thus far, burst out laughing.

Worm shot him a scowl.

Aurelius walked over to the boy and extended his hand.

"Balance! Balance! Balance! Without it, you may as well take up spinning wool," he said, pulling Worm to his feet. "Are you all right, son?"

Worm dusted himself off and rubbed his seat. "I'm fine."

Again Terryll burst out laughing. "I'm sorry, Brother Lucius!" he said. "I just can't keep it a secret any longer!"

"Are you so quick to break an oath?" the monk chided, picking up the boy's sword.

"What are you two talking about?" Worm growled. "And quit laughing, Terryll."

But Worm's command went unheeded. "You've been killed by the finger of the greatest swordsman in all of Britain!" Terryll could hardly get the words out from laughing so hard.

"What?"

"Now, Terryll," Aurelius objected.

"But it's true!"

"What's going on here?" Worm demanded, looking back and forth between them, feeling more and more like the butt of a well-conceived deception.

"Before Brother Lucius became a monk, he was a Roman centurion," Terryll explained.

"He was?"

Worm looked at Aurelius, and his lower lip fell in awe. He had never met a Roman soldier before, let alone a centurion. They inhabited the places in his mind reserved for legend and lore, for tales of great exploits. At once, images of Roman legionaries marching into battle in machinelike formation swept across his mind: each soldier bedecked in gleaming armor and scarlet cloak, scarlet brushes bristling over their helmets—the ubiquitous symbols of the power of the Roman Empire.

Reading the vision on his face, Aurelius smiled and handed Worm his sword. "Yes, I was," he said.

"He was the officer in charge of training all of the soldiers in the legions under General Aitius in Gaul," Terryll added with enthusiasm. "There's no finer swordsman in all the Roman Empire!"

"You . . . you *were?*" Worm asked without taking his eyes off the monk.

"Terryll is given to exaggeration."

"You really were a Roman centurion? And you trained the legionaries under General Aitius?"

"It is true. But I apologize for the deception," the monk said, flashing a mouthful of teeth. "It was Terryll who put me up to it. Will you forgive me?"

Worm nodded his head, still not sure of what had just happened.

Then the monk leaned close to the boy and whispered, "I will spend an extra hour in prayer for his soul tonight."

Getting into the humor of it, Worm threatened, "He'll need it!"

Aurelius straightened, and his demeanor took on a professional cast. "I met with Allyndaar last week, Aeryck, and he seems to think you have the makings of a fine swordsman—just like your father."

"He said that?"

"Yes, he did. I would like to train you and prove him right."

"You . . . you would *train* me?"

"I would teach you everything I know. I would consider it an honor," Aurelius said. "However, it would be up to you to learn it."

"I don't know what to say." Worm looked over at Terryll, who was now sitting down on the stool by the desk, still chuckling. Worm frowned at him, then faced the monk. "Where do we begin?"

Aurelius smiled. "With your stance, of course."

"Oh . . . right." Worm got back into his stance, suddenly feeling awkward with it. He shifted his feet into a different position, then held out his sword. "Er . . . how's this?"

"Fine. Except you won't be needing *this* for a while," Aurelius said, taking the sword.

"My sword! But—"

"Until you've mastered your feet, lad, your sword is useless to you," Aurelius bellowed in the practiced voice of an instructor. He walked behind the boy and helped him into the proper stance for sword fighting.

"Never stand flat-footed like you did. And never face your opponent square. When you stand flat-footed, you carry your weight on the back of your heels. As you've just witnessed, you are much too easy to knock down. Stand with your left foot a half step in front of your right, and put a slight bend in your knees." Aurelius kicked Worm's instep into position—first one, then the other. "This lowers your weight closer to the ground, making it harder for you to lose your balance. It also gives your opponent less of a target. There!" Aurelius said, satisfied.

Worm found it an intriguing paradox, if not a contradiction, that a Christian holy man, who wore the brown robes of the poor Roman peasantry—the birrus—and his hair in a tonsure, would be giving him a lesson in sword fighting. "Like this?"

"Yes. Now spring up and down on the balls of your feet."

Worm obeyed.

"Now, see how much easier it is to shift your weight from side to side."

Worm bounced from side to side. "Yes. It makes me feel lighter."

"Good. Now as I step backward, you follow me forward, taking two steps. Then get into the stance that I just showed you."

Aurelius stepped backward, and Worm followed him forward two steps, a little stiffly, but he managed to get into his stance.

"Keep your elbows tucked in to your sides this time. You look like you're trying to fly."

Terryll snickered from the sidelines, and Worm shot him a look.

"Pay attention now, son. The lesson's over here," Aurelius chided. "Now let's try it again."

Worm jerked his eyes back to Aurelius.

Again, Aurelius stepped backward, and Worm followed. This time the boy looked a little less awkward and a little less like a duck. "That's it. It will come easier with practice. Now take two steps backward and get into your stance."

Going backward was more difficult. But after several tries, Worm managed to get into his stance without bobbling from side to side or flapping his wings.

"Excellent! Now let's go from side to side."

Both Aurelius and Worm stepped from side to side, right to left, left to right, like mirror images. All the while, Aurelius called out the drill as they moved.

"Left to right. That's it—into your stance. Now, right to left. Good. Without sure footing, lad, the warrior is a cripple. He is not prepared to go into battle to defend his own life nor those around him. Left to right. He is worthless to all concerns. Better a weak woman with sure feet in battle than a strong man with weak feet! Into your stance. Again."

The old words flowed from the man's throat with perfunctory cadence, and, though tarnished with neglect, they were unimpeachable axioms honed on the battlefield and administered in the endless repetition of training for the battlefield.

After several minutes of drill, Aurelius said, "All right now, son, I'm not going to tell you which direction to take. But whatever I do, you follow me. Forward, backward, side to side, and do not lag behind. Understand?"

"Yes."

"Begin!"

For the next five minutes Aurelius moved in each of the four directions, at first slowly, making sure that Worm got into his stance properly each time he stopped. Then he sped up the drill as the boy learned the choreography. "Look in my eyes, not at your feet! Forward! My eyes! My eyes! Backward!" Worm gazed into the centurion's eyes and saw the reflection of a hundred men in military concert, each moving side to side, backward and forward, in rhythmic cadence and precision. And he was in their midst, one of their chosen number, one of the elite. He was infused with the pride of a new recruit who had suddenly discovered in his body a great purpose.

"To the right! . . . Backward! . . . To the left! . . . Forward!"

Terryll looked on from his stool and was amazed at how quickly Worm picked up the routine. The two seemed fixed by invisible strings. He wasn't sure which of them was having more fun.

Aurelius took the boy through the drill several times, five minutes at a time, with a one-minute rest period between sets. It was strenuous exercise.

Again they drilled. And again. And again the repetition: forward, backward, to the left, to the right, forward, and again. And it wasn't long before Worm was panting to keep up with the one-time Roman centurion, who, though forty years his senior, seemed barely winded.

Finally they took a ten-minute break. Worm gulped some water and wiped his brow. Terryll was grinning from ear to ear, and Worm now returned the grin heartily.

Then for the next hour or so, Aurelius taught the boy a few rudimentary principles in actual sword fighting, showing Worm how to parry an opponent's blade to one side, then how to thrust with his own sword once the opponent was exposed, all the while keeping a springy balance in his feet.

"Balance! Balance! Balance!" he thundered over and again, until the word was emblazoned across Worm's mind. *"Balance!"*

After a time, Aurelius retrieved an old bronze shield from under his bed, dulled with time and full of dents, then demonstrated to the boy its proper use, both as a defensive weapon and as an offensive one.

Worm's pulse quickened at the sight of the thing—a circular stage upon which battles were pitched and warriors fought, where each dent, the hammer blow of a worthy opponent, was returned with a greater skill. He imagined furious blows exchanged and the unfortunate men who had dared to stand against this man: the Visigoths and Franks, Ostrogoths and Burgundians, the screaming hordes of barbarians, falling before Aurelius's terrible battle countenance and hammering blade.

It was a tremendous vision. More than he could contemplate in one setting. And so went the first of many such lessons between the old centurion monk and the boy. It had gone well. Both master and student were well pleased. It became the foundation upon which a friendship between them would be built over the next several weeks, upon which endless repetition of drills would hone the boy's raw skills until he became a most remarkable swordsman.

And Terryll beamed, though he still thought swords were nothing more than clumsy slabs of metal.

It was mid-afternoon when Aurelius said his farewells to the boys. Terryll slung the leather valise across his chest, freeing his bow arm. Worm, beaming with a soldier's pride from ear to ear, held his sword in his right hand, and the dented shield that Aurelius had given him for practice in his left.

As they exited the monk's quarters, Terryll looked up at the now darkening skies. "It looks as though we are in for some bad weather," he said. "We had best be going."

Aurelius glanced at the clouds to the south, and immediately his countenance fell. The demeanor of the once Roman centurion was now eclipsed by a higher purpose.

Discerning the shift, Worm asked, "What's wrong, Brother Lucius?"

After a few moments the monk spoke in the tone of a prophet. "I see many stormy days ahead that will scatter the flocks of Britain. A tempest is brewing even now that threatens the peace that we have enjoyed for so long."

"Why do you say that?" Terryll asked. "Is it because of what I overheard the Saxons discussing?"

"Partly. But your news, Terryll, only confirms what I have sensed in my prayers for some time now."

Worm looked down at his grip on the hilt of his sword as the two of them spoke, suddenly feeling like an outsider.

"However, the Saxons are but flesh and blood," Aurelius continued. "There is a darkness spreading across the land that will take greater weapons than those made of iron, or even steel, to fight." Aurelius looked at both boys soberly. "I have been praying for you two boys . . . especially for you, Aeryck."

Worm looked up surprised. "For me? Why?"

"That God will have mercy on you. I will teach you all that I know about the sword, but there is an enemy of your soul that you cannot prevail against except with the weapons of the Spirit."

"Weapons of the Spirit? What are they?"

"There isn't time now," Terryll interrupted. "I'll tell you on the way home."

Terryll pulled on Worm's sleeve, and the two of them headed toward the pathway that disappeared into the palisade of trees encircling the monastery.

"Come again soon, my sons," Aurelius said, waving. "And keep faithful with your drills, Aeryck!"

"I will! And thank you!"

The boys waved, then called out a farewell to Brother Lupe. The jovial friar had given up on the stubborn ground and was now busy feeding some pigs and a couple of rambunctious shoats. Lupe returned their farewells with several hearty blessings of his own, trailing them with an offering of laughter that was intermingled with protests from several hungry hogs.

Soon only the wind could be heard, carrying all sounds from man and beast alike far into the mountains northward.

As the boys disappeared into the trees, Aurelius lifted his eyes to the southern horizon. He stared long at the verdant hill-scape that fell away gently from the monastery to the south, glazed now with the pinks and purples of heather in bloom. The view was breathtaking. But the serenity of the rolling heath, set against a lowering sky, belied a tension between two worlds: two spheres of reality that met in battle on the distant horizon and heralded—to all who would listen—a crimson forecast.

"God have mercy upon our land."

15
THE STRANGE CARNAGE

Worm was swept along in the pageantry of a great event. He had taken an inviolable oath to a splendid and worthy cause. He had become the pie-eyed enlistee in a sacred endeavor. He had become a disciple of the blade. A wondrous religion had been discovered, it seemed, and he, the devoted proselyte, was thundering with fiery verse: "Balance! Balance! Balance!" In his charged breast beat the rhythmic cadence of its holy creed: "To the left . . . forward . . . to the right . . . backward."

And again.

The boys made good time on their way home amid the fervor of drills, and, though the sky threatened rain, it remained but a threat.

For the better part of the journey, while Worm took out at least threescore Pictish warriors with his new catechism, they talked through a spectrum of topics. Terryll touched on the topic of spiritual weapons. But the subject of heavenly warfare winged swiftly over Worm's head, so the dialogue moved on from there, camping instead on the familiar terrain of sword fighting and Aurelius. Worm was intrigued by the apparent contradiction in the man and inquired about his past during a lull in his crusade.

Terryll explained briefly that while serving as a legionary in Northern Africa, his first duty station, the young Aurelius had come into contact with Augustine of Hippo.

Aurelius had been a member of a contingent escorting Augustine to a council in Rome, there to meet with the bishop to discuss a certain heresy that was spreading rampant throughout the Empire. During the lengthy journey, Augustine took the opportunity to teach the soldiers the cardinal doctrines of "true Christianity."

"*True* Christianity? Is there a *false?*" Worm asked, resuming his sword drills.

"Just ask my father about a monk named Pelagius, and you'll get an earful of false Christianity."

"Pelagius?"

"He's the man who started the heresy."

"What's it about?"

"I'm not really sure," Terryll replied. "Something to do with a teaching claiming that the free will of man is more significant in a person's conversion than God's sovereignty. But if you want to know more about it—ask my father. He and Aurelius discuss it all the time."

Worm raised his shield to ward off an enemy blow—a Visigoth's—then stepping into his assailant, he found his mark with an upward thrust of his sword and finished him off. It was neatly done. "Who is this Augustine? Is he a monk too?" he asked, looking for another contender.

"He was," Terryll replied. "He died about twenty years ago."

"He did? Then what made him so important?"

"Augustine was a great thinker. He wrote several essays and books on Christian doctrine, philosophy—even heresies like Pelagianism. We have one of his books at home called *The City of God*."

"Sounds boring."

"It is if you consider the fall of Rome boring," Terryll replied.

"Really?" Worm peered curiously over his shield. For just a moment, the story had become more interesting than his drill.

"Yeah," Terryll replied. "The Visigoths, under the command of Alaric, sacked the city forty years ago, and there were a lot of people who blamed it on Christianity. But Augustine goes into the real reasons behind the fall. You know—greed, immorality, and so on. It's a pretty interesting book, really, if you like history. You ought to read it."

"Have you ever . . . er . . . read it?"

"Had to. My mother made Dag and me read it for our 'spiritual development,' as she calls it. But I prefer reading the *Iliad* and the *Odyssey*. They've got more adventure in them." Terryll chuckled.

"What's so funny?"

"My mother doesn't like me reading the Greek classics because she says Homer wasn't a Christian," Terryll replied. "Well, of course he wasn't a Christian, I keep telling her. There weren't any Christians around at all back then, just pagans. Some Jews, of course, but mostly they just wrote the Bible. They weren't too fond of sea adventures, unless you consider Jonah and the whale."

"Yeah, I know what you mean," Worm lied.

Terryll shot him a queer look. "Anyway, like I was saying before you distracted me, Augustine was teaching Aurelius and the other soldiers what it meant to be a true Christian."

"So Aurelius wasn't always a Christian?" Worm took two steps forward and got into his stance. *Balance!*

177

"Not at all! He used to worship the bull god Mithras, like a lot of other soldiers."

"A *bull* god?"

"Yes. Mithras was a Persian bull god who demanded a regimen of discipline and order—two things which really appeal to Roman soldiers for some reason."

Worm stood up from his battle stance, allowing Terryll to gain some distance on him. "Really? What kind of discipline?"

"Too much for me," Terryll replied sardonically.

Suddenly remembering that he was waging a battle, Worm jumped back into position and looked from side to side for Pictish warriors. Finding the area suddenly clear of the devils, he ran ahead to catch up with Terryll. "What happened next?"

"You *are* listening to this, aren't you?"

"Every word."

"Uh-huh," Terryll said, shooting him a shaded look. "At first, during the overland part of their journey, Aurelius mocked Augustine's teaching and listened to him with only half an ear—"

"For half a year?" Worm interrupted, blocking a sword blow with his shield.

"With half an ear!"

"Right."

Terryll rolled his eyes. "When they arrived in Carthage they boarded a ship bound for Neapolis. Not much to do on a ship, except count waves or sea gulls, so Aurelius was forced to listen." Terryll chuckled. "What else could he do—swim?"

"What made him change his mind?" Worm asked.

"The resurrection of Christ."

"That was *it?*"

"'That was *it?*'" Terryll looked at Worm astounded. "No bull god ever rose out of the grave!"

Worm sheathed his sword, then ambled along pensively for a while as his mind sorted through the conversation. "Why did he become a monk?"

"After Aurelius retired from the army," Terryll replied, "he felt the call of God upon his life and took holy orders from Leo the First, the Bishop of Rome. Leo sent him—Brother Lucius now—to the monastery of St. John's in order to help guard northern Britain against the further spread of Pelagianism. He's been here for nearly ten years now."

Worm didn't hear the last sentence at all, for as Terryll was finishing the story the boys crested a knoll, and Worm was immediately distracted by something on the road ahead of them.

"Are you listening to me?" Terryll asked. "I've already heard this story, you know."

"What are those?" Worm asked, pointing ahead.

"What are what?"

"Those things lying all over the field down there."

Terryll looked to see what Worm was pointing to. The road rolled away from the knoll and down into a broad expanse of meadow about a half mile in width and a mile in length, before it climbed another hill on the far side. Off to the right of the road, several shapes were scattered across the field.

"They're sheep," Terryll said.

"Why aren't they moving?"

"What do you mean—'why aren't they moving?' I see two or three of them moving over there on the right. And there's another one walking across the road toward those bushes on the left. The rest are probably sleep—" He broke off.

There *was* something odd about the way the sheep were lying on the ground. And their coloring was wrong. Red sheep? Terryll strained his eyes, trying to make sense of it. As they drew nearer the sheep, it hit him.

"They're . . . dead."

"Dead! Are you sure?" Worm started running toward them.

"*Stop!*"

Worm wheeled around in his tracks. "Why?"

Terryll fit an arrow to his bowstring and caught up with him. "Something's wrong here, that's why." He trained his eyes on the tree line that skirted the field, looking for anything out of the ordinary, any movement, any sign of danger.

Catching Terryll's concern, Worm drew his sword and quickly rehearsed his catechism: to the right . . . forward . . . to the left . . . And suddenly the drill seemed absurd.

The closer they approached the dead sheep, the more it became apparent that something horrible had indeed taken place. When they came upon the first one lying in the grass alongside the road, they stopped to examine it. However, at first glance it was difficult to tell which end of the sheep was the head and which was the tail. There was blood all over it, as though it had been killed by some awful savagery.

"What happened to it?" Worm asked.

"I don't know, but keep your eyes open while I look at its wounds. Something butchered these sheep, and it—or they—may still be around."

Worm stiffened, and he felt the hair on the back of his neck stand on end like a little regiment of fear. He looked around the periphery of the meadow, his busy eyes searching for danger. The trees jagged up into the lowering sky like a rake of teeth. The horizon was alive, unfriendly, nearer now than a minute before. There was a grim contrast between the liveness of the trees and the deadness of the field, and the wind soughed menacingly through the dark boughs and whirled around his head.

Worm was certain that there were at least a dozen pairs of eyes or more, sheep-butchering eyes, peering at them from the tree line—probably hideous Pictish warriors amassing to swarm upon them, to hack their bodies until their heads could not be discerned from their feet. He shuddered.

The boy hunkered below the lip of the shield, with just his eyes peeking over it, as though the shield somehow bequeathed invisibility to those who bore it. *Balance! Balance! Balance!*

The words mocked him.

Terryll raked the thick bloody wool away from the wounded areas, trying to discern the cause of death. His eyes studied the carcass with the keenness of a surgeon. What he saw puzzled him. The sheep's neck was broken. It had obviously been killed by a crushing bite from some animal. But apparently just killing the sheep did not satisfy its attacker. All over the body were several more gashes and tears made by teeth and claws, as though the attacking animal was in some kind of killing frenzy. He checked the area around the sheep and found some tracks.

"Wild dog," he said, rising soundlessly to his feet. He looked across the field at the dozens of bloody carcasses and shook his head in amazement. "But there had to be more than one of them to create all of this carnage."

"Wild dogs?" Worm asked.

"From the look of the tracks, the one that killed this sheep was a big one. And it killed for pleasure, not for meat."

"For pleasure?" Slowly a bristling of fear crawled up Worm's spine as a terrible thought tore at his mind. "Do you think that it was . . . a boarhound?"

"I don't know." Terryll moved to the next sheep and stooped to examine it.

Boarhounds were the inspiration behind Worm's worst nightmares, and immediately the little regiment mustered along his nape. And to compound matters, where there were boarhounds there would be Saxons —in Worm's reckoning, just a notch down from Picts on the fear scale.

And then he was struck by a puzzling thought. "Where's the old shepherd?" he said, voicing it. He headed toward another group of sheep farther down the road as if the answer lay waiting somewhere in the grass. "Wouldn't he have driven away any wild dogs?"

"These may not be the same sheep that we saw this morning," Terryll offered as he moved from sheep to sheep. "They're probably a flock that wandered over here from a nearby farm. I've seen many sheep along this road unattended by shepherds."

In each case the wounds were similar, and Terryll's conclusions were the same: wild dogs had come upon this flock and killed the sheep out of wanton meanness. He stood up from one of them and blew out the sum of his bewilderment.

Suddenly Worm called out, "Terryll! Come here—quick!"

Terryll ran over to him. There, strewn in and among several dead sheep, were the carcasses of four large canines.

"Wolves!" Terryll exclaimed.

"Wolves?" Worm gaped at the four carcasses in a wide-eyed trance. He had seen wolves running across faraway ridges at night—or what he took to be wolves—howling and barking and carrying on in their malefic voices, but he had never seen one up close before. Wolves were larger than he had imagined. Even in death they looked fearsome, as if they could spring up out of the horrible stillness and snatch his throat before he could blink.

"It doesn't make sense," Terryll said. "Wild dogs might destroy sheep out of sheer viciousness, but not wolves. They would kill only what they could drag away and eat. This is the work of some devilish madness."

"What killed the wolves?" Worm asked, a little timorously. His mind was contemplating answers in the tree line.

Shadows were falling long across the bloody field now, and there was a sudden chill in the air.

Terryll stooped to examine one of the bodies. "It's still warm," he said, rubbing his hand across the wolf's fur. "This happened fifteen— maybe twenty minutes ago." Then he found the wound that had killed it—five parallel slashes about two inches apart across the wolf's throat. "A bear!"

"A bear?"

"A big one."

Terryll quickly looked for tracks in the soft earth to confirm his suspicions. The tracks showed that there had been a terrible struggle not long before the boys arrived, but he couldn't find a clean print from the bear.

Worm found one ten feet away. "Over here!"

When Terryll saw the track, he knew immediately who had made it. "Hauwka!"

"Hauwka? How can you be sure?"

"Look at the size of it. There isn't another bear in all of Britain that could make a track that size." Terryll placed his hand inside the track. It was easily twice as wide as his span, and more. He looked around for other signs and presently found a group of tracks heading south. "From the look of these tracks, there were several more wolves in the pack. And here," he said, pointing out another bear print, "is Hauwka's track running after them."

"How do you know that he's running?"

"See the way his claws are dug deep into the ground?—his front pads as well." Again Terryll pressed the flat of his hand into the track, this time spreading his fingers carefully to feel the contours left by the great bruin. "And here you see that the heel of his foot hardly makes an imprint at all." Terryll looked up at Worm. "Believe me, he's running— and not too long ago. These tracks are fresh!"

"What do you think happened?"

"It's hard to say. A pack of wolves come across an untended flock of sheep and for some reason just start killing them all. By the look of things here, they were probably surprised by Hauwka, who killed several of them before they knew what hit them. Then he chased the rest of the pack across the road heading south." Terryll looked at the hills southward for several moments, then glanced back across the field of dead sheep. "What puzzles me still," he said, scratching his head, "is why wolves would attack and kill like this for no apparent reason."

The dull, clanging of a bell suddenly broke through the shroud of mystery. The boys turned to see where it was coming from. Across the road was a clump of bushes and small shrubby trees. Out from behind the screen of foliage, a single sheep—the lead sheep with the bell tied around its neck—walked out into the open and looked directly at the boys.

"It's the same sheep we saw this morning," Worm said. "I can tell by the bell."

Terryll fixed his eyes on the sheep and moved cautiously toward it, his bow at the ready. Worm followed, peering over his shield at the terrain to his left. As the boys drew nearer to the sheep, it turned and disappeared behind the shrubbery from whence it came.

"Wait here and keep your eyes open, while I see where that sheep is going," Terryll said.

Terryll rounded the bushes and stopped. For several moments he just stood there looking at something on the ground in front of him.

"What is it, Terryll?" Worm asked, starting toward him.

"Stay there!"

"What?"

"Don't come over here!" Terryll reappeared, his face pale. "It's the old shepherd . . . he's dead."

"Dead? Are you sure?"

"Believe me."

182

"I want to see," Worm said, walking toward the bushes.

Terryll arched his eyebrows and shook his head. "You're making a mistake."

The first image that caught Worm's eyes was the sheep with the bell tied around its neck, bleating softly. It was looking down at something lying in the vague shadows of the grass, a shape—the second image.

Worm stood dully staring at the shape for a moment, desperately sorting through a store of references as he tried to put them together into some kind of meaningful picture in his mind. His instincts were telling him that something was dreadfully wrong, but it escaped his eyes. *What is*—?

It came to him slowly at first, and his spine prickled as a surge of recognition built quickly in waves, then rushed him with a terrible horror. He clutched his mouth out of reflex and blanched. Still holding his mouth, he staggered out from behind the bushes and said dazedly, "What on earth? What on earth?" Then he fell to his knees and vomited.

"I warned you," Terryll chided, standing behind him. "Are you all right?"

Worm spat into the grass several times. His face was ashen, drawn. Groaning, he said, "No. Yes, yes, I'm fine!"

Terryll caught a fast-moving shape from the corner of his eye. He whirled to see a large wolf, thirty feet away now and bearing down hard on them. Its yellow eyes were narrowed hatefully, its jaws snapped and flung bloody slaver, and hellish, guttural snarls jerked in its throat.

"Look out!" he heard himself scream, and he drew his bow.

Worm spun around and collided with Terryll's legs as he loosed his arrow. The shaft leaped from the shuddering string and whistled harmlessly through the air, tracing a jeering path against the leaden sky. A frustrated plea escaped into the air as Terryll grabbed for another arrow.

But the wolf was in the air, its feral eyes aimed at the vulnerable jugular of Worm, whose tragic face was now entranced—deerlike—in pathetic disbelief. A tiny gasp foundered on the air, and immediately the wolf slammed hard against a sudden raised wall of dented bronze with a deafening clang of metal. The tremendous impact of the blow hurled Worm into Terryll again, and the two of them fell sprawling across the ground like flung rag dolls, grunting and cursing.

Terryll tumbled several feet across a whirling sward of dark green, grabbing at his quiver as he rolled up onto one knee. But he found only air in his hand. To his horror, his bundled arsenal of arrows lay scattered over the ground in mocking disarray, as close to his reach as the stars.

The wolf, maddened now to rage, turned about on the run and pitched a renewed attack against the boy nearest him—Worm. The boy had held fast to his shield through the fall, but his sword had gotten flung somewhere. Panicked, he swung his head from side to side searching for it. A glint of blade about ten feet away caught his eyes. He cursed.

Again he cursed, scrambling to his feet as the wolf sprang . . . *to the right . . . forward . . .* and the boy swung his shield at the beast, striking up and hard against its flashing jowls. However, the full force of the wolf's body hit him broadside, and he was bowled over again. The shield flew one way, the boy flew the other in graceless abandon. And against the blurred sweep of time, the pristine image of a single yellow eye, peering hatefully at him as it traced a feral arc inches past his face, was caught in his mind.

Terryll frantically grabbed for an arrow in the grass but got it tangled in the leather valise slung around his chest. A battery of expletives stabbed the whorl of ground at his feet as he twisted in a comic dance.

At the same time Worm was scuttling crablike toward his sword. The violent shape of the wolf slanted into his peripheral vision, snarling and snapping at the air. The boy jerked his head toward the creature—now lunging at him—then leaped desperately for his weapon.

Clasping the haft, he hit the ground hard and swung the blade around with both hands like a scythe. Immediately the blade struck the wolf in its brisket, biting deep, rending flesh and muscle with a single long tooth of steel.

The wolf let out a blood-curdling howl as the thrust of its weight vaulted it over Worm's head, violently yanking the sword out of the boy's hands. Then, striking the ground with a jolt, it rolled several yards before coming to a halt.

Both boys sprang to their feet—panting, their bodies surging with adrenaline—and each moved cautiously toward the stricken animal.

Terryll, still tangled in the valise, stalked the creature with longbow at the ready. His eyes, quick, wary, riveted on the wolf, riveted on the dark tree line for more wolves.

Worm picked up his shield and approached the quiet, threatening shape slowly. "Is it dead? Do you think it's dead?" he asked, raking the tangled hair from his eyes.

"It looks dead!" Terryll said, circling the thing.

The wolf's body lay still, its mouth agape. A discharge of blood trickled sluggishly along its lolling tongue, and its yellow eyes were glazed in a faraway stare. The sword handle was sticking out of its chest, which had ceased its furious heaving. "It's dead, all right," he said, lowering his bow. "You killed him. That's sure."

"I did?" Worm stared at the dead wolf, reeling in the aftermath of battle. "What happened?"

"Don't ask me," Terryll replied as he looked across the field of carnage. "This is madness."

"Do you think it's safe to get my sword?"

"I don't think the wolf would object," Terryll said, forcing humor into the moment.

"I suppose not."

Worm removed his sword from the dead wolf and cleaned it with some leaves. The exercise was strange to him, and he fumbled woodenly through it. His mind, in the hollow daze that accompanies violence, clutched at scattered images whirling by his grasp like leaves on a gale. His eyes were never far from the lifeless shape as he cleaned his blade, appraising it curiously, taking only quick excursions to find another leaf or two in the cool, darkening grass. Curiously, he was struck with profound sadness. Only minutes before, the wolf was full of rage and fury, full of life, and, for reasons now lost forever in the stillness of its mind, had been trying to kill him. He felt a compelling urge to bend over and ask it why.

The wolf seemed to him now, in that moment of reflection, a tragic animal, a thing of awesome creation wasted. However, as the blurring panorama of images slowed to a discernable sequence of events in his mind—the dead sheep, the mutilated body of the shepherd, the killing hatred in the single yellow eye—he was again stricken with numbing horror. His knees trembled.

Meanwhile, Terryll strained his eyes into the fading light, looking across the meadow at the slaughter for any sign of movement. There was nothing of consequence—just a few scattered sheep grazing without a care and a few mangy birds, buzzards and crows mostly, that had gotten wind of the slaughter. Aside from these, the tree line and field were still, blackening against the turning sky. As still as death.

"What do we do now—I mean, about the old shepherd?" Worm asked solemnly.

"Nothing right now," Terryll replied. "We've got to get back to the village and tell my father. He'll get some men to come out and take care of him later."

"You want to just leave him here!?"

"He's dead, Aeryck. We can't carry him, and we don't have time to make a stretcher before nightfall."

"Then you go. I'm not going to leave him here alone." Worm was surprised that the words had escaped his mouth.

"You mean—you're going to stay here by yourself?

"I don't want any birds picking at his body."

"We can throw some branches over him to protect him."

185

Worm didn't answer. Instead, he walked over to the bushes where the old shepherd lay and set himself for his watch.

"You're not making any sense, Aeryck! It's dangerous here. There may be more wolves."

"Then the sooner you go, the sooner you'll be back with help," Worm said, steeling himself.

In truth, he wished now that he hadn't spoken so impulsively. In the aftermath of the battle his emotions were still raging, usurping control from his reason, and Terryll's words served to force some order back into his thinking. But the boy's pride—even though he was trembling with fear—would not allow him to retract. The despot was silent on the matter.

"So you aren't coming?" Terryll pressed.

"I'm staying." Worm was distracted by the now familiar sound of the bell and turned his head as the lead sheep walked up to him. The boy looked down and rubbed its wooly head.

The sheep let out a mournful bleat that had a calming effect on the boy's nerves. It was ironic that the animal that had caused him great torment of soul that morning would somehow bring him comfort that night. He looked up at Terryll and smiled. "Besides, I have a friend here to keep me company. Now, go on. I'll be fine."

Terryll shook his head. "You're a stubborn fool."

"And you're wasting daylight."

Terryll turned reluctantly and started toward the road, looking hard at the ground. After a few paces he stopped and turned back toward his friend with an imploring look.

"I'll be fine!" Worm called out. "Just hurry up and get back here!"

Again Terryll shook his head, then broke into a halting lope. As he padded along the road toward Killwyn Eden—a good five miles away— the sun began its descent behind the jagged forests off to his right, turning the dead gray sky into a wretched bloody red. He looked back one last time as he crested the hill and saw Worm, still patting the head of the lead sheep and gazing across the quiet field, keeping a silent vigil over the dead.

16
THE VIGIL

The western sky was a broken palate of blood hues, roiling in the mutating lights of sunset, a great burnished mirror reflecting in its surface the scattered shapes of death. With gleaming sword in hand and dented shield on arm, Worm patrolled the area where the old shepherd lay, dutifully walking his post in wide circles around the clump of bushes and shrubby trees.

There was a newness in his duty, and with it came a certain strength of passion—even cheer—as he paid allegiance to the rightness of his convictions. In his tread there was the strut of a brave soldier, one who was bound by honor's code, fearing only cowardice in his stride.

He saw himself engaged in a heroic exploit and hummed a happy tune as he carried out his patrol, taking comfort in the knowledge that his duty was but a small season of daring, three hours at best. He envisioned the adulations of the villagers as he returned, having faithfully discharged his duty—the son of Caelryck returning to the fine appraisal of Dagmere's blue eyes. And he made his rounds in the glory of this fine conceit.

With the passage of time, however, came a new vision: one of Terryll returning over the little hill with a band of mighty men, a vision less resplendent in glory but more expedient. It encamped securely about his mind. Twice he broke from his duty circle, walked to the brow of the rise, and looked down the endless red-washed road for the shadows to take form, almost willing them into being.

Each time, of course, there was nothing but the road and the colonnades of overshadowing trees on either side, and the long darkening corridor of stillness. But that didn't stop the willing, or the hoping, nor did it halt entirely the happy tune that had become a droning, meandering monotone.

Turning, he scanned the tree line and fields about him for any signs of danger. A crow landed nearby and hopped along the ground toward a raised mass of dark red but took off at Worm's approach, emitting a disgruntled caw. Worm brandished his sword at the thing and hurled revilements.

He grew to hate the birds. They were the hopping, black silhouettes of death, the winged morticians at wait in carrion parlors with insatiable little black eyes, squawking, always watching. They watched his patrol, their beady eyes taking his measure, sizing their take, waiting in stoic appraisal. Clucking.

Worm hated the birds. He threw stones at them, forcing them to wing. But as soon as he passed, they would hop back and continue their gruesome feast, railing at him all the while like a bunch of jeering hecklers, hurling insults as though he were some uninvited intruder, squawking, always watching, waiting.

The lead sheep followed about two paces behind, keeping company with the boy. The dull clang of its bell clapped out an incessant, disjointed tempo.

As the western horizon collapsed under the great weight of ever-darkening pigments, little voices began to whisper disturbing things in his mind, attending his thoughts with doubts and vague impressions of terror—hunched specters scratching at his shoulders, giggling, suggesting the approach of evil.

For a time, in the bright rubescent glow of twilight, he was able to shrug them off, and his circuitous roving helped to vent his anxiety and loosen his nerves. He was the brave soldier, duty driven and honor bound. The rightness of his cause sustained him, emboldened him. Of this he kept informing his mind and warded off the omnipresent whispers from behind bulwarks of waning light.

Somewhere in the passage, however, the happy tune ceased to drone.

He walked his post in the fading light, while the dull peals rattled behind him, beating out his course upon the cool, shadowy grass. The clanging gave him a comfort of sorts. It heralded life; dead things don't make sounds. Worm stopped to rub the sheep's woolly head in celebration of their common breath. The sheep was a fellow living thing.

"How're you doing, fella?" he said, kneading his fingers into the wool. "Don't worry, we won't be here much longer."

The sheep looked up into his face with dark, silent eyes. A burnished, dimming light bathed one side of its fleece. That's when he noticed it. The silence. The bell, the herald of life had ceased its clanging. The blood fled Worm's head as a terrible thought rushed him, ambushed him. *Sounds carry farther at night!*

Immediately he removed the bell from around the sheep's neck and quietly laid it on the ground. Then, flogging himself with curses, he scanned the broken tree line for movement, hoping that the sound of the

188

bell hadn't traveled too far already, beckoning distant and unwanted visitors to the scene. Worm patrolled his post in silence. His step was cautious, halting. His eyes darted in wary alertness at the darkening field and tree line that were fast becoming one. The hunched specters were now clawing at his heels, chuckling, taunting his mind with the stealthy approaches of evil.

Often he turned and walked backward, sure that he was being watched, followed. It was the same feeling he had had when he and the bear were fleeing the boarhounds through the dark wood. Something was on his tail. He was sure of it. There had been a shift. His mood had grown sullen with the dusk. The soldier was quiet, bothered now with anxious thoughts, grumbling now at his task. Cursing.

Terryll had been gone for a little more than an hour, so he was probably just reaching the village, or soon to do so. But to Worm, it seemed that he had been gone all night. He thought about Terryll now arriving at the villa—Allyndaar, Helena, and Dagmere now greeting him; how he could have been there too—right now—safe, with a bowlful of Helena's hot stew to fill his belly.

But such thinking brought little comfort and made his stomach growl, so much so that he had to train his mind on kindlier images to keep from getting sick over it. Dagmere appeared to him; her pretty feet splashed little circles in the stream, her sparkling blue eyes cast hopeful looks.

His mind whipped him again. The fine speeches drummed a distant chorus in his mind, but he knew that they were lost forever in dumb vaults. He let out long wistful sighs. And a coldness enveloped him.

He shogged to the top of the little hill, stared long and hard down the blackening road, and was suddenly smitten with the foolishness of his duty. A narrow shaft of reason had penetrated the stubborn overcast and bathed his mind with sentient light. There was nothing stopping him now from breaking into a lope and putting this field of death behind him.

The sheep were dead. The shepherd was dead. Terryll was right. The dead man neither knew nor cared that Worm had elected to watch over his grisly remains. People would probably think him foolish for being here, risking his life. And for what? A dead man. Dead sheep. What a stupid boy! That's what they would think. Dagmere too. Reason mocked him, flogged him, whipped him with imprecations, dictated a present course of action—*Flee, boy!*

But as he took a step forward, something constrained him: his cursed pride, chiding his cowardice. A bitter debate ensued between his reason and his pride—like inexorable politicians on the floor—and the despot attending his mind kept watch over the proceedings, pointing out the merits and failings of both arguments. It degenerated quickly into an all-out cat-and-dog fight, and Worm took off in a dead run.

Stricken by conscience or duty or some rampant lunacy—Worm had no idea which—the boy returned reluctantly to his lonely vigil. The sun fled below the jagged horizon, and objects that appeared farther away in the daylight gradually closed in on him with each deserting shade of light, like approaching armies of colorless, vague, phantom shapes. Soon his silent patrols encompassed smaller and smaller circles, as the waxing darkness slowly drove him across the field to the point where he now was, sitting rigid with his back pressed hard against the trunk of a scrub oak, sword and shield both at the ready, and the lead sheep lying at his side. With each anxious breath he cursed his pride, cursed the dead sheep, cursed the dead shepherd.

The night was a demonstration of voices, and Worm started at every sound. His imagination raged wild with horrible thoughts. Thoughts of demon wolves with yellow eyes and teeth dripping blood from fresh kills, stalking him from every corner of the black field. Thoughts of Pictish warriors—their painted bodies covered from head to toe with ghouls and macabre designs—lurking in the shadows, poised at any moment to attack him.

He had heard since childhood of the gruesome tortures they inflicted upon their captives, the cruel atrocities rendered, and now imagined himself the beneficiary of each one. But as these thoughts became too repulsive to contemplate, they were quickly surrendered to others, thoughts of boarhounds and Saxon horsemen and, again, the wolves.

The wolves.

His eyes traced anxious figure eights against the umbrage, keeping furtive shades at bay. He was sure that at any moment yellow-eyed wolves would leap out of the black wall and tear him limb from limb. Frogs croaked angry little boomings, growing more tympanic with every volley. Crickets raked a grating chorus. Nature opposed him in terrible symphony.

Something black—wraithlike—winged swiftly overhead, startling the boy. He looked, but the jet sky had swallowed its form. He cursed birds. Hated them. The little voices had returned, this time finding a captive ear in his mind, threading a web of fearful images, enshrouding him in fear, trammeling him in weakness.

Suddenly Worm's head jerked upward. He strained his eyes into the darkness, sure that he had just seen something move out in the meadow. Was it a night bird? A wolf? Or maybe it was just a bush swaying in the vagrant night breezes.

His eyes worked independently of his reason, playing tricks, mocking his perception of reality. And the once-little voices in his mind no longer spoke in hushed whispers. They cackled, chortled wickedly, pointed his mind at every conceivable horror.

There it is again! Something did move. He saw it for certain that time. He caught the movement in his peripheral vision. But when he looked directly at the shape, it stopped moving, and the image blurred and disappeared. And then a thought as dreadful as he ever imagined struck him, sending a legion of shudders along his spine.

The dead wolves.

He had been careful to circle wide of them during his earlier patrols to avoid looking at their twisted forms, for in Terryll's absence the beasts had taken on the most savage expressions. Their yellow eyes watched him coldly as he walked by, waiting. Why? *They weren't dead!*

Wasn't it true that Terryll had examined only one of their bodies closely? The others were certainly just lying in wait—playing the possum—until the cover of darkness fell. After all, where had the wolf that attacked them come from? They weren't dead!

And then an even more horrible thought shot into his mind. Perhaps they really were demon wolves, such as Terryll alluded to earlier, and death had no power over their bodies. Perhaps during the falling of night they had all come back to life, possessed and empowered by some savage fiend that killed not for meat but for pleasure. Worm's mind was stricken with chilling terror.

The wolves are alive!

They were closing in even now for the kill. The black forms no longer scurried into the shadows as he gazed at them. They came under full scrutiny. He could clearly see four or five . . . no, six . . . black shapes stalking him slowly, with cold, merciless eyes—yellow, feral eyes—fixed on his position. The voices in his head were screaming.

Worm staggered to his feet. His knees trembled like rattling winter twigs. His heart pounded in his chest. Somehow he remembered his battle stance. *Balance! Balance! Balance!* the cadence echoed. He would at least give them a good fight. He would defend his post to the end, even if it meant a certain and horrible death.

He found Aurelius's contradictory image in his mind, pacing side to side with him in his brown birrus and tonsure, calling out the drill, and for a moment he was emboldened by it. Then one of the nearing black forms made a most heinous, staccato, guttural sound that made his blood run cold, chasing the Roman monk away.

The sound was strange, though. Something about it struggled to be heard above the clamor in his mind. And when another of the black creatures bellowed a reply, the voices in his head were silenced.

"Sheep!" He exhaled with nervous relief, not knowing for a moment whether to laugh or cry. "They're only sheep!"

He laughed aloud as the small flock of animals, bleating out sheepish salutations, closed in around the lead sheep lying at his feet. One nuzzled his boots. After a few sniffs, it began nibbling at the hem of his woolen trouser leg, then grabbed it with its mouth and tugged as though it were something to eat or play with. It put a humor in the boy, who struggled to keep his balance, for the tenacious lamb, like some small puppy playing tug of war with a towel, nearly jerked his leg out from under him.

"Some vicious beast," he said aloud, rebuking his fear.

During the next quarter hour a few other sheep straggled into the fold and bedded down for the night, welcomed in turn by the others. From what the boy could tell, they didn't seem perturbed, at least not outwardly, that just two hours earlier most of their flock-mates had been brutally slaughtered.

Worm marveled at the thought and concluded that sheep were either very brave or very stupid.

Soon they were apparently all in and gathered around his feet, rounding off the day with sheep chatter. Looking around him, Worm realized, much to his astonishment, that he had unwittingly and by default become their surrogate shepherd. He decided then and there that sheep must be stupid.

The storm that had threatened earlier in the afternoon skirted the area and moved its front toward the villages of Brough, Greta Bridge, and points east. Trailing its intimidation were dark, broken clouds scudding harmlessly overhead, opening and closing intermittent areas of star field for the moon to shine through. This produced a blinking effect of light and darkness upon the terrain, as though a candle were being lit, then extinguished, incessantly due to some cosmic boredom.

During each of the moonlit periods, Worm was careful to scan the area for wolves. But all too soon a thatch of clouds would sweep away the light, leaving the boy and his environs wondering in darkness. Even so, he started to feel better about things, knowing that it wouldn't be too much longer before Terryll and his father showed up to relieve him of his grisly duty. Pleasant visions of Dagmere returned, sweeping murky webs from his mind.

Feeling more at ease, Worm sat down in the midst of the sheep, many of whom had fallen asleep in a careless palisade. The lead sheep nuzzled next to him and placed its head on his lap. It looked up at him with dark, soulful eyes that seemed to be searching his face for answers.

Worm stroked its head gently and pondered how just this morning he had seen this sheep for the first time. He marveled at the thought, for it seemed a year ago. Two or three other sheep lay close beside him, and it wasn't long before he was surrounded by a buttress of wool, which broke the chill of the night air. Worm relaxed his grip on sword and shield, and his mind was soon visited by more pleasant recollections of the day's events.

He thought about his visit to St. John's and chuckled when he rehearsed in his mind Brother Lupe's infectious laugh, which even now worked as a quiet medicine on the boy's temper and fears. How could anyone find the heart to laugh at such ordinary turns of life as he did? Worm smiled and shook his head and wondered if the jovial friar ever managed to finish his digging.

And then Aurelius.

The centurion monk filled his thoughts for some time—his austere but kind features and broad smile commanding respect, yet disarming fear; who, with the same powerful hand, could wield sword and pen with equal dexterity. He was an enigma to the boy. Worm's thoughts touched on the sword drills, recounting each of the lessons briefly: *to the left . . . forward . . . to the right . . . backward.*

Then he shifted to the parchments. He visualized the beautiful scenes that were painted around the borders and the words that were written with a delicate cursive hand, flowing line upon line to form the center text.

But that was a bittersweet thought. For even though the words on the pages were wondrous to look at, it saddened him that he didn't know how to read what they said—or what Homer and Virgil or any of the other books that Terryll and Dagmere read at home had to say, for that matter. He sighed at the thought, suddenly feeling very stupid.

The thought lifted the boy's head to gaze at the starry show in the heavens. Quite unexpectedly, Worm was filled with awe. He had looked at the stars countless times as he lay upon his mat in Glenryth, entertaining refined fantasies. But never before tonight had he ever really seen them. There were millions of them, hanging low in the jet sky, like sparkling jewels hurled across a blanket of shimmering velvet. He wondered, if he were on a tall mountain, whether or not he could touch them.

Worm took a deep breath to cleanse his mind of the day's events and exhaled the cool, late summer air. He felt alive, excited, as though a part of his body had been lit by a candle that had lain in darkness until this day, this moment. It was odd that he would feel so, being surrounded by such a cruel field of . . .

. . . death.

The thought of it rushed into his mind like a winter storm, bringing with it a downpour of questions. What was it? What did it feel like? What was after it? Anything, or nothing? If nothing, then why was he so afraid of it? If something, then why was he still so afraid of it? He had come close to death twice now in as many months, leading him to wonder if death were pursuing him. If it was, was there any way to fight it?

The boy had never considered the subject at any length before, for there had always been ready distractions to entertain his mind. But here, alone, in such a place, the distractions were now cloaked under a cover of utter blackness. He tried to focus on pleasantries, again the face of Dagmere, her pretty smile, the rich auburn fullness of her hair, but the thoughts of his own mortality were not to be upstaged by mortal beauty. He sought another course.

Terryll's words about a God who knew all things came to mind, a God who sovereignly orchestrated the affairs of nations, of men's lives, great and small. If his words were true, what a powerful yet wondrous God He would be: unsearchable, unknowable, certainly unapproachable. Worm was stricken with a profound uneasiness that this God was watching him even now from the canopy of darkness, scrutinizing him with a gaze of unendurable light. He immediately lowered his eyes from the stars, for it seemed to him that they too were in concert with the omnipresent Witness.

Presently he felt alone—terribly isolated—as though he were the only living being in a hostile universe, and a pervading sense of dread chilled him to his marrow. Dread not of death anymore (nothing so temporal as death), but dread of a God who was waiting just beyond the canopy, into whose terrible hands he would fall once death had found him. It was a terrifying revelation. Such a God was an awesome terror indeed.

He shuddered at the thought.

Worm looked down at the sheep lying around him to comfort his mind. Sheep were amazingly comforting animals to observe. Watching them sleep made him wonder if animals ever gave thought to such notions as gods or death—or life, for that matter. It seemed to him that they cared only for eating and sleeping and following their shepherd around without question. Maybe that was enough. Worm took a deep breath and blew it out hard.

Thoughts of the old shepherd lying dead just a few yards behind him in the bushes sneaked into his head and reopened the debate in his mind. Had the old man somehow offended the Christian God and paid for it with his life? It was hard for Worm to imagine such a thing. Just this morning the man was full of life and cheer, leading his sheep merrily along the road. Could such a God find fault in this?

Worm tried to recall what the man's face had looked like but couldn't. Several times he made the effort, but each time his mind drew a blank. It was frustrating. And then he remembered that when the old man passed by, he had been looking down at the road and never saw his face—just the lead sheep.

The realization shocked him. He wished now that he had returned his greeting and was struck hard by the reality, the grim truth, that the opportunity was forever lost. The more he thought about it, the more the loss weighed upon him, and it wasn't long before he was heartsick with remorse.

It had been a long and arduous day, one that had spent the boy's reserves. Slowly, a confluence of emotions, thoughts, and fatigue met within his breast, threatening the banks with its swell. And though the boy tried to contain the surge, it was surely, and mercifully, a losing battle. Worm buried his head in his arms and cried, whimpering softly at first, followed by weeping gasps. His body released its pent anguish. The deep was torn asunder.

The lead sheep, sensing the boy's woe, nuzzled its head further onto his lap as if to bring him comfort. It did.

Then, after a time, Worm raised his head and peeked in bewildered gaze at the stars, thinking that however terrible this God of the Christians might be, He had surely made a beautiful covering over the earth. In fact, it was glorious. Worm didn't understand why, but he was overcome with a mixture of joy and sorrow, so much so that he couldn't contain his feelings, and he wept again.

A cool breeze swept over the valley and splashed across the boy's face, removing the lines of grief from his brow and drying his cheeks. It lifted his spirit for a time, but soon his swollen eyes became too much of a burden to keep open, and Worm thought to close them for just a moment or two . . .

It was in the place between waking and sleeping that he heard them.

Worm opened his eyes with a jolt of adrenaline. At first it was a solitary wolf, baying at the moon in the distance to the west. The sheep were all awake, huddled in silence, stricken with abject terror. Even the frogs and crickets had quit their music. Worm stared at the tree line—a black, wicked-looking scar tearing across the horizon, separating earth from the night sky, also black—and shook his head to clear his senses.

Soon another wolf answered, this time not so far away and behind them to the east. Worm spun his head around to spot the direction. He got to his feet slowly, anxiously, raising his shield and sword to the ready, his right hand flexing nervously on his sword handle. Wolves!

195

The moon shone brightly over the little valley for a moment, illuminating the carcasses across the road before another mass of clouds enshrouded the night-scape in darkness. He looked south along the road to Killwyn Eden, hoping against hope to see men coming, a little line of comforting lights. Seeing nothing, he cursed.

Another howl echoed across the valley from the north. The wolves were all around him.

His body tensed involuntarily. His breath was labored, coming in shallow spadefuls now. *This is it,* he thought. *There is no mistaking these for sheep.* The clouds parted briefly, opening a flood of light upon the field. There was no movement that he could see—not yet. Then off to his right, a twig snapped. It wasn't loud, just enough to be heard. Had it not been for a soft current of wind blowing from the direction of the noise, he would have missed it. The boy spun around to see, but his field of vision was obstructed by clumps of bushes and scrub trees.

He could see nothing, but he heard it again. A crush of leaves, closer. Whatever was out there was definitely moving toward him. Then the first wolf cried out a long steady wail, trailing off with a series of staccato yelps. The sound of it was nearer than before, much nearer. The second and third wolves answered in concert, also nearer. The wolves were all around him and closing in. Courage fled from the boy like cowards from the skirmish line in twos and threes.

In a panic, Worm looked down the road for the men, and for just a moment he was again tempted to bolt. But his legs refused his mind, thus sentencing him to die on the spot. His mind envisioned the rush of wolves, their yellow eyes glowing in the dark as they pounced along savage arcs, their fangs ripping his body to bloody pieces. For pleasure. Only for pleasure. Another twig snapped.

Spinning to look, the boy caught movement through the trees. His pulse raced, his palms moistened with horror, his temples drummed the cadence of cowards, the retreat—*Flee, boy!* Courage fled en masse; it was a total rout of soul.

He could see it now, a black shape, wraithlike, moving slowly through the trees toward him. It was no sheep. But the passing of clouds overhead quickly robbed him of light, and Worm found himself facing death in blindness. His mind screamed terror at him. *Run, boy! Run, boy!*

Worm readied his stance, crouching low and shifting his weight to the balls of his feet. Numbing, paralyzing coldness shogged through his veins. He moved slowly from side to side with supreme effort, tensely, mumbling nervously to himself a pathetic catechism. He could now hear the animal scrunching the grass beneath its feet from twenty-five . . . now twenty . . . now fifteen feet away . . . now . . . And then it stopped.

196

It stopped! Worm peered into the darkness at the thing. A lump filled his throat, choking his breath as he gasped for air. He could now barely make out the shape of a silhouette even blacker than the night, one that appeared to be sitting—monstrous in size—and staring at him from less than ten feet away.

"Come and get me, wolf!" the boy rasped.

The clouds parted with a grand flourish, flooding the fields and forests with brilliant moonlight, revealing the gigantic form of Hauwka, sitting back on his haunches and looking down at the boy.

Worm reeled in horror. He screamed, then stumbled backward over a sheep and landed on the ground with a jolt.

He looked up at the bear, wide-eyed. He scrambled backward crablike over several other sheep, creating a mild uproar of bleating as they scattered, while the boy tried in vain to regain his footing. Again he fell to the ground in a graceless heap, terrified.

The sheep seemed not alarmed by the bear; they were only concerned that the boy might step on them, or worse. It was their good fortune that none were hurt by his flailing sword or shield. Most gave themselves a zone of safety and stood looking down at him. One or two bleated out their annoyance, then moved to safer places. The others followed, each bleating its contempt—all but the lead sheep, who remained faithfully at his side, however dangerous such devotion might be.

The boy looked up at the bear, round-eyed, eyeing it warily, and clambered to his feet. He brandished his sword. "You just stay where you are, bear—stay!" he threatened. "I don't care if you *are* Terryll's pet. You're not mine. Now stay." It was as though he were talking to a puppy, a rather large puppy with big teeth.

Hauwka just looked at him. His eyes twinkled with a keen intensity. Then he lifted his snout and sniffed.

Suddenly a wolf howled in the distance, distracting Worm. It was the one to the west, across the field of dead sheep.

Without warning Hauwka stood up on his hind legs and let out a terrifying roar.

Worm jumped backward, astonished. He had never heard anything so deafening or fierce. It was like the roar of a hundred furnaces, and the power of it took his breath away. He was sure that if the bear chose to kill him, all it would have to do was roar like that in his face, and he would fall over dead.

Again Hauwka sniffed the air, then lowered himself to his haunches, still gazing across the road at the tree line. The fur along his nape bristled. He snorted several times.

The air became still, and the frogs and crickets gradually resumed their furious orchestrations.

The bear continued to gaze across the road at the field of slaughter. The moon played a little dance on his eyes.

To the boy it seemed as though Hauwka's mind was pondering matters far removed from this setting, matters concerning the universe of bears. It made him feel uncomfortable, out of place, like an intruder. Finding an uneasy footing, Worm positioned himself in front of the scrub oak again, shield and sword at the ready, and watched the bear, waiting for its next move.

Hauwka's side suddenly flinched as if something had bitten into it. The bear looked over at the boy. He hadn't moved his head to do so, just his eyes. As ferocious as the bear appeared by his enormous size, there was a tenderness in his eyes that engendered trust. But Worm was not quick to trust.

Hauwka shifted his eyes back to the field, his ears twitching, the snout rising every so often to the wind.

Worm studied him warily.

The bear sat motionless, like some large boulder, staring across the field of dead sheep like a sentinel.

What is he looking for? the boy wondered. *The wolves, of course,* his mind quickly answered. *Then why doesn't he leave me alone? Go chase the wolves somewhere else?* And then it struck him. *He's standing guard over me.*

I think.

Hauwka's side flinched again. This time, however, the flinch was more of a shudder that rippled along his flank from one end to the other. In a flash the bear buried his snout into his thick fur and chiseled at the unseen assailant with his teeth, growling and snorting at the thing through the sides of his mouth. The bear paused, waiting, then dove into his hide once more with greater ferocity and snorts.

Worm scratched his head as he watched the proceedings, still unable to put it together. This huge bear that had saved him from the jaws of the boarhounds, had chased off a pack of killer wolves, again saving his life, was now standing watch over him. Why? It was a strange bear. But then again, what did he know about bears? For all he knew, all bears were exactly like this one. But something was beginning to kindle in the boy's heart, a tiny glimmer of warmth, of affection perhaps, breaking down the primal distrust, the fear. He waited until the bear was satisfied with his flea kill.

The bear blew a snort into his fur, paused again, scrutinizing the spot, licked it tenderly, then looked directly at the boy as if nothing had happened. He let out a moaning bawl, and strangely it caused Worm to chuckle. It just bubbled out of his throat before he could stop it. *Maybe he isn't such a bad bear after all,* he thought. *He hasn't tried to eat me. Just let him keep his distance, though.* But no sooner did he think that than the bear shuddered to his feet and began to plod toward him.

Worm was terror-struck. The primal fears rushed his mind again. *This is it!*

"Stay, bear!" he commanded again. Brandishing his sword, he repeated, "Stay, bear . . . you just stay where you are! Do you hear me? Stay . . . stay . . ."

But the bear kept coming. Backing up, Worm hit the scrub oak with a terrible jolt and, jerking his head around desperately for an escape, saw that there was nowhere for him to run. Even the lead sheep had wandered away from his side, joining the others. And as the bear drew in front of him, looming over him now like a black wall, his body tensed, and he held his head to one side, cringing, his eyes clenched shut, as he waited for the dreaded snap of the fangs.

What he felt, however, was like nothing he could have imagined. As the hot, fang-ensheathed snout angled toward his neck, a sudden wet slap of coarse flesh dragging up the side of his cheek nearly took the skin off his face. The sensation was horrible. *Oh, mercy!* he thought. *It's going to lick me to death!* But then he felt the bear move away. The warmth of its terrific bulk withdrew, and the cool air settled quickly over his wet cheek. Chancing a look, he peered about and found the bear sitting on its haunches a few feet away, gazing down at him as a puppy might if it were as big as a haystack. It seemed there was a thin smile along its snout.

Worm felt the terror leaving his body like a living thing, sliding off him, uncoiling the tenseness in his limbs, and becoming something altogether new. He took a deep breath and, letting it go, felt more at ease.

Hauwka let out another bawl, a sustained cry that Worm knew at once contained no ill will. How he knew this, he didn't know, but he knew, and there was a profound shift in his thinking.

This was a friendly bear, his mind reasoned, a bear that had taken to him like a stray dog, one that just wanted to be his friend. Worm looked full-face at the creature, and the flicker of warmth that had kindled earlier in his heart suddenly roared into a great blaze, consuming his fear. A fierce light beamed through his eyes and fastened on those of the bear, and the light from each entwined in a millionth of a second, knitting a bond between them. A love between man and beast was born.

"Hey, big fella," Worm said, putting down his sword and shield. Then taking a tentative step forward, and then another, he stretched forth a timorous hand, saying, "That's it, that's a boy."

Hauwka let out a snort, and Worm jumped back.

"Hey, hey," the boy said, gulping down his heart. "What you want scare me like that for?" He took another halting step forward. "You aren't going to eat me, are you?" he said calmly. And reaching the bear, he stretched his hand and brushed the fur lightly. "No . . . 'course not. That's a boy, easy now." Then gaining confidence he raked his fingers through the thick fur, rustling it affectionately. "You just want to be my friend, don't you?"

Hauwka let out a little contented moan.

"Sure you do."

The bear was looking down at him out of the corner of his eye, the white showing big, when his flank shuddered again.

The boy saw and moved his fingers to the spot. He began to rake harder. "You got another flea, big fella?" he asked. "I'll get him."

A groan escaped the bear's mouth, and hiking up his front left paw, he twisted his flank as though to direct the boy's fingers to the exact spot. His hind leg began to fan the air furiously like a hound's, obeying some phantom command. Suddenly he threw his massive head back and let out a terrific moan of ecstasy.

The boy scratched still harder. "Is that it? Did I get the flea?" he asked, digging his fingers into the fur, his elbows crooked up and kneading it with all his strength. He felt the thick hide quiver beneath his fingertips.

Several loud moans rattled about in the bear's throat, some furious snorts blew out his nose, fluttering under the loose lips and over the teeth, and in time the hind leg slowed and lowered to the ground. He shook his mane violently like a wet dog, making a tremendous noise, then grew still. There was peace again in the universe.

Looking back at the boy, he leaned over and licked his head, swiping a lock of hair over his face.

"Hey! What're you doing?" Worm laughed. "I don't have any fleas." Then, combing his hair out of his eyes, he scratched the back of his head and chuckled. "Well, maybe now I do."

The bear let out a happy bawl.

Worm looked up at him and was overwhelmed with such emotion that he threw his arms around the bear's great neck and squeezed him.

Over the next hour Worm paced happily back and forth over the road, the rightness of his cause again beating nobly in his breast. Hauwka plodded heavily alongside him. His massive head swung to the heartened tempo. Occasionally he would let out a terrific snort, startling the boy. And every so often Worm would look over at him, and he would swear the bear was smiling. But then again with the bear it was hard to tell. He might have the same expression on his face just before he was about to eat something.

For a while the sheep had followed dutifully behind, bleating out their little cares to one another, until they finally gave it up when they saw no good purpose to the exercise. Now they lay in woolen clumps along one side of the road, watching the silly boy and bear march back and forth, going nowhere. And the moon blinked on and off behind the scudding black clouds, and the frogs boomed merrily from their dewy perches.

Presently Hauwka froze. Rising up onto his hind legs, he sniffed.

Following his eyes, Worm looked down the road leading to Killwyn Eden. "What is it, boy?"

The bear lowered himself onto all fours, then turned and walked a few paces away. Hesitating, he stopped and cast an appraising look at the boy and bawled sadly.

"Where are you going?" Worm smiled, not understanding.

The bear peered down the road. Then, letting out another moan, he loped away to the edge of the trees. There he paused and gazed back across the field at the boy.

"Hey! Where're you going? Hey!" Worm yelled. "You're not leaving, are you?"

The boy ran after him a few yards but stopped when he caught sight of torches flickering through the trees in the distance. For a few moments he stared at the lights. His shoulders slumped with the realization that the vigil was over. Looking back and forth between the bear and the approaching lights, he sighed heavily. He should feel elated, he knew, but he didn't. He didn't know how he felt.

And then the clouds swept over the moon. For a few moments everything was dark, blinding the boy, but as they moved away, the light streamed silvery again over the fields. The bear was gone.

"Hauwka?" Worm called out as the panic of loss seized his mind. He ran after the bear several yards and called out again. "Hauwka, come back!" Anxious lines troubled his features as he ran several more yards, then he drew up sharply and cried out with full impassioned voice, "You are my friend!"

He waited a moment, straining his ears to the darkness, listening for the happy bawl. But there was nothing. A little breeze picked up and swirled into the tree boughs overhead, then whisked away, leaving a lonely quiet.

A great sadness fell over Worm's countenance, and he stood there in a despondent trance, marveling that he could be drawn to the giant animal who had once so terrorized him, marveling that he could now think of no greater joy than to run after this terror and embrace him with all his strength. A tear trickled down his face. Worm shook his head sadly.

Then, glancing back once or twice, he walked over to his post in front of the scrub oaks, got into his battle stance, and waited for his relief. He wiped his nose with his sleeve, sniffed, and then cleared his eyes.

They should arrive in a few minutes, he thought finally, and his mind turned introspective.

Through all the darknesses of his soul—the imprecating oratories of doubt and fear and shame—he had found in them a glimmer of light, of hope. He had stood his watch faithfully. He had not run. To know that he was not a coward was a thing of great worth. His soul rejoiced in a quiet anthem much sweeter than the adulations of any crowd.

But even so and strangely, it was not enough. A profound sorrow came over him. For looking into his barren soul, he was reminded of the terrible dread, the aching aloneness, the shuddering terror of God that caused him to withdraw his gaze from the heavens. He knew that he could never be truly happy until he came to terms with that.

He glanced heavenward, and another sigh winged off his lips.

"Aeryck!"

Worm jerked his head toward the road.

It was Terryll. He could see the haunting glow from several torches ascending over the little hill like a solemn procession, marching in broken cadence to the drummings of frogs and crickets. There was a murmur of men's voices, low and reverent. And the stars joined them in the requiem.

"I'm over here!" Worm returned.

"Are you all right?" echoed Terryll's voice across the valley.

"I'm fine! Just fine."

Worm looked down at his sword, the tip of which was dug slightly into the dirt. Immediately he jerked it up, remembering Terryll's chiding jest that morning. *Can't have the men relieving me like that,* he thought.

Then he felt something nuzzling his thigh, and it gave him quite a start. It was the lead sheep. He freed his sword arm and patted the animal on its woolly head and smiled.

"What do you say we find that bell of yours," he said. "I don't think I like you sneaking up on me like this."

The sheep looked up at him and bleated softly.

17
THE SEDUCTION
OF BRITAIN

That same night in a place many miles to the southeast, the storm that had skirted the area where Worm stood his vigil was now dumping a torrent of water on the bent shapes of miserable men. Thousands of British and Saxon campfires lit up the hillsides along the banks of the Thames Estuary, then extended westward along the meandering course of the River Thames. So bright were the myriad blazes that the very clouds seemed laden with fire.

From a distance it appeared as though the hellish sky were raining, hurling, billions of tiny firebrands upon the tortured landscape, and gave to those who could witness it a portent of the apocalypse.

Londinium itself—a small island in the midst of the terrible conflagration—appeared to be writhing in torment and crying out to the heavens for mercy. The collective moanings of war ascended plaintively upon the smoke.

It was a scene typical of war, one that had been drawn out into ten long years of killing. Miserable shapes huddled around spattered campfires, bent in abject attitudes. Each soul was wearied and disillusioned and clamoring for warmth in the chilling rain with muttering, cursing exchanges.

These tragic warriors, who at one time were fueled by a raging fire in their bellies—stoked by the glorious idealism of youth—now wore the singular expressions of despair, now were reduced by time and death and hunger to grumbling masses. Each soul craved nothing more of glory now but to return to his farm and family and once-loves and, with such, be content to live out his years in quiet solitude.

It seemed that they were a deceived bunch. The war had ebbed and flowed with victories to both armies, promising to each the surety of ultimate triumph yet giving naught to either but endless death and frustration. And now the splendor of the great war engine was grinding down at last into a bitter stalemate.

Inside the bedchamber of his hill fort, a man in his mid-fifties jabbed a poker into the hearth, separating the burning logs to give them air. He wasn't doing it with any force of will. It was clear that other matters weighed more heavily on his mind. It had been a wearisome campaign, and the weight of it had carved deep lines of anguish across his brow. He knew that his only hope for triumph lay in his knowledge that the Saxons would soon run out of supplies, perhaps as early as spring, for without the ability to resupply an army, the best and noblest strategies of generals are quickly devoured by the voracious appetites of war.

Because the Britons controlled the major ports on the island, the king was able to establish effective blockades and keep much needed reinforcements and supplies from reaching Hengist and Horsa. Time was on his side, if his army didn't collapse first from tribal bickering and disunity.

And collapse it surely would have had it not been for the leadership of Vortimer, whose bravery on the field, and comradery with the soldiers off, kept the British army from falling apart. But, alas, that valiant warrior had been felled in battle two months past by a Saxon arrow, leaving a festering void in the heart of the army and in the heart of the man now carelessly stoking the fire in his hill-fort bedchamber. This one mourned his loss to the point of despair; Vortimer had been his only son.

King Vortigern sighed heavily. He desperately wanted peace. The sealed letter he had just received from a Saxon envoy promised him such. But the news was either too good to be true or a devilish trap, and he lacked the discernment to know which of the two it was.

"Is it good news, my husband?" Rowena asked. She sat in front of a round table mirror, turning her head to one side as she brushed out her long, golden tresses. The burnished image in the mirror made an appraising sweep of her features.

"Your father is calling for a truce," he said. A wan smile curled across his lips. "He wants to sue for peace."

"That sounds like wonderful news!" she said, still brushing her hair. "Is there something wrong?"

"I'm not certain."

The man, gray-haired and haggard, looked over at his wife, easily thirty years his younger, and sighed. She was beautiful—in fact, ravishing. He knew without question that she could easily claim the heart of many a young and handsome lover. But as far as Vortigern could tell, her virtue was beyond reproach. He loved her desperately and would do anything to hold onto that love. She was all he had now that his son was gone.

She had been a gift from her father, Hengist, to seal an alliance between the two powers. But when the alliance failed and war broke out,

Rowena, though a Saxon, remained faithful to her husband and stayed by his side. Vortigern had often wondered why. This was one of those times.

"What is it that troubles you?" she asked.

"I don't know. It's just hard to believe that what I have hoped for for so long has finally arrived. If only my son were alive to see this day."

Vortigern looked back into the fireplace and tapped against one of the logs with the poker. A flurry of red-hot cinders shot from the logs, blasted upward by escaping gases that crackled and popped when ignited. They floated above the flames for a moment before the draft sucked them up the flue into the chimney. "Is it really possible?" he thought aloud.

Rowena placed her brush on the table and turned to her husband. "Only if you make it so, my love. I am sure that your chieftains and warriors would welcome such news."

"Yes, I'm sure they would," he said, laying the poker aside. He paced out into the middle of the bedroom, brooding over the matter, with one hand stroking his beard and the other behind his back.

"Then why so glum?"

Still pulling on his beard, Vortigern started to answer. "I just don't know if—" But he stopped mid sentence and let out a deep sigh. He didn't pick it up again.

Rowena stood and walked toward the fireplace. "You just don't know if . . . what?"

Vortigern stopped his pacing and watched his wife gliding across the flagstones in her bare feet. She was wearing a diaphanous silk night-gown—one imported from Persia—and as she halted in front of the glowing fire, the man could see her wondrous shape silhouetted through it.

"If . . . what?" he asked, not sure what she meant. He was distracted by her beauty.

She turned to him and smiled. "You were saying that you just didn't know if . . . then you stopped. What were you going to say, my love?"

"Oh!" He remembered. "I just don't know if I can trust your father."

Rowena's countenance suddenly fell, and she looked into the fire. It seemed that Vortigern's words had wounded her.

"What is wrong?" he asked. "Have I said something to hurt you?"

"You trust *me*, don't you?"

"Of course I do!"

Vortigern walked over to his wife's side and put his arms around her waist. Just as he did so, a tear rolled down the side of her cheek. He chided himself at the sight of it.

"You know that I would die for you, my love."

Rowena shouldered her back to him, still seemingly bruised from his words. "He is my father. He wouldn't do anything that would hurt me. I know that he wants to end this war as much as you do, so that he and I can visit one another in peace."

"You are his daughter, Rowena. Of course he wants what is best for you."

"Then you must believe that he is sincere with his offer." She turned toward him slightly, allowing the light from the fire to catch her profile. "I am your wife. My father knows that in order to make me happy, he must end this war, so that you and I . . . and our child . . . may live in peace."

Vortigern was stunned. "You are with child?" Incredulous, he grabbed her shoulders and eased her around to face him. "Is it true?"

"We shall know in another week," she replied, smiling up into his eyes.

"This is wonderful news!"

"Yes. And to have it born in peace would make it even more so. It would be our . . . our peace child!"

Vortigern stood back and threw both his arms on the mantle of the fireplace, flabbergasted, shaking his head. For several moments he gazed into the flames deep in thought. The flickering glow upon his face seemed to purge away the years of misery, of anguish, of death. In such fiery baptism he was becoming a new man; a thing once dead inside him was stirring.

"A son!" he finally said, nodding his head incredulously. "It would be good to raise him without war pressing in from all sides. Such a child would certainly secure a peace between us."

"What if it's . . . a girl?" Rowena teased.

"Would God take from me a son and return to me a daughter?" Then after giving it some thought, he laughed uproariously and threw his hands into the air in surrender. "If it is His will, then so be it!"

"Then you will accept the truce?"

The man picked up a log and tossed it on the fire with a new arrogance, a rekindled mannishness. "Only on my terms."

"Good!" Rowena agreed. "But if I were you, I would insist that my father meet with you and your leaders in a place of your choosing to discuss them."

Vortigern looked over at his wife, puzzled. "What is wrong with meeting here?"

"This place smells with the blood of war!" she said contemptuously. "I am sick of it! Can such a peace be born in this bed of violence?"

"But where else?"

"Where else? Hmm." It was a pleasant challenge. Rowena walked a few paces from her husband and began moving in easy little circles as she gave the matter some thought, twirling golden strands of hair with her finger. She felt Vortigern's ardent gaze, and she moved in a little feminine glory.

"I know!" she said, brightening. "How about—" But then she caught herself. It was as if she had suddenly realized the enormous import of her thoughts. Immediately she looked over at her husband, wide-eyed. "Oh, Vortigern! This *must* be from the gods!" She ran over and embraced him. "Our child will be born in the spring—just before the vernal equinox!"

Vortigern did some quick calculations, not sure why just yet, then nodded. "Yes . . . if you're as far along as you think. But what does—"

"Don't you see?" Her face was glowing radiantly. "The gods have given us this child to bring peace between our people! Suddenly it is so clear to me!"

"Yes . . . it would seem so," he said, trying to fit the pieces together. "But how?"

"What if we held a great love feast between our peoples at Stonehenge in honor of the spring goddess, Eostre?"

"*Stonehenge?* But that's eighty miles from here."

"Exactly! Eighty miles away from the stench of both armies." Rowena stood on tiptoe and wrapped her arms around his neck. "Don't you think that to have such a feast here would be an insult to her?"

"But my people worship the Christian God," Vortigern suddenly remembered. "I don't think they would go along with—"

"Oh, rubbish," Rowena chided affectionately. "You've said yourself that the Christians are always embroiled in petty disputes over one thing or another. This would bring them together. And besides, don't Christians celebrate the supposed resurrection of their god during the vernal equinox?"

"Yes, but—"

"Then this is perfect! What better place than Stonehenge? What better time to honor both gods? It would bring our peoples together. Don't you see, my husband?" But before he could answer, she kissed him several times around his lips, then once long and passionately. Pulling her lips away from his, she added, "Your Christian god will smile upon such a feast, and Eostre will smile upon such a feast. And both of them upon—" she paused and smiled "—our *son.*"

Vortigern looked down into her large hazel eyes, sparkling like jewels in the light of the fire, and he kissed her. It would be good to leave this miserable place for a time, he thought, before kissing her again, and again. And soon, as the man took in a long draught of her sensual beauty, every thought of the war and its misery clouded over in his mind.

"To the gods!" he said, finally releasing her.

"We will go to Stonehenge?" she asked in a feline whisper.

"To Stonehenge!"

The trap was set.

18
THE END OF SUMMER AND HORSES

The men of Killwyn Eden gave the old shepherd a Christian burial and marked the place where he lay with a little white stone that simply read:

LAIRN—THE SHEPHERD

He had no kith or kin to speak of. But, even so, he was mourned as one deeply loved, for upon his lips had ever been the kind word in season to lift the flagging heart, and in his eyes there was always a generous display. Some thought him to be an angel and grieved appropriately.

Word of his death and the manner of it quickly spread throughout the villages of the Brigantes like fire before the wind. There was a collective gasp of horror as the northlanders regarded the news, and a collective wariness that set in as the news made its way in epidemic sweeps.

However, the slaughter of Lairn and his sheep was not an isolated incident. Soon reports of wolf attacks and sightings filtered into Killwyn Eden from neighboring villages. Most of the attacks were upon livestock, but there were a few incidents involving people.

At Brough, just ten miles east of Killwyn Eden, a woman in her mid-thirties was killed on the outskirts of town. It was reported that there were six wolves in the pack, and that it took at least as many men from the village to drive them off with pikes and arrows.

Then at Bowes, a farmer, his wife, and their three children were killed while stacking shocks of grain in the field adjacent to their cottage. In this case, there were no witnesses, but it was clear from the mutilation of the bodies that the slaughter had either been caused by wild dogs or wolves.

Most of the attacks occurred at night, as would be expected, but a few—as in the two cases mentioned—occurred in the middle of day. And in every case the killings, like those of the old shepherd and sheep, had been done not out of need for food, but out of sheer wanton savagery. Nothing like it had been heard of or seen in the history of the tribe. There was some wickedness afoot, some devilry.

Several weeks had passed since the night Worm stood his vigil, and it had become his habit to visit Aurelius at least once a week—oftentimes without Terryll—to study his swordsmanship.

One day as he cheerfully made his way to St. John's he caught a glimpse of a lone wolf, white in color, shadowing him along a ridge about a hundred yards from the road. That gave him quite a start, for it was near the place where the shepherd had been killed, and the horrible image was still fresh in his mind.

The wolf kept pace with him for about three miles, staring at the boy with keen appraisal, but made no movement toward him. It seemed content with a duel of eyes.

It was a fierce duel, however, and Worm gave it no quarter. He'd had his fill of wolves and shook his sword at it occasionally, daring it to come on, to fight, to end this thing on the field of honor.

The white wolf eyed him curiously, its head lowered, its shoulders hunched in lupine attitude as it padded along the ridge with a silken gait. And then as suddenly as the wolf appeared, it moved behind a screen of trees and never reappeared. It was gone. Worm kept a cautious eye on the ridge and a firm grip on his sword until he reached the monastery.

On that particular day, however, he had come not to learn the sword but the Latin alphabet, a far more powerful weapon than any sword. For since the day when he first set foot in Brother Lucius's little hallowed room of knowledge, a desire burned within him to learn how to read and write—a belated endeavor, to be sure, but he came at it with a passion. He had put his hand to becoming a scholar.

He took lessons from Aurelius and Lupe only when he visited the monastery by himself, not wanting Terryll and, in particular, Dagmere to know that he was doing so. Both of them were well educated, as were many Romano-Britons at the time. Each of them was thoroughly versed in the Holy Scriptures and the writings of Augustine and Jerome, as well as the secular works of the Roman and Greek philosophers Cicero, Plato, and Aristotle, and the poets Homer and Virgil.

Worm was ashamed of his ignorance, and on a few occasions he stayed at the monastery for several days at a stretch to study. However, the letters came to him slower than the sword, and his lack of patience oftentimes got the better of his speech.

For the remainder of the summer Worm never saw another wolf, white or otherwise. Neither were there any more wolf sightings or attacks reported from the neighboring villages. It appeared as though whatever sickness or madness or quirk of nature had affected the wolves, it had crawled away into some hellish hibernation, sated in blood-lust, its lust for pleasure expiated for a season. And the northern tribes breathed a collective sigh of relief.

The leaves turned almost overnight with a grand flourish, setting the forests surrounding Killwyn Eden ablaze with color, marking the end of summer. The scent of autumn was an immediate thing, rushing the senses with the tart, musky, wet smell of decaying leaves. The air was livened with brisk, blustery gusts of wind.

The earth was now entering into a season of little groanings. It was slowing down, changing, adapting to the arthritic aches of the year's middle age, preparing for the coming death of winter, becoming wiser in the myriad little experiences of survival. Everywhere there was a noticeable flurry of enterprise among the woodland creatures, now aroused out of the indolence of the hot summer months: gorging, gathering, fattening up for the lean times ahead.

Autumn was Worm's favorite time of the year. It spoke to something deep within him, stirred within him profound resolutions. In it he became keenly aware of the grandeur of life and that he, though a small part in its larger scheme, was a part nonetheless. He was alive. And he reveled in the tartness of it.

Terryll's family owned several horses (mostly mares in foal), and looking after and training them was a chore that fell primarily to Dagmere.

The stables were stone based, with wattle and daub walls and a thatched roof that sagged with age, standing about fifty yards away from the villa at the bottom of a gentle, tree-studded slope. Reddish vines reached from the ground and clung tenaciously to the base and walls, giving the appearance that the earth was reclaiming the place as its own. Trees framed it with reds and yellows and browns and oranges. The stables were built to accommodate twenty horses, with individual box stalls and corrals, and included several paddocks and a round pen for exercising and lunging. The air was rife with the sweet pungency of horses.

A year earlier Allyndaar had purchased a beautiful dapple-gray stallion named Daktahr, which had in his estimation "a most perfect conformation." The stallion once belonged to an Arab sheikh, and the chieftain had paid a handsome sum of gold to a group of Celtiberian merchants for him to breed with his British mares. The mares were larger, heavier horses with gentle spirits that did equally well in front of a plow or in battle. But having substantial heads and blunted noses, thick necks and big feet, they were really too slow and somewhat ungainly in appearance.

Allyndaar hoped that he could breed a line of horses that possessed not only the easy temperament and strength of his mares but also the beauty, speed, and endurance of his Arabian stallion. The coming spring would yield the first fruits.

Worm spent considerable time in the stable area, finding chores to do. It wasn't that he was especially fond of horses or of the lowly chores attending them, but from the cover of the stables he stole wistful glances at Dagmere while she worked the horses in the adjacent field. From these shaded observatories, his mind imagined erudite conversations with her over the poets and philosophers, always envisioning her wide-eyed and attentive and marveling at his scholarly brilliance.

However, he was careful not to let her know that he was spying on her, though she knew. And of a truth, he knew she knew. But the boy couldn't help himself. The sight of her long auburn hair—her blazing, autumn hair—flowing wildly behind her as she rode bareback, holding onto nothing but their floating manes, fired the boy's spirit. But his affections were enchained in two little orbs of torture.

Throughout the summer they had played a most heinous game of "eye tag," an insidious invention designed by some cruelness in the universe to torture youths. Both Dagmere and Worm had become masters of the game wherein their eyes would meet at the dinner table, or as they passed each other in one of the hallways of the villa, "tag," then dart away, leaving them each withering in excruciating throes of embarrassment. For each knew what was in the other's mind but was too afraid to risk the first step toward breaking the terrible curse of silence. Of course, every time an opportunity passed, it became all the more difficult the next time around.

The fine speeches Worm had earlier imagined at the stream in midsummer degenerated into the tersest of salutations that died in cowardly shame ever they reached his lips. His mind became a practiced hurler of polished insults and imprecations. And so he writhed in a postpubescent madness, consumed by thoughts, feelings, and desires that raged within him like some caged and tormented demon.

Dagmere took it out on the horses.

They had become players in a little tragicomedy.

It happened one morning that, after many self-abusements, Worm finally dredged up some pebble of courage to speak with her, an act of heroism that would rival any on the battlefield.

It was driven solely by hormones. He had been carrying armfuls of firewood back and forth from the woodpile to the house. Each trip, he casually looked down to the stable area to steal a glimpse of Dagmere, who was as usual grooming the stallion before his morning exercise. With a look of impassioned determination, Worm suddenly dropped the load of wood and started toward the stables, tripping over the logs as he did so.

Dagmere had been watching him the entire time out of the corner of her eye and giggled at the sight.

At first Worm strode with the confidence of Achilles as he made his way toward the girl. But when he had reached the halfway point between them, he caught her big blue eyes peering at him from over the horse's withers, and his heart suddenly began drumming the retreat. Obediently, he cowered and veered off toward the rear of the stables.

Reading his aborted intentions, Dagmere called out to him in a little panic. "Hello, Aeryck."

"Huh? . . . Oh!" he stuttered, feigning surprise. "Hello, Dagmere. I . . . I didn't see you there." He chuckled stupidly. "I was just going into the stables to . . . er . . . feed the horses."

"Really? Didn't you already feed them this morning?" Dagmere wondered innocently. "I mean—"

The boy stopped abruptly and gestured toward the stalls. "Uh . . . yeah, but I was going to give them some oats as a treat." He turned away awkwardly, mumbled something inane, then took a few halting steps toward the stables.

"You probably know a lot about horses, don't you?" she asked, trying to keep the conversation alive. "I mean . . . I see you down here all the time watching . . . er . . . the horses."

Worm's face showed the guilt of someone caught in an unspeakable crime. "You do? . . . oh, yes! Watching the horses. Heh, heh. Everybody knows about . . . er . . . watches horses where I come . . . uh . . . from . . ." He died at this point, and his mind whipped his corpse like a slaver.

"Do you like to ride?" Dagmere asked winsomely.

"Huh?" Glorious resurrection! "Well, sure. Who doesn't? Why as a matter of fact, I was just coming down here to ride this very moment."

"I thought you were going to feed the horses some oats?" she asked, again innocently.

"Uh . . . I was going to ride first," he said, starting toward her, "then feed the horses some oats afterwards."

"Oh, I see."

Worm walked up to the girl. "Now here's a fine-looking horse," he said, slapping it on the rump. At once the horse spooked and sidestepped its hindquarters against the boy, knocking him off-balance and sending him stumbling into Dagmere. He managed to grab her just before she fell.

Both of their faces flushed red as they each looked into the other's eyes.

Worm jumped back completely flustered and stammered out the first words that entered his head. "Now this is a mare with spirit," he said, brushing his hand along the stallion's right flank. "Uh . . . mind if I ride her?"

Dagmere furrowed her brow into a puzzled expression. She thought for a moment, looking over at the stallion. Then it hit her—*he doesn't know the first thing about horses.* She looked back at Worm, who was still brushing the horse mindlessly. He had a silly-looking grin on his face, and Dagmere almost burst out laughing. She had caught onto his ruse but didn't want to embarrass him by letting on that she knew.

"I think that you should try one of the other . . . uh . . . *mares,"* she offered politely. "They're gentler and easier to handle than this one."

"Gentle?" Worm's uproarious guffaw had in it the makings of a proverb. "I love horses that have spirit!"

"But this horse has more spirit than maybe you're used to."

"It's all right. I know how to ride," Worm reassured her. Then, before she could object, he placed his hands on the stallion's right rump and withers and gathered himself to mount.

There was an ominous shuddering of horseflesh.

"What are you doing?" she protested.

"I'm getting on the horse."

"But that's the wrong side."

"This is the side we get on our horses where I come from."

"But—"

Before she could stop him, Worm jumped up onto the stallion and, with a whoop, managed to straddle its back. "C'mon, girl, let's go!"

The horse whickered and bolted out of the stable area at a full gallop before the boy could get his seating. His legs were still hanging over the horse's right flank, and his arms were flailing wildly over the left, as he tried desperately to find something to hang onto. All the while, he was flopping up and down on the horse's back like a sack of meal.

The stallion galloped across a field, heading straight for a five-foot hedge of hawthorn.

Worm screamed. "Stop, horse! Stop!"

Dagmere winced and covered her eyes as the horse cleared the hedge and the boy cleared the horse, both making long trajectories to the other side of it. The horse twisted one way, the boy careered the other.

He screamed again, flapping through the air like a pigeon. Moments later, he fetched the ground with a terrific jolt.

Dagmere ran up to the hedge in a panic. Immediately she heard a terrible moaning emanating from the other side. Peeking through the leaves, she saw Worm lying on his back, looking straight up at the sky, a dazed expression on his face. Somewhere overhead there was a twittering of birds.

"Are you all right?" she called out.

He moaned again. He sat up in broken movements, rubbing his left shoulder and head.

"Is your shoulder hurt again?"

"No. I just like rubbing it for the exercise," he replied with an edge of sarcasm.

"*What?*" Dagmere was stunned. Her face turned a peculiar shade of red. A little twig of hawthorn snapped between her fingers. "There's no need to be tart about it," she chided. "You're the one to blame."

"Huh?"

"You heard me," she scolded. "I *told* you not to get on the horse from that side, but you wouldn't listen."

Worm moved his head this way and that, trying to see her through the hedge. "Yeah? Well, the horses where I come from are trained not to do that," he remarked. Scrunching his nose, he asked, "Where are you anyway?"

"The horses where you—" Dagmere climbed through an opening in the hedge. "Why, that's the silliest thing I've ever heard." She wagged a finger at him. "If you don't know how to ride, you shouldn't have said that you could. Besides, you could have hurt the horse."

"Hurt the *horse!* How about me?"

Dagmere ignored him. Instead she looked across the field at the stallion, who was grazing contentedly in the long grass. She put her fingers into her mouth and let out a shrill whistle.

The boy winced at the ear-piercing blast.

"Come here, Daktahr! Come here, boy!" she called out.

"*Boy?*" Worm thought aloud, his ears still ringing.

The stallion looked up and whinnied, then trotted over. Drawing up between them, he lowered his head and sniffed at Worm's shoulder, nudging him affectionately with his wet nose. Then he nibbled at his sleeve.

"Now, what's it trying to do . . . eat me?"

"He likes you," Dagmere said, patting the horse on his neck. "Although, for the life of me, I don't know why."

"I'm flattered," he grumbled, struggling to his feet. "Stupid horse could've killed me."

"Stupid *horse?*" she shot back. "You're the one that was stupid enough to get on him."

"*Me,* stupid? Me? Well—"

"At least Daktahr can tell the difference between a mare and a stallion!" Dagmere interrupted.

"Is that right? Humph! Is that right?" Worm's mental arsenal seemed to be engaged in some gross insubordination and was apparently incapable of delivering a single cogent salvo. "Well, a lot you know!"

Dagmere grunted, then hopped onto the stallion's back, as if she had springs in her feet, and grabbed a handful of mane. "I know that I don't look like a fish flopping around on a horse's back when I ride."

"Fish flopping! Well—" Worm searched his brain for a quick retort, anything, but found nothing but a total rout. Exasperated, he grabbed at the only standing thought. "Well, at least I don't have silly-looking freckles all over my nose!"

Dagmere grabbed her nose, reeling in horror. Worm's little dagger had found a very tender place, and she struggled to hold back a gush of tears. "If everything is so wonderful where you come from," she said, glaring down at him, "then why don't you just go back there?" She gave the horse a sharp kick with her heels and took off across the field in a fury of thundering hooves.

Worm stood rubbing his shoulder as he watched the two of them race through the tall grass, jumping first a stream and a low stone wall, then finally clearing the same five-foot hedge on the other side of the field with effortless grace. His mind was reeling in a numbed siege of denial and disbelief and anger. The despot was in a rage but was immediately dethroned by a violent coup. Worm shook his head and cursed. Her words had found their mark as well.

He stormed away and started to climb through the hedge. But as he did so, he caught his shirt on a branch and tore it. He cursed again. As he tried to free himself from the tangle of hawthorn branches, the situation worsened. Dramatically. It seemed as though the hedge had become a living thing, a monster with no face and a thousand spindly claws that tore at him, ripping into his shirt and skin.

He became so entangled in its clutches that freedom from the accursed hedge seemed hopeless. It had him in a stranglehold. At one point he almost burst into tears out of sheer frustration, but his temper quickly got the better of him. It raged foul with a geyser of profanities.

Then, after what seemed an eternity of battle, the spent lad finally tore himself loose and dove out of the hedge, leaving a good part of his shirt behind. The monster hedgerow snickered as Worm headed toward the orchards on the far side of the villa to nurse his pride, kicking clods of dirt that got in his path, giving them curious names, tripping over them periodically, and swearing every step of the way.

The sun tilted its course over the mountain ridges to the west, sending back its emissaries of shade on long eastward pilgrimages across the autumnal landscape. Throughout the day, Worm had lazed in the cool, long grass beneath an apple tree in the orchard, watching cloud patterns promenade overhead through its branches.

In between dozings and bites of apples, he replayed the disastrous events of the morning over and again in his mind, tagging each recollection with a bite of apple and some maledictory flagellations. It was during one such oration that Terryll walked up to him, carrying his longbow.

"I thought I'd find you here," he called out. "Where'd you learn to swear like that?"

Worm was so startled by his interruption, that he nearly choked on a bite of apple. "I . . . Terryll, you s-scared me half to death wiff your sh-shneaking up on me."

"Sh-shneaking? Since when does anybody have to sh-shneak up on a log?"

Worm swallowed hard on the apple chunk. "Ow!" he said, grabbing his sore throat. "I was deep in thought."

"It looks to me like you're deep in apple cores." There were several chiseled cores strewn around him.

"What do *you* want?"

"What do *I* want? Aren't we in a foul mood today?"

"Leave me alone."

"Look, just because you had a disagreement with a horse this morning—"

"*She* told you that?" Worm shouted.

"Nobody had to tell me anything. I watched the entire circus from my bedroom window." Terryll started laughing. "That was some ride!"

Worm grunted and furrowed his brow. He saw no humor in it.

"Why're you being such a grouse?"

Worm didn't answer. Instead, he took another bite of apple and gazed at the florescent hills. His mind, however, sulked elsewhere.

Terryll eyed Worm's tattered shirt and snickered. "Hmm. New shirt?"

Worm looked down at the ribbons hanging from his arms and grimaced. He hadn't noticed it before now. He swore, then looked back up at Terryll. "You come over here just to torment me or what?"

"Look, she'll get over it, Aeryck. She's probably laughing about it right now."

"What are you talking about? Who'll get over what?"

"Dagmere, of course . . . and your argument with her this morning."

"Argument? Who said we were having an argument? Were you eavesdropping as well?"

"I didn't have to hear anything to figure out that you two weren't having a picnic together."

Worm took another bite of apple, as if disinterested, then shot back, "What do I care about Dagmere anyway, except that she's your sister?"

"Oh, come on! Any blind man can see that both of you start acting the fool whenever you're around each other."

"I do not!" he said, swallowing. And then after a moment, Terryll's words struck him. "What do you mean, 'both of you'?"

"Just what I said—both of you. As in you and Dagmere, or the 'two fools'—whichever; it doesn't matter."

You and Dagmere, Worm thought. He rolled the words over in his mind several times backward and forward. It never occurred to him until that moment that Dagmere would have any feelings for him—he just presumed that he was alone in his misery. For an instant there appeared in his mind a parting of the clouds and, peeking through them, a tiny ray of hope.

"It's just as well that you made a complete dolt of yourself early in the game," Terryll continued. "Girls are trouble anyway, especially my sister. Now come on, let's go—"

"You actually think she likes me?" Worm interrupted.

Terryll rolled his eyes to the heavens and sighed the inevitable. "I've lost my only friend to a girl."

Suddenly Worm's eyes opened. Oblivious to all but his own thoughts and audience, he rebuked himself loudly. "You fool! You imbecilic fool!"

"Now what?"

Worm let out a primal groan. "I told her she had silly-looking freckles all over her nose." He flung his apple against a tree and watched it splatter.

"You told her *that?*"

"My mind went blank," Worm answered, staring at the applesauce dripping down the trunk. "What was I supposed to say? She was winning the argument."

"What'd you expect?" Terryll shook his head at the pathetic creature.

A despondent glaze drifted over Worm's features. At length he let out a doleful sigh. "She told me to go back to Glenryth."

"She meant it."

"But I *like* her freckles." Worm moaned. "They're cute."

"Well, like 'em or not, you'd better sleep with one eye open from now on. Dagmere is awful touchy when it comes to her freckles, and she's meaner'n a sow bear when riled. Likely as not, she's riled good."

With that Worm let out a woeful "Aaaaargh!" then collapsed into his arms. The once-parting clouds in his mind quickly gathered into fearsome thunderheads, swallowing any rays of hope without mercy and pelting his soul with a sudden downpour of gloom.

Terryll laughed aloud at the pitiful sight. "Fortunately for me," he said, "my friend is an idiot. Give it up, Aeryck. Give it up. Love is for the birds, I tell you."

Abandoning the hapless fool to his misery, Terryll headed for the archery bales off to the side of the villa, shaking his head slowly and clucking his tongue.

But Worm, sitting slumped-shouldered with head now cradled in his hands, stared numbly at the dirt between his legs. His eyes were glazed over with a stupid expression—a familiar one—seeing naught but the blackness of rain all about him. His ears, also deafened by the inner storm, heard only the heartless voices of accusation that sounded like the monotonous toll of a bell, clapping out a mournful dirge. "You stupid fool . . .you stupid fool . . . you stupid, stupid fool . . ."

The despot was back in power, somewhat disheveled and bent out of shape, but back in power, nonetheless, and caterwauling in terrific voice.

19
THE PASSAGE TO BOWNESS

That night at supper, Allyndaar told the boys that he had finished the longbows he had been making for his friend Belfourt, the chieftain of Bowness, and asked if they would take them up to him in the morning.

Terryll let out a yell, for it meant that they would get away from the house for a few days and possibly even do some hunting along the way.

But Worm didn't share Terryll's enthusiasm; he had unresolved business.

He stole a look across the table at Dagmere, who hadn't eaten a bite of her meal. Throughout supper, she had rolled a boiled potato through her peas back and forth across her plate with her fork, jabbing at it every so often. Her face was shaded from Worm's view by her hand. The tension between them hung over the table like a thick cloud that threatened to break at any moment.

She knew that his eyes were on her, but she refused to acknowledge him. Instead, she put an end to the potato by mashing it. *So much for you!* she thought. Then without saying a word, she dropped her fork on her plate and jumped up from the table.

Allyndaar watched her storm away, oblivious to the tension that had been in the air. He angled his head over to Helena, suddenly aware that some secret business had developed without him. "What's wrong with her?"

Helena just shook her head and advised him to keep out of it. The man shrugged his shoulders, then looked back at Worm for his answer.

Worm consented to go on the trip with a cheerless nod, but it was clear that his heart wasn't in it.

Helena wasn't thrilled with the venture either and stated such.

Allyndaar took her hand. "It's necessary that Terryll make this trip for me, Helena," he said, patting her slender fingers. "You know that I have important business in Brough tomorrow and the next day that needs tending, else would I go with them. Besides, it's only two days' journey from here."

"Three days," she corrected.

"Not if we go on horseback," Terryll pleaded, sensing a downward shift in the proceedings.

"Horseback?" Worm shrieked.

Terryll read sabotage on Worm's face and shifted tacks without missing a beat. "But if we cut through the mountains on foot, we'd make it there even faster!"

"They'll be so close to the Wall, Allyn," Helena said, ignoring her son.

Allyndaar started to reassure her. "We've been there many times—"

"Yes, Mother, Bowness is very safe," Terryll interrupted. "Right, Aeryck?"

"How would I know?" Worm answered sullenly. "I've never been there."

Terryll shot him a hard look.

"Well, I haven't!"

Terryll tried yet another tack. "Papa, you know that I can take care of myself in the mountains. And Aeryck can certainly take care of himself. Didn't Brother Lucius tell you that in all his years of training soldiers, he's never found one so naturally fitted to the blade?"

Worm perked up. "He said that?"

Allyndaar smiled. "Last week. He also said that you were quick and agile—that you anticipated his every move."

"He did?"

"Uh-huh!" Terryll was shifting his eyes back and forth between his father and mother, working his face hard. "'A thing of beauty to watch him practicing his drills.' Didn't he say so, Papa?"

"He said that too?" Worm asked, suddenly feeling like something being auctioned off at a market in which he had much at stake but no say at all in the proceedings.

"Yes."

"He never said nothing like that to me."

Terryll shot him a scowl.

"Well, he hasn't!"

Ignoring the boys completely, Helena sighed. She knew a losing battle when she saw one. Terryll was approaching the age where more and more he would be needed to represent the civitas of Killwyn Eden as the chieftain's son. She knew that she couldn't stand in his way, regardless of her maternal desires to protect him. Besides, she did look forward to any news he would bring from Sophie, Belfourt's wife. She consented at last.

"Then it's settled!" Allyndaar said, slamming his palm on the table to seal the matter.

Again Terryll let out a whoop and jumped away from the table before anyone could change his mind.

Worm lingered a while and nibbled at his supper until the storm finally passed from his mind. He was uncharacteristically poor of appetite.

The next morning at first light, after bidding their farewells to Allyndaar and Helena, the boys left for Bowness—on foot. Dagmere was nowhere in sight.

Terryll carried the bows (five of them), wrapped in a canvas sheath and slung across his back, and a large quiverful of arrows to go with them. His own bow he held in his hand.

Worm carried a satchelful of provisions—broiled chicken, jerked beef, three loaves of bread, a wedge of cheese, and a goatskin of cider—that Helena had prepared for them, as well as a gift of elderberry preserves for Sophie that she strictly warned the boys not to sample. And with his sword and shield slung across his back, Worm looked more mule than boy.

Each carried his own bedroll. Terryll thought that they had more than they needed, for he intended to hunt along the way. But he made no noise about it. He was anxious to get out of earshot just as soon as possible.

And so they were off.

As the boys approached the center of town, the clanging of hammer and anvil called their attention to the blacksmith's shop up ahead.

"Morning, Bolstroem!" Worm called out and waved.

The giant raised his hammer and turned from his work. Seeing the boys approaching along the road, his broad face allowed a gregarious smile. "A good morning to ye, lads!" he hailed, laying aside his tongs. "And where're ye off to at this hour, then?"

The boys drew up just inside the open bay doors of the smithy, where Bolstroem's anvil was set to catch the cool breezes. The forge was lit and growling and belching black smoke up the flu like some infernal beast. Protruding from the bed were several long strips of iron, glowing bright red in the coals. Several iron barrel hoops were stacked against one wall. and one in the making was slung over the anvil.

"Making a delivery to Bowness," Worm replied, feeling a measure of pride in the duty, while also feeling a little reticence as he took in the steamy, comfortable ambience of the shop.

"Bowness, ye say? Ye wouldn't be deliverin' a load of wineskins to old Belfourt, now would ye?" The giant threw his head back and roared.

"We're taking some longbows up to him," Terryll returned, smiling.

"Some longbows, eh? Well, that's good! That's good! That old war-horse'll have better use of 'em than a good drunk." Bolstroem chortled. "Ye lads best be mindful of them northern lands, hear? There's a scalawag or two skulking along them walls, ye can be sure of it."

"We can take care of ourselves," Worm boasted.

"That, I'm sure." Bolstroem grinned, and he clapped Worm on his shoulder. "You're fillin' out strappin' like your father, Little Bear. Won't be long before you'll be settin' up your own smithy, I'll wager."

"I've got a lot more to learn before I ever do that," Worm said, smoothing his toe over the dirt.

"Aye. But you're a bright lad. It comes quick to you."

"We'd best be going, Aeryck, if we're going to make Whitley Castle by sundown," Terryll interjected. The two of them were getting mighty chummy with their metal talk, and he was anxious to be on the road.

Bolstroem laughed. "All right, boys! All right! Off with ye, now! And make sure ye give old fat Belfourt and his little woman my regards, hear?"

"We will."

The giant blessed the boys with a wave of his tongs, then resumed the happy cadences of his toil.

The boys dipped with the road leading into town. Ahead of them to the left a gaggle of women and girls was standing next to the large marble fountain near the great hall. Here most of the women in the village came to draw water in the early morning and at dusk—and to catch up on the latest news and gossip. A few girls looked in their direction, and the boys could see trouble as sure as they were in for it.

The girl with the mass of raven hair and flashing green eyes spotted them. Immediately she set off on an intercepting course.

And the boys knew that they had appraised the situation correctly.

"Where you going, Aeryck?" she asked, ignoring Terryll.

"Huh? . . . oh . . . hello, Fiona."

"So you *do* know my name!" she said, batting her eyelashes. "I'm flattered."

Worm shot Terryll a shaded look.

Terryll rolled his eyes and looked the other way.

"But you didn't answer my question, Aeryck," she teased.

"What?"

"I said, where are you going? It looks like you're leaving on a trip."

"Uh . . . yeah," he said, quickening his stride.

Undaunted, Fiona kept pace, walking backward in front of Worm, with arms folded behind her back. "You've been avoiding me all summer long! Don't you like me, Aeryck?" she asked coyly.

"*Like* you?" His face flushed beet red. The rest of him flushed as well. The truth was he was scared to death of the raven-haired girl, and not scared in the way he was scared of Dagmere. Dagmere was certainly a beautiful girl, and being scared of beautiful girls came naturally to Worm. But this creature, this stunning apparition, was no mere beautiful girl. In her flashing green eyes were the ancient movements of the earth, the furious upheavals of nature that cause the stout hearts of men to quake. Looking into her eyes gave Worm the cold, terrifying shivers of doom.

"I like *you*, Aeryck," Fiona said with a coquettish lilt in her voice. She trailed it with a coquettish fluttering of eyelashes. "Ever since the first time I lit eyes on you, I've thought of no one else."

Worm gulped. In desperation he looked over at Terryll, who, with a certain loathsome smirk on his face, had deserted him and had begun to whistle a little tune. Worm stood alone in his trial. "When are you coming back?" she asked in her lilting voice.

"Not for a *long* time!" he retorted with some found braveness, hoping that it would satisfy her enough to leave him alone.

Instead, she stopped suddenly and opened her arms, and Worm walked right into her trap. What happened next remained a mystery with the boy for some time, for in the twinkling of an eye Fiona grabbed him and kissed him long and hard on the mouth.

Worm was too shocked to move. He had never been kissed by any girl before, let alone by a ravishing beauty like Fiona, and all he could do was stand there staring bug-eyed while she initiated him. Then, after what seemed an eternity, it ended.

"There!" she said, releasing him. "There'll be more of those when you come back!" Fiona giggled, gave him another quick peck on the cheek, then ran back to the well, leaving Worm standing in the road, stunned and unblinking and about ready to pass out.

"Wake up, Aeryck," Terryll teased, waving a hand in front of Worm's face.

"What?"

"Are you still breathing? It looked like she sucked all the air out of your lungs!"

Not hearing him, Worm looked back at the girl, dumbfounded. She waved at him from the well and blew a kiss. "Good-bye, Sweet Lips! I love you!" she called out, loud enough to wake the entire village. It elicited a rise of laughter from the womenfolk, who quickly added the new business to their chatter.

Worm's face burned a brighter red than before, and his ears were on fire. He spun around to see if anyone from the villa had seen him, and the sight that met his eyes caused him to groan loudly.

Sitting on Daktahr at the edge of the villa estate, about a hundred yards away, was Dagmere, staring at him. When his eyes met hers, there was that unspoken moment of "knowing" that hung in the air between them. He could read the hurt and anger, even at a distance. She pulled back on her reins, spurred the horse toward the hills, and galloped away.

"You've done it now, Sweet Lips," Terryll ribbed.

"Shut up!" Worm snapped. "And if you ever call me that again, I'll hit you on the mouth!"

Terryll laughed as Worm stormed ahead of him. "I told you before, but you wouldn't listen," he called out. "This love business is for the birds."

It was clear from the outset that they were both in for a wonderful adventure.

The boys reached St. John's in a little under two hours, the fastest time either of them had ever made the distance. It took the entire stretch for Worm to cool down.

One of Helena's concessions in allowing the boys to go at all was that they take the route through Whitley Castle instead of the more direct road through Old Penrith. She wanted Terryll to ask Brother Lucius to pray that they have a safe journey and to commission him to transcribe another gospel for her.

Terryll had winced when his mother stated her demands, for it meant the loss of at least an hour at the monastery. But he was in no position to barter. Besides, he enjoyed the northern route more because of the higher mountains and many forests, where there was plenty of game and many fish to be pulled from the South River Tyne.

So the boys visited with Aurelius and Brother Lupe and shared a meal with them out of their provisions. Afterward, Aurelius took Worm outside to discuss a defensive sword maneuver, while Lupe cornered Terryll with an anecdote involving a mule, three chickens, and a pig.

Terryll was patient to the point of tears, but Lupe wasn't aware. He laughed between every sentence, each time getting louder and longer. The boy thought he was doomed for the rest of the day and sought desperately for an opportunity to escape. Fortunately for him, Lupe forgot what the end of the story was and thought that the funniest part yet. And while the friar was doubled over in a loud guffaw, Terryll stole away.

Outside, he asked Brother Lucius to say a quick benediction over them. The monk obliged. And thus fulfilling their charge, the boys were on the road again, hoping to reach the outskirts of Whitley Castle by sunset.

Leaving the monastery, the road climbed through a brilliant show of autumn, winding as it did through rock-infested hills and pasturelands. These were forested with the hardiest of trees and vegetation indigenous to the wind-blasted highlands of Northumbria. Speckled across the landscape were hairy sheep, hairy cattle, some horses, and an occasional farmer and his family stacking sheaves of grain from a scant harvest.

Worm was careful to greet each one as Terryll and he passed by, paying particular attention to each of their faces. He had never been this far north—though they were just a few miles outside of St. John's—and it wasn't long before the weighty concerns behind him were put aside, replaced now with a lighthearted step and the thrill of glorious adventure.

Caring little for deep conversation, the boys laughed and joked and took note of the upward shifts in the terrain. The mountains rose sharply to the west like great muscled shoulders, then sloped into the gentler, more blunted ranks of hills to the east.

They were ascending a northern ridge of the Pennine Chain rapidly, and Terryll pointed ahead to Cross Fell, the highest point in the mountains. "From the summit you can see the ends of the earth in every direction!" he exclaimed. Oftentimes, in the cool of a summer's night, he lay there on his back and marked the passage of black clouds or counted the shooting stars that were hurled across the jet of night. It was his favorite place in all the earth.

In a few miles the road would pass by Whitley Castle, level off for a few more miles, then fall away sharply to the wall of Hadrian, where it connected with the east-west road at the wall-fort of Stanegate—an important trade and military route. But the boys would not take it, for it would add at least a day to their journey. Instead, once arriving on the outskirts of Whitley Castle, they planned to veer off-road through the mountains to the northwest, camp for the night, then drop into Bowness the following afternoon.

As they crested a low rise, Terryll caught a glint of light off the antlers of a small fallow deer grazing in a meadow along the tree line ahead. He quickly fit an arrow to his bowstring. A kill would add the fair taste of venison to their now depleted stores—a tribute to Helena's cooking and Brother Lupe's appetite.

But as he drew the nock to his cheek, the deer startled and bounded into the cover of the forest. The boys didn't spook it, however, and Terryll knew it. They were downwind of the animal, and never once did the stag look in their direction.

Suddenly Worm spotted what did. "Terryll, look!" He pointed to an outcropping of boulders north of where the deer had been. "It's the white wolf that I told you about!"

Terryll caught its movement in the rocks. The wolf, obviously uninterested in the deer, threaded its way through the boulders, then came to rest on a flat rock jutting out from the formation. It sat down on its haunches and stared directly at the boys with its yellow wolf eyes.

"Are you sure?"

"It's the same one, all right," Worm replied as he studied the creature. "It's following us."

"Us? How do you know it's not following *you?*"

Worm thought about that until his nape bristled, at which point he forced it out of his mind. "Can you hit it from here?" he asked.

"It'll be difficult with it staring at us like it is."

Terryll raised his bow in a slow unbroken arc, hoping the wolf would not be wary of his intentions. He raised the tip of his broadhead just over the wolf's head and a little to the right, allowing for trajectory and windage, and loosed the arrow.

Immediately the wolf jumped to the side, and the shaft skittered harmlessly across the rocks. The wolf sat down again, lowered its head, and stared at them.

"He's a wily one," Terryll said.

"I wonder if there are any more of them?" Worm scanned the tree line.

"I don't know. Maybe." Terryll started up the road and fetched another arrow from his quiver. "This one might be a scout or something."

As the boys drew nearer to the rocks, the wolf casually loped into the forest heading north, the same direction they were heading.

"Do you think he's had enough of us?" Worm asked.

"I hope so. One thing's for certain, though."

"What's that?"

"It wasn't running away from us!"

It was a chilling thought. The boys talked about the nature of wolves for the next few miles, keeping a sharp eye out for any that might be lurking about.

They spotted the white one once again that day about a mile south of Whitley Castle, padding slowly along the tree line to the west, just out of bowshot. What did it want? Were there others? If so, where were they? Why were they waiting to attack? Perhaps they were waiting for nightfall. Such were the questions that attended Worm's mind.

The boys made the outskirts of Whitley Castle about two hours before sunset and veered northwest into the hills. Dusk was the time when deer and boars could be found rooting around in the thickets for berries and nuts before bedding down for the night. It was the hunter's hour.

Once leaving the road, Terryll metamorphosed into a different person. His eyes immediately took on a wary gaze. A wild sheen glinted in them. They were quick, carving filigree patterns against the darkening shrubbery and trees as they searched for game. His movements became stealthy, fluid like a cat's, scrutinizing, finely tuned to the wild rhythms about him. He was no longer a dweller of villas, a user of fine and comfortable things; he had become the hunter, the predator, a wilder thing. He was in his glory.

Worm, on the other hand, began seriously regretting his part in the endeavor.

They had hiked a mile or so into the hills when Terryll abruptly dropped to one knee. "Here," he whispered.

"What?"

"Boars."

"*Boars!*" Worm yanked his head back and forth. "Where?"

Terryll studied the sign for a moment, then looked away to the west. "Over there," he said, pointing. "A small herd. Probably rooting around in those oak trees along the river."

"Really? I don't see any boars."

Terryll chuckled. "I doubt you would at a half mile." He stood up soundlessly and unshouldered his bedding and the bundle of longbows. "You want to come?"

"Er . . . no. I'll stay here and watch the bows and supplies—make camp."

"Suit yourself." And Terryll was gone.

It suited Worm just fine. The memory of the wild boar glaring down at him in the great hall was still fresh in his mind. The thought of running into one of its relatives out in the woods didn't sit well with him.

Presently he found a suitable place to set up camp, next to a small stream and under the canopy of several climbable yews. He didn't relish any uninvited guests dropping in during the evening. But if any did, he wanted a number of stout trees nearby that he could shinny up.

During the first hour, Worm stacked enough firewood to last them a week, then sat down on a fallen log and waited anxiously for Terryll to return. He gnawed on a strip of jerky to pass the time. Finishing, he unsheathed his sword and began to polish it. While running his fingertips along the engraved relief on the blade and hilt, he sifted slowly through a small library of memories.

The sword strengthened his bonds with his father. Then, as his eyes swept over the exquisite details of the crest for what must have been the thousandth time, it hit him. Like a revelation. He was amazed at himself for not seeing it before. But now that he had seen it, there was no retreating from the image. The bear's head was the very likeness of Hauwka!

And then he stopped himself. How could that be? His father would had to have seen the bear more than ten years ago, gotten close enough to him to have studied his features. It wasn't possible. Was it? Not likely at any rate. He shook his head and decided that it just had to be a bear that bore an uncanny resemblance to Hauwka. After all, didn't all bears look alike? He reasoned that they did. But then again, what did he know about bears?

Worm studied the face for some time, marveling at the incredible likeness. It had the same blunt snout, with just a hint of smile curling at the corners of the mouth, the identical shape of head, broad and flat on the fore-brow, the very ears and eyes—*the eyes!* The boy blinked at them incredulously.

It *was* Hauwka, his mind demanded. There was no mistaking it. The image had the same watery eyes that seemed to glisten with laughter, that stared out at you so intently that you could swear he understood your every word.

As he sat gazing at the bear's head, amazed at the wonderful skill of his father's hands to have carved it so perfectly, he pondered the mystery that he could never know. Was it possible? Could his father have somehow met the great bear and, like him, forged a bond of friendship with him? It seemed impossible, but Worm's face glowed with the bittersweet reverie of it. Then thoughts of his father churned within him until a terrible ache swelled in his breast. He held onto the ache for several moments, then let it out with a sigh.

It wasn't long before the day's light faded, leaving a sunset cast across the sky. Long fingers of red-orange light slanted through the canopy of yews overhead, igniting the autumn foliage into a bright twilight conflagration, keeping the umbral shadows of night at bay, and the leaves were black and crisp against it. He built a fire to help in the losing effort.

Studying the Greek chi-rho on the crest had given Worm an idea. Finding a stick nearby, he cleared an area in the dirt and started to practice his Latin alphabet. He worked the letters A-B-C into the dirt, sounding them out as he drew them. But as soon as he got to the letter D, he stopped.

Images of Dagmere flooded his mind. He thought about her name and wondered if he could write it. He had never tried before. The thought brightened his mood, and he set into the task immediately. Again sounding out the letters, he started writing D-A, then paused. He wasn't sure of the next letter, so he guessed—K. At first it didn't look right, so he scribbled it out with his stick, and replaced it with the letter Q. But that looked even worse, so he resurrected the K.

"That's it!" he exclaimed. Somehow it looked better this time, and he left it. Then he added M-E-R to finish the name. He sounded out each one of the letters again—D-A-K-M-E-R—making sure that he hadn't left any out. Satisfied, he said the name out loud, "Dagmere!"

"That's not how you spell Dagmere!" a voice spoke from behind him.

Worm screamed, nearly falling into the fire. He spun around in the dirt and looked up to see Terryll standing behind the log with a wild boar draped over his shoulders. Worm rebuked him with a string of profanities.

Terryll lowered the animal onto the ground and studied Worm's handiwork. "I am impressed," he teased. "I knew that you could swear, but I didn't know that you could write. When did this happen?"

Worm jumped to his feet and scuffed out the letters with his toe. "None of your business!" He scowled. "And besides, you ought to know better than to always be sneaking up on me!"

"Sneaking! There you go with the sneaking again! I made enough noise coming in here to wake the dead!"

"Well, I didn't hear you."

"No doubt, because the little love fairies were whispering in your ears."

Worm jutted out his chin and made a threatening gesture with his fist. "If you tell Dagmere about this, so help me, Terryll, I'll . . . I'll . . ."

"You'll . . . you'll . . . what?" Terryll mimicked. Immediately he began aping Worm's gestures in gross exaggeration. He thrust out his lower lip and shuffled from side to side in a mock pugilistic dance, jabbed at the air with his fists, and screwed his face into impossible expressions. Mostly he made a grand imitation of a fierce idiot.

When Worm saw how silly Terryll looked, he burst out laughing.

Terryll dressed out the boar in the retiring light of the day. It was a small boar without tusks that weighed about a hundred pounds. He had seen larger ones. One brute in particular probably weighed more than three hundred pounds—a real tusker—but to kill more than they could eat would have been a waste. He cut two filets from high on the back of the pig that he called the "butterfly" and gave them to Worm.

Worm knew them to be the choicest cuts from the hog and was moved by Terryll's generosity. He took the filets and roasted them over the fire on a spit, turning them slowly to perfection, then gave one back to Terryll.

The evening showed promise.

Sitting next to a generous fire under an awning of yews and a host of silver stars, free from the confines of home and chores, the boys spent the rest of the night eating their fill of boar, talking through their now-familiar spectrum of subjects, laughing and pondering deep mysteries that thundered in their breasts, and simply basking in the revelations and wonders of boyhood. They took the night with a joyous passage. Taking turns at watch and sleep, they saw no more of the white wolf that evening.

Morning greeted them with an unexpected rain, and the boys got an early start on their journey. Gray clouds, like cotton batting, draped low over the ridge and into the vales, obscuring vision. The rain—more a hard drizzle—depressed their spirits. Neither spoke much as they ascended westward across the backbone of the Pennines, and, when they did speak, it was only to point out an obstacle in the path or to inquire of the distance remaining or to curse a wet tree limb in the face. Leaves clung to their feet like little paper starfish, stones jumped out of hiding to strike and trip, little rivulets of sweat mingled with rain and trickled down their spines.

All in all, it was a cold, wet, and miserable day, a day for roaring hearths and hot drinks. But they made good time in spite of it. Because of it. They both knew that the quicker their progress, the sooner they would be warm and dry in the home of Belfourt ("Bellie" to Terryll and Dagmere) and his wife, Sophie, drinking hot cider and eating a heaping plateful of her delicious venison stew.

Terryll had told Worm many times that there wasn't a finer cook or friendlier people in all of Britain, but to watch out for Bellie once he'd had a few mugs of ale. He could get so boisterously friendly that it hurt. One night on their last visit, he had slapped Terryll on his back after telling a joke and sent him sprawling across the floor. The old war-horse, as the men of Killwyn Eden called him, laughed at his own joke a solid minute before he realized what he had done.

Terryll also warned Worm to be kind to their daughter, Gwyneth. She had red, stringy hair and teeth that stuck out a little too far. And if her homeliness weren't enough against her, she had a terrible temper to boot. She did have one redeeming quality—she could ride a horse like no one he ever saw.

Worm looked forward to meeting them all, even Gwyneth with the teeth. The horses, however, he'd give a wide berth.

They had begun their gradual descent into Bowness, skirting the wall-forts of Caer Luel (Carlisle), Burgh by Sands, and were now just west of Drumburgh, last of the wall-forts before reaching their destination.

Worm noted the change in the air about five miles back, as they climbed through a thick wood toward a rolling, treeless ridge below the summit of Cross Fell. But the boy had been too soaked and sour to think much about it, focusing his thoughts instead on the distance to the top and how many wet leaves he had to trudge through before he got there.

But as the boys exited the trees at the ridge crest, a bracing wind from the west smacked them hard in their faces and livened their spirits. Terryll knew the smell at once, but to Worm, who had been landlocked his entire life, it was an entirely new sensation. He asked Terryll what it was.

"The sea."

Actually it was the Solway Firth, a wedge-shaped estuary more than twenty miles wide at the mouth, which drew the salt air inland from the Irish Sea like a large funnel.

It was an exhilarating smell, and Worm instantly forgot his misery. Even in the rain. He had heard songs telling tales of seafaring warriors who traveled great distances to exotic lands peopled with races of strange color and culture—rugged, fearless men who brought back with them treasures of unfathomable worth. The thought of finding treasure had entertained his mind more than once. But even so, Worm often wondered why men would leave hearth and heath to do such things. His first taste of the briny magic upon his lips beckoned him—like a distant siren whispering on the wind—to come and see.

But seeing would have to wait, for the whole area was socked in with a fog so thick that there were barely twenty feet of visibility, leaving the boy to the inventions of his mind.

"What does the sea look like?" he asked Terryll.

"The *sea?*"

"I've never seen it before."

"Well . . . uh . . . hmm. Just imagine a lake so wide you can't see the other side of it," Terryll explained. "Water everywhere you look. No trees, no mountains, no rivers—nothing. Nothing but water and more water. Boring, if you ask me. You haven't missed much."

Worm had trouble picturing the image in his mind. He had seen some large lakes but none so wide that he couldn't see across them, and none that smelled like this. He took in a deep breath and exhaled. "Why does the sea smell so different than a lake?"

By the look on his face it was obvious that Terryll hadn't ever given it thought before now. "Because the sea is bigger, that's why. And because there are just more things in it that make it smell the way it does."

The answer satisfied Worm at first, but after a moment's thought he realized that Terryll didn't know any more about it than he did.

"What's on the other side of it—more land?" he pressed, taking a different tack.

"Beyond Ireland, I don't know. Probably nothing. Why concern yourself with such things?"

"Just curious, I guess." With that, Worm decided to wait until he got to Bowness to ask someone there. They'd know about the sea.

The ground began to level off, and the rain thinned to a heavy mist. They were only about four miles outside of Bowness, leaving less than an hour of travel. The boys took heart and quickened their stride, keeping mindful of the uneven terrain. Each of them had stumbled over an unseen rock more than once, so their eyes were kept busy at their feet.

Suddenly Terryll froze in his tracks, and Worm nearly collided with him. Worm started to protest but was motioned still. Terryll cupped his ears against the fog and listened—sight was impossible. Immediately he spun around and, grabbing Worm by an arm, bolted toward some oak trees up the slope.

"What—"

"No time!"

The trees grew out of a flat, grassless scarp, about fifty feet in diameter, that cut into the grassy slope and butted up against a fifteen-foot-high natural retaining wall made of large boulders. The boys clambered up into the rocks and scrambled for cover. They prostrated themselves in the wet grass behind a low screen of rocks on top of the wall and waited.

"What is it?" Worm asked in a low, raspy voice.

"Shh!"

Seconds later the ghostly shapes of six men glided gracefully—like Stygian shades—through the thick, swirling mists along the rocky incline below. They appeared to be moving in slow motion, for the fog slurred the extremes of movement as well as muting sound.

Terryll and Worm watched anxiously from their vantage point, each with weapon in hand, as the darkening wraiths slowly came into focus. To their horror the men veered from their course and were now approaching the very place where the boys had sought cover. Men's voices could now be heard, mumbling, disgruntled.

Worm's heart began to pound, and he feared discovery because of it. His breath came in shallow wheezes. The hecklers of his manhood were returning in fine voice.

"Who are they?" he whispered nervously, barely audible.

Terryll couldn't make out their features just yet, but he could tell by their gray silhouettes that they were warriors of some kind. They carried spears and battle-axes and swords, and what appeared to be ball maces swinging pendulously from their belts by long tethers. Also, several of them carried large sacks slung over their shoulders. But it was too difficult to make out any more detail in the milky haze.

"I think they're Picts!" Terryll whispered.

"*Picts!*"

Terryll could have said any other word—Saxons, wolves, demons —and it wouldn't have stricken him with a tenth of the horror that presently worked on Worm's mind and soul and body. Death was coming for him again. The third time. Immediately the blood rushed from his head and collected in his throat, as though that area were some kind of sanctuary. Death was coming for him, and his whole body took the moment to revolt. His brain barked out a thousand commands to face it, but his body was in a great demonstration of protest, of terror. It convulsed within itself. Everywhere, members were abdicating their stations as the wondrous network collapsed into a million sparks. Death was coming for him. Fear had taken him. Worm thought he might run.

He shot a shuddering glance at Terryll, who was lying still on his side with his bow set across his thigh at the ready, unflinching, apparently calm, self-possessed. Like one of the rocks. The reverse image of himself.

At once Worm was surprised by a profound pride. To him, Terryll was a sudden revelation of manhood, of bravery, of everything that he was not, and he loved him for it. Somewhere in the hollowness that was his chest, he discovered that there was left in him a little strength. He clung to it desperately.

Terryll whispered again, "They *are* Picts!"

Worm looked down at his own weapon to insure that it was still there, for he had lost the feeling of the thing in his hand. His bloodless fingers were clenched white around the haft like a vise, so tight that when he tried to relax his grip he couldn't. He was too cold and too scared to let go. His arm trembled, and he noted that one of his legs was shaking involuntarily.

As the warriors, like demonic apparitions from the netherworld, wended their way through the dreary veil to within twenty yards of the boulder wall, Worm's deepest fears took flesh. But what kind of flesh? His nightmares had understated the case. Evil had become incarnate.

His mind refused to believe what his eyes were telling it. The Picts were long-haired and bearded and had paintings of fiendish designs and faces covering their bare torsos and exposed limbs—designed, no doubt, to instill fear in the minds of their enemies in battle. The desired effect was certain, for they looked more like monsters than men. At first Worm thought that their hands and forearms were painted also but soon realized that they were covered with blood up to their elbows. Apparently they had just come from some killing place.

Then, as his eyes fell on the round objects tethered to their belts that he had thought were maces, he realized to his horror that they were actually human heads dangling by their hair. The boy's stomach turned at the appalling sight. He clutched at his mouth until he got hold of himself, knowing that to vomit would mean certain death. He blinked in stark astonishment as they came out of the fog.

The Pictish warriors filed into the grassless area and walked straight up to one of the trees, about thirty feet from the boys. The tree held their rapt attention for several moments, as though it were an object of some sizable interest. A few grunts attended the appraisal. Presently two of the warriors began jerking their bloody fingers to the north, and the grunts swelled to an angry debate.

Apparently the tree had given them some piece of unfavorable news. It was a relief to Worm, for it was clear that the men had come to dialogue with the tree and had not seen them. However, he was bewildered.

"What are they doing?" he whispered to Terryll.

"They're looking at the moss on the trunk to determine which way north is."

"Why?"

"They're lost."

Then a large warrior who had been trailing the rest, walked up to the tree, noted it briefly, and cursed. That he was the leader there was no doubt, for the others fell away at his approach. He turned to the warrior who had been in the forefront—a smallish man who seemed the most concerned with the tree business—and at once an altercation broke out between them.

Worm tried to make out the words, but the men had such thick accents that it was difficult. From what he could ascertain, the argument had something to do with the smaller warrior—a man referred to as Tork—having led the group in a direction that separated them from a larger body of Picts. The smaller man was busy making a furious defense, indicating the density of the fog with several sweeps of his hand. But the others assailed him with insults.

During the argument, one of the men walked over to the wall and stopped right below the boys, so close they could have tapped him on his helmet with a long stick. Worm's heart, certain that they would be discovered, quit his chest and boomed heavily in his temples.

But the man merely set his sack down on the ground beneath Worm, then relieved himself. The mouth of the sack opened slightly, revealing to the boy some of its contents—articles of jewelry, clothing, some earthenware mugs, and a child's doll made of painted wood sitting on top of the pile. Worm thought it a curious assortment and wondered how and why such a man, who looked more brute than human, would be in possession of such things. His thoughts were interrupted when he heard an outburst of shouting. The altercation had come to a boil.

Worm glanced up in time to see the Pict leader backhand the other man across the face, sending him stumbling backward. The smaller warrior grabbed his ax and raised it halfway out of its frog. His face twisted into a glowering scowl. This roused a cheer from the others, who were champing for a fight. Not wanting to miss any action, the Pict by the wall quickly rejoined the others, adding his voice to the bloodthirsty chorus.

"Go ahead, Tork. You want to kill me? Try it!" the large Pict taunted the smaller man. He laid his palm lightly upon his ax. "If you think you're man enough!"

The others, driven by some insatiate cruelty, egged on Tork to oblige him. But the smaller man, hearkening to a greater wisdom that now worked across his visage, let his ax slip back into the frog. The bystanders groaned as one man, then proceeded to hurl more taunts and insults at him. A blood chant ensued.

"Kill him! Kill him! Kill him!"

And then a curious thing happened. The leader's sack fell to the ground behind him, spilling some of its contents. As he bent over to collect them, he turned his back slightly—carelessly, Worm thought. The man Tork grabbed his ax and lunged at him.

But a small sword magically appeared from the large Pict's sack. With the striking swiftness of an adder, he thrust it upward into Tork's stomach, burying the blade to its hilt.

The large Pict held up the man on his sword with brute strength and sneered into his face. "You always were a little fool, Tork," he chortled. "Seems it's caught up with you now, hasn't it?" Then, spitting into his face, he let him fall off his blade to the ground.

This brought wild howls from the others. It was clear that the large Pict had played this ruse before. With a fearsome scowl, the leader grabbed Tork's sack and his own, then strode northward out of the clearing. The others rushed to the dying man like jackals, clawing and cursing among themselves until they had picked him clean of anything useful—his ax, knife, helmet, shield, and even his grisly head trophies. Then the Picts left their fallen comrade staring up at the misty tree limbs, while they—like specters—spirited away into the fog in search of whatever hellish place they called home.

The boys waited until they were sure that the Picts were out of earshot, then quickly scrambled out of the rocks and made their way to the fallen man. When they reached his side, he was still alive but lay groaning in the final throes of death.

Hearing their approach, the man Tork rolled his swollen eyes over to Terryll and tried to focus on him.

"Who are you?" he rasped.

"We are Britons."

"Have mercy on me." The Pict looked over to Worm, standing at Terryll's side, and whispered in a hoarse voice, "Run me through with your sword, mannie. Do it. Run me thr—" He broke off, coughing.

"You will die soon enough," Terryll interposed. "You were in a battle today, weren't you? Where? Tell us where!"

The Pict looked back at Terryll and gazed into his anxious face. He obviously read the fear and empathy in the boy's eyes as weakness. Slowly, a thin, proud smile formed on his pale lips, which seemed no more than a wicked scar of flesh. "There are many more Britons in Hades today, mannie." The man tried to laugh, but coughed instead.

Terryll dropped to his knees beside him. "No doubt you will soon be there yourself. Now, tell us what wickedness you have wrought!"

The Pict sneered with the last of his breath. A low gurgling noise rattled in his throat.

Terryll grabbed him by his hair. *"Tell me!"* he screamed into the Pict's face.

But the man merely stared at the boy with glazing, unseeing eyes, hearing nothing now but the wailing of lost souls in torment.

"Is he dead?" Worm asked.

"He's dead," Terryll said, letting go his head. He stood to his feet and looked gravely toward Bowness.

"What do you think he meant—many more Britons in Hades?" Worm asked.

"Bowness."

"Bowness?"

"It's the only village in the direction they came from."

The boys gathered up their equipment and left at once for the home of Belfourt and Sophie, hoping against reason that their fears were unmerited.

237

—— 20 ——
BOWNESS

B y the time the boys reached the outskirts of Bowness, the fog had begun to lift from the earth like a great white tarpaulin, allowing a low ceiling of visibility beneath. Descending a blunted hill abounding in rocks, Worm, ever mindful of his feet, was startled by a man's face suddenly gazing up at him from the grass. He pulled up sharply as their eyes met and, for a few moments, held a curious exchange.

Worm thought to jostle the man on the shoulder to ask him of his circumstances. But as his eyes glanced over his body, the gaping wound in the chest prevented him. He could scarce comprehend the revelation as his eyes crept back to the face, to the eyes.

Death was here.

With a shudder Worm looked away from the dead eyes and saw another man not far away, lying on his face, one arm folded peacefully under his body, the other stretching out from his side. A dark red clot obscured the back of his head. Death was there too.

And there. And over there, and here. And everywhere on the rocky slope it seemed there were grim soliloquies of death, assailing the boys' minds with astonishment and horror.

As they approached the village, they threaded their way surreptitiously through little groupings of bodies that were strewn across the gray-green battlefield and lay tendered amid the purple-pinks of heather.

The contradictions of life and death were everywhere apparent and overwhelmed their sensibilities. Some of the dead wore placid expressions, as though they were not dead at all but merely lazing about in the wet grass in peaceful repose, picnicking perhaps. Their glazed eyes stared dully at the ascending fog, or the trunk of a tree, a rock, or a single blade of grass. Others were twisted into impractical postures, their faces contorted. Others, still, were impossible to look upon. Death it seemed was the master of hyperbole.

Each boy, with appalling deference, was mindful where he placed his foot, not wanting to touch or to offend the gray appendages of the dead that stretched here and there in their last desperate clutchings for life. As they moved along in some abstraction of mind and will, each boy was strangely stricken by a feeling of alien remoteness, as though he had suddenly entered a forbidden place and was there met by the quiet eyes that gazed at them from every quarter, inquiring as to their business, admonishing them to leave—to flee.

Worm found that he could not endure the scrutiny of the dead. He felt as though he should somehow make an apology for his trespass, a trespass not of soil, however, but one for having thrice escaped death, thrice having been the beneficiary of some inarticulate cleverness of which he had no inkling or control.

They entered the village precincts through a wooded area with profound wariness, not wanting to chance an open approach by road. Likely as not, small bands of Pictish raiders similar to the one they had just encountered were still at large, pillaging the dead and dying.

Soon they began to hear sounds—ghastly, moribund groanings that emanated from a place beyond the woods, hailing them through the dark, forbidding shapes of trees, alerting them to depart at once. The boys knew that each step brought them closer to a shocking vision. Each footfall was a labor accompanied by strong protestations from their minds and legs and the anxious tread of their soles.

Fallen logs and rocks hidden by leaves hurled themselves before the boys, impeding their progress. Limbs and branches joined in concerted objection to their progress, whipping against their faces and torsos, warning them of impending horror.

As they drew near the edge of the woods, Worm nearly tripped over the body of a dead Pict lying in a pile of wet leaves. A small knife protruded from his back. Next to him was a young woman sitting against a tree with knees drawn up to her chest, rocking back and forth slowly, staring straight ahead and wild-eyed, naked but for a piece of torn cloth that she clutched about her. Worm's mind rejected attempts to acknowledge a connection between the dead Pict, the small knife, and the girl. It was a startling scene.

The girl was shivering from cold and shock, but Worm had no experience with such situations as battle scenes or girls sitting violated in the midst of them, and he felt terribly ill-suited to deal with either. Awkwardly, he pulled off his cloak and called to Terryll to help him—who, seeing right away what was needed, disappeared into the trees. Worm knelt beside the girl and covered her gingerly, daring not to look upon, or touch, her resonate shame. "This should help until Terryll . . . er . . . my friend gets back," he said haltingly. "Are you all right?"

The young woman made no reply. Instead, she continued to rock back and forth, swaying to the tempo of some private anguish.

Worm rebuked himself for such a stupid question and began scouting the immediate area for her clothes. Finding nothing, he concluded that the girl had been stripped elsewhere, then dragged into the woods.

Presently Terryll returned with a fur manteau that he found on a dead Briton and handed it to Worm. Wrapping the young woman in it, the boy picked her up, then followed Terryll out of the trees.

The woods opened into a large clearing, three hundred yards deep, that skirted the village on two sides. North of the village was the Solway Firth; to the east was Hadrian's Wall; to the west, the sea was obscured by a bank of clouds.

The village itself, a Roman-built wall-fort similar in design and layout to Killwyn Eden, sat atop the promontory, having an escarpment that rose from the clearing to the earthen berm and wooden palisades encircling it. Long tongues of fire jumped from thatched roofs, lapping furiously at the fog, and these were attended by great plumes of curdling black smoke. Across the clearing and escarpment, scores (if not hundreds) of Britons lay dead and dying, the cries of whom ascended heavenward through the tendrils of fog. A few dead Picts were among their number, and some wounded. But it was clear from a glance that the day had gone to the painted men from beyond the wall.

As Worm slowly took in the drama of spent battle, the first fetching image were the birds—Death's little sycophants. There were thousands of them—so many, in fact, that the slaughter was obscured mercifully by the shapes of crows and buzzards, cawing exultantly as they hopped to and fro inspecting the dead. The sky was filled with sea gulls as well, swooping and floating up and down through the dissipating layers of mist and smoke, like some well-rehearsed choreography, before lighting on the dead in groups of five or six.

Worm had never seen gulls before and thought it interesting that they kept to themselves, and the crows and buzzards likewise. Their high-pitched screeching, mixed with the obnoxious cawing of the crows and buzzards, was mind-numbing.

Everywhere he gazed upon the horrific escarpment his senses were assailed by pain and suffering and death. It seemed to him a vision of hell. Children and babies, newly orphaned, were crying for their mothers and fathers. Mothers and fathers were crying for their children. The burdened, bent shapes of survivors (mostly old women and men) moved woodenly through the mist, their dispirited husks sifting through the dead for loved ones. The birds hopped out of their paths, annoyed, always cawing, but returned quickly.

Here and there a new chorus of wailing would erupt from different quarters of the battle, as the body of a friend or relative was found. Piercing the clamor were the cries for mercy by Pictish warriors too wounded to move. But they were quickly bludgeoned by these same survivors, who were driven by anguish to commit deplorable acts.

Surprisingly, Worm was enveloped by a numbing dispassion. Death's appalling artistry had somewhere along the way ceased to shock him with its excesses, and the boy looked away.

"I'm going ahead to look for Belfourt to see if he's alive," Terryll said. His gaze was hard; his eyes, quick with cunning. "I'll meet you by the gates."

Drawn out of some dark and distant thought, Worm nodded, scarce aware that Terryll had been standing beside him.

"Will you be all right with the girl?"

Worm nodded again, and Terryll ran ahead. Worm watched his friend thread his way through the aisles of tragic shapes. Then, sighing deeply, he looked down at the young woman in his arms.

"We'll be fine," he reassured her. "Won't we?"

The girl didn't make a sound. She just stared at him, stared through him, for her mind was far removed from his face, lost to the witness of her eyes.

Worm smiled at her, and for the first time he noticed that she had red hair and green eyes. Her face was smudged with dirt, and he could see where her tears had made pale little tracks of trauma down her cheeks. On the corner of her mouth was a scab where she had, no doubt, been struck by her assailant, and there was a yellowish-purple swelling over her left eye. She wasn't beautiful, not even very pretty, but the boy saw, even through her abject circumstances, that she had a kindly face.

He hefted her weight in his arms and began a circuitous trek through the grinning gauntlet of death. Again, he was mindful of his feet.

"Yes, we're going to be just fine," he said aloud, and he thought he might cry.

Terryll found Belfourt just inside the gates, sitting propped up against the base of a Roman catapult, holding a sword in one hand and a battle-ax in the other. He was babbling some chant. There were five dead Picts littered around his feet.

Belfourt had apparently been wounded several times. His skin was of a sallow complexion, and, at first glance, he appeared at the end of things. When the chieftain saw Terryll rounding the gates, he stared at him blankly for several moments, while his mind sifted through the shock and grief for his name.

"Terry," he said softly. "Is that you?"

"It's me, Bellie. What hap—" But his words were snatched from his throat as he caught sight of Sophie, lying dead at the chieftain's side.

The man shook his head slowly, then all at once his chest and shoulders and huge back began to heave, as the old warhorse gave in to his despair.

Terryll moved to his side and inspected his wounds with a closer eye. He would live if treated quickly. Then he looked down at Sophie. Poor Sophie. His mind refused to believe that the woman who had been so cheerful, so full of life and bloom, now lay gray and lifeless on the ground, the spark flown. A thought swept into his mind that she was just sleeping, and that all he had to do was just shake her a few times and she would wake up and fix them all a glorious supper. But the thought was fleeting, mocking him in flight, and it left a great hollow aching in his chest.

"They've taken her, Terry. They've taken her," Belfourt cried out.

But Terryll was distracted by the wonder of Sophie's still face and didn't hear him.

"They've taken her, Terry," Belfourt cried again. "By Toutatis, they've taken her."

"Huh?" Terryll looked away from Sophie. "Who, Bellie? Who have they taken?" Then the answer came to him on a blazing bolt. "Where's Gwinnie?"

"The filthy devils have taken my little girl!" Belfourt wailed. "They've taken my little Gwinnie!" A trace of unspent fury glinted in his eyes as he hefted his battle-ax. He let it fall heavily into the dirt next to a dead Pict, spraying the face with sand. It was the only vengeance his languishing strength and rage could muster.

"O God, have mercy!" Terryll cried out, then buried his head into the man's chest and wept.

Just then Worm walked through the gates carrying the girl with the red hair. He stopped. It took him a moment to survey the scene, before the full impact of the horror registered in his mind. Worm had never seen Terryll cry before, not really cry, and he stood gazing stolidly at his friend, empty of any feelings. They had all been used up. It was as though his emotions were tangible things, little pieces of scattered articles that were quickly gathered up into a bundle, then cast far from his body, leaving him without reserve, without empathy.

And all at once Worm was overwhelmed with a profound weariness. He sighed deeply, wanting nothing more of this day but to retreat into some quiet faraway corner, curl up into a little ball, and summon his shadow friends, then disappear with them into some sleeping fantasy.

Terryll's head jerked up suddenly. It was as though some dark and imperious call had sounded from an unfathomed depth in his soul, startling him. His eyes were reckless, it seemed, full of resolve and glinting with a cold darkness unknown to the young hunter. The dark cast swept across his face, like driven shadows before an oncoming storm, and he sprang to his feet.

"You, there! Old man!" he yelled, pointing to an elderly couple who were attending to some wounded nearby. "Come quickly! It's your chieftain."

The old man and woman hurried to his side, and when they saw their chieftain sitting wounded behind the catapult, and Sophie lying dead beside him, they gasped. The old man called to some others to quickly bring a litter, and soon several people were tending to Belfourt's needs.

Terryll pulled a crippled man aside and began to question him as to the morning's events, and the darkness was in his eyes as he listened.

Worm asked one of the women helping Belfourt where he should take the girl. Immediately the girl grabbed him around his neck as though stricken with a jolt of animation, and she began to whimper. "It's all right," he said, taken aback. "You're going to be fine, I promise!"

But she clung to his neck as one drowning would cling to a floating limb. She jerked her head back and forth, darting wild looks at those around her, and held fast. Her eyes, now reunited with her mind, were panicked, full of terror, imploring Worm to save her from some remembered trauma. She was a tragic thing. Worm felt completely useless and sighed despondently.

"There, there," the old woman said, comforting her. "Everything's going to be just fine now. Giselle, isn't it?" The woman extended her arms to take her, and her husband drew alongside to help.

"Aye! Sure, 'tis," he said, with a smile in his eyes. "Come, now, girl. 'Twill go kindly with you! Aye! There you go now."

Giselle's eyes danced from face to face, collecting information, little bits of buoyancy. As they lighted on Worm's face, freshets of tears glistened over the dried tracks of her cheeks. In her eyes a recitation of pain was crying out for a single ear to listen.

That the boy understood her agony was a revelation to him, and he gave her a reassuring smile. It was all that he had left to give.

It seemed enough. As the old man and woman took her, the girl stiffened and whimpered a little, but at last fell limp into the man's arms and grew quiet.

"That's it, girl. You'll be fine now," he said, hefting her weight. "Aye. We'll take bonnie care of you, little Giselle."

As the old man and woman carried her toward a nearby cottage to care for her, the girl looked back at Worm with rabbit eyes. He gave her a little wave and smile and stood watching until she was taken out of sight. Again he sighed.

He scanned the village, saw the buildings on fire, saw the plumes of black smoke churning, ascending, drifting eastward with the offshore wind and the gulls showing white against it.

All around him people were running here and there, yelling, crying, calling, some mustering in terrified little knots, some carrying wounded, some huddled over their dead, wailing, moaning. Some wandered aimlessly in dazes, some stood and stared. A baby sat in a puddle, splashing playfully, and standing next to it was a small child who was crying and digging a fist into its eye.

Worm was about to go over and attend to them when a woman arrived to do so. He looked over at Terryll, who was still listening intently to the man telling him how the Picts had come in a rush before sunup. He was pulling on his lower lip.

And looking around, Worm suddenly felt out of place. He was merely an observer, a shade among the living. He wanted to leave, to return to his shadow world. But he was condemned to stay, to observe, to listen to the warnings of the living.

There was a welter of activity around the chieftain as several women worked their furious ministrations on his wounds. One woman covered Sophie's face with a towel. This seemed to trigger some spent madness in Belfourt. He gesticulated wildly, demanding that someone tend to her needs as well. At one point he growled, "Get up, Sophie! Let's go now. By the gods—up with you, woman!"

But he was quickly restrained by some men, who hefted him onto a litter and carried him away. Belfourt continued to rail in his madness, battling Picts, hailing the gods, and beseeching his wife to get up and look lively about things.

Terryll rejoined Worm, and they walked alongside the litter. Terryll stared into the chieftain's wild eyes with a detached scrutiny. The boy's countenance was dark, brooding, and concealing a little madness of his own. His lips were compressed into a punishing slit. He had learned from the cripple that several other girls had been taken as well—perhaps as many as twelve.

Terryll's eyes started with a purpose. "Don't worry, Bellie," he said, peering into the chieftain's rolling eyes. "I'm going after them. I'm going after those Pictish butchers, and I swear I'll bring Gwinnie and the other girls back safe. I swear it!"

But the chieftain was too stricken to hear or protest.

Worm, on the other hand, couldn't believe his ears. "You're going to do *what!*"

Terryll ignored him and fell away from the group. Quickly he gathered up a few essentials for his trip—the remaining food in the satchel, water, a good supply of arrows, and his longbow.

Worm was on his heels, dumbfounded.

"You heard me!" Terryll said, reading the protest on his face.

"You're going to go after an army of Picts—to who knows where—and rescue a dozen girls?"

"No one asked you to come along," Terryll said, slinging the satchel around his chest.

"That's right! And don't even think it!"

Terryll started away as though Worm weren't there.

"You really think you're going to save those girls?" Worm said, striding after him.

Terryll stopped for a moment. "Look around you!" he snapped. "You see anyone else who can go after them?"

Worm glanced about the village again. It was the grim truth. The fighting men who had survived the ordeal were either wounded or too exhausted to be of any help. Those who could walk were needed to tend the wounded and to protect the village from further harm.

Worm shook his head incredulously. His brain began to swirl with thoughts and voices and ghastly images until his mind was a disquieting buzz. He wanted to sit down and hear his thoughts out, study their arguments, reason with them, reason with Terryll, but Terryll had started away again, creating an urgency in his mind that prevented him from rational considerations. He needed time to think. His mind was screaming at him for a command, a direction, a purpose, anything. But he couldn't think. Even the despot was mute with his rulings.

"Wait!"

"Can't!"

"We have to talk about this!"

"No point!"

Worm cursed. Panic razed his thoughts. He grabbed at straws in the whirlwind. "What am I supposed to tell your parents when they hear you were killed by a bunch of Picts?"

"Tell them whatever you want."

"Tell them *what!*"

Terryll broke into a lope, heading east toward the wall outside the village.

"Stop!"

"No!"

The panicked swirl gathered into a furious squall. "What if I just knock you out!" Worm yelled, keeping pace behind him.

Terryll whirled in his tracks and glared. A savageness burned in his eyes that Worm had not seen before. "While there's life in my body, I'm not going to let them die! And there isn't a man alive that's going to stop me! Including you!" With that he took off.

Worm stood in the middle of the road, staring horrified at Terryll's shape growing smaller in the distance, and he cursed again. Panic enveloped his thinking, as though a swarm of mosquitoes had suddenly gotten loose in his skull. He looked back at Bowness, then ahead at Terryll, then back and forth.

How could he venture forward? Death was waiting there, grinning at him. How could he go back? Cowardice was there, mocking him. He was caught. Kicking the ground, he cursed yet again. Then a rage kindled in his breast, touched off by the desperation that burned in his mind, and he began to hurl obscenities at Terryll, hurled obscenities at himself and the world.

And then he began to cry. Through his tears he scowled at the diminishing, loping shape of Terryll, small against the autumn foliage, and all he could imagine was catching up to him and pounding sense into his stubborn head.

"You're gonna get yourself killed!" Worm yelled. "Don't you see that?"

But Terryll hopped a low stone wall without breaking stride.

"You're nothing but a pig-headed fool, you know! You're just like your stupid sister!"

The young hunter made his way along the base of the escarpment and headed for the outlying trees.

"Terryll, stop! Please!"

And as the rage grew, it was fueled by a terrible sucking fear that burned out of control in his belly, consuming him now until nothing was left to burn of the fear but smoke. And the smoke smoldered and swirled and was whisked away by a little wind, and in the midst of its clearing there was left standing a single salient resolve.

"Oh, why?"

Worm wiped his eyes and gritted his teeth and struck out slowly, as his mind wrangled his feet to the trail and drove them like an obstinate herd of range cattle. Each step fell with a waxing resolve, each dragged with a waning hope. Then his footfalls quickened, and the pounding, jolting impact of them against the earth sounded in his brain like distant knells, tolling out his doom, dulled and deadened as they were over the great passage of his body. He was running now.

"Wait up!" he shouted, scarce hearing his own voice. "I'm coming with you!"

And so he ran toward the land of painted men, toward his greatest fear now becoming incarnate, toward some great and living darkness that was waiting somewhere beyond the wall. The death that had been pursuing him, thrice failing, he was now pursuing with abandon, running headlong and wide-armed into its gaping maw, and he felt powerless to alter his course.

He shuddered. And glancing behind him at the smoldering, wailing, bird-infested village of Bowness, he shuddered again. Death was behind him and before him, to the left and to the right of him, and he was running.

Strangely, a chuckle escaped his lips.

PART THREE
THE THRONE OF DEATH

21
PURSUIT INTO THE DARKNESS

The wall had been built by Emperor Hadrian in the second century after Christ to repel Pictish and Scottish invaders. It ran across the entire width of the island from Bowness, on the Solway Firth, to Wallsend, on the North Sea. It averaged ten feet in width and twelve to fifteen feet in height, built of stone and brick and surmounted with crenellations. At every mile was a mile-castle, a stone fortification where Roman troops were garrisoned, spaced between the larger wall forts such as Bowness. Between these were spaced two turrets, stone structures in which even more soldiers were stationed.

All in all, it was a tidy defense against the northern invaders. But since the departure of the Romans forty years earlier, maintenance of the wall-forts and mile-castles had grown weak and were frequently overrun by Picts.

When the boys reached the first mile-castle outside Bowness, they were not surprised to find the men who had been guarding it slain and their bodies mutilated. They quickly passed through the north gate in the wall, climbed the earthen berm opposite, then disappeared silently into the forests beyond—a counter-invasion of two.

Terryll found the Picts' trail at once—a wide swath of broken soil that wriggled across the terrain like a great serpent. It was obvious that they weren't trying to conceal their passage. Why should they? He estimated that there were at least two hundred in the party, beside a dozen or more horses.

"How long do you think since they've been through here?" Worm asked.

"About three or four hours."

"Any sign of the women?"

"Too many tracks," Terryll said, stooping to examine the spoor. "It'll be difficult finding any particular prints. But here's something."

"What?"

251

"There's a lot of blood along the trail." Terryll looked ahead. "We'll have to watch for their wounded."

The warning wasn't necessary, for Worm was watching for everything.

The boys followed the tracks east along the southern bank of the Solway Firth. The fog had cleared, giving Worm his first full view of the sea, or at least the estuary leading to it. The surf boomed ancient cadences along its shores, and sandpipers flirted with the wash and foam, stabbing here and there at bugs and skittering after fiddler crabs. A skein of geese winged southward against a sky of reds and yellow-oranges and purples, honking. Two brown pelicans skimmed inches over the glittering rubescent surface of the water, racing somewhere.

Worm paused to acknowledge the day's adieu. Never had he imagined such sights, such roaring of sea and wind that swallowed the shrill screeching of gulls. And the brisk, biting tang of salt air was to his spirit an invigorating liquor, a magical potion. He lapped it in greedily as one dying of thirst. But the dark, hazy smear of land brushed across the northern horizon at once diminished it, caught the draught in his gullet, and reduced it to a shuddering gasp.

Picts dwelled there.

The trail paralleled the wall, giving Worm a comfort of sorts. He knew that Britain and safety lay just two miles south. But Terryll told him that the trail would undoubtedly swing north once rounding the tip of the firth, then head deeper into Pictish territory. It did. And from that point onward, Worm's mood darkened with every step. He was heading directly into the blackness of his deepest fears, and the jeering hecklers were keeping close.

A wet, biting wind from the north picked up suddenly, whipping across the moors, and tore through his clothes, rousing regiments of chills along his limbs and spine. This did little to console his sullen mood. The boy cursed under his breath—at what, or whom, it didn't matter. He was too miserable to sort it out. It seemed to him they were trudging into a monstrous oppression, a certain doom. Shooting the back of Terryll's head a sour look, Worm pulled the hood of his cloak over his own head and hunkered down for the long haul. His shaded eyes kept a busy watch amid the darkening shifts of Pictish soil.

The trail hit a road heading northwest opposite the old Roman fort of Netherby. A settlement of Picts had occupied the site after the Romans abandoned it in the late part of the fourth century, but Terryll said that these were not the ones they were pursuing. The blood spoor bypassed the village and led the boys farther into the highlands of the north country.

Not wanting to be discovered, they cut west, keeping to the forests and gullies whenever possible but always following the course of the road. Terryll kept their gait at an easy hunter's lope, hoping to close the gap with the Picts as quickly as possible. How far would they have to travel? There was no way to tell. But they would continue until they found Gwinnie and the other women, and somehow effect their rescue.

It was a fool's errand.

In a secluded inlet on the Solway Firth, just east of the Pictish village of Glenlochar, a large group of fierce-looking Picts landed their boats (five of them, with twenty men to a boat) in the light of a waxing crescent moon. They were returning from a raid that had begun several months earlier along the eastern coasts of Ireland. But their good fortune had taken them deep into the heart of the isle to the village of Armagh, and there they took plunder beyond their wildest expectations. Because of it they were long overdue and no doubt feared dead by their kinsmen.

The leader, a commanding figure with a terrible countenance, was tired, battle-worn, and anxious to see his wife. He led his warriors on a northeasterly course from the great River Nith that would at some point intercept the path of Terryll and Worm.

Terryll heard the noise about two hundred yards ahead—a low moaning that sounded either like the wind blowing through the trees or demons in torment. After hearing it again he knew that they had caught up with some wounded Picts.

"What do we do now?" Worm whispered anxiously. "Circle around them?" Wounded Picts were the same as unwounded Picts in his estimation.

"No. We sneak up on them."

"Are you serious?"

"I want to know how many of them there are, and if they're able to cause us any trouble," Terryll replied. "No point worrying about mischief behind us as well as in front." Then he took off.

Worm was near exasperation at this point, but he followed.

Under the veil of night, the boys—two black silhouettes—stole from cover to cover like thieves until they finally reached a clump of bushes at the brink of a muddy declivity overlooking the road.

Below them, and against the opposing bank, were four blacker shapes. The miserly light from the moon glinted here and there off their weapons and armor and other shapes. Worm's rapt appraisal gave to their truculent outlines the definition of ogres. It would take his imagination some convincing to allow otherwise.

From what the boys could gather, two of the ogre shapes were in a bad way and had probably taken their last steps forward in this life. They swayed and stiffened and carried on in an awful way, moaning and cursing and filibustering the inescapable call upon their souls with tantrums. The other two ogre shapes hovered nearby, one of whom picked at a shoulder wound like some great simian fretting over fleas.

The fourth didn't appear to be wounded at all. He seemed to be nursing another matter altogether, and as soon as the third man finished dressing his shoulder, the matter was revealed. He and the fourth man stood up, bade their stricken fellows farewell, and ran them through with their swords. Then they proceeded to divide up their spoils, grunting and chortling over their finds as if they had just sat down at table to eat.

The boys were too far from the Picts to hear what they were saying, so Terryll stole to the other side of the road to eavesdrop, hoping to glean information as to the whereabouts of their village. The arrangement was fine with Worm. He didn't want to get any nearer to the Picts than was required, and he set himself behind the bushes to await Terryll's return.

Presently one man let out a coarse laugh. Apparently he had found something amusing in one of the dead men's sacks.

Worm, driven by insatiable curiosity, leaned forward on a branch to get a better look. But as it happened, the branch snapped beneath his weight, and the boy tumbled down the bank like a barrel, landing face-first in the mud next to the road, about twenty feet from the men.

The two Picts whirled to their feet, swords at the ready. But when they caught Worm's figure, a mere lad lying sprawled in the mud, they began laughing.

"What's this, then?" the fourth man queried.

"Dunno! Appears a British cub what's strayed too far from his home," the other said, moving closer to Worm. " 'Tis a pity that such a bonnie face has gotten mud all over it." The man let out a throaty chortle. "Still, his head would look right smart hanging from my belt, wouldn't it, Larth?"

"Or mine." The other man laughed.

Grabbing his shield, Worm struggled to his feet and raised the tip of his blade with something that resembled a threatening gesture. He tried desperately to remember his battle stance and drills. But his mind was a-blow with terror, and his catechisms had fled. It seemed he could only find a focus on the severed heads dangling ghoulishly from the man's belt.

"If—if you come a-any closer to me," he managed to say, "I-I'll be forced to k-kill you."

"Is that right then, lad?" The third man laughed, still edging toward the boy. "Did you hear that, Larth? The whelp means to stick me with his shiny sword."

Worm hedged backward to keep the distance between them, his knees nearly buckling from fear. These were no wolves he was facing, no Saxon boarhounds. They were Picts—black ogres, glinting in a ghoulish light—who stood before him, drenched in fresh murder, sneering devilishly. Their eyes were fixed on his and glinting more violence.

Worm's heart leaped furiously in his chest like a caged ferret, adrenaline raced through his arteries, and his mind was a riot of desperate thoughts. *To the right . . . backward . . .* And he retreated one step and to the right.

"It might do you well to have some of your air let out," the fourth man ribbed, making sport of the situation. He started toward the boy at an oblique angle, so as to outflank him. "Are you sure you can handle him alone, Grendahl?"

"I'm . . . I'm warning y-you to stop!" Worm demanded. However, his voice was barely more than a hoarse whisper. As he shot his eyes back and forth between the men, a sudden urge to run stabbed his mind. But the mud about his feet seemed to be sucking him into the earth.

Grendahl inched toward the boy and chortled throatily. "You're warning me to—"

"You heard what he said," Terryll's voice interrupted from the opposite bank. "If you take another step forward, I swear it will be your last."

Both men froze. The third man had closed to within eight feet of Worm; the other to about the same distance, but on the far side of the road nearest Terryll. The men searched the embankment for this new shape, but the boy was obscured in the shadows behind a tree.

"What? Another cub what's lost his way?" the fourth man said, his eyes warily scanning the trees along the bank. "Come and show yourself, boy. We mean you nay harm." Still peering into the tree line, Larth continued, "I think the boy means it—eh, Grendahl? Perhaps they wish to rob us of our booty." Larth turned to Worm. "Is that what you mean to do, boy? Are you to rob us, then?"

While the fourth man was talking, Grendahl shifted his weight subtly to his hinder foot. It was an old trick, and Worm fell for it. The boy turned his eyes from Grendahl to the one who had asked him the question.

Seizing the moment, Grendahl sprang at him with a howl, and his blade traced a thin curve of light at Worm's head.

Instinctively, Worm drew his sword up and caught the man's blade with a clash of sparks inches from his face. But the man's attack found Worm completely surprised and flat-footed, and the force of the blow hammered him backward into the mud bank. Adding to Worm's horror, his sword had gotten entangled in his cloak. Cursing unabridged, he struggled frantically in the mud to free himself, expecting to be run through at any moment.

Out of the corner of his eye he caught the man's black shape lunging toward him, and he rolled to his right in a desperate maneuver. The action freed him of his cloak, and with an angry outburst he scrambled to his feet in a panic. Expecting an immediate blow to fall, he ducked behind his shield and swung his sword blindly in a broad scything arc, but his opponent had disappeared.

Worm spun around, thinking himself flanked, and nearly tripped over the man's body. To his bewilderment, the Pict lay at his feet with an arrow imbedded in his chest.

The moment was short-lived, for immediately Terryll came bounding down the opposite bank toward him, yelling for help. Larth was on his heels with sword poised to strike. Apparently the Pict had run up the bank the moment Terryll loosed his arrow, and the boy hadn't time to fit another to his bow.

Without thinking, Worm jumped in front of the man as Terryll passed him like a shot, and set immediately into his battle stance. The man pulled up short, stunned to see the boy alive, astonished to see his confederate prostrate and in a dying way. Without hesitating further, he drove his sword furiously at Worm's chest.

The boy parried the thrust sharply to his right, exposing the Pict's right flank. Then, with a single fluid motion, he sidestepped left and came up under the other's sword with a short jab to the man's rib cage. The Pict didn't know what hit him. But none was more surprised or terrified than Worm, who, standing over the man in his battle stance, was numbly still chanting the battle hymn as he waited for the next blow to fall. *To the left . . . forward . . .*

"It's over, Aeryck!" Terryll said.

"What?" Worm yelped, startled.

The young hunter stood behind him with his longbow now drawn and pointing at the twisted black form lying at their feet. "He's dead."

Worm looked down at the Pict, then at his own bloodied sword, stunned that there was a connection between the two. His eyes edged over to the pathetic head trophies that were strung about the man's side. Their faces seemed locked in ghoulish taunts, now avenged by his death.

It was difficult for Worm to fathom the gravity of the moment. He had just fought a hideous-looking foe—a Pictish warrior, a murderous ogre that had assailed him in night visions—and had prevailed against him.

"What happened?" he asked Terryll.

"You just saved my life!"

"How?"

"I don't know. It happened too fast. One moment I'm fetching an arrow, and the next there's a Pict lying at your feet, staring up at the trees," Terryll said, looking down at the body. There was no mirth in his voice. "Aurelius has taught you well." He shook his head solemnly.

Not wanting to leave any evidence of their presence behind, he leaned over and drew his arrow from the man's chest. "Let's go."

As Worm stood watching him, the swirling images of the last few minutes slowly came into focus, revealing to his mind the terrible chronology of events. "You saved my life as well," he said softly.

Terryll let out a deep sigh. "God be praised for His mercy."

Without further delay, the boys dragged all four bodies off the road and hid them in the bushes. Curious as to what the fourth Pict had found amusing, Worm looked in his sack and saw, sitting on top, a small wooden cross with some kind of animal shape carved against it. In the dim moonlight he couldn't make out what it was and didn't have time to scrutinize it, so he stuck it in his pocket.

Anxious to make up lost time, the boys took off at a lope, sticking to the road as much as they dared. This time, however, Worm welcomed the pace, for it helped him burn up the adrenaline and the nausea that was pitching and rolling in his stomach.

As the earth tilted its broad belly to the first gray light of the morning, the night with its shadows fled ever westward. However, the sun was kept at bay by an overcast of dark clouds that was oppressive. Worm began to wonder if the sun ever shone upon this wretched soil, and he had only trod upon it now less than twenty-four hours.

It was then and there on the broken and disconsolate moors that they saw it again. Keeping pace with them, a hundred yards off their left flank, was the white wolf. With his thoughts and fears focused on the Picts and the impossible endeavor before them, Worm had completely forgotten about wolves.

Terryll shot it a quick glance and shook his head. He was just as puzzled by it as Worm was. But there was no time to give it thought. He drew up suddenly when he spotted the remains of several fires alongside the road.

Worm kept his eyes on the wolf, while Terryll examined the coals.

"They're about an hour ahead of us," Terryll said, sifting through the cooling embers with his fingers. "We've made good time. They've picked up some more horses along the way, I see," he added, inspecting some droppings. He got up and sorted through the littered remains of the hasty campsite—scraps of chicken, partridge, mutton, and pork. Apparently the Picts had stopped just long enough to break for a meal.

Terryll had hoped to catch up with the warriors during the night, expecting them to make camp somewhere along the way. But they hadn't. Why not? Surely they needed the rest. Terryll pondered the question and arrived at a conclusion: either the Picts planned to set up an evening camp farther down the road, or they were close enough to their village that a night camp wasn't warranted. Either way, the boys would soon be upon them.

Suddenly he stooped in a clearing next to a stand of sycamores. "Over here!"

Worm ran over to him. "What is it?"

"Look at these tracks!" Terryll exclaimed. "It's the women!" He pointed to several small footprints imbedded in the soft, wet earth next to the trees. Some were made by bare feet, some by sandals, but each of the prints was clearly made by a woman. The news was welcome and cleared Terryll's brow somewhat.

"You don't think any of those could've been made by a man?" Worm asked.

"There's no man I know that makes a print that small. Take a look at your own feet. One of those hog stompers is big enough to swallow up any two of these. And you're not even full-grown yet."

Worm looked down. There was no arguing with him; the evidence lay out in front of him like two sides of beef. "Can you tell how many women there are?" he asked, changing the subject.

"At least eight—maybe more. But we don't have time to stay here." Terryll grabbed a chunk of roast boar from the food satchel and tore off a piece for Worm and himself. "Let's go," he said, taking off in a lope.

Worm remembered the wolf. He looked back to where it had been, but the animal had disappeared. The boy shook his head, then stepped into a jog behind Terryll.

Over the next two hours the boys stayed off the road as much as possible. However, foliage on the moors was as sparse as the hair on their chins, so, road or no road, there was precious little cover anywhere. It was a contrary land, this berth of Picts and Scots—hard, masculine, virile. It seemed opposed to the tread of their British feet and smote them at every turn with rocks and untoward terrain, and the wind was an incessant howling banshee in their ears, voicing its antagonism in a thousand angry inflections.

A couple of times they had to scramble for a rock or a scrawny bush as people approached them on the road. Once, a farmer and his son came along, driving a few milk cows. They never once looked in their direction.

But on another occasion, a lone horseman trotted over a rise about a hundred yards away, catching them by surprise. The boys ducked into a shallow cleft in the ground but feared they had been seen.

They slowly peeked over the edge of the crack to catch a view of the passing rider and found to their horror that the man had stopped his horse no more than fifty feet from their position. Moreover, he was standing up in his stirrups, shielding his eyes, and staring right at them.

Worm nearly passed out.

The man held that position for a solid minute. Terryll was about to fit an arrow to his bowstring when the rider took his seat and continued down the road.

The boys breathed a sigh of relief. However, neither knew if the man had seen them or merely thought them a curious aberration in the terrain. Both wondered what mischief he might cause them later on.

Fortunately for Terryll and Worm, the bleak, tree-scarce moorlands slowly gave way to undulating hill-scapes lush with forests and vegetation, affording them ample protection.

It was a good thing. They were now into the pasturelands, and the frequency of farmhouses and people had increased dramatically, making progress difficult and adding hazard to their absurd mission. But on the positive side, the growing congestion also suggested that there was a village nearby. Hopefully, it was the one they were looking for, and so they quickened their pace.

As the boys crested a hill, keeping as always just inside the tree line, Terryll spotted them.

"There they are!"

"Where?"

"There," the young hunter said, pointing to a spot on the road about a half-mile ahead.

Worm followed his point and found the long column of Picts—more a loose collection of four groups—plodding slowly up a hill, twin to the one they had just scaled.

The boys ran ahead inside the tree line and quickly bypassed the Picts on the far side of the rise, then made their way over several smaller hills beyond.

They discovered a fair-sized knoll well ahead of the column, that jutted into the course of the road. Several large boulders were flung casually about the crown, and clumps of heather clung tenaciously around them by their gnarled roots. The boys hid in these, catching their breath as they lay in wait, battling growing fatigue with grim determination and the favor of youth. Small birds rustled about in the bushes, chirping happily.

The road curved around the base of the knoll below, giving them an ideal vantage point from which to survey the column, both coming and going. Then the trail stretched northward about three hundred yards before it dropped out of sight behind a screen of trees. While waiting, the boys refreshed themselves with the last of the cider and cheese.

"What are we going to do now?" Worm asked anxiously.

"Wait."

"I mean—do you have a plan or something?"

"Not yet."

This didn't set well with Worm. He thought that they at least should have a plan of some kind. Even he used to devise a plan before he went about to steal something. Without a good plan there was no telling what might happen. He began to wonder whether or not he should take charge of this rescue, since he had had more experience in the area of subterfuge and thieving than Terryll. He put his mind to some scheming but came up without a single scheme. It seemed that stealing women from Picts was a sight more complicated than stealing bread from fat bakers.

"What do you think the Picts plan to do with the women?" Worm asked, abandoning his former line of musings.

"There's no way to tell," Terryll said, glancing up the road. "Maybe they want them for wives or slaves or—" He broke off.

"Or what?" Worm pressed.

"Nothing."

"Tell me."

Terryll gave him the same look he had when Worm insisted on looking at the remains of the shepherd, and Worm returned to him the same look he had before he had gone to see.

"Many of the Picts still practice the ancient druidic religions," Terryll said, obliging him. "The Romans weren't able to wipe out all of their practices as they did in Britain."

"So . . ."

"Some of the young women may be sacrificed to their gods."

The thought of it turned Worm's stomach. It also made him angry, so angry that it caught his fear off-guard, and for just a moment he felt the burden of their task weigh upon him like a heavy mantle. "You come up with a plan yet?" he asked.

Terryll shot him a shaded look. "I might, if you'd quit yapping about it."

"We just need a good plan is all," Worm muttered. "A good plan."

"Whatever we do," Terryll said, "it would be best done at night—and better still on the open road. Wait! Here they come."

The first group in the broken column—one hundred fifty warriors strong—made the summit of a low hill, followed soon after by another, smaller, group. There were easily two hundred warriors in all, as well as several packhorses loaded with plunder. The column had the appearance of a great black dragon, snaking sluggishly along the road, its belly swollen with a consumed village.

It was certain, however, that the reptile was possessed of some harnessed strength and could strike in a snap if need be. Here and there the sun, when it poked through the overcast, glinted off armor, glimmering like plates of scale across the broad, heaving back of the leviathan. The sounds of scraping feet, the clinking of weapons and other accoutrements grew more distinct as the beast slithered toward the boys' position. Its voice was a low, hissing murmur. It came inexorably.

Worm beheld the monster in rapt wonder. Never would he have imagined such a sight.

Terryll strained his eyes to pick out the forms of the women amid the column, and he spotted them finally. There were nine, straggling far behind the horses. From what the boy could fathom, they were being goaded forward by only two warriors. In the midst of them Terryll found a single brand of fiery hair, but from the distance there was no way to tell if it was Gwyneth.

Minutes later, as the Pict's faces came into focus, Worm grabbed Terryll's sleeve and whispered, "Look! It's the same man."

"What?" Terryll asked, distracted.

"The one who killed the man in the fog."

Terryll studied the large warrior at the head of the column. He was now astride a gray horse. He rode with an arrogance that played well over the distance, his head tilted proud to the heavens, looking this way and that, his gestures sweeping and deliberate. Clearly he bore the persona of a Pictish commander, perhaps even a chieftain.

"You're right," he said. "Looks like he found his way. Found a horse too."

"Do you think he's the leader of the whole party?"

"Looks like it."

The boys studied the warriors as the first group cornered the bend below. They were a savage lot, as inhuman in appearance as ever were clothed in mortal flesh, but men nonetheless. Battle-worn and journey-spent, they reeked of vainglory, telling it by their flinty faces and the confident strut in their gait.

Trailing in the wake of such hellish splendor was a smaller group of fifty men, many of whom appeared near exhaustion or debilitated by battle and wounds. But they struggled through the humility of their misfortunes to keep pace with the others. Terryll knew by looking at them that, unless their village was nearby, many would soon collapse. It did not bode well for a night rescue out on the road.

Following the men were the packhorses, clopping along at a sleepy gait, sore-ladened with a bloody harvest of spoils. They were tended by four horsemen, whose interests lay on points forward, not on the women behind.

Terryll looked ahead on the road. The leader of the column had reached the point where the road fell away from view behind the shield of trees. Soon they would be out of sight altogether. He then looked below as the last of the horses made the bend in the road, and a plan took shape in his mind.

He shot a look back. The women were now shielded from the column's view by the jutting knoll. There was a chance—a small one—that they would not be missed for some time, giving the boys a chance to flee with them into the forest. With Godspeed they could put several miles between the column and themselves by midafternoon. Come nightfall they could rest, then steal away southward under its cloak. Only two men stood between the women and their freedom, and Terryll could take care of them before they knew what hit them.

It was a daring plan, but therein lay its strength. The others wouldn't expect such a rescue so far into Pictish territory—and in broad daylight besides. It was worth a try.

Terryll quickly whispered his plan to Worm, who, in light of his own failure to come up with anything better, agreed resignedly that it was their only chance. He didn't relish the idea of having to effect a plan from inside the Pictish village.

Terryll fetched two arrows from his quiver. He held one against the back of the bow with his left hand, for a quick second release, and fitted the other to the bowstring. The two men were within bowshot now, and the wind was in Terryll's favor. They would be easy marks.

The boy raised up onto one knee, still shielded by the bushes, and drew back on his longbow.

And then the unexpected happened.

One of the women caught her foot on a jutting stone and stumbled to the road, letting out a loud shriek. Grabbing her left ankle, she writhed on the ground, screaming.

Terryll ducked behind the bushes and looked up the track. Three horsemen had heard the screams and reined their mounts. Two headed back toward the women at a gallop.

The two footmen lifted the woman to her feet, but she was unable to walk. She had either broken her ankle or badly twisted it, and in either case Terryll's plan was foiled. They would have to wait and hope that another opportunity would present itself. The men put her up behind one of the horsemen, and once again the women dragged forward.

Terryll chewed on his lip in frustration.

Moments later the women were right below the boys, giving them at last an unhindered view of their faces. Most appeared to be in their teens; two or three, perhaps in their early twenties. Each wore a mask of quiet terror.

Terryll's eyes fell upon the one with the red hair, thinking she must be Gwyneth, but there was nothing in her appearance that was familiar. Quickly he searched the other women in the group for her face, but it wasn't there. Panic welled up inside him. What had happened to her? Had she been killed, and they missed her body somehow? Or was there another group of warriors ahead of this column with more captured women in it? Didn't the man in Bowness say that there may have been as many as twelve girls taken?

"What is it?" Worm asked.

"She's not there."

"What do you mean, 'she's not there'?"

"She's not there, I tell you! Not one of them even resembles Gwyneth."

"Are you sure? Not even the one with the red hair?"

"Especially the one with the red hair."

"People change, you know."

Terryll shot Worm a look that closed the matter.

Worm shrugged his shoulders. "What do we do now?"

"We follow them. She might be in another group up ahead."

"Some plan," Worm mumbled again.

The boys waited until the women fell out of sight behind the trees, then left.

Terryll and Worm shadowed the column from the tree line for another two miles. When they came to the Roman ruins at Birrens, the Picts veered off the road and headed due west, taking a path that followed the north bank of a river. The boys kept in the trees on the south side of it and shagged the warriors for three more miles to where the river cut a gorge through the hills, leaving steep bluffs on either side. The path along the river narrowed, allowing only three men abreast or an ox-cart's width to pass through at a time.

The boys, on the other hand, were forced to scale the ridge opposite, halting once they reached the summit. They had known for some time before reaching the crest what they would see below, for soon after they veered from the road they picked up the telling smell. Wood smoke. The Pictish village would lie just ahead.

They were not disappointed. Spread out below them on the far side of the river lay the village of Loch na Huric—"lake of the yew." It was a fair-sized hamlet that was nestled in a river valley, surrounded by steep, forested hills—sometimes sheer cliffs—on all sides, with a half-mile clearing for pasturing sheep and farming that stretched northward for miles on either side of the river.

From what the boys could see, there was a varied collection of thatched huts, mostly built of wood, though some were of stone also. An earthen berm about five feet high encircled the village, but without the usual wooden palisades surmounting it.

Given its natural defenses, man-made defense works would have been redundant. The pass leading into the village was easily secured, and the hills enclosing it would be difficult, if not impossible, to negotiate an army over. But the primary source of protection was obvious—the river itself. The broad, serpentine watercourse bowed around the granite bedrock upon which Loch na Huric sat, wrapping it on three sides, affording it a natural barrier from assault.

The boys would have to cross it later that night and somehow mount their own assault, a thought that troubled Worm to the bone.

From their vantage point the boys watched the column of Picts snake its way along the river, then pour out into the clearing before the village a good quarter-mile below them. Scores of people (mostly women and children) ran out of the gates to greet their husbands and fathers. Loud shouts and cries of victory sounded from the gathering throng and continued unabated as the returning warriors—in time-worn tradition— were welcomed home by their kinsmen. Following on their heels, the terrified captives, like sheep, were driven along a corridor of mocking celebrators to some unknown fate, ogled and poked the while by laughing women and children and leered at by men and boys, their eyes gleaming with lustful intentions.

The festivities began in earnest and would surely carry long into the night, as clan by clan—in order of status and merit—would take their turn under the moon to tell their tales of valor and to take what was theirs by right in the division of spoils.

The sky behind the hills to the west was ablaze. Sunset now bathed the slopes around the village with an eerie, reddish glow. It seemed the river was a course of blood. Elsewhere the clouds hung upon the hills like ribbons of black smoke.

Worm looked up and followed the course of another skein of geese heading south to warmer climate, to Britain. The boy let out a wistful sigh, then hunkered down into his arms and closed his eyes. There was nothing that Terryll and he could do now but get what rest they were able and wait anxiously with their own thoughts until the cloak of darkness fell upon the day.

22

THE SUMMIT OF BADONSWARD

A sharp autumn breeze swept through the sapless boughs of a sycamore, culling a handful of brittle leaves from the hardy remnant, then scattered them carelessly to the earth. The bear padded silently through them. He rose onto his hind legs and sniffed the air for scent. Curiously, there wasn't any. For the past few miles it had been the same. It was as though every scent of animalkind had been spirited away without a trace.

It wasn't natural. His instincts tingled because of it, bristling with the knowledge that he was being pursued, stalked by some creature or creatures that were cunning. Hauwka snorted. Then, lowering himself to the ground, the great beast lumbered up the trail toward the summit of Badonsward.

There had been much wolf-sign in the area, much more in fact than when he and Terryll journeyed through here on their way to Glenryth a few months earlier. But there was no scent in the air. And now the wind was strangely silent with news of others who moved about in the night, betraying nothing.

Whatever was trailing him was very clever; it wasn't man, he knew. Men were clever, but in the ways of the forest they were as clumsy as cattle, out of tune with the wild symphonies. No, this was something else.

They moved like spirits through the trees, their feet whispering soundlessly over the earth with effortless grace. Their heads were lowered in feral attitudes, their yellow eyes sweeping the black shapes of the night with the honed instincts of predators. Each mind was attuned to the whole, and the whole was a killing thing that came stealthily and without fear.

As they passed, Nature looked on with a collective hush.

The moon was just a sliver of light in the sky—a waxing crescent— and the hills were bathed in a ghostly half-light. Thin shadows flickered behind the leaves, and every so often dark clouds glided slowly overhead, gathering in the shadows. It was the time of night when gray mists creep over the land and collect in the dingles and vales.

Hauwka scanned the trees on either side of him for danger, peered into the umbral recesses for telling shapes, a still bush or tree or boulder that might conceal an enemy crouching in ambush, waiting for the instant his guard was lowered. But there was nothing. Not a bird feathering its nest, not a squirrel rustling in the leaves. Nothing. Only the quiet sullen mists.

More than once he stopped and looked back on his trail, waiting for any quiver of movement that might betray life. But the thin shard of moon made visibility difficult at best, even for the keen eyes of the bear. A chill fingered along his spine. Again he stood to his feet and sniffed. Nothing. The absence of scent was, in and of itself, a new kind of scent, a dangerous one, and he pursued it with the knowledge that he was being hunted, that the hunter was a wiley one. His senses tingled with this knowledge.

Sensing the nearness of the kill, they quickened their pace, the predators. For at once the scent hit them, the wild clarion sounded the deep impulses in each breast, the drumming of instincts impelling them, exciting them now to a hot blood-lust, burning through their fevered eyes with a crackling of electricity. In their brains the killing synapses fired off images of the rush, the taking hold of the throat, the scream of terror, and the warm gush of life over their snouts. The scent was heavy now, a crimson heat snapping through their veins that drew them through the mists with invisible cords. Guttural sounds began to jerk in their throats, and the heated slaver bubbled along the mouths.

The bear soon reached a clearing at the summit, broad and pale with light. Then, padding over to the brow overlooking the hill-fort, he gazed down upon the fires of Badonsward below, noted the florid light flickering on the tiny faces of men. There were many Saxons encamped on the plain, gathering here in greater numbers, more than he had seen in many years.

Hauwka cared nothing for the affairs of men, their politics and industry, but he sensed that these men, this new and violent breed that had come to the island, would bring harm to the domain of bears.

Something deep and imperious stirred within the great heart of the bear, something born of instinct and subject to the Creator's decree. He blew out a snort of contempt. Though he could not reason it with words or define it with images, he sensed something dreadful in the air—some wily aberration in the natural order stalking the wild peripheries—much the same as a cat or dog might sense some impending catastrophe and slink to cover. But he would not slink to cover.

It was why he had come to this place this night—to study these new men, to stalk them, to kill perhaps. Kill, and the men might go away. Thoughts sifted quietly through the mind of the bear, and his eyes, the wet, laughing eyes, narrowed with a cunning hatred.

Suddenly his shaggy mane bristled with alarm. Reeling to his feet, turning with the hackles up, the massive head thrust forward, he saw a wolf, and then a dozen others as they moved swiftly through the trees, coming at him, racing over the clearing in snarling fury.

The quickest of the wolves leaped at the bear, and Hauwka caught it with a swipe of his paw, breaking its neck as though it were a piece of kindling. Whirling about, he came down on the nape of another with a powerful snap of his jaws, and two wolves were dead.

Then the bulk of the creatures were upon him in a frenzy, attacking from every quarter, leaping onto his massive back and stabbing at his neck and throat with their fangs.

But the bear's great size belied a terrific speed. Stripping the wolves from his flanks and limbs with long, razor claws, he fell upon them with stunning ferocity, rushing into them and slashing at them, rending flesh and crushing bones.

For just a moment the wolves fell away, and those that could encircled him warily, regrouping, their heads low and their keen yellow eyes fixed on those of the bear as they rethought their strategy—one that so far had left two of them dead, three others mortally wounded, and the bear with only a few surface wounds.

Hauwka glared at them, the great arms raised and bowed with the two-inch claws pointing at the wolves, the snout thrust forward with the cup of his lower lip quivering, revealing long ranks of gleaming sharp teeth that clicked with hatred. He eyed one wolf, the gray one with the black nape, who seemed to be the leader. A growl rattled in his throat.

The wolves rushed him again, three darting in low from behind, converging at once, the rest waited, eyeing the throat beneath the ranks of teeth—and as Hauwka spun to break the rearward assault, they leaped from the circle like thrown daggers and bit hard into the bear's exposed hind leg, drawing blood. The bear lurched in pain, his back arching, twisting. Then, swinging down, he thrust his jaws over the wolf's back and snapped the life from him.

But the diversion had worked—a single wolf sacrificed, and the others were again upon him in a rabid flurry, coming fast in darts, turning, biting with quick stabs, and leaping back beneath the terrific swipe of claws, darting in low again, now tearing at him, wearing him down, ripping deep slashes along his flanks and back, snapping at the nape, tearing little hunks of flesh from the hide, their gleaming fangs gnashing closer and closer to the throat.

A flash of crimson light suddenly burst in Hauwka's brain as the fangs found the soft part of his neck, just over the right shoulder. A terrific shudder rippled over the length of his body, and, reeling, the giant bear flung the wolf clear of him. A flow of blood now streamed from his neck.

Unconcerned with the wound, he tore into the wolves with renewed savagery, snapping at those on his limbs and slashing at those on his back. His eyes burned red with unbridled wrath, his teeth flashed in the wan light. Wolves screamed as the bear's sharp teeth and claws found their vital marks, tore through them with blinding speed. His gargantuan weight crushed those that fell to the ground.

Again the wolves drew back to regroup. However, as they turned to face the bear, they were stunned by his ear-splitting roar. For a moment the moon was blocked, and then the black-and-gray wolf let out a startled cry as the great bear fell upon him, out of the sky it seemed, crushing him and two others that were frozen in terror. The rest fled yelping into the trees.

Hauwka stood to his feet and let out another terrible roar, the exultant cry of victory, the sound of which pierced the still night-scape and shook the earth, then came rolling back as though from a great distance. Several men below turned and gaped up at the hill, astonished. It had seemed to them a clap of thunder.

Gazing after the wolves, Hauwka blew out several snorts of disdain, then lowered himself to all fours and looked about the clearing at the dead wolves and at those who soon would join them. Panting and weakened from the battle, he glanced over his wet flanks. Several thin courses of blood oozed from deep lacerations, glimmering wickedly in the pale sliver of light. As he craned his head to lick at one of the wounds, a sharp pain knifed his right shoulder high up near the neck. The shoulder flinched involuntarily. Hauwka knew instinctively that he needed rest, that he needed only to find a soft bed of pine needles, lie down, and let the wounds heal.

Limping slowly to the brow of the hill, the giant bear cast a scornful look at the men below, teeming in the lurid firelight. He would come back later and deal with them. Turning away, he labored back over the clearing. His shoulder smarted painfully under his weight.

The wind stirred now. It rustled out of the trees and carried into the nostrils of the giant bear a deadly scent, yanking his head to it. A movement caught his eyes, and, starting to it, he saw another wolf, a large one. Hauwka froze.

The wolf snarled through bared fangs as he stepped truculently out from his cover into the clearing, allowing the moonlight to collect his features. Then he moved to an old snag about twenty feet from the bear and deftly leaped onto it.

Hauwka eyed the thing warily as its black shape silently padded along the snag's incline. The wolf was powerfully built, with a deep chest and thick, muscled shoulders and neck, and moved with the confident bearing of one both cunning and battle-wise. Its rufous fur stood out in thatches around a network of old scars, one of which jagged across its left eye from a torn ear, discoloring it, so that his one good eye was a wicked ocher and the other pale gray. Indeed this was a veteran fighter, the dominant, or alpha, wolf of the pack. The bear recognized him at once as one of the wolves that had killed the shepherd and his sheep.

It was Gray Eye.

When the wolf reached a level place on the snag—eight feet or so above the ground—he sat down into a hunched position and gazed about at the dead wolves strewn over the clearing. Then, lowering his head, he narrowed his eyes menacingly on the bear, revealing smoldering contempt as he studied him. The moonlight sifted through the wolf's thick coat and illumined a mane full of grizzled tips, found the old killer teeth clenched and gleaming beneath the bent snout. A low growl rattled in his throat. It was a taunt.

But Hauwka was too shrewd to fall for such a trick. He sensed others were in the shadows, watching. He could smell them now. Moving just his eyes, he looked away into the thickets to the left. There were two dark wolf shapes that had not been there a moment before. Their yellow eyes, like little suns glaring in the dreadful hurl of space, peered suddenly out of the blackness. Then the bear's eyes shifted to the right of the snag and found three or four more wolves moving into the periphery of the clearing from behind some trees. Several more were beyond them, creeping silently behind the snag, adding their yellow orbs to the growing constellation.

Several lank shapes moved toward him from behind and found their places along the dark circle that was forming quickly around the bear. They sat deathly still under the black canopy of trees, like chiseled stones. The wan moonlight edged weakly against their feet, pushing against the darkness, as it were. And the wolves silently watched the giant bear with hateful eyes.

Hauwka eyed them back, looked intently into each face, measuring the length and breadth of their threat. Many of the younger wolves held his scrutiny with defiant, unblinking eyes, but the older, more seasoned ones were less secure in their position. They respected the bear for his formidable prowess in battle (the ten dead wolves before them bore testimony to this), and they quickly broke from his gaze as his eyes met theirs.

Soon a murmuring of low growls rose among them, but each held his place as though by a silent command. One, however, a younger wolf—Kill Deer—crept forward a few steps out of the shadows, arching his back.

Hauwka took a step toward him and snorted a challenge.

Kill Deer backed up two steps before he realized what he had done. His eyes darted along the circle to see if the others had noticed. They had. The young wolf turned back to Hauwka and let out a menacing growl, then moved toward him a step, baring his fangs. He was careful, however, to maintain a respectable distance. Several along the circle growled, and more than one of the younger ones seemed ready to rush the bear. But they were kept at bay by a fierce look from Gray Eye.

Gazing into the eyes of the veteran fighter, the bear wondered why Gray Eye was waiting. Why did he not attack? Surely he had the clear advantage. And then again, perhaps that was the very reason for not attacking. The bear was surrounded, sorely wounded, and spent from battle. Why not savor the moment? It is often the way of the predator to play with its prey before killing it.

But Hauwka too was a predator, a hunter of living flesh. He too knew the game. However, unlike his enemy, he was not playing with his prey—he was playing for time, time that he desperately needed in which to regather his strength. His earlier fight had weakened him terribly. The bite of pain in his right shoulder grew with each chug of his heart.

And so he waited, quietly observing his opponents, studying them, calculating their strengths and weaknesses, strategizing his defense and attack, eyeing possible routes of escape. He appeared calm, placid even. However, his mind was buzzing with the instincts that had kept him alive through many perils, and his blood simmered with pent ferocity, churning from the bellows of his heart over the loose muscles and sinews, warming them, stoking them for the rush that must come. He waited for it, the predator did. The wildness in him even wanted it.

His eyes left Gray Eye's to survey the trees and shrubs along the periphery. He picked up at least a dozen more wolf shapes that had moved into the shadow-line, swelling their number to more than twenty. The fight or flight instincts burned hot within him, each striving for dominance, for the slightest tip of the scales. He sensed in that moment that the sum of his skills in battle would soon be tested. But his mind was not on death; it was on the eyes of the veteran wolf, on the throat of the young one called Kill Deer, and on those two older wolves off to the right.

And he gathered himself for the rush.

Suddenly a howl cried out from the hill-fort below and echoed across the night, a cry unlike any wolf that the bear had ever heard. It was wolfish to be sure, yet at the same time human, though altogether unnatural and hell-born. It was unnerving, even for the stout heart of the giant bear. However, as Gray Eye turned his attention from it, a thin, baneful snarl curled across his snout.

The wolves rushed him from the shadow-line. But Hauwka had anticipated that and, in a blink of time, reared to his full height and let out a deafening roar.

Several of the beasts shied at its thunderous power and fell backward to the ground in awe. Others stood dumbfounded in their tracks, gaping stupidly up at him. The great bear took advantage of the moment and lunged into their midst, and the summit again became a killing field.

The first to fall was Kill Deer. Three others around him were quickly dispatched, before they knew that death was upon them. Then the bear turned and, like a raging juggernaut, cut an indiscriminate corridor through those behind him, forcing the terrified creatures into one another. Some turned on each other in panic. Hauwka had taken their advantage and turned it against them.

Gray Eye quickly let out a rallying cry that pierced through the whirling confusion. Then he raced along the old snag and leaped onto the bear's massive back and bit deep into his wounded shoulder.

Hauwka jerked upward with a growl and flung the animal to the ground as he might a small rodent.

Gray Eye hit hard and rolled across the clearing. But he came up on all fours, unscathed, a line of bloody foam frothing around his mouth. And immediately the wolf sprang again.

Hauwka roared and hurled his gargantuan bulk into the fray, felling many of the puny wolves. But his advantage was short-lived. The wolves quickly recovered from his initial attack—inspired as they were by the fury of Gray Eye. They regrouped, and in an instant two dozen were upon the great bear in a frenzied, snarling counterattack. Their terrible fangs snapped and clicked like a thousand little sabers in his ears and tore the very life from him.

Hauwka reeled in pain and with the last discharges of his strength obeyed the primal instinct to flee. The giant bear clawed his way through one of the older wolves and bolted into the trees, and the wolves were fast upon him.

___ 23 ___
ACROSS THE RIVER

I t was fortunate for the boys that the moon was but a crescent. It allowed a cover of darkness as they sneaked down the hill overlooking the village, yet afforded them a sliver of light in which to pick their way to the river's edge.

Terryll led the way and soon found a sandy crook of beach on the leeward side of a jutting sandbar, plenteous with sedge and cattails. At once, the water's surface was pelted by a broadside of frogs jumping into the river from a blind of reeds. The young hunter quickly wrapped his longbow and quiver of arrows in his cloak to keep them dry during the crossing, then scanned the opposing bank for a suitable place to make shore.

The river was wide and black, save for the shimmering highlights of the moon, which skittered across its surface in a wild erratic dance. The mesmerizing play of light, however, belied a treacherous current beneath.

Terryll suspected as much. He carefully waded to his knees through the eelgrass and bottom rocks slick with algae and soon felt the pull of it against his legs. He looked back at Worm, still standing on the bank, and signaled for him to follow.

Worm thought it appropriate to inform Terryll that he didn't know how to swim.

"*What!*"

"I never learned."

"This is a fine time to tell me!" Terryll rasped above the flow. "Why didn't you tell me earlier? We could've found a better place to cross—or even doubled back to the road."

"I figured I'd just pick it up as we went along," Worm said, shrugging his shoulders. "I mean—how hard can it be?"

Ten minutes later Terryll dragged him up onto the far bank, blubbering and coughing and near drowned.

During the crossing Terryll had lost him once and feared the worst. Worm had been holding onto Terryll's waist-belt with one hand and thrashing at the water with the other. He did fair until they reached midstream, at which point the satchel of provisions he was carrying was torn loose by the strong current. Making a grab for it, he let go of the belt.

Had it not been for the weight of the sword and shield strapped around his back, the torrent would have swept him downstream to sure doom. As it was, he sank like a stone. Fortunately, Terryll was able to grab a handful of his hair and yank him to the surface.

"You could've been killed," Terryll chided, hitting the beach near exhaustion.

"We made it, didn't we?" Worm sputtered, after which he hacked up a mouthful of water. He thought he might vomit for a moment and spit at the sand a couple of times in preparation. But the feeling passed. Instead, he rolled over and groaned. With his shield still slung across his back, he resembled a rather large upended turtle lying on its shell and pondering its miserable fate.

"I think I've about got the hang of this swimming business."

"Remind me to take the *road* out of here when we leave," Terryll countered.

Finding their wind after a few minutes, the boys peeked over the embankment through a screen of bulrushes and surveyed the village and grounds.

Earlier that day, from their vantage point on the hill, they observed the area where the women were taken. There were three small huts on the eastern periphery of the village, set apart from the other buildings by a hillock and surrounded by several trees and shrubs. From what the boys could tell, the women were led into one of the huts—which one, they didn't know for certain, but at least they had a direction.

They had studied the layout of the village—its various landmarks, buildings, and other structures—and committed their positions to memory. They knew that come nightfall they could easily get lost or disoriented, and their situation was grave enough without adding confusion to it. Even so, the change of perspective to the ground level put a troublesome slant on things.

Terryll strung his longbow and fit an arrow to its string. Worm slipped his arm through the leather straps on his shield, unsheathed his sword, then got into his battle stance and practiced a few of his sword maneuvers. He spent a full minute slashing and jabbing at unseen opponents, before sensing Terryll's eyes on his temples. Looking up, he grinned broadly, deflecting Terryll's stare.

"Are you ready?" Worm asked nonchalantly.

"Am *I* ready!" Terryll said, not believing his ears. "You're the one who's been standing there swatting mosquitoes nearly all night!"

"I need to keep loose," Worm said.

"Let's go!"

"Anytime you're ready."

Terryll moaned under his breath.

The boys moved silently from their place of concealment and crept delicately along the top of the embankment as though mindful of eggs scattered about their feet, heading east toward the black wall of hills that rose sharply behind the village. As they picked their way through the bulrushes and tall river grass, they kept a wary eye on the village, though they couldn't see much of it but the berm and a few rooftops, standing out in dramatic relief against the fireglow that came from somewhere inside.

Something dark slithered through Worm's legs and brushed lightly against his instep, causing him to jump to one side and let out a startled gasp. Immediately a dog commenced to bark near the village gates, and the boys froze. Thinking it had gotten wind of their approach, they quickly scanned a route of retreat and prepared to bolt.

However, the dog seemed more intent on a wayward hedgehog than on the two young Britons and from all appearances was about to separate the thing from its life after a few moments of artful quartering.

The boys let go sighs of relief, then Terryll shot Worm a censuring look.

"It was *something*," Worm whispered defensively.

Terryll shook his head, and the two hurried along their course. Worm kept a sharp eye on his feet.

A jangle of strings, drums, and high-pitched instruments that whined and wailed—making a most ghastly, haunting music—swelled up into the cool autumnal air and smote it with a clangor. It sent shivers up Worm's spine as he imagined what manner of instrument could produce such a frightful noise. It had in its voice the timbre of demons shrieking out of hellholes.

However, the music gave the boys a cloak for their stealthy approach—and the guarded comfort that everyone inside would be distracted by song and drink and not suspecting their bold scheme. It was a small edge.

Terryll and Worm soon reached the road that paralleled the river and opened into the village precincts. At this point they were forced to leave the cover of the bulrushes and begin a hazardous trek across the skirt of land between river and village berm, a breadth that seemed a great impassable chasm.

Out in the open, the boys were vulnerable to discovery, and, sure that there would be pickets about, they put a fair clip in their gait. But as soon as they reached the midpoint, the music stopped abruptly. Again the boys froze, and their hearts leaped into their throats. They crouched to the ground and listened intently for any sign of danger. Their eyes were busy around the gates.

Presently there came a bloodcurdling outcry from within, and the hills resounded with a terrifying echolalia. It lit a fire under the boys' feet, and they sprinted—cares to the wind—across the field and dove into some bracken near the base of the hills.

"What's happening?" Worm rasped, panting. He was unfettering himself from a tangle of fern fronds and vines.

Terryll peeked through a frond and said, "How should I know?"

The boys scanned the village, fully expecting to see a horde of Picts storming through the gates any second. But their dread expectations were met only with an uproar of laughter and cheers. The strange music quickly climbed again to its frenetic tempo, and more spirits were let loose out of their black holes, wailing and moaning.

Terryll stood up, shaking his head, angry at himself for having been so easily unnerved.

Worm had no such remorse.

Then the music dipped for a moment under the breeze, and a sound in the thickets above them had his rapt attention.

"What's that noise?" he asked, wide-eyed.

"What noise?"

"I thought I heard something up on the hill."

Terryll cupped his ears and listened for a few moments. "I just hear bullfrogs," he said, with an edge of sarcasm.

Worm was indignant. "It wasn't bullfrogs I heard—"

"Shh!" Terryll ducked into the bracken, and a look of intensity swept over his face as he surveyed the darkness. "I heard it too," he admitted, though it pained him to do so. He prided himself on his keen hearing and didn't like being upstaged by Worm, whom he considered deaf as a tree stump. Worm grunted with a little smirk on his face. He knew what Terryll was thinking, and he took great pleasure in it. Suddenly his eyes jerked wide. "There! Something moved behind those bushes!" he whispered, pointing to some shrubbery far up the slope. "Are you sure?"

"I saw a glint of light—like off a helmet. I think there's more than one—there! Did you see that?"

"Yes!" Terryll raised up onto one knee. He drew back on his bow and found his mark on one of several black shapes angling obliquely across the slope.

"Are they Picts?" Worm asked, clenching his sword.

Terryll immediately eased the pull on his bowstring, and his expression fell. "If they are, then they're the first Picts I've ever seen with udders!" He stood to his feet. "We have no time for this. Next, we'll be jumping at beetles." He waded out of the ferns.

Worm furrowed his brow. "Udders?"

At that moment four cows crashed through the bracken and nearly trampled him.

He dove through the fronds out of their path. Scrambling to his feet, he observed that the cows were headed toward the long grasses along the river, undoubtedly for a quiet evening graze. "Well, they looked like helmets," he remarked, noting their curved horns. But his efforts to convince himself were short-lived. The sight of the cows plodding away into the darkness mocked his defense at once. He shook his head, castigating himself for his stupidity, then hurried to rejoin Terryll.

The boys moved surreptitiously from trees to rocks along the base of the steep incline until they reached the point opposite the southeast corner of the berm. From there they climbed the hill partway, then traversed its rocky flanks, thick with wildwood trees and shrubs, until they came to a sizable outcropping of boulders, a quarter mile from their starting point on the slope.

The site commanded a panoramic view of the village below—principally the eastern edge of town, not far from the three small huts where the women had been taken—and for the first time they were able to see the gathering of Picts. What they saw filled them with dread.

Below their position was a broad expanse of cleared land, surrounded by dense groves of oaks, that rose to a low, blunted hillock thronged with people. Many of the revelers—mostly women and teenage girls—were dancing to the strange, wailing music against the lurid, blazing lights of several bonfires. Bangles chinked at their feet. Their black-and-red silhouettes cast indecent shadows across the ground and over the watching men, who sat hunched like bacchanalian satyrs in large clusters around the fires with insatiable, leering eyes.

These, mostly drunk from ale and mead, cast lewd comments and gifts from their spoils at the more seductive dancers, who in turn snatched up their prizes from the dirt and hurled back vulgar retorts.

The men howled with laughter. The women howled with laughter. The children squealed and played games. Fights broke out. At one point a man was felled by an indiscriminate blade. But this did little to dampen the mood of the festivities. On the contrary, it seemed to impel it to a more riotous abandon.

The boys stared in wide-eyed disbelief. It was a haunting spectacle.

Suddenly the crowd roared in unison as though cued by some unseen stage prompter, and all heads turned toward the area of the three huts.

Small children and three robed men came through the trees, leading a girl dressed in a white ceremonial gown. They had apparently exited one of the huts, though the boys couldn't determine which of the three it was.

The children led the small procession, skipping gleefully and singing songs as if playing some new game, while scattering mistletoe leaves and berries onto the pathway in front of them. They were followed, several paces behind, by a white-haired man with a long beard and stoic face—the high priest?—who droned an incantation heavenward. Every so often he reached into a woolen pouch at his side, pulled out a handful of light-colored ashes, then tossed them into the air as if to purify it from some unseen evil.

Trailing the high priest by several more paces was the girl—wild-eyed and screaming in terror—who was flanked by two other priests. These men, also bearded and devoid of expression, held fast to her arms as they escorted her toward some grisly fate.

As the girl and her entourage wended their way through the press of gawkers, she tried desperately to free herself from the leather thongs binding her hands behind her back, but her efforts were in vain.

On either side of the procession, against a backdrop of roaring celebrants, the women dancers began to make high-pitched yodeling noises at the passing girl. They were devilish, unearthly sounding cries, altogether inhuman.

Worm looked over at Terryll. The young hunter's countenance was drawn into grim lines of horror.

"What're they going to do to that girl?" Worm asked, needlessly.

"They're going to sacrifice her," Terryll said, turning his gaze to the area of the three huts.

Worm felt the blood drain from his head. He glanced back at the ghastly cortege, which had begun its slow ascent toward a fifteen-foot-high ring of crude monoliths, set in place perhaps hundreds of years before, that was situated at the crown of the hillock.

Located in the center of the ring was a large stone altar, overlaid with a granite slab and worn smooth from centuries of exposure to the elements and use. Runic lettering honoring the sun and moon gods was chiseled around the edge of the slab. This was chanted by the high priest on each of the solstices and equinoxes before the quarterly sacrifices were made.

This eve boasted neither a solstice nor an equinox but a waxing crescent, and yet a pyre of branches and wood had been built to one side of the altar to consume a sacrifice. It was an aberration, if not a breach, in the druidic rites.

"Is she—is she one of the women we've been following?" Worm asked haltingly.

"She's the one who fell and hurt her ankle."

Worm shot a look at the girl and took note that she favored her left ankle. It was she, all right, one of the Britons they had pledged to save. Worm felt his stomach tighten; they had failed her.

As he gave thought to her plight, the girl stumbled again and, unable to brace the jolt, fell hard to the ground. The crowd cheered drunkenly.

The girl looked up into the seething, undulating wall of leering faces and begged for mercy.

But they laughed her to scorn. Quickly the two priests—oblivious to all but their task—whisked her to her feet and ushered her along toward the mount.

"Isn't there anything we can do?" Worm asked, desperation edging into his features.

Terryll didn't answer. Instead his eyes swept the area by the huts with an intensity that shut out all but a tapered focus.

Worm pressed. "What about the girl? Can't we—"

"Forget about her!" Terryll snapped. "She's *dead!* Now be quiet so I can think, will you!"

Worm's hands doubled into fists as he watched helplessly from the rocks. And then a fit of rage swept over him and took his fear by surprise, chasing it away, metamorphosing mind and body into another thing, a nobler thing. His body was suddenly charged with a terrible bravery, and in a single glorious moment he felt as though he could overpower the entire Pictish village.

He was about to burst from his hiding place and charge down the hill into their midst to inflict furious punishment upon them, but he hesitated—just a moment—and in such pause a voice of protestation shouted at him to reconsider his folly. Quickly the voice reminded him of his youth, pointed out each of the Pictish warriors by the bonfires, their painted faces, their horrible, devilish torsos, the gruesome trophies dangling about their waists, described to him in vivid detail his many inadequacies, his myriad fears, and the treasure of life, his life.

And before he was aware of it, the fit of bravery had been whipped and had somewhere slunk away into a shadowy recess. Then, as he lay pressed securely against the rocks, considering what he might have done, a shroud of terror enveloped him, and he shuddered.

Looking down at the girl, who, gripped by shrieking hysteria, was now being dragged between the priests, Worm bit hard on the grim truth. A great pain seized his chest and tears fell from his eyes. "Do you have a plan?" he asked, resignedly.

Terryll had come to a resolution. "We find out which of those huts they're keeping the women in," he said, "sneak them out into the bushes, then climb over the berm and escape into the hills."

"*That's* your plan? We'll be killed!"

"You have a better one?"

"What about the Picts? They're all over the place down there."

"Everyone will be watching the sacrifice. They won't be expecting anything," Terryll said, turning to leave. It seemed a cold and heartless appraisal, but, in truth, it was quite pragmatic. The girl would provide a most necessary diversion. "Come on! We don't have time to argue about it."

Worm grabbed him by his arm. "Wait! There're bound to be Picts guarding the women!"

Terryll whirled around and glared. His eyes were wild and burning with cold fury. "If you want to stay behind and watch, you can!" He yanked his arm free. "But if Gwinnie's down there, I'm not going to let those butchers kill her!" Without waiting for Worm, he climbed out of the boulders and slipped into the underbrush.

Worm grabbed his head. "This is madness!" he muttered, blowing the air out of his lungs. "Madness!" Then he followed Terryll.

The boys sneaked to the bottom of the hill, hurried across the open ground to the berm, then crept along its base until they came to the place where they estimated the huts to be on the other side. Quickly they climbed up the slant of the berm and peered into the compound.

Spread out before them were the three small huts—though they were much larger than they had appeared from the hillside—nestled in the midst of an oak grove. The trees, along with the dense shrubbery between the huts, would provide the boys with ample cover in which to move, thus honing their small edge.

They scanned the three huts. From what they could determine in the scant light, the one closest was empty.

"Come," Terryll said. "Let's take a look a the other two."

The boys crawled lizardlike over the berm and hid themselves in some brush to the left of the middle hut. The area around the wooden structure was dark and shadowy, save for the dappled patterns of light on the ground cast by the thin shard of moon slanting to the west.

The boys took advantage of the cover. Worm stood guard behind a large oak, keeping an eye out for Picts, as Terryll crawled through the underbrush toward a small window. A torch was burning inside, hinting that there might be occupants.

Reaching the hut, he pressed his ear against the rough-hewn planks of the wall and listened. Hearing nothing, he raised up to the windowsill slowly, careful to keep his face hidden in the shadows, and peered inside.

Meanwhile, Worm's attention was fixed on the tiny procession trudging up the hillock, now passing the halfway point to the summit. The high-pitched music wailed a feverish dirge. But curiously, it drew him to inquiry.

The boy was scanning the throng to locate the source of it when his eyes at last fell upon several men holding what appeared to be bags under their arms. There were sticks coming out of the bags, and the men were blowing into them like pipes. The instruments looked as devilish as they sounded, Worm thought. However he became entranced by their haunting melodies.

The girl let out a shriek and fell again, drawing his attention. As before, the priests bent to lift her up. However, in a final desperate clutch at life, she went limp in their arms and refused to walk farther.

Undaunted, the larger of the two scooped her up and continued the ascension with her in his arms, like a powerful torrent whisking away the opposition of a little twig.

Worm let out a sigh and cursed the sight of these hellish people with their hellish religion and hellish instruments. Pure hatred burned in his eyes.

"It's empty," Terryll whispered.

Startled, Worm shrieked.

"Shh! Quit doing that," Terryll rasped. "You scare me."

"Scare *you?* What about me?"

"Come on, the women must be in the far hut."

Worm grunted.

The boys made their way furtively to the third hut, keeping to the shadows and cover. They pulled up behind a thick oak several yards from the rear corner of the building and peeked around its trunk.

Terryll's eyes narrowed at once. "There's a guard," he whispered.

"I see him. You think he's the only one?"

"You stay here and keep an eye on him, while I circle around to the other side and find out."

Terryll's silhouette was swallowed by the dense foliage before Worm even realized he had left. He marveled at his friend's stealth and for a moment was reminded of the times they had hunted game together during the summer.

He remembered how Terryll tried desperately time and again to teach him the art of stalking and reading tracks, but to little avail. Worm invariably spooked the animal by stepping on a dry twig or generally making too much noise, frustrating Terryll no end. Terryll had faced him one day with the facts: "It's a good thing you're learning metalsmithing from Bolstroem! You'd starve as a hunter!"

Worm found himself smiling. Those were good days. His thoughts turned briefly to Dagmere. *I wonder what she's doing right now? Probably sleeping. Probably dreaming about some other boy in the village, now that she hates me.* He let out a sigh, then glanced at the guard standing near the front corner of the hut.

The man's attention was fixed on the business on the hillock.

The procession had just reached the summit, and all but the children entered the wide circle of monoliths, bathed in the sulfurous effect of several torches. The priests, like soulless automatons, lifted the girl onto the altar and began fastening her ankles and wrists to each of the four brass rings sunk into the slab.

The girl was now unable to scream—her strength was sapped by the ordeal—and marshaled only a soft pleading whimper.

If the high priest heard her cries, his expression did not betray it, for he continued his monotonous incantation without skipping a syllable.

The crowd grew deathly still. In the clear hush of night air the words of the high priest wafted to the heavens in solemn ascent.

"O fearsome and terrible Dagda—great warrior god who goes before us into glorious battle, and Boann, your wife, whose rivers nourish our bairns and protect us from our enemies. We have seen your sign in the heavens each night—the wandering star which moves across the night sky through the Bear and its cub, toward Canis on the southern mountains. We have taken this sign as your pledge of victory against the Britons. You have not disappointed us, powerful Dagda, and tonight we bring to you the firstfruits of our plunder . . ."

Worm felt Terryll at his side.

"There's only one other guard," Terryll whispered. "He's inside with the women."

"What should we do?" Worm asked nervously.

The guard outside the door, like the two who had led the girl to the altar, was dressed in a ceremonial robe for the sacred occasion—a hooded garment made of coarse wool, gathered at the waist with a cord and falling to a few inches above the ground. He, too, was a priest. His expression, like the others, was drawn in placid lines that betrayed no emotion as he gazed intently at the proceedings on the sacrificial mound.

Suddenly his eyes jerked open, and he let out a short cough. He staggered backward into the wall of the hut, then slumped to the ground.

From the cover of the thick oak tree, the boys searched the crowd for any sign of alarm. To their relief, everyone's attention was riveted on the words and gesticulations of the high priest, just as Terryll had hoped.

"Help me drag him into the bushes," Terryll whispered. "Then put on his robe and stand watch in front of the hut. I'll take care of the other guard inside."

Worm pulled on the robe and cast a look at the altar. Then the two of them moved silently toward the hut, one more silently than the other.

Inside, the women sat huddled in the shadows against one wall, clutching one another, their eyes white with terror as they watched the movements of their priest guard.

He had just fashioned a laurel wreath of mistletoe and turned toward the girl standing alone in the center of the room. She was dressed in a ceremonial gown, her hands were tied behind her back, and she stared at the man approaching her.

"Do not be afraid, my child," the priest said in a sonorous tone. "It is a great honor to be offered to Dagda." He set the wreath in place, then lifted her long, thick tresses into the light of the torch, sifting the strands slowly through his fingers. "Such fire in your hair," he remarked, admiring the palette of red hues glimmering radiantly in the torchglow, "as though the sun god himself has kissed the crown of your head. Dagda will be pleased." The priest shifted his eyes in a furtive glance heavenward, then moved closer to her face. "'Tis a pity, though," he whispered, "for I would have gladly taken you for my wife."

The girl glared into his eyes defiantly. "I would slit your throat on our first night."

"Tsk, tsk, tsk. And a fiery spirit to match her hair!" the priest said, caressing the porcelainlike skin of her cheek. "I do hope that Boann will not be jealous of such beauty and temper!"

A sudden scuffling outside caught the priest's attention, and he turned. "It cannot be her time so soon, Cadryll!" he remarked, irritated.

"It is *your* time," Terryll said, as his black shape filled the doorway, his bow drawn.

Before the priest could utter a protest he was struck in the throat by Terryll's arrow and fell backward to the floor.

The girl looked down at the body, stunned, then up at the boy. Terryll had shut the door behind him and was treading from the dark periphery into the pool of light where the girl stood. At once, she brightened.

"Terryll!" she gasped. "Is it really you?"

"Yes!" he answered, surprised. As he crossed to the girl, his eyes shifted back and forth between her face and the line of eyes gazing at him from the shadows, not sure which of the women had spoken his name. "How did you know it was—" he started to say, but as his eyes rested on the lighted features of the girl before him, they widened in disbelief. "Gwinnie?"

"Yes, Terryll, it's me—Gwyneth!" A wave of relief softened her features.

Terryll felt a lump suddenly swell in his throat as he gazed into her emerald-green eyes. "You—you've *changed*."

His expression was not lost on the girl. "I'm not so little anymore."

"Uh . . . no. You aren't." He averted his gaze from her eyes, then quickly escaped around to her back to cut the leather thongs with his knife.

A contagion of hope murmured across the line of women as the boy then moved to the first one and cut her bindings as well.

The high priest dipped his fingers into his pouch and sprinkled the girl with ashes.

Her body jerked as the ash fell lightly upon her skin. Then, growing still, she at last succumbed to the monotonous drone of his incantation and spell. She looked up at him, a confused expression replacing the one of terror, as the high priest smudged ashes on her feet, her hands, her forehead, across her throat.

"We purify her now, O most powerful Dagda," he intoned, "that she might be an holy offering in your sight . . ."

Worm's shaded eyes peered from beneath the priest's hood as he watched the ceremony on the hilltop. Upon his countenance there writhed a lurid play of lights and shadows, cast by the many well-stoked bonfires before him. And though their heat touched him, they warmed him not, for it seemed that some dark and indiscernible thing had reached from the pit of his soul, through the length and breadth of his body, and grasped his throat with a stranglehold of chilling terror. He had the appearance of one caught in the throes of great torment. As he stood in such reddish, brimstone light, with such a vision of devilish propitiation before him, the thought occurred to him that he was nothing more than a sentinel at the gates of hell.

He glanced at the throng smothering one side of the mound, too agog with the proceedings before them to notice the subterfuge forty yards behind. Then he shot his gaze back to the summit where the drama moved quickly toward its horrifying climax.

His heart chugged heavily in his chest, then quickened. Brimming with emotion, the boy's moist eyes darted back and forth between the crowd and the girl, lying quiet and shivering upon the altar. His weight shifted anxiously from foot to foot as a familiar chant echoed through his mind. Never had he felt so utterly helpless. He blinked back the tears and, gathering his features into a grimace of despair, gritted his teeth.

"Is the army waiting outside the village, Terryll?" Gwyneth asked.

283

"There is no army," Terryll answered, cutting another girl free.

"No army? Then how many others are with you?"

"Just one," Terryll answered, moving to the next woman. "A friend of mine."

"There are only *two* of you?" Gwyneth asked incredulously.

Terryll did not answer, though something was kindled within him to rebut. However, he busied himself with the thongs around a woman's wrists and ankles.

"Then how did you propose to get us out of here?"

The other women commenced murmuring, and there was a sudden flurry of eye exchanges and wagging of heads.

Terryll glowered. "No one's getting out of here alive if you all don't keep quiet."

"*What!*"

"Look, when your father told us that you had all been taken captive yesterday, we didn't have time to wait around for any army. But if you'd prefer to wait for one, Aeryck and I will—"

"My father?" she interrupted. "My father—he's alive?"

"Er—yes," Terryll replied, cooling down. "At least he was alive when I saw him last."

Gwyneth's countenance fell at once. She covered her face with her hands to hide her anguish but did a poor job of it.

Terryll cut the last girl free, then walked over to Gwyneth and patted her on the back, awkwardly. Clearly he was out of his element.

At his touch Gwyneth threw her arms around him and began to weep. "I saw him fall next to . . .next to my mother as they carried me away," she labored through her tears. "I thought them both—"

"There will be time to mourn later, Gwinnie." Terryll pulled away from her gently and looked into her glistening eyes. "We're in grave danger now. We must flee quickly."

Gwyneth looked up into his eyes and apparently found comfort in them. Then, gathering her emotions, she embraced him warmly and said, "It is good to see you, Terryll."

"Uh . . . you too," the boy stammered. His arms hung from his shoulders like two planks.

Releasing him, Gwyneth turned to the girls. "Whatever he tells us to do, we must do quickly and without noise."

"What about Corrie?" one asked.

Gywneth looked back at Terryll. "The girl they took before me," she explained quietly.

Terryll shook his head. "I am sorry about Corrie," he said. "But we must leave at once."

Sadly, the girls glanced at one another, then gathered behind him at the door.

"One at a time we're going to sneak into the bushes just off to the side of the hut," Terryll explained as he reached for the latch. "My friend Aeryck will show you what to do from there." He opened the door a crack and peeked outside, but Worm wasn't at his post. He opened the door further, slipped outside, and checked the area around the hut, but still he was nowhere in sight.

"What's wrong?" Gwyneth whispered from inside the doorway.

"He's gone!"

"Gone? What do you mean 'gone'? Where'd he go?"

"I don't know," Terryll said anxiously. "He's supposed to wait right—"

Terryll spun toward the hillock, and, to his horror, his eyes fell on the hooded silhouette of someone creeping up the backside of the blunted mount toward the circle of monoliths. "What is he doing!" he rasped. A grim look fell over his face as he suspected the worst, and he chastised himself severely for not having observed the signs of it along the way.

"That's your friend?" Gwyneth asked. "The one who's going to help save us?"

Terryll just stared at Worm, who looked about as stealthy climbing up the hill as a wild boar sneaking into a porcelain shop. "Yes, that's him."

When Worm reached the summit, he hurried to the nearest menhir and dipped into the shadows behind it. The great stone thrust upward on the far side of the mound like a monstrous headstone, shielding the boy from the crowd's view below. He sat with his back against it for a moment to catch his breath and to take stock of his dire predicament.

It puzzled him what manner of madness had driven him to this place, to this very place at the core of his deepest and darkest fears. But the voices in his mind were strangely silent, as though reason and emotion had abandoned him, deserted him down at the hut, leaving him for once with an unchallenged resolve. Surely it was Death driving him, summoning him here to its very throne. Or was it?

He looked away into the black void of night as though for an answer. It seemed the sky was an immeasurable loneliness, touching the hills about him with a glistening of tears, weeping for him. He sighed in concert.

Never before had he felt so utterly and terribly alone, so despondent and without hope. The sum of his life read an epitaph of futility against the great headstone. Sadly, it was true. So terrible was the loneliness upon him, he felt cast away even from his mortal sheath. It was as though his body was an inert thing set apart from himself, from the hillock, even from the world, and he, some excarnate soul, was now hurling across the vast and awful desolation of space like an insignificant speck of cosmic dust, without cause, without purpose, without end.

Surely there must be a purpose, he cried out to the heavens. He perceived a great truth there. But the heavens were mute. A chilling draft of wind brushed a tear across his face, like a touch from the very finger of God, drawing his mind from the heavens to the earthy weight of the shield on his arm, to the familiar heft of his sword, and there was nothing left for him to consider. These were enough. They gave to him a clarity in his mind, a focus as pristine as anything he had ever seen, and he knew what he had to do.

Quickly he shed the priest's robe, took a deep, cleansing breath, then peered around the stone and scanned the altar now fifteen feet away. His eyes were burning with unquenchable indignation.

The two priests stood at each end of the altar with their backs to the boy, framing his view of the high priest, who stood on the other side, gazing down at the girl lying bound and abject before him.

The high priest removed a long, curved knife from his belt-sheath and held it outstretched to the heavens between his hands. As he did so, the blade caught a glint of light from the torches, and its gleam shone across the face of the girl, causing her to wince. Again she cried for mercy, but to no avail. Mercy, it appeared, was a thing of deafness.

"And now, O venerable Dagda," the high priest continued, "we present to you this holy offering—this virgin daughter taken from our enemies to grace your hallowed courts."

And with these words the high priest's incantation ceased. The time had come. He looked down and placed the edge of the blade deliberately against the girl's throat.

Corrie closed her eyes, waiting.

But the raging figure of Worm was already halfway to the altar. His legs, churning like furious pistons, impelled him forward with tremendous speed. His shield caught the firelight and became a brazen sun, and the sword of Caelryck brandished against the jet sky seemed a bolt of flashing silver falling across the heavens.

"Stop!" he screamed.

The high priest reeled as the boy leaped onto the altar and drove his sword into the man's chest.

"Take *that* offering to your gods, you blackhearted swine!"

The girl's eyes jerked open in wonder. The two priests on either side of her stood gaping at the fallen length of man between them, frozen in disbelief.

The crowd, also locked in a confused stupor, was unsure of what had just happened. They stood gazing at the figure of Worm atop the altar, entranced in profound astonishment as the horror of the transgression slowly swept over their number.

Worm straddled the petrified girl, shifting his eyes back and forth over the crowd, glaring imprecations at them. His body, at once taut and limber, stood heaving and gathering its stores for the imminent rebuttal. He was a picture of the consummate Celtic warrior, the image of his father, Caelryck, as he stood in resolute dignity atop the blasphemous altar, his weight forward, his shield and blade up, and the voice of Aurelius hammering in his brain as he waited for the spell to break.

His eyes found Terryll's incredulous gaze in the recesses of the doorway below, and both boys knew in that minute exchange that their hour had come.

"I'm sorry, Terryll. I couldn't let her die!" Worm cried out over the crowd. "Not like this! Now flee for your lives! At once! Flee! Flee!" It was a sweet voice, sublime, and his words composed a little hymn for the brave.

"May God have mercy on you, Aeryck!" Terryll returned. His chest swelled with a great love for his friend—his boon fellow. And though death was upon them, he knew that it would be a glorious passing. He was fairly bursting with pride.

"What's happening?" Gwyneth asked.

"Get back inside!" Terryll yelled. He pushed her into the hut, shut the door behind him, then drew back on his longbow and found a mark.

"You have killed the high priest!" the priest nearest Worm said, rousing from his trance. Jerking his head up at the boy, he added, "You've desecrated the altar of Dagda!" And with that he drew his own knife and struck at the young Briton like a snake, shrieking, "Death! Death! Death!"

Worm leaped from the altar over the man's careless blade and landed in a crouched position a few feet away. Then, springing upward, he thrust his sword into the startled man's side. The other priest flew at the boy, flailing his knife, but was struck in the thigh by Terryll's rifling shaft and fell headlong into the dirt.

The spell was broken. All at once the crowd became an unpenned beast, a savage revelation, and they let out a battle cry that shook the earth. The Picts nearest Terryll raced toward him as one man, whooping, shouting, brandishing battle-axes and spears. As many others stormed the hill after Worm.

Terryll loosed several arrows at the wall of charging Picts, thirty, twenty-five, now twenty yards away.

They came at him with demonic fury. Their faces twisted and contorted maniacally as they howled and shrieked.

But he stood his ground, even though the hail of deadly shafts from his longbow did little to impede their attack.

The boy shot a final look at the summit, now swarming with warriors, and saw Worm fighting gallantly in their midst, his flashing blade parrying, thrusting, and striking swift and true. He heard the boy let out an exultant cry to his father, Caelryck, then watched him fall silent to the blow of a Pictish war club. Terryll turned back on his attackers, loosed his last arrow, and threw his bow to the ground.

"Lord Jesus, receive my spirit!" he cried out to the heavens. Then the young Briton flew into their midst with nothing but his hunting knife and was quickly overwhelmed by the deluge of painted warriors.

Gwyneth let out a piercing scream, and it was over.

24
THE AFTERMATH

Sarteham moved to the window of the hut and leaned his weight against the sill with both hands. Looking across the clearing at the base of the hillock, once ablaze with revelry and abandon, he brooded over the recent turn of events. All that remained of the celebration were a dozen scattered piles of glowing embers cooling in the night air, a handful of men curled in sleep around their once-comforting warmth—too drunk to find their way home—and a few skinny dogs scavenging through the littered debris.

After a time, the large Pict raised his eyes to the jutting stone sentinels standing watch over the altar on the summit. The lines across his leathery brow furrowed at once, and he cursed under his breath.

"The sun god is angry. Shunloc-Taz should have waited until he showed his face before offering a sacrifice to Dagda. I warned him, but he would not listen."

"The high priest wanted to honor the warrior god for the great victory against the Britons," a voice answered from across the room.

"You seem to have forgotten that Shunloc-Taz forbade me to go against the Britons," Sarteham countered.

"He merely advised you to wait until Brynwald returned with his warriors," the voice replied.

"Hypocrisy!" Sarteham bellowed, now glaring at the man across the room. "Shunloc-Taz was jealous of my victory. Do you not remember how he tried to dissuade my warriors from following me into battle? 'Belfourt is too strong,' said he. 'His warriors are many, and ours few.' He told our people that many children in Loch na Huric would be fatherless—that there would be great weeping among the widows because of me. He laughed me to scorn. But when he saw that Dagda went before me and granted me glorious spoils, he knew that he had become a fool in the eyes of the people. He wanted to entreat Dagda's favor and power for himself while the sun god slept—to regain his face before the village."

"So you say," the voice retorted.

"Are you also a fool, then? Why then did he not wait until the morrow and honor the sun god as well?"

"Perhaps the high priest did not realize that—"

"That what?" Sarteham laughed. "That the sun god could see at night?" Then he added in a mocking tone, "Perhaps he did not ken that the wandering star was not a messenger of Dagda at all but a servant of the sun god sent to watch him."

The man across the room did not answer.

The large Pict stared intently at him as though taking a measure of his mind. After several moments the man averted his eyes from his truculent stare and gazed at the wall beside him.

A thin smile curled across the Sarteham's lips. "Have you nothin' to say, Tolc?"

Still the man named Tolc did not answer.

Sarteham let out a grunt of contempt. Looking back upon the hillock, his eyes were a smoldering ocher as he pondered the circle of monoliths. His cruel hands—still stained with the innocent blood of Britons—clutched and unclutched the battle-ax at his side, as though to either check or coax some pent beast within him. "Dagda has smiled upon me and has made my right arm strong against my enemies! Aye," he spoke after an interval of silence. "Shunloc-Taz has blasphemed, and now he is dead!"

"You speak boldly against the high priest, Sarteham," the voice dared to chide.

"So, you have found your tongue at last," Sarteham retorted coolly. Then added, "I am chieftain. It is my right." His frame seemed to shudder at the utterance.

"Brynwald is chieftain," Tolc countered.

"Brynwald is dead."

"Perhaps."

The large Pict drew his powerful bulk from the windowsill and took two predatory steps toward the other man. An animallike ferocity burned in his eyes. "Do you challenge me also, Tolc?"

But Tolc held his tongue.

"Shunloc-Taz stood against me," the Pict continued, "and now he and all his priests but you are dead. Slain by the two British cubs. The gods have vindicated me. They have declared my right to rule as chieftain."

"The cubs killed many of your warriors also," Tolc said, shifting his weight on the bed. It seemed madness had taken his tongue. "Or have *you* forgotten?"

A terrific violence breached upon Sarteham's brow, and his arm leaped at the haft of his battle-ax.

"But we need not quarrel further about it," Tolc hastened to add, sensing that the preservation or the forfeiture of his life lay upon his tongue. "It bears little fruit. I will not contest you."

The large Pict grunted and paused. The beast within crouched, gathered itself together for a launch, waited.

The priest sat upright in his bed, adjusting his back nervously against the wall opposite Sarteham, mindful of the man's feral eyes upon him.

Next to him, in the thick yellow light of a wax taper, an old woman sat quietly, apprehensive and wary as she applied a poultice of herbs and mud to the jagged wound that had cut deep into his thigh. Her eyes paced furtive arcs between the two men and her business.

Tolc raised his leg, allowing her to wrap a linen strip several times around it to bind the wound, and winced a little as she pulled taut on the ends to make a knot.

"Your victory against the Britons proves that the gods have favored you, Sarteham," he allowed, addressing the large Pict guardedly. "I would not challenge their will."

"You have answered wisely, Tolc," the Pict said, relaxing his grip upon the ax. "I see now why the sun god has spared your life." Sarteham continued over to the bed and cast a pitiless glance at the man's leg. "But he has given you fair warnin'."

"How do you mean?"

"The wound in your leg—'tis a sign you are to watch your path before the gods."

The priest smiled wryly. "Does the 'chieftain' now speak for the gods?"

Sarteham grunted. "Now that Shunloc-Taz is dead, you are the new high priest. But I trust that you'll listen to my counsel," he said, thinly veiling his intent. Then he strode back to the window to cast his gaze once again on the circle of monoliths at the summit.

The old woman quickly finished her business. When Tolc dismissed her with a nod, she cleaned up the excess bandages and poultice, placing them in a wooden bowl, then shuffled stoop-shouldered slowly across the flagstones toward the door. But a glint of light from an object lying against the wall caught her eyes, and she paused to see what it was.

As she did, Sarteham stood at the window mulling the last few days over in his mind, trying to determine how they had led him to this fateful moment—a point of destiny, he decided, that could no longer be ignored by his enemies in the tribe. He had been lost in such thoughts, oblivious even to the woman's shuffling behind him. But when she stopped to examine the glimmering object, the silence distracted him, and he turned to see why she had not left the room.

"Are you still here, old woman?" he asked, irritated. But seeing what interested her, the man softened his tone. "'Tis a beautiful thing, is it not, Myrna?"

The old woman flushed with embarrassment and turned to leave.

"Bring it to me!"

Picking up the object, she tottered over to Sarteham with it in her hands, stealing looks along its lustrous beauty the while.

"There's nothing like it," the Pict said, taking it from her greedily.

He turned the sword in his hands deliberately, allowing the light to catch the delicate workmanship along its blade and hilt.

The old woman stood gaping at it, until a sideways look from Sarteham informed her that the time of her service was spent. She turned without hesitation and shuffled out, leaving the two men alone.

"Never have I seen such a blade," he said, testing its balance. "It cannot have been made by a man."

"Perhaps it is a gift from the gods," Tolc said.

"Right you are!" Sarteham returned, gazing at the crest on the hilt. "Delivered to me by the hands of one who has no further use for it." He glanced at Tolc and chortled wickedly.

The new high priest forced a smile.

"You'll be well enough to continue the sacrifice on the morrow?" Sarteham asked him.

"Perhaps."

"See that you are. We will offer a sacrifice to the sun god first. 'Tis his will, I'm sure of it. Then we will thank Dagda for his great victory against the Britons!"

The large Pict glanced at the two huts off to his right. A few warriors were stationed out in front, having replaced the slain priests, and others milled about among the oak trees behind, biding their time gambling until the dawn's relief.

"There are yet three hours before the sun god rises," Sarteham grunted after a time. "It will be a glorious day. Aye. And the gods will be pleased!" Then, turning to the new high priest, he added, "You must rest."

"And you also," the high priest returned, halfheartedly.

"Ha! I will sleep well!" the large Pict said, striking his bare breast. "Aye." Then he strode out of the room, carrying the sword of Caelryck and feeling a wealth of pride.

Tolc was left to himself in the flickering shadows to brood over the events of the evening. What had begun in celebration had ended in disaster. He pondered Sarteham's words. Was he right? Had Shunloc-Taz offended the sun god? Is that why he and the others were killed? If so, then why was he—Tolc—alone spared? He had certainly cast his lot with the others. Questions.

Tolc glanced across the large room at the four empty beds, once warmed by the other priests, his friends, men whom he had known since boyhood, when they were each chosen by Shunloc-Taz to serve in the priesthood. A sad smile played over his lips as he thought about the early days. They were good days. Proud days. Days of honor. He sighed wistfully.

From his earliest memories, Tolc had served the gods to the best of his ability, faithfully, wishing never to offend any of them, for they were easily offended. He had hoped that some day he would find a measure of joy in their service.

In many of his waking dreams he even dared to imagine himself becoming high priest one day, if he found favor with the gods—a difficult task, to be sure, given their capriciousness. However, such dreams moved him to pride, and he was careful to bridle them lest he attract unwanted attention. The gods were always watching, and they were known to be jealous.

But today was no waking dream; it was real. Shunloc-Taz was dead, the friends of his boyhood were dead, he alone was alive to wear the mantle of the high priest. It seemed he had found favor with the gods, after all. Hadn't he?

However, it was clear from his troubled expression that the man found little joy or pride in this day. Instead, there was a great heaviness upon his soul, as though something unknown, something terrible, was about to happen. And though he tried, he couldn't shake the feeling of dread.

Tolc sadly shook his head. He had many things on his mind. Many things to consider. Many questions.

"Who can know what pleases the gods?" He sighed. Then he blew out the taper and gazed into the darkness.

At that same moment, many miles to the south of Loch na Huric, the chieftain of Killwyn Eden was looking out the window of his Roman villa, gazing upon the highlands to the south of his village. He was deeply troubled. Off in the distance a terrible battle could be heard as the wind carried its death sounds over the mountain ridges and down into the sleeping Eden Valley. This, however, was not a battle fought between men, but between wolves—scores of them.

Helena walked up to her husband and placed her arm around his waist. "What is it, Allyn?" she asked. "Is it the wolves?"

"Couldn't sleep."

"They kept me from sleep also," she said. "There must be hundreds of them out there fighting. What do you suppose it means?"

"I don't know that it means anything," Allyndaar replied. "Just a large pack of wolves stirred up about something, is all."

Helena looked out upon the black hills beyond their village. Letting out a sigh, she said, "My spirit is troubled, Allyn. It sounds strange, I realize, but it's almost as though it's a battle between the forces of good and evil."

"Good and evil?" Allyndaar considered her words for a moment. It was true that he had never heard such a hellish fury in all his years as a hunter. But a conflict between good and evil? Between wolves? It was absurd. He dismissed the notion at once. Something other than wolves fighting in the hills weighed heavier on his mind.

"Why would the wolves fight amongst themselves?" Helena asked.

"Who knows? It could be a number of things—food, hunting grounds. Wolves are very territorial, you know."

Helena simply accepted his answer; Allyndaar knew about such things. However, in her heart she debated another matter, an issue she was reticent to reveal to her husband. She knew clearly how he felt about the subject; it had been settled. Still she couldn't shake the dark foreboding in her spirit. It compelled her. "Allyn, I know that I worry more than I should about Terryll," she said, setting her feet squarely. "And I know that he is old enough now and able to take care of himself. But even so, I sense that the boys are in some kind of danger."

Allyndaar looked at her, startled. "What?"

"I said—well, I know—"

"I've been feeling the same thing all day, even as I journeyed home from Brough," he interrupted.

"Really!" Helena was surprised. A great relief rushed her heart. "Why didn't you tell me?"

"I don't know. It's . . . it's just a feeling," he replied, suddenly awkward with his words. "Something I can't explain. I didn't want to trouble you with it."

"Allyn, could we go to Bowness?" Helena asked. "I shan't be able to sleep until I know the boys are safe. Besides, wouldn't it be delightful to see Belfourt and Sophie again?"

Allyndaar looked over at her and smiled. Then, squeezing her hand, he said, "It was already in my mind to do so. We shall leave for Bowness at first light."

"Oh, Allyn," Helena said. Then she hugged him and kissed his cheek. "I'll go and pack at once."

"Helena, would you wake up Dagmere and have her saddle the horses?"

"You don't have to wake me up, Papa," Dagmere said, walking into the bedroom. "There's no way I could sleep with all those wolves howling and yapping out there. Where are we going?"

"To Bowness," Helena said. "Now quickly get some things together, then saddle up Daktahr and two of the mares. We're leaving at first light."

Dagmere's eyes grew as big as saucers. "Bowness! This is wonderful!" she exclaimed, then ran out of the room, squealing with delight.

Helena and Allyndaar exchanged smiles. Then, as the women made preparations to leave, the chieftain looked out upon the hills and listened to the distant battle, the baleful contest that raged somewhere between wolves, and he pondered Helena's words.

It was black as pitch inside the middle hut, save for a small pool of wan light on the flagstones near the window, cast by the now moonless starfield. Only the sound of chains lightly scraping over the floor every so often betrayed the presence of someone in the room.

"You awake?" a voice whispered.

No response. The hut was still, deathly still, like a charnel house, so black and still and deathlike that sight was impossible. Minutes passed in a procession of funereal despair. A dark malignancy presided in the gloomy vault, and in its cold, clammy clutches the air was choked of its breath and hope. Hope was a dying thing. In time the sound of chains brushing dully over the stones broke the awful silence.

"You awake?" the voice repeated.

No response. More minutes passed. The malignancy endured, grew. Hope waned. Again the chains stirred; it seemed with vigor.

"You awake?"

There was a groan, and the chains rattled about as though by a rousing will. "Thank God!" the voice whispered. "I didn't think you were going to make it."

Another groan. A curse followed. "I can't see a thing in here. Where are we?"

"Middle hut. You must have a skull as hard as iron."

"Very funny." Another groan. "I feel like I've been kicked by a horse."

"It looked more like a war club."

Worm gingerly felt around the blood-matted lump on the back of his head and grimaced. "Ouch! There's a knot on my head the size of a goose egg."

"That must be your nose."

"You can jest? How can you jest?"

"It's a wonder you're alive."

"You sure I'm not dead?" Another groan. "I take it we're captured, right?" Worm said, testing his manacles.

"Good guess."

Worm grunted at the sarcasm. "What happened to you anyway? Last I remember, it seemed the whole village was attacking you."

"I charged into them like a fool," Terryll said. "I was knocked to the ground right off, then all at once there were a bunch of them on top of me, beating me up. They did a good job of it too. My jaw hurts, my ribs are killing me, both my ears are stinging, my lip's bleeding, and it feels like my right eye's just about swollen shut. Nothing's broken though, I don't think."

"Why didn't you run when you had the chance?"

"Couldn't."

"You mean *wouldn't.*"

"What's the difference?"

"You're the most bullheaded person I know."

"Besides you, you mean?"

Worm grunted. "Did you find Gwinnie?"

There was a pause, after which Terryll chuckled. "Remember the girl with the red hair?"

"You said she didn't look a thing like Gwinnie," Worm objected.

"It was her, all right." In the darkness Worm couldn't see the wistful gaze stirring in Terryll's eyes. "She's—she's kind of pretty, you know."

"You said before she was homely—red stringy hair, bucktoothed—"

"I never said she was bucktoothed," Terryll interrupted. And then with some indignation he added, "Besides, people change."

Terryll couldn't see Worm's eyes rolling or his wry smile. But these faded quickly in the oppressive black gloom of the hut. Worm fell silent for a long interval, during which time he grew morose. "If I didn't go after the girl," he said quietly, "we could've all gotten away."

"Maybe," Terryll said. "One thing's sure, though. She'd be dead now if you hadn't tried to save her."

"She's alive?" The information lifted Worm's spirits somewhat.

"I saw them carrying her into the other hut before they threw us in here."

Worm's spirits sank once his thoughts cleared on the matter. "They'll probably just kill her in the morning. And us too, no doubt." He shifted his weight against the wall and let out a great sigh of remorse. "Everything I do, or touch, or say is cursed. Now I've brought a curse down on you and Gwinnie and everyone else."

"What are you talking about?"

No response.

Terryll waited. "It was a brave thing you did, Aeryck."

"Brave?" Worm grunted. "I don't even know what happened up there. One second I'm surrounded by dozens of Picts, feeling like I could take on the whole army. Then the next, I wake up shackled in these chains, shaking like a bird in a net. Brave?" He grunted. "I'm not brave—I'm scared to death."

"I'm scared too. Who wouldn't be in this hellhole? You fought well, and being scared now doesn't take anything away from that!"

Worm reflected upon Terryll's words, reflected upon the short, furious battle waged a few hours before. It seemed in his recollection a blur. His eyes blinked heavily against the chilling black wall of air before him. "I suppose." He sighed. "Why is it I feel like a coward?"

The boys were quiet for a few minutes. In the oppressive stillness of the night they could hear the guards' muffled conversation outside. They listened, hoping to learn something pertinent to their situation.

But from what they overheard and could understand of the men's thick, trilling, northern burr, it seemed the Picts were interested only in bartering their spoils from the raid, in timeworn tradition: a knife for a place setting, a string of beads for a carved wooden god, and so on, back and forth. Every so often the voices rose in heated debate over the supposed value of an object, each man hearkening to some unwritten rate of exchange in the universe that supposedly fixed the value of such things, each man appealing to those around him to bear witness to his interpretation of said exchange. After much wrangling and waffling and cajoling, they usually struck some sort of trade agreement that seemed fair to both parties.

At one point, however, the boys clearly heard a man say that his child's doll made of painted wood was worth two bronze lampstands.

"You're either an idiot," the man with the lampstands countered, "or you take me for one."

"Iffen I parted with these shiny jewels, would you be thinking it a fair trade then?" the one with the child's doll countered, holding up three glass marbles in front of the other man's eyes. "You'll notice how they sparkle—how they capture the light from the stars!" The man rolled them around in his palm, trying to capture any hint of light. "Aye. They're of great worth! I can see the want of them in your eyes!" Then he added reverently, "It'll pain me deeply to part with 'em."

The man with the candlesticks fell into a blank stare as he looked at the marbles rolling about in the first man's hand until one of them overshot his palm and fell into the dirt.

"There's nay doubt about it, Spang," he said, shaking his head. "You are an idiot! Take your worthless trinkets and baubles and go trade 'em with the pigs. Who kens? Maybe you'll strike a good bargain with one of 'em!"

"I don't think so," another man chimed in. "The pigs sent him over here to try his luck with us!"

The guards laughed uproariously, then returned to their bartering. The first man, Spang, cursed loudly and threatened each of them with violence, shaking a big fist in each face.

The men respected his fist and backed off. Spang was a large fellow—more, a mesomorphic brute—who had the misfortune of possessing a small brain—certainly a dangerous combination, especially when it came to delicate matters likely to end in dispute, such as bartering and gambling.

But he gathered up his goods without mishap and moved to the rear of the hut where others were engaged in a game of dice. Perhaps he would fare better with them, though it was unlikely.

"Why didn't they kill us last night?" Worm asked, thinking how cruel-hearted these men were.

"They have their reasons."

"What do you think they're going to do to us?" Worm pressed, not satisfied with the response.

"You were right about that Pict at the head of the column we saw yesterday," Terryll said, deflecting the question.

"What're you talking about?"

"The man you thought looked like a chieftain. When you were still unconscious, he came in here to get a look at us. He looked at us real hard—for a solid minute—then left. One of the warriors referred to him as chieftain."

The thought of it struck Worm odd. *What was he wanting to look at us for?* he mused. "Well, he can't be much of a chieftain if he can't find his way through a little fog," Worm said, finishing his thoughts on the matter.

"I don't think he's the real chieftain, though," Terryll said. "I got the feeling the real one had either gone off somewhere—or was dead—and this fellow had taken his place."

"He probably slit the other one's throat."

"You two—shut up in there!" a man yelled into the window. "Or we'll come in and get some early carving on ye!"

The other guards laughed and added a few threatening comments of their own.

The boys complied, and a tomblike hush fell over the hut.

But the Pict's words had managed to secure a toehold in Worm's mind and wouldn't let go. It wasn't long before the boy's imagination was running wild with all sorts of heinous possibilities. His curiosity finally got the better of his fear, and he leaned over to Terryll.

"What do you think they meant by 'early carving'?" he whispered as quietly as he could.

"You don't want to know."

"You always say that. But tell me anyway," Worm insisted.

There was a pause, and then Terryll said, "When the chieftain was in here earlier, he told me he was going to flay us alive in the morning."

"Flay us alive?" Worm asked, incredulous. He hadn't considered *that* black possibility. "You shouldn't have told me."

"It would've been better if we were killed last night," Terryll said, regretfully.

Worm let out a groan as he gave thought to the vivid imagery of it. He had helped Terryll skin more than a few deer after their summer hunts, and the image of a bloody deer carcass hanging from a tree limb took up residence in his mind.

It had always amazed Worm how quickly and skillfully Terryll worked his knife between the animal's skin and muscles, separating the two as though he were peeling away some article of clothing. Terryll referred to the process as "dressing out the game." Worm had always considered it an appropriate description. He thought about the Picts skinning Terryll and him in the same manner, dressing out the game as it were, and he suddenly felt nauseous. He didn't make another sound for about twenty minutes.

During that time his thoughts shifted to the large Pict again, particularly to the time, outside Bowness in the fog, when the man had tricked the warrior Tork into making a move for him. Worm could still see the cruel smile on the chieftain's face as the smaller man slid mortally wounded from his blade to the ground. He was obviously a man who enjoyed inflicting pain and looked for opportunities to do so. If he could enjoy such cruel sport with men of his own tribe—men who had fought under him—what would he do to his enemies? The boy shuddered to think and tried to put such thoughts away from him.

But then another thought, one more tormenting than any conjured by a cruel Pictish chieftain, invaded his mind, a thought so pervasive, so tenacious its hold, that the boy could neither flee from it nor shake the thing. A profound uneasiness overwhelmed him, a dread. The thought became an obsession. Worm commenced to tremble, a little at first, building progressively to an uncontrollable shaking that tyrannized his length and limbs.

"Terryll," he whispered anxiously.

"What?"

"You afraid of dying?"

"What kind of question is that?"

"Just answer me."

"I think everybody is."

"I'm not talking about the actual dying part," Worm corrected, "but what comes after it. You know . . ."

"You mean—what happens to your *soul* after you die?"

"I guess that's what I mean—yes. What happens to your soul?"

"Like I've told you before, it will either go to heaven or to hell," Terryll replied. "One place or the other."

"You're sure?"

"By faith, I am."

Worm pondered the notion for a few moments. "Do you know where *you're* going to go?"

"I know that I'm going to heaven," Terryll said calmly.

"You're sure?"

"Yes."

The idea of being sure about such a thing once infuriated Worm; now it intrigued him. Before he met Terryll and his family he had never given it a thought. He believed that people were born, lived out their lives under a cruel sun, beat out whatever living they could, grew old if they weren't killed by disease or sword, then died. At which point, only the worms made a sizable profit. Such knowledge was enough. It was simple. Beyond that, it was a mystery that could not be fathomed, a mystery best left to stargazers and fools.

But of late, the mystery had deeply troubled him. His pat answers no longer sufficed. Since the night when he stood his vigil over the field of dead sheep, the mystery ambushed his mind on what seemed an exponential scale, pervading his thoughts, ruining pleasant fantasies, souring otherwise tolerable moods. The thing would not give him rest.

It was as though it were a vicious spectral beast that had been created with the sole purpose of pursuing and capturing and devouring his soul, however worthless his soul was esteemed in his mind. Relentlessly the beast hunted him, haunting him in night dreams, preying upon his reflective respites from chores or other distractions.

And always without fail, as he sought escape, he was brought, or driven—yes, driven—to the terrible warp and woof of the tapestry, where his mind's eye was made to gaze upon the man and woman in their threaded flight, and upon the writhing dragon and the bloody slash of crimson gaping at the throat of the lamb.

Each assault of his mind left him quivering in mounting terror. It seemed the Christian God, the awesome Otherness, who was waiting just beyond the wall of blackness, was pouncing now, was upon him.

"Do you want to talk about it, Aeryck?" Terryll asked.

"Huh?"

"Your soul. Do you want to talk about your soul?"

Worm did not answer Terryll's question. He lacked the strength or will or ability to engage. Instead, he let out an anguished sigh. Even in this place the spectral beast had come, the thing that would not give him rest, that would not allow him to live out what little remained of his life in peace. In his mind he cursed the thing. Too exhausted from the night's ordeal to focus any longer on the matter, Worm laid his head against the wall of the hut and fell, or wandered, into deep musings, still wrestling with the stalker of his soul.

And the terror of it drove him.

25
THE DYING

A t once Worm found himself standing before a garden—the one he had seen many times before in the tapestry—and knew not whether he was awake or asleep, for the imagery was so lifelike and sensorial. He pinched himself on the wrist, expecting to waken from the fantasy, but felt only the bite of pain instead. The boy looked about the garden, full of wonder—being more curious than afraid—and yielded without mental inquiry to the transports of whimsy that had carried him to this place.

Worm looked to the area in the garden where he expected to see the naked man and woman running, but they were not there. Neither was the serpent in the place where it had been. He was alone. And the aloneness startled him. He looked over his shoulder. Perhaps the man and woman had run behind him. But all that he could see was a vast desolation stretching beyond him for what seemed an eternity, without the least shard of relief breaking the pale horizon.

It seemed a wasteland scorched by some fiery judgment. It was a vision of soundless solitude, a soulless isolation that was even more startling to the boy, and the sense of it burdened his soul with unrest and melancholy. He turned immediately toward the garden with a budding hope.

In stark contrast to the bleak wasteland, the garden was everywhere a vision of resplendent creation, everywhere bursting with vibrant colors and fragrances as cascades of flowers and vines laden with berries spilled onto its many paths. All around Worm, as he made his way into its midst, were fruit trees weighted—boughs bent—with all manner of fruit shining with lustrous beauty. There wasn't a place he laid his eyes where there wasn't a cornucopia of beauteous fare, ripe for the picking.

The sight quickened the boy's appetite, so he took a piece of fruit from the nearest tree and bit into it. As he did the sweet nectar squeezed from the pulp, gushed over his lips, and dripped down his chin, brightening his eyes, for the fruit was cool to the touch and delightful to his taste, such as he had not known. But curiously it did not satisfy his hunger. If anything, it left his mouth sour and parched. He took another bite, but again his appetite was not sated. Looking down at the fruit in his hand, he was shocked to see it crawling with worms that had eaten through the pulp. He spit out the piece and saw that it too crawled with worms. The boy nearly retched at the sight, but so parched was his throat that he managed only to choke out a windless cough. He threw the fruit to the ground and cursed the worms, then journeyed farther into the garden, driven now by his thirst.

The boy knew that given a garden of such bounty, there had to be a source of life to nourish it. No sooner was the thought framed in his mind, than he heard the babbling lap of water against stones and smelled the cool scent of foliage dripping wet with spray along the muddied banks of a river.

Worm marveled that his quest was so brief, and he wended his way through the garden toward the river, rejoicing at his timely fortune. But as he approached its banks, the Lamb with the crimson slash across its throat was suddenly standing in the way before him, blocking his path.

So fierce was the Lamb's gaze upon him, so penetrating its stare, that the boy reeled backward several steps as though he had run into a wall. Recoiling from the fright, Worm gathered his wits and thought that he might circumvent the Lamb and run to the river beyond it. But whichever way the boy turned, this way and that, the Lamb was standing in his path, watching him silently, its bloody wound gaping horribly across its throat.

Worm was repulsed by the wound and sought a place to avert his gaze. He chanced a look into the Lamb's eyes but at once felt a burning light piercing into the very pit of his soul, revealing a vast desolation. It seemed his soul was a mirror to the wasteland hinder, and the Lamb's presence the fiery source of its scorching. He found that he could not endure the Lamb's scrutiny, so tormenting was his soul's vision of itself, and he knew that he would certainly die should he not find relief. Terror struck him. The boy raised his hands to shield his view of the Lamb and fled from its presence.

Immediately Worm found himself in a broad expanse, fleeing as fast as he could from the terror of the Lamb. At first he could not tell whether he was running or flying, for there was no sensation of ground beneath his feet. He looked down to see which it was and was surprised to see the terrain fleeing beneath him at a blinding speed, though there wasn't the slightest hint of wind playing against his face. Although he didn't understand it, it pleased him, for he knew that he was putting a great distance between him and the Lamb.

Worm glanced over his shoulder to see if it was so and was amazed to behold a multitude of people as far as the eye could see, traveling along with him—or perhaps he was along with them. He couldn't tell. There were people of many colors and exotic appearance, the like of which he had never imagined. He saw in their midst many who were beggars and thieves like himself, as well as merchants and commoners, noblemen and noblewomen, kings, queens, and not a few men of religion: pagan, Jew, and Christian. Of these latter travelers, he was able to discern which from which by the catechisms they broadcast with zealous eloquence and by their proud carriage and the scornful looks they cast at one another.

Worm didn't know if those in the multitude were also fleeing from the wrath of the Lamb. However, it did not matter, for their presence gave to him the comfort of numbers, fellow sojourners as they were, and in their entertaining distractions he soon forgot its terror.

The boy had no idea where they were headed, so he made inquiry of a man drawing near to him.

"I was just about to ask you the same," the man said with an affable shrug of his shoulders. Then he smiled and continued on his way jauntily.

"But we'll be there soon enough, I'm sure!" a woman spoke from behind him. "Just you wait and see."

"I'm on my way to give a dissertation," one of the religious fellows intoned. "I trust you will be there, lad. Your soul, your soul, tend to it!"

The answers puzzled the boy, but he fell in step with the others just the same, not giving the matter another thought.

Then all at once, enthusiastic cries of *"Look! Look!"* rang out from the multitude, and many were pointing ahead.

As the boy looked, he saw a great city sitting upon the circle of the earth—a splendid vision of light, stretching from one end of the horizon to the other. It reached high into the heavens through tiers of shimmering clouds, so that its zenith could not be described or fathomed. The city appeared to be fashioned with stones cast of pure gold, and it shone with a blaze brighter than any sun, though there was no sun in the sky.

As the multitude drew near the city, another shout rang out from their midst. It became apparent that the walls of gold were not fit with stones at all but with people, as many as the blades of dewy grass glistening across ten thousand fields.

The sight was of such sublime majesty that it brought Worm to tears. The people were clothed in garments as white as snow, each bursting with a splendor that was a mere reflection of some greater light radiating from within the city.

Worm could not see the source of light but knew that it must be too awesome to behold, for he could scarce hold his eyes upon those before him without squinting and shading his brow. As he scanned the peopled edifice—now close enough to discern their features—his eyes halted upon the figure of a man whom he recognized at once.

"Father! Father! Is it you!? Is it really you!?" Worm cried out, rejoicing to see Caelryck's radiant face. Immediately the boy ran ahead of the others to greet him, his arms flung outward with idiot abandon. And a stream of joyous tears flowed upon his cheeks.

Cries of joy ejaculated from the multitude as loved ones were recognized here and there along the city wall, and soon there was a deafening crescendo of rapturous shouts. The throng quickened its pace, and the ground thundered beneath. It seemed a great surge of humanity was rolling and cresting and breaking, impelling the boy forward with a terrific rush toward the wall. Never before had he known such elation, such ecstasy of joy, as he considered the delinquent embrace of his father awaiting his arms, and he shrieked in concert with the billowing waves of happy faces behind him.

From a distance, the ground between the city and the multitude appeared unbroken, a terrain of unblemished distribution. But as they drew nigh, it became apparent that a great chasm yawned in their path, cutting off the wall before them.

Worm saw the abyss in time and pulled up abruptly at its edge, teetering a few horrifying moments over its lip. But the remainder of his company did not see until too late and fell headlong into the chasm, screaming out in astonished terror.

The boy peered over the terrible precipice to behold their fate, and immediately the horror of it struck his face like a furnace blast, filling his nostrils with the foul stench of burning sulfur. An involuntary gasp rushed from his throat.

Below him was a raging conflagration. Billowing plumes of thick, black smoke belched menacingly and without cessation from some bottomless furnace. Awesome displays of fiery brimstone vomited into the flues like a myriad candles blazing upon relentless arcs.

In the midst of the terrible demonstration there writhed the twisting, scaly shape of the serpent who had been conquered by the Lamb. The reptile appeared in great torment as it burned without consummation in the fiery gorge. Even so, the serpent cried out blasphemies against the Lamb with whom it had warred, all the while fattening itself on the burning flesh of those falling to their destruction. The screams and wailings were terrifying, and the boy reeled backward from the noxious updraft along the face of the chasm to escape their horrible lot.

But to his added horror, the blissful multitude behind him, blind to their impending doom, pushed him ever closer to the brink as they clamored for the city.

"Can't you *see?*" Worm cried out, as he fought desperately through their midst away from the edge. "You will all perish! Turn back!"

But either they could not hear him, or they refused to heed, for they made no adjustment in their course.

The affable man he had seen earlier smiled as he stretched his jaunty foot over the lip. "Come on, lad! This is the way! What a wonderful—" And he was gone, followed by two clerics who were arguing some important point of catechism.

Suddenly a creature of strange design and terrible to behold flew out of the clouds overhead crying, "Woe! Woe! Woe to those who are not clothed in the raiment of the Lamb!" And a great chorus of woe ascended from the pit in response.

Worm was bewildered as he shied away from the strange creature. *Raiment of the Lamb?* he wondered. Then, looking at those who were plunging into the abyss, he saw that every person was clothed in filthy rags. It was an astonishing revelation, and he marveled that he had not noticed it before.

And then a thought struck him. He glanced down at his own clothes and saw that he too was wearing rags. At once shame welled up from the depth of his soul like a black spring that overwhelmed him, an accusation so weighty that it pressed hard against his back and caused him to bow low under its oppression.

He gazed across the great chasm at his father, hoping for a look of comfort to ease the torment of his guilt, but instead he found only the expression of pity in his eyes, a visage Worm could not bear. And beside Caelryck there stood a kindly woman whose radiant face bore the self-same expression of pity. In a terrible rush of horror Worm knew her at once to be his mother. He turned away and wept bitterly.

Immediately he was enveloped in darkness, and the memory of his father and mother and the glorious city was swallowed up in despair.

And the terror of the Lamb pursued him.

Worm wandered into the blackness of night, his hands extended outward to protect him, for he could see no farther than the end of his nose. Voices cried out in anguish all around him—though he could not see the contorted faces that must have cast them—and he hurried to escape these and the Lamb, who was surely gnashing at his heels.

However, at once he fell into a quagmire of such foul decaying stench that it caused Worm's head to whirl. The boy struggled to his feet but found that they were now leaden, pulled downward by the sucking mire and making it near impossible for him to move. Yet the terror of the Lamb impelled him onward.

After shogging only a few steps, Worm felt a ceiling of some kind pressing hard against his back, so much so that he cried out. Apparently he had entered a tunnel or cave—he couldn't tell which—but he couldn't turn back for fear of the Lamb and the anguished wailing of voices. So the boy pressed forward into the blackness, stooping into a crouch in order to make progress.

It wasn't long before the vault of the ceiling dipped further, and then again it might have been a thousand years, or ten thousand years, for in this place there were no temporal reference points, and time had no measure.

Again Worm lowered himself, and once more after only a few paces he was pressed downward by the slant of the ceiling. He stretched out his hands to his flanks to determine his bearing and to his alarm realized that the walls were narrowing—like the ceiling—as though he were inside a lightless cone, moving steadily toward its vertex.

Soon he could move forward only on his hands and knees. But even such comfort was short-lived, for the closing vault quickly forced him to his belly, and Worm wriggled forward by inches through the putrid slime to escape the wrath of the Lamb.

And then he could move no farther at all. He had reached the tip of whatever hellish place he had crawled into and lay there in the muck with barely room enough for his head to move. At once Worm began to gasp for breath in the oppressive air.

His only recourse was to back out the way he came, but he had managed only an inch of retreat when he butted up against a wall blocking his exit. This struck him with a new comprehension of terror. He was trapped, incapable of the slightest movement, and so he lay there swathed in a cocoon of impenetrable oppression, it seemed, for time without measure. The loneliness became a soundless solitude, a soulless isolation. And the isolation was an insufferable torment.

His soul began to cry out for a single glimpse of humanity, a touch of human flesh, a casual brush of an elbow, a shoulder. He would beg for a smile, crawl to behold the glint of warm sun upon the liquid eye. But even a human slap across his cheek would be most welcome, and in this desolation of loneliness even the vilest of fellows he would consider a boon companion. In such a wretched sheath of clay there would yet beat a human heart, alive, coursing with human desires, pulsing with tomorrow's hope, yet redeemable. But in this place, if it could be called such, there was no one, not a soul but he, and there was certainly no hope. Hope was a forsaken thing.

And immediately, as though in response to his pleas, there were all about him the grotesque faces of the damned, startling him with the suddenness of their appearance, conjuring up unimaginable horrors within. Apparently they had been there all along, for it was these whose shapes had composed the ceiling and walls of the cone, or cocoon, that had so confined him.

Each face bore a singular aspect that befit its personality. On the one was a raging expression of hatred and murder, his eyes burning red with all manner of violence. On another was a lurid visage of lust and adulteries, his bulging, leering eyes wandering to and fro incessantly with insatiable cravings, never to find rest or contentment.. The narrowed looks of avarice and his twin, stinginess, slanted across the countenances of two others, pinching their expressions into ever-tightening piggish scowls. Scores of other faces encompassed Worm—the faces of pettiness, slander, gossip, jealousy, idolatry, witchcraft, each pressing heavy against his soul.

"What do you want with me?" he cried out, panting for breath. "Why are you tormenting me so? Why have you been following me?"

"We are not following you, Worm," the faces answered as one voice. "You have been pursuing *us.*"

"I don't even know you!" he protested. "Why should I follow you?"

"Oh, but you do know us, Worm," the faces answered. "For we have come out of your heart!"

"My heart! You're lying!" Worm screamed.

"What do you know of truth?" asked another face, its features a constant metamorphosing of deceitful expressions.

Worm did not answer, for he knew this one at once to be a liar. Instead he turned to the others and asked, "Who are you?"

"We are the many facets of unbelief," they replied. "Merely look into your self, and you will see the whole."

And it was true. The more Worm studied their visages, the more he recognized them. Some were more familiar than others, for he had often seen their reflections in a certain look, thought, or deed that he had labored to achieve. Others were more distant—filial strangers—yet he knew in his heart that the shadow of each had passed over his countenance at one time or another—a murderous thought here, a lustful thought there.

Worm covered his face to hide from their glaring introspection, but there was no escaping them. Each face moved freely about in his mind—every one of them claiming the right of access—for every one of them was named Worm.

The boy sought death to flee the fire of their torment, but even such hope was denied, and Worm writhed without hope beneath their unending accusations.

And then another face appeared quite unexpectedly, a face completely foreign and yet completely familiar to Worm, a face at once terrible and kind. It was an unsearchable paradox, or mystery, that troubled the boy, and yet there seemed to be but a thin veil between Worm and the knowing of it. As he gazed into its myriad features, his spirit was strangely quickened with a desire to penetrate the veil, a desire that burned to the very marrow of his soul, one giving birth at last to a flicker of hope.

"Who *are* you?" Worm asked.

"Behold," the Face said.

At once a wreath of thorns encircled its brow, causing rivulets of blood to drip without end over its swollen eyes and down its cheeks and mouth. The face appeared to have been beaten with many rods, such that it was marred beyond human recognition. And its beard was sparse and bleeding, where the hair had been torn from the flesh by handfuls. It was a visage of abject horror—one cursed and forsaken—and the boy could scarce look upon it without feeling the presence of the walls and ceiling of faces pressing even more upon his back.

"Have you come to torment me as well as these others?" Worm cried out in despair. "I cannot bear the shame of this burden any longer, for my soul is crushed beneath its weight." Then he buried his face in his hands and wept.

"I have not come to torment but to take away your sins," the Face said.

"To take away my sins? Who are you then?" Worm asked.

"I am the Face of Grace."

"And I am but a worm."

"You are mine. I have bought you with a price, a great price. Behold, the Lamb of God," the Face commanded.

Slowly, obediently, Worm lifted his eyes to the Face. He was startled to see that the Face, though scarred from its wounds, shone now with a glorious radiance, more brilliant than the noonday sun. At once the veil that cloaked the knowing of it was rent in two, and the boy could see him at last!

"Woe upon me!" Worm cried out in terror as he comprehended the gravity of his transgressions. "Many woes upon me, for you are the Lamb who has been pursuing me! You have found me!"

"Do not be afraid," the Face answered. "For I have sought you that, through dying, you might have life."

"How can I die and yet live?" Worm asked, once again bewildered at the paradox.

"Believe in me."

As Worm looked intently into the face of the Lamb, the tiny hope flickering upon the wick of his soul grew steadily stronger. Then all at once, as though moved by a breath of wind, the flicker burst into a blaze.

Faith took hold of the boy, impelling his mind and body and soul. Reaching out to the Lamb, he clung to his feet and would not let go.

"Have mercy on me!" he cried. "Have mercy on me!"

As the Lamb touched the crown of the boy's head, a bolt of light shot through the length and breadth of his soul, first revealing, then purging, every crimson stain of sin and vestige of shame, now consuming every dark and wicked facet of his being. So fiery was the bolt, so intense was the Lamb's omniscient gaze into his soul, that he could not endure it, and immediately the beggar boy named Worm died once and forever. It seemed his greatest fear had, alas, come true.

But then in the twinkling of an eye, the fire that had just consumed him now radiated throughout his person with a glorious re-creation, transforming him from something old into something altogether new and clean, and clothing him overall in brilliant white raiment.

Aeryck slowly opened his eyes and blinked heavily several times while collecting his bearings in the cheerless light. Some time had passed since he laid his head against the wall, for the first gray light of predawn was now spilling through the window of the hut, bathing the flagstones with the day's promise. He breathed in the air, tasted it. It felt good in his lungs, and hope rushed him. There was yet hope of soul.

"Are you all right?" Terryll asked. He was staring at Aeryck, wide-eyed. "You've been having the strangest nightmare. One with serpents and lambs and—"

"I'm fine," Aeryck said, turning his head to his friend. And with a smile he added, "I've just been thinking about the tapestry on your parents' wall."

"The tapestry? Oh. You sure you're all right?"

"I'm sure," Aeryck replied. And as his eyes began to brim with tears, he added, "As sure as I've ever been of anything in my life!"

And the once beggar boy was no longer afraid.

26
THE DESPERATE
HOUR

Sarteham threw open the door of the middle hut and strode into the room with several of his warriors, who in the wake of his all-consuming presence, his primal masculinity, seemed but caricatures of their former savagery. The large Pict glanced down at the boys as though they were nothing more than two sacks of grain needing to be moved, then addressed one of the men nearest him.

"Unshackle the Britons," he commanded, tossing him a key. "Then stretch 'em out between the flogging stones. We'll have some sport of 'em—eh?"

The man hesitated for a moment too long—he had paused to look at the boys—and Sarteham cuffed him alongside the head.

"Do it *now!*" he barked.

"Ow . . . er . . . as you wish," the man said, rubbing his ringing ear. Then he quickly stooped to unlock their chains.

Turning to leave, Sarteham drew his sword and added, "You other men will be mindful of your charges, won't ye now? For if either of them escapes, I'll prick each of your gullets with the tip of my blade!"

They nodded obsequiously as the chieftain strode out. Once left to themselves, each man discovered a withered pugnacity and made an ostentatious show of his bloom before the others.

The first man, the brutish fellow named Spang, glared into Terryll's eyes as he worked the key into the locks around his wrists. His right ear was now a bright scarlet hue, and, while fumbling with the locks, he touched it every so often as if to coax it back into shape, grunting curses into the air.

Aeryck recognized him at once as one of Sarteham's men who had been lost in the fog the morning the boys approached Bowness.

"It'll be a pleasure seein' your hide shaved off your bones, mannie," Spang chortled wickedly.

"Just like strippin' a grape!" another man added.

"Aye. Or peelin' the skin off a blood sausage to get to the good-and-tasties inside!" another taunted. He smacked his lips as if he were sitting down to supper and elbowed the men around him, giving to each a clever wink.

"I fancy the fair-haired one's liver," a fourth announced, to which the men declared other portions for themselves.

"You ever seen what a man looks like without his flesh?" Spang grabbed a pinch of Terryll's cheek. "It's too ugly to even think about."

"You're probably quite an authority on what's ugly, I'd expect," Terryll countered, undaunted.

This got a rise out of the men, and they broke into laughter. Spang bristled, then backhanded Terryll across the face.

"Yeah? Well, we'll see how funny you are, once't you're stretched between the stones!" he snarled. Then the Pict leaned close to the boy's face and added, "And I'll be the one doin' the stretchin', mannie! And you ken somethin'? I'm right good at it. What do ya think about that, then?"

Terryll didn't answer. Instead, he stared back at Spang's eyes until the man turned away.

The Pict looked over his shoulder. "What do ya ken?" he chortled. "He not so funny anymore now, is he?"

"Go easy on him, Spang," one of the men joked. "It ain't his fault you lost all your booty last night gamblin'!"

"Well, he wouldn't have had such bad luck iffen he'd gone to tradin' with the pigs like I told him to!" another chimed in. "At least the pigs would've given him an old cob to take home to his wife."

"His wife's already got an old cob. What would she want with another one?"

This got another rise out of the men as the banter degenerated into foulness, and they all had a good laugh.

"Yeah, well, just shut up—the lot of ye!" Spang growled. Then he jerked Terryll to his feet. "Come on, whelp! You've got some stretchin' to do!" The Pict tossed the key to one of the men as he hauled the boy toward the door. "Here. You unlock t'other one and bring him along, iffen ye think ye can manage."

As the man stooped to unlock Aeryck's manacles, still chuckling to himself over the pig joke, Spang blindsided him with his fist and knocked him across the floor into the wall.

"There! That oughta teach you to be makin' jests on me," Spang snarled, stabbing his thick finger into the air at the dazed man and then at the others. "I don't like it! Do ya hear? I don't!"

The others quickly backed away to give Spang a wide berth as he dragged Terryll out of the hut.

A small crowd had already assembled at the base of the hillock for the ceremony. Others, who suffered from the painful harvest of too much drink the night before, came stumbling from their homes and cursing the day's intrusion. Gone was the festive mood of the preceding night, replaced now by a dour cast that hung over the village like a mantle of gloom. There was no sound of flute and harp, there were no dancers luring the men to lechery. There was only a cold and cheerless murmuring sweeping among the people, many of whom blamed Sarteham for the disastrous developments.

A mist fingered low over the ground, curling around trees and shrubs and cloaking the debris strewn about from the previous night. The hillock pushed through it, and the ring of monoliths was gray against the sky.

The flogging stones—granite totem menhirs rising eight feet from the ground and carved with all manner of gods and goddesses—stood three in line at the base of the hill. Each menhir had several recesses hollowed out in it in which the skulls of past ceremonial victims had been placed, facing north, south, west, and east, each direction corresponding with the druidic death and life cycles.

To the druid, north (or winter) was the beginning, not the end, of the cycle and represented death. East (spring) represented new life and followed death. South (summer) was the season of growth, which was followed by west (autumn), bringing the cycle to maturation. Such was the balance of life, and any intrusion into or deviation from it—plagues, natural disasters, war, and the like—required a propitious offering to bring the cycle back into balance, hence, an animal or human sacrifice.

However, the sacrifice at dawn was not a propitiatory offering but one of thanksgiving, thanking the gods for their favor of victory over the Britons at Bowness. Failure to do so could quickly tilt the scales off balance and draw calamity upon the village. A good druid would be mindful of such things.

The boys were stripped to the waist and relieved of their boots. Then they were spread-eagled, standing, between the stones and secured by leather thongs to brass rings. Their shoulders and joints strained in their sockets from the pull of the leather, which cut mercilessly into their wrists and ankles.

The boys were already in a painful way from their battle wounds— Aeryck's head, clapping at once a dull throbbing yet piercing knell of pain beneath a mat of bloodied hair, and Terryll's eye, now hidden within a swollen skin-lump of blue, purple, and red-brown hues, among other facial and body contusions. Adding to these, both had discovered new injuries and pains that had lain in ambush until they were moved and were now barking fiercely. All in all, death seemed a welcome suitor.

Many of the sluggish crowd gathered around the menhirs and were enlivened somewhat by the brutal display. Others came just because it was something to do.

Mindful of his audience, Spang thumped each of the boys on his taut midriff to test his work, as though he were sounding the ripeness of a melon. He turned to the men behind him, and a sneer worked across his cruel face.

"I'd say they was ripe enough, what d'ya think?" he chortled.

The men laughed, then several poked and slapped the boys all over their bodies.

"I don't know," one of them said, pinching Aeryck's stomach. "This one here's still got a bit of looseness round his brisket!" Then he flat-handed the boy in his solar plexus, knocking the wind out of him.

The torturous games continued unabated for a while, but the boys held their tongues and took it without any word of protest, any cry of pain, for such would only draw another battery of brutality.

Satisfied with his duty, Spang claimed the boys' tunics, cloaks, and Aeryck's boots (Terryll's were too small for either Spang's or his wife's feet) as his rightful plunder. No one contested this, for the charge had fallen to Spang to carry out Sarteham's orders, and with such came whatever plunder was available.

Spang was busy entertaining the men by tracing the tip of his knife around Terryll's stomach when Sarteham strode up to the stones and shoved him out of the way. The chieftain didn't shove hard, but Spang wasn't prepared for it and stumbled to the ground. As his luck would have it, his head hit hard against one of the stones, and he was knocked senseless.

He was unconscious but a few minutes, just long enough to be fleeced of the boys' outfits and the handful of glass marbles that he carried in his pocket. Sarteham had two men drag the brute off to the side by the third hut where he would be out of the way, then turned his attention to the boys.

"Aah! You seem to have fallen into a bad way here, lads," he said, checking the thongs binding them. "Aye, to be sure!" A low, guttural chortle rattled in his throat, like a lion's rattle, as he gazed into each of their faces.

Aeryck noticed the length of his arms, the muscles and sinews beneath the tattooed layers of leathery brawn, how they flexed and jumped to his brutal will, how his torso rippled with ranks of animal strength. He was a vision of masculine virility, however bent, and his scowl was a terror to behold. Energy seemed to crackle from his frame into the crowd about him, charging them with his vigor.

"What did ye hope to gain with such a vain show, lads? Answer me, then," the large Pict continued. "Perhaps ye were seeking the favor of the warrior god."

"More likely the favor of the wenches," one of the men jeered. The boys held their tongues.

"Perhaps. Perhaps not," the large Pict said, studying Terryll's face. "At any rate, you are mine now to do with as I please. And it pleases me to kill you." He chortled sadistically. "Aye, and it'll go none too easy for you, I'll warrant!"

Sarteham moved over to Aeryck and held the sword of Caelryck out before him, once again admiring its beauty. Looking up from the blade, he gazed into the boy's eyes. "You distinguished yourself in battle, young Briton," he said, tempering his voice to an almost paternal tone. "If I had an army of men like you, I could sweep the island. Aye. 'Tis a pity that such a warrior must die between the stones."

Sarteham reached over to the third stone in line, grabbed the skull facing east, and held it up before the boy's face.

Aeryck shot a quick look at the thing, feeling compelled by morbid curiosity to do so, then looked back at the Pict, wishing he hadn't.

"But I shall place your own crown in the place of honor," the Pict continued, tossing the skull behind him to one of his men, "where the hollows of your eyes shall forever feast upon the rising of the sun god." The man looked closely into Aeryck's eyes and let out a throaty chortle. "But not until I've first had a draft of ale from it, you understand."

Aeryck held his gaze for several moments, trying not to think of the imagery of his words.

The large Pict suddenly lowered his eyes to the bronze medallion around Aeryck's neck.

"What's this?" he asked, lifting the pendant away from the boy's chest with the tip of his sword. "I'm surprised that our ox of a friend lying in the dirt missed this when he stripped you down. But then, he's too stupid to realize the value of such things, isn't he?" With a flick of the swordtip, Sarteham cut the leather thong holding the medal and caught it as it fell. "But I'm not!"

"Give that back to me!" Aeryck demanded, pulling against his bonds.

Ignoring the boy, Sarteham studied the crest on the medallion, then compared it with the one on the hilt of Aeryck's sword. "Where did you get these, lad?"

"My father made them," Aeryck returned with a bit of pride.

"*Made* them? I think not. I think that you stole them."

"I'm not a thief!" Aeryck protested and was surprised that such words had come out of his mouth.

"Then your father was," Sarteham countered.

Aeryck glared. "You're a liar!"

Sarteham chuckled as he moved again to Terryll.

"And you're the archer who shoots fire from your bow," he said, eyeing him. "Some of my men fear you," he added, casting a scornful look at the group behind him. "They say that you're a son of the Great Mother Goddess, Modron. Perhaps even Mabon himself. Ha! But I say that my warriors are not men, but old women."

The large Pict leaned in close to Terryll's face and looked him in the eye. "The archer kills his enemy from far away so he doesn't have to look into his eyes. I say that such a one is a coward. The true warrior kills his enemy up close, so close he can look into his eyes and see his soul—smell the fear skulking there."

"Or the foulness of his breath," Terryll said.

Sarteham narrowed his eyes. "You're not only a coward, but you're impudent as well." He scowled. "I will enjoy separating you from your soul, Briton . . . one strip of impudence at a time." Then he pressed the edge of the sword against Terryll's cheekbone and drew a line of blood across his face. "And I'll do it with your friend's sword. It's got a fine edge, dinna you think?"

The men laughed, and they sensed matters coming to a head.

At some point in the exchange Spang woke up and stumbled over to the group, rubbing his sore head. While the others were taunting the boys, the brute stooped to a crouch and looked around the area for the tunics and boots, all the while grunting and casting suspicious scowls at each of the men. But his plunder had long since been spirited away.

Spang stood up with a furrowed brow and scratched his head as he tried to solve the riddle. He was totally bewildered. At that moment one of the men helping Tolc ran over to Sarteham and told him that the high priest was ready to begin the ceremony.

"Good! Step lively to it then, and let the sacrifice begin!" Sarteham yelled over the crowd. He turned to Terryll and Aeryck and added, "You lads'll no doubt enjoy the proceedings. After which you'll make a fittin' sport. Think on it."

Spang had grabbed a smaller man by his earlobes and was about to pound an answer out of him, when Sarteham took the brute by his collar and jerked him over to the menhirs.

"You watch the Britons during the sacrifice," he commanded.

"But I just—"

"See to it!" Sarteham barked. Then the large Pict took his place at the head of the crowd.

Spang watched him leave. His lower lip hung open and quivered petulantly. He let out a curse, folded his thick arms, and leaned back against the middle stone. He shot each boy a sour look. His hopes for recovering his newly acquired wardrobe were clearly gone.

No children broadcast mistletoe leaves and berries in front of the procession this time, and there was no sound of timbrel or lyre. There was only Tolc, the new high priest, who limped along horribly on his leg wound as he led a small procession out of the third hut. He chanted incantations heavenward, earthward, and to the ground below his feet like a good druid, being careful to address each of the threefold realms of deities. His expressionless countenance, however, belied a great turbulence at work.

Following Tolc came two warriors escorting the girl to be sacrificed. The chieftain had told the new high priest that the girl with the twisted ankle had been an unsuitable offering to make to the sun god, and for this reason Shunloc-Taz had incurred his wrath. In Corrie's stead, Sarteham had chosen Gwyneth for her beauty and thick red hair, a combination that would undoubtedly please the sun god.

When the boys saw her exiting the third hut, between the warriors, their spirits sank. Aeryck looked over at Terryll and sadly shook his head.

Even in the gray light of predawn, with the laurel wreath crowning her fiery head, the white ceremonial gown draped fluidly about her comely form, Belfourt's daughter lighted the morning with a glorious radiance. As her bare feet whispered along the smooth path leading to the hillock, the mist swirled about her ankles. She carried herself with the grace and dignity of a hind in the mountains, and every moist and living eye in the crowd—man, woman, and child—was transfixed by her beauty. By the look of wonder upon their faces, it appeared that a goddess was walking in their midst, enthralling each soul, and every heart of man was a temple devoted to her singular worship. As she passed, a collective aching sigh was exhaled; it seemed a prayer.

As the small procession angled in front of the boys, Gwyneth met Terryll's eyes. She hesitated for a moment as she held his tender gaze and winced at the sight of his pained form.

Terryll's heart swelled in his breast as the two of them shared unspoken words with their eyes—words like poetry, expressing heaven's truth and soul's passion, honed to their purest essence in a single tragic glance.

And as he perused a little volume in her eyes, the young hunter found, quite to his surprise, that he was forever changed. Something fierce and insatiable, certainly inscrutable—he knew not the name of the beast—had stalked and found and captured the wildness in his soul, subduing the dominant impulse by a greater and more perfect wildness.

Never before was he struck with such a comprehension of life's driving mystery. Never before had he ever been so dumbfounded and undone by a revelation. It was at once a terrible thing to behold, though full of wonder, a thing at once hither and thither, transcendent and familiar, frightening and yet altogether sublime and overwhelming him with exhilarating joy. A flow of tears coursed down his cheeks from the suddenness of the thing.

But the moment was short-lived. Gwyneth's face was stolen from his view by her two Pictish escorts, who quickly, brutally, goaded her forward. Terryll looked after her until he could bear the pain no longer. He was filled with rage and strained against his bonds to free himself.

"Gwyneth! Gwyneth!" he cried.

She looked over her shoulder for him, desperately craning her neck. But it was to no avail, and the men pushed her along.

Again the boy cried out her name, but Spang punched him in the stomach to shut him up and threatened him with his monstrous fist. Then the brute slumped back into his glowering pose against the middle stone.

The crowd yawned open lazily to allow passage for the small procession. Some women managed the spirit to cry out in their high-pitched yodels, but it was a pathetic comparison to the previous night's offering, and they soon gave it up. Even the men, though encouraged by Sarteham's wild shrieks, gave a lackluster performance that soon trailed off into a low, rumbling drone, punctuated here and there by an occasional hoot or howl. Sensing the emotional rout of the people, the large Pict was furious and stormed over to the new high priest.

"What have you done?" he shrieked. "Have you called down a curse over the people, that they would dishonor the gods so? Och, but the gods will burn with anger!"

"If the gods are angry, they are angry," Tolc answered flatly. "If there is more that I can do to appease them, tell me, for I have done all that I can do."

Sarteham's countenance registered profound incredulity. "You are not fit to be the high priest!"

Tolc laughed bitterly. "I am not fit to be the high priest? Who can say with the gods? One day they smile upon you, the next day they slay you. I am not fit to be the high priest? Ha, such a thought!"

Immediately the procession came to a halt.

Sarteham glared at him. "You mock the gods!"

"Nay, but the gods mock us," Tolc countered. "We dance the fool in their courts, only to be cast aside when they grow weary of the tune. Ask Shunloc-Taz and the others. Aye, they would tell you the truth of it, if they could but launch a word or weep a tear of regret." Lowering his

318

eyes, he let out a rueful sigh. "Aye, the gods mock us, and I cannot bear it longer. It is madness! Madness!"

"You blaspheme!" the chieftain thundered.

"Then strike me dead, for my life is nothing but a blasphemous lie," Tolc answered contemptuously. "Send me to the gates of the underworld, if you have any mercy in your soul, and I will be quit of the blasphemy. There at least Cernunnos will guide me along the dark waters to truth. Ha! Truth! Can such a devil as truth be found?" He shook his head. "I think not."

Sarteham stared blankly at the man, his mouth hanging slightly agape, his shoulders drooping under the weight of astonishment. Never had he heard such words from a man, let alone from a priest! He began to tremble with rage. "You must die!" His voice strained quietly through the anger. "Yes, you must die!"

However as he began to draw his sword, a disturbance at the far side of the clearing caught his attention.

It had started with one or two people shouting across the camp, followed by several more who relayed their words to others until an excited buzz rippled through the crowd. Everyone's head turned as one man, and a great cheer went up from their midst, so loud in fact that the hills shook from the uproar and continued unabated for what seemed a score of minutes.

Sarteham and Tolc turned to see what was happening, and immediately their eyes widened, the one's in horror, the other's in disbelief.

Sarteham sheathed his sword at once and headed across the camp, completely forgetting his business with the high priest. The cause of his memory lapse was no small matter, for coming toward him through the ecstatic throng were the chieftain of Loch na Huric and his warriors, returning at long last from a raid along the eastern coasts of Ireland.

27
THE CHIEFTAIN OF LOCH NA HURIC

Brynwald! You live!" Sarteham managed to choke out, eyeing the towering Pictish chieftain as he angled through the crowd with his warriors.

"More than you ken, Sarteham, you old serpent!" the chieftain boomed over the crowd. "More than you ken!"

Terryll and Aeryck blinked in awe at the man and at those with him, then cast dubious glances at one another around the middle stone. There were at least a hundred warriors, by far the fiercest-looking Picts that either of them had seen.

Brynwald met Sarteham in the midst of the crowd and looked him in the eyes with an intensity that the boys could feel even from the stones. "What? No 'Hail and well met' after so long and prosperous a journey?"

Sarteham immediately offered his right arm to the man, realizing his breach of protocol. "Hail and well met," he added.

Brynwald ignored the gesture and turned his attention to the beaming faces around him. "Ha! Ha!" he howled, as he threw his massive arms into the air. "'Tis grand to see your bonnie faces—and the smell of heather off the hills! Aye! 'Tis a bonnie grand! What do ye say then, men? A hoot for the heath and ale a'round!"

At this the crowd roared another five minutes.

The boys stared at the man in awe, for he consumed the very hills and sky with his presence.

The chieftain of Loch na Huric turned to Sarteham and glanced down at his still outstretched hand. "Word has reached m' ears along our journey, Sarteham, that you have things well to hand."

Sarteham lowered his arm awkwardly. "I have done what I had to do in your long absence," he retorted coolly.

"Perhaps—perhaps." Again he turned to the crowd. With his voice booming like thunder, and his eyes flashing and hurling bolts, and with a gregarious smile the chieftain continued. "Since our boats touched shore on the firth, we have heard of nothing but 'Sarteham has doon this' and 'Sarteham has doon that.' Aye! 'What a ruddy kipper this Sarteham must be,' I say to m' men. 'Surely this cannay be the same clansman we left behind to coddle the bosom of our fair heath!' 'Aye, but 'tis!' says they. 'The selfsame!' 'How is it, then, that he's off to raiding the likes of Bowness and not minding his own?' I ask, and they have nary a word for me! Imagine that, if you will. They become quiet as dead men!"

Sarteham searched the chieftain's eyes warily for his intent, then countered, "We took much plunder."

"So I see," Brynwald said, eyeing the sword of Caelryck at his side. At once the humor left his eyes, and there burned in them a deadly coldness. "And does the plunder include my life and limb, Sarteham?"

Brynwald's words played curiously across Sarteham's face, but he made no reply. He shifted in his stance.

"*Och!* Have you gone deef?" Brynwald pressed. "Or perhaps you'd only be answering to '*Chieftain,*' then?"

Brynwald presumably expected the man either to deny it or to take an offensive posture. Either way he would have him.

But instead, Sarteham sidestepped the point and smiled. "'Tis a glorious day for the people of Loch na Huric, now that their chieftain and his warriors are returned to their hearths!" he exclaimed, choosing his words carefully. "It was feared that Eire had taken you to harm or to some other mishap, and that were the truth of it. The people needed a surrogate in your absence, Brynwald."

Brynwald grunted as he fingered his ax-haft. "Shunloc-Taz was here to lead the people," he countered, glancing over the crowd for sight of the man.

"The high priest had many concerns with the spiritual needs of the people," Sarteham retorted. "He could not be tending to every little fox in the coop, so I stood in the gap to help him with his task. You would have done the same, Brynwald, and you ken it."

"Aye, that I would," the chieftain conceded. Then leaning forward he thumped the man once on his chest with his finger. The sound of it carried as far away as the boys. "But Bowness is nay little fox!" He scowled. "And I would not've left m' hearth and heath defenseless while traipsing over the hill and gone winning glory for m'self—nay! 'Twere a proud thing to do and foolish, and you ken *that!*" And he gave Sarteham's chest another thump for good measure.

A low murmuring spread among the people as the words of Brynwald and Sarteham were passed from person to person, finding profit with the telling, until everyone in the camp had heard some version of the confrontation.

321

Sarteham bristled under the rebuke. His body tensed and gathered for a leap, and his brow darkened. It seemed for a moment that he was going to jump at the chieftain.

Brynwald waited, his eyes fixed on the other's. And waiting, he beat the man's stare.

Sarteham cleared his throat. "'Twere a proud thing to do,' you say. Then perhaps you contend with the gods, Brynwald," he rebutted evenly. His temper cooled some. "They've granted us favor. Aye. A boon of plunder to show it!" And pointing to Tolc and the small procession, he added, "We are about to honor their foolishness with a sacrifice."

"The gods—*faugh!*" Brynwald grunted. Then he turned away from the man and headed toward Tolc, followed by his warriors and the great crowd of jubilant people.

Sarteham muttered something contemptuous under his breath.

As Brynwald drew up to the procession, he scanned the scene aloofly, as though his interest lay somewhere else.

Tolc bowed slightly and offered a perfunctory greeting.

But the chieftain appeared not to see or hear him. His mind was elsewhere, and his eyes were in pursuit of it. "Where is she, then?" he muttered under his breath. Making a full sweep of the crowd, his eyes settled at last upon the face of Belfourt's daughter standing proudly before him. Appraising her with a glance, he let out a grunt.

The girl stiffened and glared back at the Pictish chieftain as defiantly as she could. However, she knew that she could not withstand his fierce eyes long, and so she jerked her head away proudly with a "Humph!"

Ignoring her insolence as he might a fly, Brynwald turned to the new high priest. "Where is Shunloc-Taz?" he asked gruffly.

"He is dead."

"*Dead!* Shunloc-Taz is dead?" Brynwald was stunned and stepped backward a half step. "This I did not hear on m' journey. Nay," he said, suddenly pensive. He shook his head and added, "I had hoped to tell him—" Then he broke off. "How did it happen? When?"

Tolc glanced over at Sarteham, who was approaching, then turned back to the chieftain and indicated the flogging stones. "He was killed by one of the captured Britons who raided our village last night."

Brynwald shot a startled glance at the boys, now twenty-five yards away. "We were raided by Britons!" Not waiting for Tolc's answer, Brynwald again searched the crowd for the face of his wife. "Were there any women and—"

"No. The women and children are safe, Brynwald," Tolc interrupted, sensing his concern. "But eleven others were killed and several more wounded." Then he added almost apologetically, "I, alone, am left of the priesthood."

322

The chieftain's countenance burned as he whirled around to Sarteham. "We lost twelve men—one of whom was a dear friend of mine, and you say that the gods have favored you?" he thundered. "How else have the gods favored you in my absence?"

But Sarteham held his peace.

"*Paagh!* You're either a fool or a madman!" Turning to Tolc, Brynwald jabbed his finger toward the ground and snapped, "You stay right here until I say otherwise!"

Tolc nodded.

As Brynwald headed toward the boys, his ire burning, Sarteham stood glowering at the man's back. His hand fondled the pommel of his sword. He shot a scowl at Tolc, then strode after the chieftain.

Tolc looked on for a moment, then glanced dolefully into the bowl of mistletoe leaves and berries in his hands, shook his head to a rueful cadence, and sighed.

Gwyneth, however, sensing the peculiar shift in the dynamics, turned and watched Terryll and Aeryck fearfully, biting her lower lip.

Reaching the three menhirs, Brynwald cast no more than a glance at the boys, then barked at Spang. "Where're the British warriors?" he demanded. "Tolc said there were captives."

Spang stepped back to give him space, nearly tripping over his feet again. Then, fidgeting with the frayed hem of his tunic, the brute tried desperately to muster his thoughts. "Uh . . . they are . . . uh—"

"These are the Britons who *raided* our village and killed the high priest last night, Brynwald," Sarteham interrupted, sardonically. "As you can see, they do not constitute much of a threat."

The chieftain looked at each of the boys' faces, first at Aeryck's, then at Terryll's. "These are only boys," he said, not sure what Sarteham meant. "Where are the men who were in their party?"

Sarteham hesitated a moment to consider an answer.

Spang, however, brightened with a thought and jumped right in. "'Tweren't no men a-tall! There's just the two sucklings!" he said, jerking a big thumb at the boys. Then he added through a proud, tooth-scarce grin, "But we caught 'em good, all right!" Spang looked over at Sarteham for his approval but was met with a sharp scowl.

Brynwald, on the other hand, was astonished. "*Och!* Can it be?" he asked Sarteham.

"Aye. But it was night, and our attention was on the cer—"

"These two kippers are the entire raiding party?" Brynwald interrupted, almost shrieking. "I cannay believe it!"

"Your dead warriors have little trouble believing," Terryll cut in.

Brynwald jerked his head toward the boy, and his eyes flashed murderously. "May I be cursed with the ten plagues of Cernunnos iffen I don't cut you doon as you stand!" he roared as he reached for his battle-ax.

Immediately one of his warriors leaped forward and grabbed his arm. "Wait, Brynwald! 'Tis the deffil's game you're playin' here," he said with a fire equal to the chieftain's. "Wait, I say, till you've heard the whole of the matter."

Huffing and fuming, Brynwald glared at Terryll and, unmindful of the pull at his arm, was set on cleaving the boy's skull.

"Do ya hear me, Bryn?" the warrior persisted. "Quit your wroth now, lessen it steal your very mind and blacken your soul straightway!"

The man was stout of frame and strong of heart and withheld the chieftain's arm.

Brynwald, coming to himself in degrees, cast a sideways glance at the red-bearded fellow, and at once his fury broke with a little jolt of his head. The deadly blaze in his eyes flickered a moment, then sputtered out.

"Aye. Aye. Right you are, Dunnald," he said, gathering his wits. "Right you are. I'll hear the lad on the matter." Then the Pictish chieftain stepped up close to Terryll and arched his brow into a menacing black scowl. "Is it true, then, kipper, that you killed the high priest and eleven of my people?"

"I wasn't keeping score," Terryll replied.

"Answer me, lad, or so help me I'll split your insolent skull!" Brynwald roared, and again the stout warrior had to constrain his arm.

Terryll stared at the man, unflinching at his threats. "After your people killed hundreds of ours," he said, then added scornfully, "not to mention those that were raped and maimed by your brave warriors. We came here only to bring our women home—we'd hoped without bloodshed."

"*Och!* Leave me be, Dunnald!" Brynwald growled, pulling his arm free of the stout warrior's grasp. "Are you m' wet nurse, then? Back off with you!"

Dunnald heeled to, then Brynwald turned and stared at Terryll for several long moments as he considered the boy's words. "To kill an enemy in battle is just and honorable, to be sure," he said evenly. "Aye. But to kill the high priest is an act of blasphemy against the Pictish gods. It carries with it the bane of death."

"Then kill me and get it over with, you butcher!" Terryll yelled. "I do not fear your death, nor your accursed gods. And I certainly don't fear the likes of you, Pict!"

Brynwald marveled at the boy's pluck. "You're an arrogant colt," he said, strangely cooling his tone. "What's your name, kipper?"

"What?" Terryll wasn't sure he'd heard the question.

"Come, come, lad, you speak Gaelic, don't you? Your name . . . how're you called, then?"

"I am Terryll, the son of Allyndaar."

Brynwald reeled slightly. "Allyndaar!—the chieftain of Killwyn Eden?"

Terryll did not answer. He hadn't expected a Pictish chieftain so many miles from his village to have heard of his father. The thought at once intrigued him and gave him a twinge of pride. But then his conscience smote him, and he realized that perhaps he had spoken too much.

"Like the trunk, so the limbs," Brynwald said, looking closer at the boy's face. "'Tis said of Allyndaar that he is now a wise chieftain," he added, casting a look over to Dunnald. "Though once he was the deffil on the wind."

The chieftain waited for a retort, but Terryll only eyed the man curiously. "'Tis also said he makes a fine bow," Brynwald continued.

"And that he knows how to use it," Terryll added, dryly.

Brynwald tossed his head back and laughed uproariously, startling the boys and those around him. "Aye! Of a truth, kipper! Of a truth!" he howled. "When I was a struttin' buck not much older than you, I fought against your father and his longbowmen on the wall. 'Twere a day I'll not soon forget!"

Terryll was astonished.

"I wouldnay lie to you, kipper!' the chieftain continued. And as he did, his voice thundered and boomed, and his eyes flashed with fury.

"The army of old Germanus come against us like a scourge with their eyes a-blazing fire and their teeth a-flashing sparks, and the whole lot of 'em were singing the hallelujahs to their God—*och!* 'Twere the deffil of a row, it was—like the beginnin' of Time itself. And there was your father, a-hurlin' his bloody bolts from heaven, it seemed, for all we could see of him and his fierce longbowmen, and the sky was like soot for their arrows. Of a truth, kipper, the terror of their God was upon us, I'll warrant you, and we fled. Aye, we fled like old women."

The chieftain paused to reflect on the battle, and his eyes moistened. "I rue the day, kipper, I rue it—I swear. Many of m' kin are now clothed with the sod for the likes of your father's terrible longbow, the cursed thing that nary missed a mark."

"Oh, but he missed his mark once, didn't he?" Terryll returned with a wry expression.

Brynwald grunted. "Of a truth," he replied, taking his meaning. A malicious light seemed to kindle in the chieftain's eyes as he added, "I vowed an oath on the man as we limped and bled the way back to our hearths in disgrace. And by the providences, here you are then, kipper, the limb in m' grasp to do as I will. Aye. 'Tis a marvel."

325

Then turning to Aeryck, Brynwald asked, "And who is this other mannie, then?"

"Ask him yourself," Terryll said.

But as the chieftain moved toward Aeryck, Sarteham stepped in front of the man and protested. "Can this questioning not wait till after the sacrifice? 'Tis the moment for the sun god to rise, and the girl is not made ready yet on the altar."

Brynwald stared at Sarteham, ignoring his question, and waited for him to move aside. Sarteham did so under protest, then the chieftain stepped up to Aeryck. "And what's your name, kipper?" he asked, studying the lad's features.

"Aeryck," the boy said with conviction.

"And who is your father then?" Brynwald asked. "Perhaps I owe him a vengeance as well."

"Caelryck!" Aeryck almost shouted. "My father's name was Caelryck of Glenryth."

"*Caelryck!*" Brynwald was taken aback.

"Caelryck of Glenryth?" Dunnald was equally astonished.

The warriors who had come with Brynwald immediately turned to one another and wondered at the boy's answer with grunts and queries.

Brynwald narrowed his eyes on the boy. "You're lying!" he said. "Caelryck had nay son!"

"You're the liar," Aeryck shot back. "He stands before you."

Brynwald turned to his warriors. Several shrugged their shoulders, others raised their eyebrows and shook their heads, but none of them had any answers. "How can I be certain of this?" Brynwald asked, looking at the boy.

"I don't care whether you're certain or not," Aeryck snarled. "I am Caelryck's son, and I don't see what it matters to the likes of you!"

"Aye," Sarteham concurred. "Who is this Caelryck but some British dog to be whipped? The sun god will not wait on such fribble!"

"To the pit with the sun god!" Brynwald roared. "If you want to go talk to the blazin' thing, go right ahead! Right now, I'm talking here to the lad!"

Sarteham fell back in horror, as did many of those nearby. The crowd immediately boiled with feverish scuttlebutt, as those who heard the chieftain's words quickly passed along to others what they supposed he meant by them. Certainly they had misunderstood the man. It seemed he had cursed the sun god—but that wasn't possible, for he was, after all, the chieftain. So it was dismissed summarily.

Since none of the people had heard of Caelryck before, they supposed him to be one of the Scotti that Brynwald had met in Ireland—or perhaps a Briton who had sent the boys after the women. Therefore many insisted, in lieu of a more plausible explanation, that it was Caelryck who had cursed the sun god, and that Brynwald was simply retelling it. But mostly everyone was confused.

The boys glanced at each other, completely bewildered.

Brynwald turned from Sarteham to Aeryck with a confluence of confusion, fatigue, and wrath knitting his brow. "I've been away from m' hearth and heath longer than I ought, kipper," he said deliberately. "M' bones are weary. M' belly's empty—and who kens where that woman of mine has got to. So I'll nay longer have you playing the fox with me, do ya hear?"

Aeryck stared into the Pict's eyes and beheld a madness lighting in them like a smoldering fury taking draft with each word.

"Now what proof do you have that you're the son of Caelryck?" the chieftain continued, stabbing the boy's chest with his finger. "Tell me straight, or, so help me, I'll run you through m'self for the lying serpent you are!"

Aeryck blinked at the chieftain a few times, sure that the man meant his threat, then shifted his gaze to Sarteham. "That man has the proof of it hanging at his side and around his neck. My father's crest has been engraved on each."

Glancing at the sword and medallion, Brynwald stretched his hand to Sarteham. "Let me see those."

But Sarteham backed away and grabbed the haft of his sword, ready now for a fight. "These are spoils of war!" he snarled. "They are mine by right, and I'll not let you have them!"

The crowd choked quiet with the falling of the gauntlet. Brynwald's men immediately grabbed their ax-hafts and set themselves for battle. Spang and those with him did likewise. The crowd backed away nervously to give them room.

Both groups of warriors eyed each other warily, choosing their opposites, as the possibility of civil bloodshed hung suspended in the air like the sword of Damocles. The air was rife with the anticipation of violence.

Sarteham stood in the middle of a cleared area before the three menhirs, facing Brynwald and waiting for his move.

"They are yours if I deem them yours," Brynwald said. "Now let me see them. Or shall I come and take them from you?"

Every eye was fixed on the two men, each standing equal to the other's height and stature, each clearly a head taller than everyone else in the village.

Sarteham glared at the chieftain with unmasked hatred. Brynwald narrowed his eyes, and for a moment the two stared at each other in a dreadful silence—like two bulls in the arena—weighing the other's mettle, looking for weakness, battling the other's will.

Brynwald's words had in them the power of life and death and, with a piercing, implacable gaze he searched his rival's eyes to see which way the sword would tilt. It mattered little to him either way.

Clearly the moment had come for each man to declare himself before the people. Certainly to the victor the spoils would fall, the clan would be won. The onus lay upon Sarteham to act, for he had thrown down the gauntlet.

And Brynwald waited, cold and resolute, waited until there was a slight twitch in one of Sarteham's eyes, a dullish glint of reticence curling atop the flushed cornea. It was imperceptible to the crowd, to the boys mere feet away, but Brynwald caught it. He had seen the glint in scores of eyes upon the battlefield.

Then Sarteham broke his gaze, shifting it instead to the ring of Brynwald's warriors encircling them. His shoulders seemed to roll downward into two great heaps upon his frame, with his heavy limbs slackening and hanging loose at his sides. Then, as a haughty sneer twisted his face, he handed over the sword and medallion to the chieftain.

Brynwald grunted. "A wise decision, Sarteham. Aye . . . aye."

The crowd released the tension in the air with a collective breath, and the warriors shifted their stances. At once a contagion of murmuring swept through their midst.

The Pictish chieftain looked down at the sword and medallion in his hands and carefully examined the crest on each one. After a moment of scrutiny he looked up at Aeryck as though thunderstruck. Searching the boy's face, he said, "Can this be true? Can it, then? God have mercy on my soul!" And immediately he took the sword and began to hack through the thongs on Aeryck's wrists.

"Wait!" Sarteham cried out. "What are you doing!?"

"There'll be nay more blood sacrifices in Loch na Huric!" the chieftain bellowed indignantly. "Not as long as I've breath to draw!"

The crowd gasped as Brynwald moved over to Terryll and began cutting him loose.

"What do you mean, there'll be no more blood sacrifices?" Sarteham demanded. "Have you taken the plunder of madness in Eire?"

"Nay, but we plundered *something* there, I'll warrant you!" Brynwald boomed, as he cut the last of Terryll's bonds. Then he turned to several of his warriors. "Take the kippers to the hall and guard them till I send for them. Look lively to it, lads."

Sarteham shot a fierce look at the boys, who stood next to the menhirs, rubbing their wrists, as bewildered as everyone else. Then he glared back at the chieftain. "What is the meaning of this? This is blasphemy!"

Brynwald ignored him, and quickly several of his warriors surrounded the boys.

"Iffen anyone troubles you, Dunnald," Brynwald said, pulling the stout warrior aside, "strike him doon!"

"As you wish, Brynwald," Dunnald replied with a generous smile. Brynwald shot a look of contempt at Sarteham as he brushed past him to the center of the clearing, then held up his hand to quiet the crowd. "People of Loch na Huric! Give me the duty of your minds and hearts," he shouted over the din.

The crowd simmered to a hush.

Looking into their faces, Brynwald said, "There are many things I wish to speak to you concerning our journey to Eire—many strange and wondrous things, I'll say. But they must wait till I hold council this eve. I'll not confer on such weighty matters till I've seen m' wife and hearth."

Brynwald dismissed the crowd, then strode over to Tolc and Gwyneth. "Cut the girl loose and take her to where the others are being kept," he commanded Tolc. Then, as he turned to leave, he added, "And dinnay let anyone near them, Tolc. Do you hear? Nary a one!" And with that the chieftain headed alone across the camp toward his home through a corridor of astonished eyes.

Tolc, dumbfounded, watched the man until Brynwald disappeared behind some trees at the edge of the clearing, then he looked down at the bowl of mistletoe in his hands, a vacuous look on his face. He was suddenly filled with the realization that he held in his hands the sum total of his life and beliefs—a bowlful of leaves and berries. He tossed the bowl to the ground unceremoniously, then set to work untying Gwyneth's hands.

At that moment the boys, led by a contingent of Brynwald's warriors, passed in front of them, and Terryll paused to look at Gwyneth. She met his gaze with an uncertain smile, which Terryll returned warmly, adding to it a shrug of his shoulders. Then the boys were led off with the warriors across the camp, and Gwyneth toward the third hut with Tolc—each entertaining his own thoughts as to what had just happened, and each with private concerns for the future.

The dawning sky was a gray oppression, sullen and overcast, and the crowd slowly broke apart into small huddles of bewildered chatter. However, none could explain the upheaval during the last few hours that had shaken their village to its very core. It was as if a mighty storm had suddenly blown into their midst, tearing loose every vestige of familiarity that had moored their lives to security and hope.

In all their memory there had never been anything like it, and it would be talked about in the great hall of Loch na Huric for generations to come. Some of the people were filled with dread, saying that the gods had gathered from the three worlds to vent their wrath upon them. Others believed that the chieftain brought with him something new and wonderful, though they couldn't imagine what. Still there were those who simply didn't care—their heads still ached from the night before.

The huddles soon dispersed from the clearing in groups of twos and threes, and most gradually filtered back to their hearths to await the evening council.

Sarteham, on the other hand, stood alone in the middle of the clearing, looking up at the monoliths upon the hillock. He shook his head in disgust as the first rays of the sun broke through the gray ceiling and crept along the avenue of stones to greet the barren altar. Then, without so much as a glimmer of pause to observe the affairs of men, the rays continued ever westward along their predetermined course.

The large Pict narrowed his eyes and cursed by his gods. Spang and the men with him edged to his side and waited for his orders.

The landscape had suddenly become obscure.

28
THE PLUNDER

A pall of uncertainty hung over the hall of Loch na Huric as the elder men of the village, and those men of standing, filed into the timbered edifice to find whatever space they could. The place buzzed with apprehension as information and innuendo floated over the milling press.

The hall was about half the size of the great hall in Killwyn Eden, so many of the people from the village were crowded outside around the doors and windows. The sound carried well from inside, and the Pictish villagers, being a hardy lot, preferred the cool of the early evening air to the stuffy confines of the hall anyway.

Inside, the people stood elbow to elbow, and several persons deep, in a semicircle around a long oak table that was set against one wall. A broad clearing was left before it to accommodate the often-spirited ambulation of the chieftain. A score of Sarteham's warriors were lined noticeably in front of the crowd at one end of the semicircle, awaiting the arrival of the Brynwald. Each proud figure fidgeted anxiously with his battle accoutrements as he mumbled to his neighbor.

Sarteham stood to one side of these in the shadows. His visage was a cold and vacant exhibition that betrayed nothing of the man, good or ill, as he scanned the room deliberately. It was a cunning perusal he was making, subtle, with apparent geniality, as though he were calculating a measure of the room or its occupants for some innocuous purpose. But to any discerning eye there winked about his person the treachery of a snake.

Spang, on the other hand, broadcast his thoughts with every twitching contortion of his face. His eyes were wicked and lively, squinting about the room in furtive leaps and darts, fitting every foul description of a fugitive. He shifted his weight nervously from foot to foot as though the flagstones were a bed of coals and, coping unsuccessfully with his discomfiture, blustered pugnaciously about, here jostling an elbow, there returning a nudge with a poke, and grunting curses the while.

At the other end of the room, near the doorway, many of Brynwald's warriors were positioned inside and without the hall. They were a stolid lot, fierce and rough of cut. Each man stood his ground with wary eyes fixed on Sarteham's men and with his hands ever hovering near to hilt and haft. Of a truth, they appeared ready for a fight and wore the taut expressions of men at the brink of battle. They were a magnificent group, and Aeryck frequented their rugged visages with rapt wonder.

Terryll, who nursed his swollen eye with a slice of raw meat, and Aeryck stood along the periphery of the cleared area, perpendicular to the midsection of the long table, and were surrounded by some of Brynwald's warriors as they had been all day. The old woman Myrna, who had bandaged Tolc's leg, had tended to their wounds with poultices and medicinal broths, and both boys were clothed again in their own tunics and boots—they had been tossed mysteriously through a window in the hall about midday. They looked and felt considerably better than they had at sunrise.

The hall was abuzz with banter—loud banter—mostly anticipating the council at hand, though there was talk of crops and sheep and other pedestrian concerns intermingled with it. After all, it was harvest time, and the seasons wouldn't wait for political or religious matters to be settled, no matter how interruptive they might be.

The boys, on the other hand, kept their conversation low and focused warily on the situation at hand, for though their lives had been spared for the moment, they sensed a blow in the air. Aside from a few shelves beetling about the room—lined fantastically with human skulls—the trappings in the hall were sparse and nondescript. Earlier in the day, Aeryck had taken note of one skull in particular, off to his right, that still had a wispy thatch of yellow hair sticking out of it. He wondered how a skull could grow hair and glanced at it periodically with a new thought on the matter.

Terryll nudged his arm while he was again giving consideration to the thing and whispered something into his ear.

Immediately Aeryck looked across the room and found Sarteham staring at them with cold, unblinking eyes, and the look sent a ripple of shivers along his spine.

Suddenly a cheer arose outside, heralding the coming of Brynwald, and at once the crowd at the doorway opened to make way for him.

The chieftain strode into the hall with a thunderous "Hail and well met!" and his greeting was returned in unison. He was carrying Aeryck's sword and medallion and, shooting Sarteham a shaded glance, he placed them on the oak table across from the boys.

Trailing behind him were Tolc, who stopped just inside the doorway, and Brynwald's wife, a plump, rosy-faced woman, who squeezed into a spot along the wall near the long table. She glanced over at the boys and gave them a quick smile. Terryll returned her kindness, but Aeryck's attention was on the Pictish chieftain, and he missed it altogether.

As the chieftain stood bathed in the waning glow of twilight, Aeryck was struck by the size of the man. He was huge, dwarfing everyone in the room but one with a masculine vigor and confidence that described his every movement. The man's hair was long and wavy, the color of burning coke. He wore a thick braid dangling from either temple, and his eyes were stern and of the ruddy hue of brick. He was bare-chested and bronzed by the elements and wore only a pair of woolen trousers that were twilled with the tartan plaid of his clan. A small ceremonial ax—one that was more ornamental than his battle-ax—hung from a leather belt about his waist and was worn only for decoration on such occasions as this. Draped over his shoulders he wore a coarse woolen cloak, scarlet of color and fastened at the neck with a brooch of bronze, and his feet were shod with a pair of stout leather moccasins that hit him high at the ankles.

The boy wasn't intrigued by these, for Brynwald's attire was common for men of that day. What intrigued the boy—nay, horrified him— were his tattoos.

Brynwald's muscular arms were ringed with designs like armlets, and his thick chest and torso were covered with all manner of illustrations—some depicting themes of nature, others depicting the horrible gape-mouthed faces of various gods. The overall effect gave to the chieftain a terrible appearance, one that might quell the fiercest of hearts in battle. Aeryck could only imagine what manner of designs might be etched across his back, and he was in awe of the man.

Brynwald cleft the air with his arm, motioning the people to order, and he scanned the room with a fiery gaze until there wasn't a sound in the hall.

A brisk autumn breeze picked up suddenly and whistled through the windows, carrying with it the tart smell of heather on the hills that cleared the suffocating air somewhat. Then, just as quickly, it dropped off, leaving behind a fragrant hush to settle on the crowd.

At last his austere gaze fell upon the boys and harbored there a moment. There glinted in his eyes a different light, edged with humor it seemed. Even so, the hair stood up on the back of Aeryck's neck, and he averted his eyes.

"Men of Loch na Huric!" the chieftain began in a slow, resonant baritone. "At long last we've returned from that rocky blast of isle to our fair heath and loch—to our kith and kin. 'Twere a prosperous journey we had, and I ken you're wanting to hear the sum of it."

"Aye! Aye!" the hall returned in fraternal unison.

"To the straight of it, then!" Brynwald bellowed, and he began in earnest to tell his strange tale. "We fell at once upon the coastal villages of Eire like a storm and ravaged the land—aye! and we taken a boon of plunder during our raids. And as ye ken our custom, men, we left naught but burning rubble in our wake, to be sure. Aye. Ne'er had a people seen such a bloody rake as ours—'The gods have come against us with a vengeance!' they cried, and before our battle-axes and swords they fled in stark raving terror. Those who couldna flee—" Brynwald broke off, paused momentarily, then continued in a grave and sober voice. "Aye. Those who couldna flee, we cut doon without mercy."

At this point several men in the hall grunted their approval with head nods and great exaggerated winks to one another. To them, Brynwald's words had promise and took some of the edge off their apprehensions. The chieftain glanced over at Sarteham in the shadows to gauge his reaction but was met with a cold stare and a lurid glint lighting here and there upon his quiet orbs.

"From the coast, we turned our faces inland toward the city of Armagh, the very bosom of the Scotti, to take even greater plunder," Brynwald continued, searching each face in the crowd. "But as we drew nigh to the outskirts of town, we were there met by an old Briton of curious description. Aye, he looked to us but a smoldering wick, frail and life-spent, though he stood as cold and still as ever there was a stone betwixt us and the city—a madman we thought, come to find his end, perhaps a peace to his railing.

"Of a truth, the old Briton raised his hand and bade us stop our pillaging, as though 'twere nothing but a wee tow of bairns come against him. Then lifting his dimming eyes to the heavens, he cried out to some god whose name were strange to our ears. 'Have mercy on these wayward sheep! They ken not what they do!' cries he to his god, and I ordered Dunnald to strike him doon at once. Aye. But Dunnald—my very thunder in battle—stood trembling at my side like some old woman and, verily, refused my command, saying he could not even look upon the man."

Immediately the hall buzzed with amazement. Heads wagged this way and that, and tongues clucked. Many thought they had misunderstood Brynwald's words and sought clarification from others who sought the same.

Aeryck, his mouth a little open to suit his eyes, looked over at Dunnald and found it hard to believe as well. The stout warrior was of such terrible countenance, and so built like a heap of boulders, that the boy wondered what manner of man this old Briton might be to have withstood him.

"Och! 'Tis the truth—I swear—and my wroth were kindled," Brynwald returned, "and I raised my ax to cut the old man doon m'self.

'Twere in my mind to turn upon Dunnald after the duty. But as I gazed into the Briton's eyes, I saw in them not a smoldering wick—nay, but a blazing consumption which took my very heart and soul. I tell ye, by troth of the oaks, my fury was vented of a sudden, and a chilling shudder whipped my bones. Aye. My ax hung shiverin' betwixt and between heaven and earth and withheld from its wicked purpose.

"Men of Loch na Huric, ne'er have I faced such a one in battle, though I've stood against and felled many a worthy foe. And—ho! there was nary a soul in our party who dared stand against the old man either. For there was a mystery in his bearing and a sword in his tongue, which slew every manly skin of us, though he ne'er lifted a weapon in his defense."

This drew another chorus of bewilderment from men who again thought they had misunderstood Brynwald's words. They knew well the man who stood before them. They had seen him in battle, wielding his ax from light to light with unabating wrath, cutting down the fiercest of warriors and razing the most impregnable of strongholds, never flinching, never wavering, always merciless. Sarteham revealed the first hint of expression on his face, a thin smile.

And the chieftain raised his arm once again and waited until the room simmered to a quiet. "This Patrick of Ireland, as he is kenned to the Scotti, spake to us of a God who is laird over all gods and beside whom there is nay other god, One who created the heavens and the earth and things under the earth, One who is all-powerful and everywhere at once, full of unsearchable wisdom and mercy, though brimmin' with terrible wrath to all who reject His Son—who is Jesus the Christ." Brynwald broke off for a moment to give thought to his next words.

Every eye in the room was riveted on his stalwart visage, and there was no misunderstanding him now. His speech was clear and spoken with such force that no one could move. His countenance shone with a radiance never before seen upon the man, and many whispered to one another that he looked like the god Belenos, "the shining one."

Even those outside were caught in the spell of Brynwald's address, many of whom stood gaping at him through the doorway and windows as though they were struck stupid.

Terryll and Aeryck exchanged looks of astonishment. Never could either of them have imagined such a thing as this.

"As we hearkened to the awld Briton, we kenned his words to be true," Brynwald continued, "for our hearts were pricked with fiery pangs by the deeds we had done, and we fell on our faces as dead men and begged for mercy. For we were stricken with a sudden terror—aye!—that this strange and terrible God would surely strike us doon lessen we turned our hearts.

"The old man bade us rise. Then, lifting his withering hands to the heavens, he blessed us with a kindly word and gave to us plunder beyond our fathomable hopes. *Och!*—I am telling ye the truth. For immediately we found our legs, our souls were filled with such joy and gladness as we have never known—nor can I tell it with the words of men!"

As the chieftain spoke, many of the people were amazed that such a thing was possible, and their eyes clearly betrayed their wonder. Others shook their heads with uncertainty; these would need more information before they came to an opinion on the matter. And there were those who were not so easy to read, whose blank expressions remained ungiving throughout.

"The old Briton welcomed us into the city to sup with him and with other men of his persuasion," Brynwald said, shifting his gaze to Aeryck. "We stayed with them in Armagh these past many months, learning the ways of this religion, which is the sole reason for our painful delay. In time our hearts burned within us for our families and the beauty of the highlands, and so here we are—we have now returned to the loch and heath, bringing to ye grand news of such glorious plunder.

"Men of Loch na Huric! There can be nay course for our people but the right and true, so I say to ye now that, from this day forward, we will follow the one true and only God and His Son—Jesus the Christ! It is my troth as your chieftain that we will serve nay others!"

And with such words Brynwald ended his address.

Immediately the hall boiled with a jangle of noise and confusion. More than once Brynwald tried to quiet the crowd in order to answer questions, but the din was unstoppable and continued for several minutes unabated. People inside and outside the hall were grabbing Brynwald's warriors and asking them for clarification and details.

Terryll and Aeryck looked around the hall in amazement. Although hearing with their own ears the wonders that God had wrought, they still found it difficult to comprehend how He could show mercy to such a pagan and savage people, and they wondered if they weren't in some devilish waking dream that had taken their minds.

Aeryck glanced over at Tolc, whose head was shaking in thoughtful consideration. And though he couldn't be certain, he thought that he could see a glistening of tears in his eyes. And the stout warrior Dunnald was nodding to and fro at a barrage of inquiries and discoursing favorably. The boys looked at each other with tears streaming down their cheeks and shrugged their shoulders, as their souls welcomed the news with the profoundest joy.

It happened at some point in the furor of the aftermath that Aeryck remembered Sarteham and looked over to catch his reaction. What he saw startled him, for the large Pict seemed unmoved by the address one way or the other. The boy had expected a strong protest from the warrior, having witnessed his confrontation with Brynwald earlier. Instead, Sarteham was speaking calmly to one of his men, as though giving him some counsel on the proper method of shearing sheep.

It occurred to the boy that Spang was missing. He had been so enthralled with the chieftain's words that he hadn't noticed him leave. And though such was of little consequence, none perhaps, it raised the specter of curiosity in his mind.

Aeryck glanced around the room to see if maybe the brute had skulked to some other spot, but, searching for his form, he found him nowhere in sight. Returning to Sarteham, he noticed the large Pict nod to someone across the hall. Aeryck thought that an odd gesture—not the nod itself but the execution of it. It was curt, martial, secretive, as though he were signaling a clandestine order. Aeryck clung to a mischievous thought and followed the man's eyes to the doorway.

And there was Spang, standing just outside the hall, returning the gesture. Darting a look back at Sarteham, the boy beheld the large Pict slowly raise his hand to the pommel of his sword, and his hackles bristled.

Suddenly there was a terrible uproar outside, as though a wayward flight of banshees had suddenly descended on the place. Men were caterwauling and women shrieking, and there, in the midst of a furious brawl, was Spang, hurling a battery of blows and bellowing curses and inciting a small riot.

While everyone else's attention was affixed on the melee without, Aeryck shot a look back at Sarteham and saw, even through the press of men around him, the large Pict surreptitiously removing his sword from its sheath. To his rekindled horror, the man's eyes were glaring murderously at the back of Brynwald's head.

It was in that instant that Aeryck saw the trap. Immediately a thought flashed through his memory of the foggy day outside Bowness, when he and Terryll had watched secretly from the cover of rocks as Sarteham tricked the Pictish warrior Tork into making a play for him. Aeryck had marveled then at the man's deception, though he—like Tork—had not seen it coming. But he saw the ruse now and blanched at the prospects of it.

He looked from Sarteham to Brynwald, back and again, hoping that the chieftain was also aware of the devilish trap. But Brynwald's gaze remained fixed on the doorway, oblivious to the impending treachery.

Aeryck didn't know at what point he decided to act, but he feared he had acted too late. As he bounded across the floor toward his sword, he could see Sarteham's blurred shape out of the corner of his eye, bearing down on the unsuspecting chieftain, with his own sword poised murderously over his head to strike him down.

"Treachery! Treachery!" Aeryck cried out as he reached the table. Then, clasping his sword, he swung the blade around with a quick scything curve to meet the falling hammer of Sarteham's broadsword, and a shuddering clang of steel followed with an explosion of sparks, that shook the hall to silence. Sarteham's blow hit the boy with such terrible force that he fell backward into Brynwald, knocking the chieftain off balance. Aeryck himself rebounded aright.

Sarteham was stunned to see his blade caught in the air before him, hanging there as if by its own will, defying his, and it took him a moment to realize what had just happened. The crowd gasped in horror as the drama shifted to the clearing in the center, and the people fell back to give the combatants room.

Grabbing for his ax, Brynwald reeled to face his would-be assassin, but Sarteham still had the edge of surprise and quickly pressed his advantage with a quick recoil and a second strike. His eyes burned with hatred as he sidestepped the boy to strike down the chieftain, but Aeryck jumped in front of the man to break his attack with a skillful parry of Sarteham's blade.

Enraged at Aeryck's doggedness—for, truly, the boy seemed but a lap dog before the terrible fangs of a wolf—the large Pict turned his fury from Brynwald to the boy, more to rid himself of a nuisance than for any consideration of threat. "Take Brynwald!" he cried out to his warriors, as he swung his blade at the minor interruption.

But every one of his warriors held fast in his place, as did Brynwald's men, as though each was prevented from interfering by some unseen hand. Even Brynwald's efforts were thwarted, for as he reached for his ceremonial ax, he fumbled clumsily with the smaller haft, and it fell clattering to the floor. The net of it was that Aeryck was left alone with his wits and holy grace to do battle against the seemingly invincible Sarteham.

As the fight commenced, the boy was encircled by a lightning blur of colors and shapes, of faces yawing and pitching over the human turbulence, and of sounds that gathered a muted ambience like that of a distant furnace roaring. These collectively provided the backdrop to the intense drama before him.

However, in the midst of the swirl, Aeryck's mind was clear and serene, fixed to a narrow point on Sarteham's eyes and the glinting tip of his deadly adder blade. He could see them both at once, pristinely, for as adrenaline heightened his senses, everything appeared to move in a slow-motion mockery of time and space. Every movement was defined with supernal clarity.

Balance! Balance! Balance! thundered the Roman catechist in his brain. *To the left and feint! To the right and thrust!* And the boy devotedly obeyed each line and verse.

Sarteham's blade fell upon him with a battery of exchanges, challenging his drills with stunning inquiries, and each blow was fairly answered by the counter and parry of Aeryck's tempered steel. A furious contest ensued between the swords.

Their blades met time and again, with surfaces of polished metal catching the fire from the torchlight and igniting them like fiery shards of lightning as they ripped through the air with terrible rushes of wind. And the hammering clangor of metal against metal was deafening, and animal snarls and grunts jerked and coughed in human throats as the heavy blades were hefted and poised and brought down again, rending the space between them, followed by the report of metal and flashes of blue and red and yellow sparks that careered off the edges.

The blades were hefted and poised time and again. To strike. Then parry. Now thrust. Now jabbing, cutting, slashing. Now and now. Circling, eyeing, waiting for the moment, now parrying, now thrusting and hammering, and pounding . . . pounding . . . pounding. And the resounding clang was deafening in the little hall, and the song of the anvil hammered in Aeryck's mind, and his feet danced to the driving cadence. *Balance! Balance! Balance!*

With a glance the boy saw Sarteham's face snarling at him through clenched teeth, his eyes red and squinting with unbridled wrath. The man cursed him by his gods, cursed him by his mother's grave, though the words penetrated the boy's mind as distant echoes, jumping out of the furnace roar.

And so Sarteham pressed his attack with inexorable force. But the sword of Caelryck gave little quarter, and neither did the boy, who soon found ground to press a counterattack with a lightning-quick thrust of his blade to the man's throat. Sarteham had not anticipated the move, nor the speed of it, and staggered back awkwardly to escape the fatal cleft.

It was then that Aeryck saw in the Pict's eyes a glint of uncertainty coloring his rage, of such hue he had not seen before in the man. But such a glint seemed only to kindle a greater rage in the large Pict, and, letting out a terrible howl, Sarteham began hacking with renewed fury, laughing uproariously with each slash and swipe of his blade. He wore the expression of a madman, or a demon, loosed from his chains as he came at the boy ranting and railing and cursing him with a raft of blasphemies. The fury of Sarteham was a terrible thing to behold. Relentless he came, and at one point Aeryck glimpsed the bolt of his life pass before him.

The boy was forced back from the renewed attack but still held his ground. He faltered once, nearly stumbling to the floor, then again, and though he caught Sarteham's punishing blade each time, it beat and hammered the strength from his body to the point where his limbs burned hot with fatigue and wonder. Never had the boy imagined such devastating power.

The room fell away from his mind in savage jolts. Gone were the whirl of faces, the muted sounds. All the world might have been ruined and ablaze and lapping at the door, but the whole of the apocalypse was a ten-by-ten square to the boy, and his judgment a blade's length away, and he knew that he would soon fall to it.

Sarteham did too.

The large Pict drew his sword through the air with the surety of victory, and, roaring drunkenly, he brought the edge down with all the force his brutish strength could muster. But as his blade charged against the sure edge of Caelryck's steel, it snapped in two with a horrible ring, and the end of it skittered across the floor, clanging harmlessly into the gallery of onlookers.

Sarteham looked at the thing amazed, then he let out a maddened war cry and lunged at the boy with the jagged remains of his weapon.

Aeryck parried the blade across the man's chest with a single, fluid motion, spun around on his heels like a wily matador to avoid a sure collision, then swung his blade down onto the Pict's exposed sword arm as he passed by, severing it at the wrist.

Sarteham jolted to a stop. A horrible look contorted his features. It was as though his mind were yet unaware of, or disbelieving, the dreadful mishap to his body. Clutching his gushing arm with his left hand, he let out a violent scream, fell hard to the floor, and was quit of the battle.

The crowd let out a gasp as they stood gaping incredulously at the scene. Sweat poured from Aeryck's face, and his chest heaved like a bellows as he stepped back from the battle line, not sure what had just happened, for his senses were veiled by surges of adrenaline. He looked over at Sarteham writhing like a beheaded snake, but his mind refused the witness of his eyes, and he set himself for the next battery of blows.

Presently the boy felt a large hand on his shoulder, and he spun around to face the intruder. As the sounds and colors of the background clambered into focus, there was Brynwald beaming down at him, and hinder to him was a wall of gaping moons, wagging in awe.

"Easy, kipper! Easy! It's over! I mean you nay harm!" the chieftain said, patting him on the shoulder. "I'm not your enemy!"

Aeryck looked from Brynwald to Sarteham, using the pause to clear his mind, to collect his breath. He stared blankly at the vanquished foe who lay at his feet and was startled at the turn of fortune. The large

Pict had seemed an indomitable enemy. But now he looked like any other man wounded in battle. Curiously, the boy felt pity for him.

The chieftain patted Aeryck's shoulder again. "You've saved my life, kipper," Brynwald said, broad and beaming. "Aye! 'Twere as fine a piece of swordplay as ever I've witnessed—and by nay more'n a mannie at that! I owe you a trove of gratitude! By the oaks, I do!"

Then a terrible color jumped into his face, and, stepping around the boy, the chieftain glared down at Sarteham and raised his ax to finish him off. But he hesitated. On his brow there worked a curious design—a merciful one, it seemed, and certainly a stranger to his countenance.

Sarteham crawled up onto his elbow, still gripping his bloody stump with his other hand and snarling like a wounded animal. "Go ahead . . . kill me!" he spat defiantly. "I wouldna waver a hair's breadth to strike *you* down!"

Brynwald seemed to wonder at himself for not cleaving the man's skull right off, for that clearly had been his intention. Sarteham had defied his authority, plotted his murder, and would lead an insurrection against him. He deserved nothing but swift and final justice.

Instead, the chieftain lowered his ax slowly and turned to the stunned crowd.

"Men of Loch na Huric! Ye must now make your choice. Those of you who would stay and learn of this new religion—welcome, say I!" Then he gestured to Sarteham with his ax. "But those of you who would follow the old ways of death—here is your chieftain. Follow him!" Then he grunted and added, "What's left of him!"

Brynwald glared at Sarteham's warriors, who stood gaping at their fallen leader with lamenting expressions. "But if you follow this old serpent," he continued, "you must ken that from the morrow's first light, you and your families are forever banished from our fair loch and heath. Should any of your kind be seen treading upon our tribal lands, it'll be taken as an act of war. Aye, they'll be cut doon at once!" Brynwald let out a grunt. "Consider the matter now, men—and look lively to it!"

Sarteham seemed as surprised as the others that Brynwald had withdrawn his blade. But as the disabled Pict struggled to his feet, the trace of a proud smile played at the corners of his mouth.

"Aye, my brothers! You must choose betwixt us!" he shouted. "I follow the gods of our fathers who have made us strong. Brynwald's new god is a weakling! See how it has made a woman of your chieftain, who can no longer kill his enemy! Is this coward the Brynwald that left us? Nay, but this is some old crone who has returned to bewitch you with some strange madness! Those who follow me, I will lead to glorious victories as I did against the Britons! By my troth, there will be great plunder for all!"

"Och! These are pretty words coming from one who was fairly beaten by a lad!" Brynwald roared. "Perhaps the men of Loch na Huric would prefer to follow the kipper instead." Then turning to the stout warrior, he commanded him, saying, "Take charge of this usurper, Dunnald, for I'll not look again on his face."

As Dunnald took hold of Sarteham's sound arm, the large Pict glared into Aeryck's eyes. "Do not think that this is over, Briton," he growled. "Whenever I look upon this foul stump, I will be reminded of your face. You may have taken my hand, but I swear by all the gods that I'll soon take your head and have it swinging about my belt!" Sarteham looked back at Brynwald and snarled. *"Paagh!* I'll need only one hand to kill the both of you!"

The chieftain turned to Dunnald and gave him strict charge concerning Sarteham and his warriors, adding, "If any of them would stay, Dunnald, you must show them kindness."

Dunnald nodded, then led Sarteham out of the hall under guard. Brynwald's warriors had already subdued Spang and the other insurrectionists and were holding them at bay with their swords. Others of Sarteham's men were quickly rounded up, having offered little resistance, for the fight had gone out of them. One man, however, drew his sword on Dunnald as the stout warrior escorted Sarteham across the grounds, but Dunnald made short work of him.

Most of the villagers returned to the quiet of their hearths to discuss Brynwald's words with their wives and families, some to make ready for the morrow's hasty departure. However, many lingered around the hall, debating the strange news with one another long into the night.

Tolc was one of these. He cornered two of Brynwald's men and pressed them on the issue of Christ's sacrificial death and resurrection. Such notions intrigued the man, for he saw in them some similarities to the Celtic god Mabon, known also as "the son of light."

However, what intrigued him most were the dissimilarities—the idea that this holy and awesome God was also merciful and loved men, such that He would willingly sacrifice His only Son in their stead. Such a notion, though completely foreign to the mind of the new high priest, struck a chord of truth in his heart.

29
THE HEARTH OF BRYNWALD

Brynwald, the boys, and a small contingent of warriors left the thinning hall under the first light of the crescent moon and made their way through silvery birches toward the chieftain's home. The air was bracing, scented with the highlands of autumn, and it quickly washed the clamor of the crowd from Aeryck's mind.

Many had gathered around him in the hall to see what manner of boy he was and to gape at his wondrous sword. Some believed that the sword had magical powers, for surely, they thought, no man (let alone boy) could wield a sword with such skill without the aid of magic.

It was all rather suffocating to the young Briton, and he was glad to finally be away from there where he could cull quiet thoughts from the tumultuous day and entertain them privately under the starry heavens. But there was little time for such musings. No sooner had they started on their way than the ground swelled before them to present the humble estate of Brynwald.

The chieftain's home—more a farmer's cottage—was set amid an orchard of apple, plum, and peach trees, stands of rowans, ashes, and elms, and a fair array of old oaks that dotted the place in clumps of twos and threes. About the cottage were holly and heather bushes and fresh plantings of pansies, betraying the woman's touch.

Terryll caught the glint off the antlers of a fallow deer in the apple orchard and paused to watch as the animal stood up onto its hind legs to snatch an apple. The young hunter's mind took him at once to the mountains and rivers of his homeland, where he and Hauwka had spent many such nights hunting and fishing and reveling in the joys of life. He realized in that moment how much he missed his old friend and wondered of his well-being. He let out a sigh, then quickly caught up with the others.

The estate was surrounded by fields of harvested barley, straw, and oats, though the earth had played the miser this year with its yield.

Shunloc-Taz had told the people that was because they had stolen seven girls from neighboring clans to sacrifice at the feast of Beltane, the May Day festival, which honored the setting of the seven goddesses of the Pleiades in the southern sky. The high priest went on to say that to receive from the earth they must give to the earth and that by stealing the girls, instead of using their own, they had shown their selfishness and greed.

It was then that Tolc began to secretly doubt his words. After all, he thought, why were the neighboring clans suffering the wrath of the sun god as well? Surely they had given to the earth.

The cottage was made of wattle and daub inside and out and was roofed with straw thatch, though it was sorely in need of rethatching and other repairs that had been left to fallow until Brynwald's return. All in all, it was a far cry from the sprawling villa estate of the chieftain of Kill-wyn Eden, though there was a certain hominess about the place that appealed to both boys.

Inside, Aeryck and Terryll waited at the table with mugs of hot apple cider in front of a comfortable peat fire, as Brynald's wife—Tillie—prepared supper.

Brynwald had gone outside to post his warriors around the estate in case any of Sarteham's men tried to finish his work, then to collect wood for the hearth.

The boys had offered to help with the wood gathering, but Brynwald refused them flatly, saying that they were his guests and to sit tight until supper. Neither boy dared counter the man, even politely, for the Pictish chieftain looked just as fierce in front of his hearth as he did in front of his warriors—perhaps even more so now that they were alone with him and in such close quarters.

Presently the door was kicked open, and Brynwald came into the cottage with an armload of firewood and dumped it unceremoniously next to the hearth. "That ought to be enough for the night," he said, casting the boys a wink. "I wouldnay be wanting the fair skin of you Britons to be takin' a draft!"

The boys weren't sure if they were expected to make comment on his words. It was the kind of statement that didn't need remark or rebuttal, but etiquette seem to demand some kind of retort—even a grunt might suffice—so there was an awkward pause. They took the safe route and just nodded at him politely.

Brynwald supplied the grunt, then, breaking up the peat bed, he proceeded to throw logs onto the fire.

The boys rolled their eyes at each other and retreated into their mugs of cider.

Aeryck glanced over at Tillie, who was at work in the kitchen area, and wondered that there weren't any children about to help her with the chores. He thought of offering to help her with the heavy cooking pot that she carried to the fire but thought better of it in light of Brynwald's austere rules of hospitality.

Brynwald finished stoking the fire, then tossed the poker carelessly to one side and sat down at the head of the table, pleased with his handiwork.

Terryll thought he had placed too many logs on top of each other, which would surely smother the fire, though he wasn't about to mention it. Perhaps Pictish flues drew differently than British ones, he reasoned diplomatically, and let it go.

The chieftain turned to Aeryck and slapped him across the back. "*Och!* Never have I seen such swordsmanship!" he said, abruptly finishing an earlier thought he'd left dangling back at the hall.

Aeryck coughed, choking back a swallow of cider.

"Aye! How is it then, that you being a mannie could have learnt the blade so well?" Brynwald asked, eyeing the lad. "It has my mind in the mirligoes!"

Aeryck was embarrassed by both the attention and the suddenness of the praise, and he squirmed noticeably. Wiping his face, he said, "I had a good teacher."

"The best in all Briton!" Terryll added with pride, pleased with the upswing in conversation. He too had marveled at Aeryck's victory, for there were not many who could have (or would have) stood against a mighty warrior such as Sarteham and lived the telling of it.

"You have a gift, kipper!" Brynwald countered. "A master can only help a student to find it. Aye, I ken of a certainty now that you are the son of Caelryck! 'Twere nay buckie you were crossing blades with! Mayhaps 'twas the deffil himself!"

At that moment Tillie entered the room with a potful of steaming stew and set it on the table before the boys. "Supper's on!" she said in a singsongy voice.

Terryll's eyes lit up at the sight. "Boar stew! It's one of my favorites!" he exclaimed, sniffing the vapors.

Tillie giggled. "'Tis really just one of our old sows I got tired of kicking out of my garden," she said, wiping a strand of hair from her face. "We had many battles over the rhubarb and squash these past three years. She won most of 'em too!" The woman winked at the boys as she ladled stew into bowls, adding, "But I reckon she's made her peace now, hasn't she?" She let out a big laugh, then hefted the pot over onto the hob.

Tillie wasn't exactly pretty, though she wasn't homely either. Although she was past the flower of her youth, still she was a bosomy woman, with alert little blue eyes set into a friendly face, and she took advantage of her charms. Her hair was a wild snarl of reds and grays that kept falling into her eyes, which she was constantly wiping or blowing away. And when she smiled she revealed a small gap between her two front teeth, though it fit her looks. The boys liked her at once.

Once she joined them at the table, Brynwald said a blessing over the meal, and both boys stared at the man with irreverent wonder. The idea of a Pictish chieftain saying prayers to Christ would take some getting used to, especially one who had depictions of his former gods tattooed all over his body.

It wasn't an eloquent prayer such as Aurelius might offer, Terryll thought as he listened, but it was said with as much heart, and the boy was impressed. And so the blessing was said and ratified with a round of "amens," and consumption of the stew began in earnest.

Sometime during a pause in the meal, Aeryck managed the courage to broach a subject with Brynwald that had been gnawing at him all day. "How is it that you know of my father?" he asked.

The chieftain looked at him and smiled. "Aye! I was wondering when you'd get around to that, kipper."

Presently smoke began to billow out of the hearth and curdled about the low-beamed ceiling. Brynwald shot a fierce look at the fireplace and jumped up to tend it. Grabbing the poker, he stabbed at the logs wildly as if they were rodents under foot. Cinders popped, sparks flew everywhere—some even landed on the table—and smoke continued to boil and belch out of the hearth unchecked, troubling the breathing air.

Tillie pushed away from the table in a panic. Rushing to the hearth, she said, "Hoot, Brynnie, the stew! Here, let me take care of that!"

"I've got it, Tillie," Brynwald said, kicking a burning log back into the fireplace.

"You were never suited for such domestics, love!" she said, grabbing a log from his armload.

"Away with you! It needs more fuel, is all," he countered, tossing the logs onto the fire.

"You're going to burn the hame doon!"

"Leave me be, woman! Or you'll vex me to ill temper!"

Tillie threw her arms into the air and stormed to the door and flung it open.

The boys watched helplessly as the round-faced woman charged around the cottage throwing open windows and talking to herself, while Brynwald maintained his post at the hearth, stabbing logs and tossing more fuel onto the problem. He finally gave it up and returned to the table but not until he had used up the entire stack of wood.

After the cottage had cleared of smoke—though a thin pall of it hung over their heads for most of the night—Tillie brought out a trayful of drinks for everyone: hot cider for the boys and a flagon of mead for Brynwald. And though the fire continued to smolder defiantly, refusing both flame and heat, nobody dared mention it further.

Soon, as Brynwald's spirit was refreshed with drink, and peace reigned sublime, the fierce-looking chieftain picked up his aborted thoughts as though nothing had happened.

"Aye!" he began cheerfully. "During our sojourn in Eire, the brothers there took us to their bosoms to feed and care for us. 'Twere a kindly thing to do in light of our pillaging along their shores—" Brynwald broke off and glanced momentarily into his flagon, shaking his head thoughtfully. And when he looked up, his eyes were moist. "*Och*, by the oaks, it were a kindly thing."

The boys looked into their mugs.

"Dunnald and I stayed in the hame of old Finn MacLlewald," Brynwald continued, "a blacksmith, and a man of quiet humors, I taken, though mighty bold of the tongue. 'Twere in his hame that I learnt of your father, Caelryck."

Aeryck started. "How so?" he asked, intrigued that someone in Ireland would know of his father.

Brynwald seemed surprised at the question. "*Och*, kipper! What do you ken of your mother's kinfolk, then?" he asked curiously.

The boy shrugged his shoulders and sighed. "Er . . . nothing," he said, ruefully. "Nothing of my father's family either, for that matter. I just know that I was born in Glenryth, and there my father and I lived until he was killed by the Saxons."

"And does your mother live, then?" Brynwald asked.

"No," Aeryck answered, haltingly. "She died giving birth to me."

"'Tis a shame," Brynwald said.

"Aye," Tillie added sadly, and she wiped a tear from her cheek.

"How is it, then, that your father didnay tell you of your mother's kin?" Brynwald pressed.

"He may have, but I don't remember," Aeryck replied, not sure where the Pict was heading.

"It makes sense now, it does," Brynwald said.

"What makes sense?"

"Yes—what makes sense?" Terryll jumped in, eager to know the answer to the riddle.

"Finn MacLlewald told us that he had a sister who died in child-birth away back," Brynwald answered. "What he didnay tell us was that she had given birth to a son." The chieftain studied the boy's features thoughtfully, then added, "Aye! I can see it now. You favor your mother's side of the tree."

"I've been told I look like my father," Aeryck said, not making the connection. When he did make it, his hand leaped to his face and stroked the side of his chin. "You mean—"

"Aye! The MacLlewalds are your mother's kin—your blood an' bones—and of the Scotti, nay less!"

Aeryck shot a mystified look at Terryll, then asked, "How can this be? Why didn't they come for me when my father died?"

"Like I said t' you, kipper, old Finn ne'er kenned that his sister's bairn had lived—only that Rebecca had died in the birthing. What profit were there, I ask you, in comin' for a ghost?"

Aeryck perked up when he heard the name. "Rebecca? My mother's name was Rebecca?" he asked thoughtfully. He sounded the name in his memory, but no image returned.

"Aye, it were," Brynwald said. "And a bonnie name at that!"

Then the boy scrunched up his nose, thinking. "But if she was from Ireland, how—"

"Did she meet your father?" Brynwald interrupted.

"Aye . . . er . . . yes."

"Old Finn—that rascal—told us that when your father were not too many years older than you, he came to believe in Christ," Brynwald said. "He went on to say that he learnt of the faith from some holy men of Patrick, sojournin' amongst the British. Caelryck gang with 'em back to Eire to hear the words of Patrick firsthand.

"Being a blacksmith as he was, he was presented to the MacLlewald clan—also of the trade—and, there a-boardin' with the stout Scotti, he met fair Rebecca." Brynwald let out a hearty laugh. "Aye. She was a bonnie lass, I'm told, blessed of figure and bold as brass, and the ground moved betwixt 'em, sure! *Och!*—the tales still told—"

He was cut off by a scowl from Tillie.

Brynwald cleared his throat and continued. "But to the straight of it, kipper, Caelryck and the lass were coupled in a flash—to the sorrow of many an Eire-born lad—and returned to Britain some time behind, and Rebecca bein' great with child."

Aeryck lowered his head with a great heaviness. "Where she died giving birth to me."

"Aye, she did," Brynwald said matter-of-factly. "And the Saxons come and killed your father no' too many years later." He looked across the table at Tillie, who, apart from the odd scowl or two, had been quietly listening to the story. In the flickering candlelight, he could see that her eyes were wet and glistening, the sides of her round cheeks shimmering with a fine glow.

The chieftain turned again to the boy. "Life is hard, kipper. You've lost your parents . . . we've lost our only bairn. But they are gone now, and we cannay bring 'em back. Aye. We are not always given the wisdom of such things, but 'tis enough to ken that God is the sovereign Laird, and that we are alive to accomplish His purposes."

The room was quiet for a spell, save for the snapping and crackling in the hearth and the muffled roar of the river, coursing along the perimeter of the steading. It seemed a sad and melancholy place where the four of them sat at table, and for a time they conversed in sighs.

"How did you lose your child?" Aeryck spoke his thoughts at last, before realizing the impropriety of such a question. But it was too late, the words were over the table, and he couldn't take them back.

"We were raided three years ago by warriors from Old Glenlouden, seeking bairns to sacrifice upon their altar," Brynwald replied, without offense taken. "Our Brian was taken—aye." The chieftain shook his head as he formed his next thought. "We've lang been at war with their clan and have done the same ourselves. By troth of the oaks, we suffered an accursed religion."

"Troth, and it was why I was not there to meet you, Bryn," Tillie said bitterly. "I'll be a part of its cursedness nay longer!"

Aeryck looked at Tillie and felt his heart tightening with sorrow.

She reached over and patted his hand and gave him a warm smile, though he could see in her eyes the grief that she still carried.

All of a sudden he felt like crying. He would have too, had Terryll not changed the subject.

"This morning it looked as though you recognized Aeryck's sword," Terryll said to the chieftain. "Is that true?"

Brynwald asked to see Aeryck's sword. "Not this sword, but one akin to it," he said, taking it.

"You mean there're more than one of them?" Aeryck asked.

"There are three," Brynwald replied, admiring the weapon's beauty in the candlelight. "Finn MacLlewald has one just like it."

"He does?"

"Aye, your father fashioned it for him in the MacLlewald forge," Brynwald said, studying the hilt. "'Twere then that your father designed his crest. *Och!*—such a beauty! When I saw the likeness of the bear's head on your sword and medallion, I kenned in a trice you were telling the truth."

"It is Hauwka," Aeryck blurted out.

"What is Hauwka?" Brynwald asked.

Aeryck looked over at a surprised Terryll and said, "A friend of my father's."

Until that moment, he had never mentioned to Terryll that his father must have known the bear. Aeryck turned to the chieftain, leaving Terryll with a puzzled look on his face.

"You said there were three swords that my father made," he said.

Brynwald returned the weapon to Aeryck. "Aye. Finn told us that Caelryck fashioned three swords in their forge—each being a tribute to one of the Trinity. Yours is the sword honoring the Holy Spirit as ye can see, for ye'll note the tongues of fire engraved at the base of the blade."

Aeryck had studied every inch of the blade countless times, though he had never understood the meaning of the tongues of fire. He had presumed them to be solely a design of beauty.

Terryll angled his head to get a closer look at the engraving. "I never noticed it before," he said.

"I'm surprised you noticed that it had a blade at all," Aeryck countered.

"Very funny."

"Finn MacLlewald's sword honors God the Father," Brynwald continued, "for it were the first one Caelryck made. On its blade the tablets of the Law are engraved."

"Then there is yet another sword," Aeryck said. "The sword honoring Christ."

"Aye," the chieftain said. "Though I ken not of its whereabouts."

Terryll brightened with a thought. "Your father must have carried it with him into battle against the Saxons!" he suggested. "It was either buried with him or lost—or perhaps it was stripped from his hand on the field of battle."

"Yes . . . perhaps," Aeryck said, pondering the notion. Then he asked, "What did my father engrave on its blade?"

"*Och!* This I dinna recall," Brynwald said. Then he drained his flagon of mead.

As the evening waned pleasantly with such talk, Tillie rose from the table and fixed each of the boys a soft bed of furs next to the hearth.

Brynwald took his cue and stood up. "Ye kippers will sleep here the night," he said, feigning a yawn.

"What of the British women?" Terryll asked, for Gwyneth was on his mind, and thoughts of her well-being had troubled him throughout the day.

"Dinna ye fret over them, mannie. I've already given orders that they are to be given food and comfort," Brynwald said. Then he added, "On the morrow, by m' troth, ye'll be free to return to your hames." With that Brynwald retired to his bedroom.

350

"Ye gang ahead," Tillie said. "I'll be right there after I tuck these lads in."

The boys frowned at each other and mouthed her words. *Tuck these lads in?*

Tillie quickly repaired the fire in the hearth and swore the boys to secrecy. She kissed each of them on the cheek, pinched the spot to make sure it took, then blew out the candles, leaving them standing alone in the light of a blazing fire.

They looked at each other, rubbing their cheeks embarrassedly, though secretly neither of them minded at all.

Then the boys laid their heads down on the soft, warm furs and listened to the fire crackling. They talked in whispers, mostly about the journey home on the morrow, though they touched on each of the day's events briefly.

In time the fire died down to a small mound of glowing red and black embers, and the muted roar of the river outside was calling them to sleep with a gentle song. It struck Aeryck odd that only the night before he had nearly drowned in its torrential flow. It seemed a lifetime had passed downstream since then.

Indeed, it had.

Finally the day's activities caught up with their bodies, and each retired to the quiet sanctum of his thoughts.

Terryll pondered Aeryck's words concerning Hauwka and Caelryck, then soon fell asleep, dreaming of the fire-haired beauty with the flashing emerald-green eyes and comely shape, rejoicing in his spirit that he would see her well in the morning.

Aeryck lay on his back, thinking long on his father's three swords. He wondered what became of the one honoring Christ. Perhaps it lay buried somewhere, as Terryll had suggested, on the Hill of Badon, waiting for someone to resurrect it. It saddened him to think that it might lying somewhere unattended and fouling.

He moved from these thoughts to those of Dagmere. But no sooner did he picture her face than the beautiful raven-haired Fiona moved into the scene with her wet, pursed lips and kissed him. Presently he felt a queer stirring deep within his body, as though his youth were revealing to him an ancient and profound mystery. It troubled him.

More, it frightened him, and he quickly tried to replace Fiona kissing him with Dagmere kissing him. But he kept getting their features mixed up in his mind, and soon their faces became an inseparable swirl. It wasn't long before he couldn't remember what either one looked like, and he grew weary of the challenge.

The boy rolled over onto his sleeping side and immediately felt a curious lump beneath him. At first he thought it was a fold in the furs, but upon investigating the matter he came up empty. Then he realized that the lump wasn't in his bedding at all but in his pocket. Reaching into it, he pulled out a small wooden carving, the one he had taken from the dead Pict's sack of booty on the night they had begun their pursuit of the women. He had forgotten all about it.

Holding it up to the light of the fire, he noted as before that it was carved into the shape of a cross with the figure of an animal upon it. But what he couldn't see before on the near-moonless road was that the carved animal was a lamb, one with a slash crudely cut across its throat. He was stunned.

And as he turned the little carving in the firelight, thoughts of the tapestry and the sweeping images of his waking dream filled his mind.

Aeryck smiled. *You have found me,* he mused, *or I have found you. I know not which.*

Lying down again, he reverently placed the cross next to his head. And when the boy could no longer keep his eyes open, he offered a short prayer to Christ—one without eloquence, yet one with heartfelt gratitude —then fell asleep dreaming of Ireland.

30
THE HEART OF
THE MATTER

Under the same crescent moon—though many miles to the south of Loch na Huric—the squat, bandy-legged figure of a man could be seen climbing up the ridge that overlooked the hill-fort of Badonsward. His little arms chugged as he came at the untoward slope with grim determination, puffing and wheezing, sometimes on threes, sometimes on all fours like a small ape, twice stumbling and losing advantage, cursing his adversary the hill.

Once reaching the summit, the little man threw his head back, nursed a stitch in his side, and blew out an oath, then quickly toddled over to another figure, one that stood brooding in sullen meditation at the edge of a broad clearing.

This one was taller in stature and, though manlike in appearance, he cut a sinister, wolfish shape against the night sky. His shoulders hung in a forward stoop, and the angle of his head was bent in a contrary attitude, as though the wind were laying several loads upon his back, each an immeasurable burden. And his eyes were two cold stones attending the vaults of his humorless visage, staring out from beneath the snout of the wolfskin shroud at something distant and unseen.

Below him the bonfires of Horsa's army burned bright against the hills, outlining the hill fort, reaching up and under the snout to color the grim-set jaw with sulfurous hues. But the sullen figure's mind was far beyond the fires of tiny men, his reach stretched into the eternal with a terrible grasp, one forbidden.

Boadix came panting up to Norduk's side and paused to collect his breath, throwing his stubby hands onto his knees. *"Phew!* Is there a reason my liege wishes to meet with me here instead of in his chamber?" Then, looking out over the brow of the hill, he added, "The bonfires of Horsa wash the stars from the sky."

His words seemed to waken the Saxon underlord from a preternatural trance. The wolfish head rolled heavily up, and the eyes glimmered

353

to life beneath the snout. "I do not need a stargazer to tell me what my own eyes plainly see," he rasped.

"Perhaps not," the druid retorted, still winded. He puffed up his chest and blew the air out hard. "But the eyes do not always see what they are beholding, and they do not always behold what they see."

"I'll not suffer you tonight, little man," Norduk chided angrily. "Say what you mean plainly."

"I have."

"Then your journey to Londinium has addled your pate. Is it not enough that Horsa has taken over my chambers, that you must now return to crowd me out of my senses as well?"

"Tsk, tsk. I see that much has flowed down the River Trent since I have been away."

"Indeed," Norduk said, gazing at the glowing plain below them. His eyes worked quickly over the bonfires, scrutinizing the tiny shapes of men moving about, as though wakening from another reality and seeing them for the first time. He immediately fell to what seemed a truculent air, a very human and violent air. "Each day more of Horsa's warriors arrive from the south, choking the air with their campfires," he growled. "I am growing weary of it."

"Such inconvenience is necessary to fulfill your plans," Boadix assured him.

Norduk grunted. "Even so, I loathe how the man seduces my warriors to his side. Even Olaf is bewitched by his cunning."

The little druid chuckled. "It is only a matter of time before you will be free of Horsa's arrogance. For many things can happen in battle—an arrow flies one way, it flies another. It cares little, either way." Boadix removed the glass orb from its eye-socket and held it up to the northern sky toward the constellation Ursa Minor, the "little bear."

"Tell me, little man, what you have learned in the south," Norduk demanded. "And be quick about it—my humor is foul."

"I have news of two kinds, my liege. One is good—the other concerns me," the druid answered. "Which would you prefer to hear first?"

The Wolf turned a threatening shoulder to him.

Boadix chuckled. "I will tell you the good news first," he said with a wry smile. "The daughter of Hengist is going to have a child."

"*This* is the good news! I have already learned your 'good news' from Horsa. The oaf boasts of it every day at council."

"And did the 'oaf' tell you that she will have a son?" the druid asked.

"A son? How do you know this?"

Boadix rolled the orb between his fingers, then swung it south toward the constellation Taurus. "Ahh, the Seven Sisters of the Pleiades

354

begin their ascent," he said. "Soon Orion the Hunter will pursue, followed by Sirius, the Great Dog Star."

"*Paagh!* You will drive me mad with such talk, druid!"

"There are many things one can learn when his eyes are not fixed on the earth," Boadix returned smugly.

"What has Rowena's male child to do with me?"

"Did you know that her mother was a druidess from Gaul?"

Norduk shot a skeptical look at the man. "It is not possible," he said. "You know as I do that Hengist hates the druidic religion. He would have killed her."

"The eyes of Hengist roll across the earth seeking lands to conquer," the druid said. "The fool would do well to master his own bed."

"What does this have to do with Rowena? Surely her loyalties lay with her father."

"She has the gift of sight like her mother," Boadix said, then paused to gauge the reaction on Norduk's face. "It is true! And she will go to great lengths to see the druidic priesthood reinstated," he added. "What's more, she loathes Vortigern . . . and his child within her womb."

Norduk's yellow eyes flared with a sudden heat. "She told you these things?"

"Of course," the druid replied haughtily. "It seems the gods have provided us with a sacrifice at Stonehenge." He chuckled with enormous satisfaction. "Ah, yes! Indeed, the wisdom of the gods is higher than ours, and their purposes beyond our comprehension." Boadix cast his gaze heavenward. Then, peering at the constellations through his glass orb, he added, with a slight edge of sarcasm, "This will teach us to trust our eyes less and our sight more."

Norduk ignored the comment as he fell to silent meditation; the news was indeed good.

The druid returned his prized, although recently nicked, orb to its fleshy crypt and secured it behind the little lolling veil of skin. After a calculated span of time, he remarked, "Rowena is a beautiful woman, but she is no fool. We talked of many things."

Norduk looked at him sharply. "What is her price?"

Boadix appraised the look, then turned away, folding his stumpy hands behind his back. "It is but a small request."

"Name it before I lose my patience, little man."

The druid shrugged. "She would have only the child of your union," he said, glancing over the hill fort below. He was rocking on his heels with the confidence of a banker.

Suddenly the Wolf was before him, glaring intently into the druid's single living eye.

It so startled Boadix that he jumped and nearly fell over backward.

"Our union?" The dark malignancy now burning in the Wolf's eyes clearly betrayed his thoughts. "She has asked for the kingdom."

"A kingdom that she could give to you," the druid hastened to add, chuckling nervously.

Norduk glowered fiercely at the little man, like a predator. It seemed at any moment he might leap upon the druid and snatch his throat.

Boadix faltered backward a step, but he stood his ground, for he knew well the man who stood before him. Several moments passed, and his eye darted uneasily beneath the underlord's wild stare as he waited anxiously. Then, beholding the familiar transformation over the other's countenance, the eye steadied, fastened, and narrowed into a sneer.

"Indeed," Norduk mused as a wistful reverie swept over his brow.

Presently the revelation of Rowena's beauty took root in his mind with seducing images, each working her secret craft upon his senses. His eyes became transfixed in a servile, faraway gaze, the lids of which genuflected obediently over the flames as he worshiped the goddess from afar.

Norduk shook his head incredulously as lucidity returned to his eyes, cooling them. "Indeed," he mused. With his own plans maturing splendidly on the vine, it was apparent that the gods would reward him with not only the vineyard but with the choicest fruit as well. Such wisdom was indeed higher than his sight.

"Yes," he agreed, his voice sonorous. "I will pay such a small price."

"I thought that you might." The druid grinned.

Norduk took his leave of the druid to mull over this first piece of news. He headed through some trees and across the clearing, threading his way bemusedly through the dark wolf carcasses near the old snag, the grisly evidence of Hauwka's desperate stand against Gray Eye.

Then he stooped to examine one of the bodies. Raking his fingers along its lacerated neck, he whispered, almost paternally, "Foolish Kill Deer, I told you many times never to underestimate your enemies— especially that enemy. But I see that you did not listen." The man was silent for several moments, pondering matters, then he stood and turned back to Boadix. "You said there was other news which concerned you."

"It concerns a boy," Boadix said as he toddled over to him, but seeing the slaughter of wolves he staggered in horror. "What has happened?" he gasped. "The wolves—there are so many of them, dead."

"A bear," Norduk answered flatly.

Boadix was stunned. "A bear? A single bear killed all these wolves?"

"It was a rather large bear," Norduk said, gazing to the north. "One that has been troublesome of late."

The druid's bulbous head bobbled with a jolt of light. "Could it be?" he wondered out loud, looking into the heavens. As he gazed intently at the constellations, his expression twisted with perplexity.

His mind began to quickly sort through a raft of puzzle pieces, heretofore scattered in vague disarray, now scrutinizing their shapes, arranging them, rearranging them, now brightening as a picture began to take form in the cerebral mists. "Yes . . . yes . . ." And then his face twitched with astonishment. "Ahh, yes!" he exclaimed. "Yes, of course, the bear! It is true!"

Norduk had been watching him curiously. "What is true?"

Boadix began to pace in tight circles, scratching his shapeless nose as he laid the star-scape over the images forming in his mind. "Of course—the bear!" he exclaimed with the sudden joy of revelation. "There was a bear . . . I remember that there was a bear! The gods are good!" he ejaculated. "They are wise!" He clapped his hands like a child given a shiny treasure.

Norduk began to lose his temper. "What are you talking about?" he demanded. "What bear?"

"Caelryck."

"Caelryck?" The Wolf's expression grew even darker. "What about Caelryck?"

Boadix hopped about in a little jig, mindful however of the wretched carcasses at his feet. "Don't you see? I have been pursuing the meaning of why the wandering star passed through Ursa Major before traveling on to the Dog Star, and now I see it."

"Yes?"

"It is the bear, of course—this bear, the one that has killed your wolves! It was a rather large bear, you say?"

Norduk's German mind was near exasperation. "What has that got to do with Caelryck?"

Boadix chuckled happily. "Do you not remember the tales of a very large bear that was often seen with the metalsmith from Glenryth?"

Suddenly a thought struck the underlord. "The metalsmith from Glenryth," he mused aloud. Then he drew his sword and looked down at the engraved relief on the hilt. "A bear's head," he rasped darkly, making the connection as he studied the crest. His eyes shifted inquiringly to the druid. They were glinting a deep ocher in the shadows of his face. "But what does it mean?"

"I did not understand it until tonight." The druid giggled, mindful of the sword in Norduk's hand. "But now that I do . . . hoo, hoo, hoo! I see it plainly. It is Arthgen!"

"Arthgen?" Norduk was bewildered again.

"Your enemy! Arthgen is 'the son of the bear' of which the Celtic myths speak." The druid paused, allowing this knowledge to set in the underlord's mind. Then he continued. "On my journey to Londinium I met with some Gaulish traders who had spent much time trading in the north. They told me that the Britons there sing songs of a certain boy— not just any boy, mind you. No. This is a boy whose father led a small contingent of men against your army at the Battle of Glenryth." The druid saw Norduk's head jump. "Yes, it seems the dead have risen to trouble us again."

Norduk stared at him incredulously. "Caelryck had a son?"

"Yes, a living, breathing son of his flesh." Boadix laughed.

"I fail to see the humor in this," Norduk snarled.

"Perhaps you might see the humor in it if you knew that the boy was once in your grasp, but that he escaped? Yes, yes, I see by your expression you think I have gone mad." The little man giggled again. "No, no, no, I have not gone mad. When I learned that Caelryck had a son I journeyed to Glenryth on my way back here, to inquire into the veracity of the story.

The druid resumed his banker's posture again, rocking on his heels and folding his hands behind his back. "There was a certain baker there, the magistrate, I believe, who was most loquacious. Oh, yes." Boadix chuckled at the thought of the fat man's eyes bugging open when he told him that he was an envoy of the underlord—how he kept powdering his brow with a floured rag as he stuttered an effluence of information.

"It seems the boy had been living there for the past ten years," he continued, "until a patrol of horse-soldiers chased him out of town not six months ago. That he escaped is certain. Indeed. The Gaulish traders assured me that he is alive and well today."

Norduk did some quick mental calculations.

"Yes, my liege, the timing fits," Boadix said, smiling smugly as he observed the other's expression. "It seems the patrol was under the command of a fierce-looking warrior—wearing a winged helmet, the baker said." Boadix cleared his throat and rolled forward to a stop. "Did Olaf tell you that he had failed in this, this proud Viking who is bewitched by the oaf Horsa? No? I thought not."

He waddled over to one of the dead wolves and, standing at a safe distance from it, peered ironically at its wounds. "But here is the point in the Gauls' story where it becomes most enlightening," he said, turning away with a little shudder of disgust. "For, you see, the son of Caelryck escaped with the help of a rather large bear."

Norduk followed him with a searing look. "Still, I fail to see what concern the boy is to me?"

358

Boadix swung wide of the man, maintaining a prudent distance. "Did I not overhear Horsa briefing the Viking commander that Killwyn Eden is the key to the success of your northern campaign?"

"What of it?"

"Interesting . . . most interesting." Boadix was relishing his power. "Isn't it peculiar that the son of Caelryck would flee to the very place that is crucial to the success or failure of your plans?"

"So the boy is in Killwyn Eden. Still, I fail to see—"

"He must be found and killed at once," the druid interrupted, "lest he thwart our plans as his father did."

Norduk glared.

"It is the second bit of news, my liege," the druid said seriously, "the bad news. The wandering star has veered from its course."

"So?"

"So before it veered, it first passed through Ursa Major and its cub."

"You said it was supposed to," Norduk argued.

"Ahh! I said that it would pass through the Great Bear, not the Little Bear," the druid corrected. "But before the wandering star left our skies to continue his journey across the heavens, it touched the head of the cub, telling me that his destiny is linked with yours."

"The cub?"

"Yes," the druid said, "the cub . . . Arthgen."

"Perhaps you've misunderstood the sign."

"The heavens do not lie to me, nor do I misunderstand their speech," the little druid said with supreme arrogance. "Your destiny is linked with the son of Caelryck. Kill the son—break the link."

A savage scowl gathered across Norduk's countenance as he turned his sword in his hands, studying the blade in the light of the moon. The reflected light shimmered up its length and caught the masterfully wrought design. Grunts of inexpressible contempt attended the revelation of each detail.

Raised upon its base were engravings of a broken loaf of bread overlaid with silver and set on a bronze platter, and an ornate chalice of wine overlaid with beaten gold. Both of these elements were enwreathed by a brazen plait of thorns. Its motif was carried down the length of the blade on both sides, along the sword hilt and around the pommel of the handle. Norduk let out a summary curse, then shifted his yellow eyes to the druid.

"I will not suffer a second defeat by the man," he spoke at last.

The druid watched him. The moon glistened anxiously in his glass orb.

"Killwyn Eden," Norduk mused aloud, as he looked north from beneath his wolf's cowl. His eyes burned with terrifying ferocity. A low growl rattled in his throat. "My wolves will track him down and tear him to pieces."

The underlord moved to the edge of the hillside and gazed down upon the scores of Saxon campfires dotting the plain below. Moments later Boadix tottered to his side, placed his stubby hands on his hips, and let out a sigh. The wind echoed the sigh as it shifted course, and for a moment a muffled babble of voices could be heard wafting up from the encampment like distant thunder. But whatever words were carried by the wind were lost on the two men, for each stood in quiet reflection, weighing the thoughts of his own mind.

At length the druid spoke. "The wolves must not fail you," he said. "Your kingdom hangs on the son of Caelryck's life."

"They will not fail me," Norduk growled. "They have never failed me. Besides, as my powers grow, so do my resources, resources of which even you have no knowledge. No, the son of Caelryck will not escape!"

Boadix glanced at him suspiciously. *What resources?* he wondered. He didn't like surprises. But what he said was, "Then may the gods grant his death soon."

Norduk was in a brooding silence. A dark look swept across his countenance as he left the business of men and sank again into a preternatural trance.

Boadix took note but did not let it trouble him. He had unraveled a deep mystery and was confident that the gods would reveal everything to him in time. The underlord would have no secrets from him. He puffed up his chest with the night air, then blew it out, immeasurably pleased with himself. "It is a lovely air, isn't it?"

But Norduk did not hear him.

Boadix cleared his throat several times. Still there was no response from the underlord. Indeed, it seemed as though he had turned to stone.

A span of several minutes passed. During the silence the druid viewed the constellations Ursa Major and Minor through his glass orb, viewed the Dog Star pursuing Orion the Hunter with his sword. Replacing it at last, he waddled happily along the brow of the hill, glancing occasionally at the fires and occasionally over at the wolfish figure that was bent in some wretched contemplation. "Druid, what do you know of this religion of the Romano-Britons?" the Wolf asked, finally stirring from his dark thoughts.

Boadix halted abruptly, startled out of his own thoughts. "Christianity?"

"Yes."

"It is a weak religion," the druid replied. "Look what became of the Romans once they embraced it. Why do you ask?"

"I had a dream last night that has been troubling me all day. I believe it to be from the gods, for it bears the clarity of divine spark and clings to my very soul—haunts me—it gives me little ease of mind." Norduk looked over at the druid's searching eyes. "I know not, however, whether the dream speaks to my favor or presages some disaster to befall me."

"Ahh!" the druid said, brightening. "Tell me your dream, and I will interpret it."

Norduk turned Caelryck's sword in his hands slowly. As he did, the moonlight shone radiantly along its polished surface and picked up the exquisite detail of the plait of thorns.

"I dreamed of a sword—much like this one—one that descended from the heavens to the earth," he began. "Once reaching the earth, a tongue of fire spread along its length until the entire sword was engulfed in flames. Then the blazing sword turned slowly in a great circle, pausing at each of the four corners of the horizon to touch off a small fire—one that immediately spread outward to consume all of the land. Finally the sword pointed south where it came to rest."

Norduk paused, then added, "And this is the part of the dream which troubles me. The sword came to rest with its flaming tip pointing directly at me, and I was consumed by a terrible fire."

The druid looked into the man's eyes a long while, searching them, waiting for another word. "Is this the sum of it?" he asked.

Norduk continued to scrutinize the crest on the sword hilt for several moments, then returned it to its scabbard. "Yes. That's the sum of it."

"Then it is a good dream," the druid said confidently. "The sword was pointing at you, because you are the chosen sword-bearer. And the fire that consumed you is your terrible wrath that awaits those who resist your will.

"Now, behold the bonfires of the Saxon army," he added, spreading his little fingers across the glowing horizon. "These are the tongues of fire that will set the sword blazing with your fury. And from this point in the south of Britain, you will lead a great and holy army to each of the four horizons, where you will consume every last vestige of Christianity that the weak Romans have left smoldering in their wake! It will be a terrible conflagration—one sent by the gods, and out of the ashes will rise a glorious new age."

Boadix paused and let out a shrill little laugh. "You shall be the gods' only son upon the earth." He giggled. "And I . . . I shall be your high priest! Yes, it is a good dream! A wonderful dream!"

Norduk turned his face northward and stared into the distance as he gave thought to the druid's interpretation. "Your words are good, druid," he said, without looking at the little man. "Yes, they are good. Now, haven't you some mistletoe to gather?"

Boadix chuckled. "The time of the moon's sixth house is preferred. But still, I have many preparations to make before the sacrifice at Stonehenge in the spring."

"Then leave me be," Norduk said curtly. "I am hungry."

"As you wish, O chosen one."

And without another word the druid bowed sharply, then wobbled away into the forest, leaving Norduk's brooding figure still staring toward the north like some stone statue, impervious to its surroundings.

After a time—the length of which traced the moon's descent from its zenith to a point on the horizon—Norduk, as if by command, began to walk in a large circle around the lighted clearing with an unnatural and broken gait.

As he walked, he marked each of his footfalls slowly, deliberately, and with such calibration that he was obviously measuring the spans of earth around the circle to fulfill some arcane ritualistic numerology. It was not apparent whether the man was awake or entranced by a mystic power that at the same time held his mind captive and yielded animation to his limbs. His eyes, once large and luminous, peering keenly from beneath his wolfskin shroud, were now veiled by a fixed, dull, and occultic sheen.

Moving steadily along his course, he chanted an incantation to the horned god, Cernunnos, lord of the animals and keeper of the gates to the underworld. However, the man spoke not in the harsh, staccato tongue of his Teutonic ancestors—for such would have been blasphemous to the gods of the island—but in the ancient tongue of the Celts, a pleasant-sounding language given to soft-tongued consonants, softened further with guttural vowel sounds that were discharged from the back of the throat.

Each time he completed a circle, the man turned, stepped toward its center, and began another smaller one, defining his course as a series of rings within rings within rings, which would culminate upon the closing of the ninth ring. And with each completed circle he quickened his gait and the tempo of his chanting until, finally, his mouth poured forth utterances with such an ecstatic frenzy that his body began to quiver.

The air immediately became still—not calm but choked to a hushed, irredeemable silence as though smothered by the clasp of a hand over its breath. The sounds of the cricket, the squirrel, even the screech of the nighthawk overhead were cut off by the forbidden intrusion into the nocturnal order. It was as though the created realm were suddenly retaken by the Adamic transgression and looked on from sylvan balconies with unblinking horror to witness the aberrant scene.

At first many of the animals were curious about the strange and insidious scent, and they flirted unnaturally, like moths to the irresistible charms of the flame, with the boundaries of their instincts. Then all at once, as the terror of their dilemma wakened their lulled senses, they fled wide-eyed into the protection of the forest. But those pitiful creatures who lingered too long in morbid curiosity were—like Lot's wife—suddenly caught in its terrible spell and unable to turn away. The badger was one of them.

As Norduk closed the ninth circle, the muscles around his vacant countenance twitched slightly. And amid the dark shadows of his stonecast eyes there began to emerge tiny lights dancing to a feverish reel, as though something rampant and imperious, something altogether malignant, had gotten loose about his visage. A small shudder shot down his spine, then another larger shudder. And for a moment, nothing. There was a pause, and he coughed.

Then suddenly, with the full fury of its demonic source, his body began to shake violently. He stumbled backward from the convulsion but managed to set his feet against the tottering onslaught. He was ready for it, he knew what to expect, and they came. The devils came in legion and found the portal to his soul unattended. Rushing in at once, they rampaged in the void.

Another pause.

Norduk looked down at his gnarled hands and let out a throaty chortle. He could feel the dark magic coursing through his blood vessels as it worked its hell-spawned power throughout his body. A violent jolt of pain shot to his brain, and the man cried out. He rent his clothes and clawed at his face and arms like some animal seeking to free itself from a snare. Then he fell helplessly to the ground as the madness took his mind and seared it. Pinkish foam bubbled about his mouth where he bit his lips, and dribbled unheeded.

The Saxons sitting huddled around their teeming campfires on the plain below were unaware of the transformation of horror taking place on the summit, though their lives were inextricably linked to its dark and sinister design.

They were men doubtless unaware or unconcerned with the great treasure they each possessed. For within each earthen sheath there burned that touch of the Creator's very likeness, which separated the man from the creature and gave to him an eternal purpose and dignity. And though his scant years under the sun be laden with toil, hardships, poverty, and ills, eased only with the familiar levity around a warming fire and the fruited hopes of home and hearth, he was man nonetheless.

363

Not so the pathetic and depraved soul who groveled miserably in the dirt upon the brow of Badonsward like a beast, lost somewhere in the penumbra between light and darkness. This unrepentant branch of Nebuchadnezzar's root, having yielded the birthright of his humanity to the fancies of forbidden councils, writhed drunkenly—both in ecstasy and torment—with the draft of devils. Another charge of pain, searing hot and excruciating, shook his body with sickening paroxysms. He stiffened his limbs and arched his back, screaming out blasphemies—at first sounding pitifully human, then demonic—as the last glimmerings of his divine image flickered on the wick, then finally succumbed to darkness.

The sky was bejeweled with a starry host that seemed to look askance upon the wretched hill as though with an infinite horror.

Although not given to fear, the badger was filled with gripping terror and tried desperately to flee. But it was too late. He was caught in the snare that had tightened its spell-grip upon his eyes, such that he could not command them longer. Both mesmerized and appalled, the badger watched intently, helplessly—terrified to stay, unable to leave—as the miscreant sprang to his haunches, snarling and flinging bloody slaver into the air, ripping the remains of his clothes from his body. Then with unbridled blood-lust the demoniac tore through the carcasses on the ground, hurling bodies, rocks, and tree limbs mindlessly into the air with superhuman strength.

Even the deadened air was stirred by his frenzy. Fierce blasts of wind currents rushed up from the plains and along the ridges, bending trees, stripping leaves from their boughs, and then crashed upon the summit and whipped the awful stillness into a maelstrom of fiendish hilarity. Standing in the midst of the maleficent swirl, the man stretched his hands exultantly to the heavens, threw back his head, and let out an orgiastic cry of triumph. Then at long last—spent from the devilish trauma— he crumpled to the ground, gasping. Moments passed.

The air quickly deadened again to a baleful calm.

Then, slowly, purposefully, as though a black wraith were rising from the depths of the underworld, the accursed man raised his body, shoulders first, followed by the head, the canine head of the hideous cowl with its long snout and pointed ears, and with something dark and otherworldly rattling deep in his throat, he snorted.

And rising to his full height, he glared hatefully at the northern horizon through feral eyes now, and grabbing the wolfskin cowl from his head he flung it violently to the ground.

The demoniac climbed onto the old snag and raised his face to the northern heavens. He let out a piercing howl, which carried long into the mountains, echoing up and down the ridges and wolds of the Pennines, over Badonsward, and through the village streets and alleys of Glenryth beyond, until it could be heard no more. The howl was sinister, malefic, and it sent shivers down the backs of the men below, who turned and stared bewildered at the hill. They had heard tales of strange creatures inhabiting this island, creatures of old that inhabited the dark forests and long barrows and river pools, that dwelt in caves below the earth and came out under the moon to feast upon human flesh, and they retold the tales now around their fires.

But the wretched creature cared nothing for their tales of fear and myth. And there was a scratching of nails clicking against the old snag as he turned to the east and let out another howl, likewise waiting until only the whisper of the wind could be heard through the trees. He turned to the south and finally, to the west, each time sending out the heralding cry of his coming kingdom.

The creature waited in brooding silence as he communed with the gods of his realm, the threefold deities that inhabited the sky and the earth and the regions under the earth. Listening. The time was coming, they promised, as they flitted about his ears. Soon the terrible breach would be opened, the kingdom revealed. Soon. At Stonehenge.

Then lowering his gaze to the carcasses below the snag, he scanned the tree line for his prey, for he knew that it was there. He could smell it, could smell the fear on it, and soon he found the badger's trembling shape, frozen in the shadowed periphery of the clearing. The Wolf's yellow eyes widened almost imperceptibly, then narrowed at once.

He sprang.

PART FOUR
STRANGE GOINGS

31
TIES THAT BIND

Things would never be the same in the village of Loch na Huric. Things never are, following the death of a loved one. Though the human spirit is resilient, imaginative, finding infinite and clever ways to cope with its loss, the void is long in passing, nonetheless. It is the inheritance of the kind.

Sarteham took with him a third of the people, and by sunup was headed northeastward to the village of Old Glenloudon near the headwaters of the River Tweed.

It was as if a great sword had cut through the village and, like the terrible death angel of biblical epic, was seemingly indiscriminate. It separated family from family, husbands from wives, parents from children—taking one, passing over two. Throughout the night the sounds of confusion, anger, and weeping, amid the plaintive cries to sundry deities, had been heard from every quarter of the camp, for there wasn't a home that wasn't touched by the great divorce.

Terryll and Aeryck watched silently, amid a throng of onlookers, as the dispirited line of people filed past on their way out of the village like a procession of dead limbs, carrying what possessions they could, leaving behind their homes and lands and roots, and the bulk of their material goods because of the hasty exodus.

A few in the line glared proudly at their onlookers, and these were mostly old men, women, and a few coached children. But the men of stout frame, those warriors who had known the taste of war-glory, wore only the drawn look of disgrace upon their faces as though leaving a battle in shame, having neither conquered nor died with honor. The heels before them held their rapt attention. The ground hurled incessant imprecations at their faces.

The mood was somber, oppressive, like that of a dirge, such that Aeryck felt his breast tighten with sorrow. Several times he was compelled to avert his eyes from the passage of misery before him to wonder at the trees, the hills, the thatch of a roof. A falling leaf took on tremendous significance. Sighs took wing in profusion.

One little boy began to cry loudly. His mother grabbed his hand and scolded him, telling him to hold his head up and to look straight ahead. Instead he looked back at his father, who stood resolutely—though teary-eyed—with the company of Brynwald, and cried all the louder. An expression of panic tore at the little boy's face, contorting his features between astonishment and terror. Then, jerking free of his mother's grip, he raced back into the arms of his father and clung to his legs. The woman didn't break stride or even look back. Instead she jerked her head as though casting a weight.

Passing through the northern gates of the village, Sarteham, in a final gesture of bitter hatred and defiance, turned, and with his only hand brandished his broadsword to the heavens.

"Hearken, Brynwald! By my troth, before all the gods of the heavens and the earth and below the earth, we rightful sons of Loch na Huric shall return as a mighty scourge and scrape you and your Christian vermin from the earth! And dinna think, bairn of Caelryck, that you can hide below the great wall. Whither you go, whatever rock you crawl beneath, I'll find you sure. Aye! And when I do, you'll wish that you had met death between the stones!" Sarteham wheeled about and, with an ugly sneer, rejoined his army of downtrodden souls.

Aeryck knew the threat to be born of pride, but even so the words made the blood drain from his face and the hair stand up on the back of his neck.

He knew that he had made a bitter enemy—an enemy that perhaps he would have to confront again some day—and he was immediately filled with a prescient dread. At once a thought flashed through his mind, rebuking him for not killing the man when he had the chance. Then he rebuked the thought and turned away, clearing his mind to focus on the day before him.

Many people tarried about the village gates long after the northeastern hills had taken Sarteham and his followers from view, looking on with bewildered gaze, like so many excarnate souls lingering at the graveside in mortal cling, awaiting a voice, a direction, a light. Tolc, the new high priest, was in their number.

The morning sun had thrown a crimson display up from behind the rim of hills looming over the village, shooting fingers of fierce red and orange hues through the broken clouds into the autumn landscape and casting a reddening sheen upon river and valley. The length and breadth of the valley seemed blood-washed, clean, newly attired.

An exhilarating wind picked up from the south and blew through the village, scattering leaves and ferrying birds to and fro on opened wing. It had a renewing effect upon the hamlet, taking with it the sullen mood that clung tenaciously to each heart while lifting spirits to hope. And though most of the people had retired to their farms and cottages to take stock of their lives, some to take stock of their stock, children were soon playing in the streets, chasing swirls of leaves and sending laughter echoing against the hills, filling the air with youthful merriment.

The wind also heralded a coming storm.

By early afternoon, a black, threatening thunderstorm had marshaled its clouds to the south, stretching a massive front from one end of the horizon to the other, consuming the sky with an intimidating show of force.

Brynwald, still attired in his finest chieftain's cloak and trousers for the occasion, cautioned the boys to wait until it blew over before leaving, perhaps in a day or so.

But Terryll was troubled in his spirit and pressed to get underway. It had been five long days since he and Aeryck left Killwyn Eden for Bowness, and it would take another five to return, much longer than the allotted time for the trip. His parents would worry. And besides, Belfourt's condition weighed heavily on his mind, and he was anxious to learn of his well-being. He could see it in Gwyneth's eyes as well.

Convincing the chieftain that they couldn't wait another day, storm or no, Terryll and the others made ready to depart.

Aeryck saddled a large, gray draft horse with a blunt nose and huge feet named Sullie. She was one of Tillie's horses, and her favorite at that, for the mare, though ungainly in appearance, was sure of foot, possessing a sweet temperament and a friendly ride. Earlier, the boys had had a choice between the mare and a powerful-looking black stallion named Tempest—a spirited horse that was constantly throwing his head back and forth and casting his mane and snorting and stamping with furious objections, as though he couldn't tolerate the notion of standing still.

Without any deference to Terryll whatsoever, Aeryck chose Sullie right off, leaving the "demon horse" for his friend. Whether his choice was born of humility or of a sound judgment of horseflesh wasn't clear, but the decision was made, and it stuck.

Dunnald and a contingent of twenty-five heavily armed warriors were soon mounted and ready to begin their short journey. They were to escort the Britons as far as the Solway Firth, giving them protection from robbers and cutthroats and other dangers that might befall them. Nine British women and twenty packhorses loaded heavy with goods, protected by only two boys, would be a ripe plum for the picking.

Most of the women were also saddled on their mounts and waiting anxiously. Several were apprehensive as to their sudden change of fortune and were as yet unconvinced that they were really going home. A few even harbored thoughts that Dunnald and his men were taking them to some other Pictish village to be sold into slavery or worse. And a webbing of fear clung to their secret hopes.

Corrie, the girl with the hurt ankle, was helped up behind one of the women, for she was still too much in shock to ride a horse on her own. She sat rigid, holding on tighter than she needed, and looked straight ahead with nervous, darting eyes, not alighting on anyone's face for more than a flitting moment. Her visage was an exposition of terror.

What tortures might be wracking her mind, however, were a sentineled mystery, for she hadn't spoken a word to anyone since her harrowing ordeal. Gwyneth had grave misgivings concerning her and said as much to Terryll, another factor that weighed heavy on the scales of a speedy departure.

Terryll watched Gwyneth hop onto the back of a sorrel mare and settle neatly into the saddle. She sat a horse as naturally as any he had seen. A gust of wind caught her red hair and threw it about her face and shoulders, giving her a wild and reckless look. And as her eyes found Terryll's, she flipped the hair away from her face and flashed him a broad, radiant smile. Her bright green eyes sparkled with a timeless invitation.

Immediately the boy felt his ears burning. His pulse quickened and, returning her smile, he wondered about the journey that lay ahead.

Brynwald's men finished loading the packhorses with the plundered goods as well as with items that would be sorely needed by a razed village: foodstuffs, blankets, and clothing, which were contributed gladly by the villagers. Sensing the coming torrent, however, the horses were restive and had made the men's task difficult. They stamped and whickered and snorted their protests into the air with great nostril blasts, though their warnings went unheeded.

"I'm sending ye back to Belfourt with everything that 'twere taken from his people," Brynwald said, scanning the group of women riders. "Though, by m' troth, it pains my eternal soul that I cannay return the lives of those lost." Then turning his gaze to the boys (as yet unmounted), he added, "Tell old Belfourt that we nay longer wish war betwixt our people. Iffen he's of a mind to it, I would offer a council of peace."

"I know that my father would agree to such a council as well," Terryll offered.

Brynwald let out a hearty laugh. "That would be somethin', wouldn't it? Ha! Ha! It would!" he bellowed. "Aye! Two old enemies meeting after so many years to break bread instead of skulls! Ha! Tell me, kipper—we dinna speak of it last night, but is the old longbowman still as true with his aim as he was, or have his eyes fallen beneath the mark?"

"He is still the finest bowman in all of Britain," Terryll said with a burst of pride. "Let not a Saxon warrior show his colors within two hundred paces of the man, lest he find another set of colors sticking out of his breast."

Brynwald let out a booming laugh, and his eyes blazed with kindled zeal. "*Och!* That I would like to see. Aye!" Then, clasping Terryll's arm heartily, he added, "Tell your father that if our people'll stand together against those crafty deffils, we can drive 'em back to the sea from whither they come. Troth, we'd make a grand show of it!"

"I'll let him know of your pledge," Terryll promised. "Friends are difficult to find in these times."

Brynwald let go his grip and said, "Now, kippers, is there anything you're forget—"

Tillie elbowed him in his side and cut him off. "Hoot, Bryn, you'll talk the light away. They've got everything they need but the loving arms of their mothers. Now, be still with you and let them go hame to their kin."

Brynwald furrowed his brow at her and grunted. Then, cocking his head to the boys, he said, "*Och,* now it seems I talk too much, so I'll bid ye kippers farewell, and Godspeed."

The boys smiled and returned his kindness. Then, as they turned to mount their horses, Tillie grabbed Terryll and gave him a hug.

"Take care of that eye of yours," she said. "It'll be hard to catch the eye of a bonnie lassie with the likes of that hidin' your handsome face."

"At least I can see out of it again," he said, flushing pink.

Tillie smiled and gave him a pat on the cheek and an impish wink. "Hoot! Then can you be seein' the one over yon with the hair full of fire?" she asked, gesturing to Gwyneth. "She's been giving you the queerest looks all morning lang!"

Terryll's pinkish cheeks burned bright red.

Tillie was pleased with the effect and flashed him a broad grin. Then she turned and looked into Aeryck's eyes. "Ye lads are welcome back here anytime," she said, suddenly with a maternal voice.

Stretching out her arms to the boy, she gave him a long hug, longer in fact than Aeryck had anticipated (using Terryll's hug as a measure), and he felt a little uncomfortable with it. As she pulled away, he noticed that her eyes were moist and her cheeks wet. The boy felt awkward and didn't know if he should say something. Then all at once his tear ducts took over and gave his own eyes a good washing.

Tillie caught hold of his hand and placed a small, cloth-covered pouch in it.

"I want you to take this with you, Aeryck. It belonged to my son, Brian." She searched his eyes thoughtfully. "He would've been about your age if he were still alive, and I ken that he'd be pleased for you to have it."

Aeryck stared down at the pouch.

"Gang ahead, open it," she said.

Aeryck glanced over at Terryll, then up at Brynwald.

The chieftain gave him a sharp nod and put his arm around Tillie's waist.

Aeryck shrugged his shoulders, embarrassed, then carefully opened the folds of cloth.

"Brian couldnay read, but he used to look upon the pictures and make up his own stories about them," Tillie said.

Aeryck pulled away the last fold of cloth to reveal a leather-bound copy of the *Iliad and the Odyssey*. He thumbed through the leaves idly, and they fell at once to a picture of Odysseus standing on the prow of a boat, braced against a sea wind. The page was worn smooth and colored with a darker hue than the others from handling. Young Brian had obviously spent much time there. Aeryck wondered what stories the boy might have invented, for the picture was given to grand inspiration. Closing the book, he handed it back to Tillie.

"I can't take this from you."

"Hoot! Such nonsense your talkin'!" she countered, sticking it into his pocket. "Take it now! 'Twould better serve a young lad like you with his whole life before him than the likes of us. Besides, neither of us crumblin' bricks can read." She took his hand again and patted it gently. "Perhaps you'll think of old Bryn and me from time to time as you read it," she said quietly. "Aye—now, be off with ye, before I burst!"

Aeryck compressed his lips and nodded, then climbed up onto Sullie's broad back. "Thank you." He sighed, turned the large mare to the south, and immediately put her into a trot without looking back.

A swarm of squealing children—and barking dogs—chased the long column of horses through the village as far as the gates, inventing games as they skipped happily. Each one extolled a perfect devotion to some splendid cause. They were met there by others who had turned out to see the riders off (mostly wives and kin of the men leaving), who stood waving, calling out blessings and farewells and giving gifts to their loved ones to comfort them along the way. As the column exited the gates, Dunnald immediately angled eastward across the broad clearing encircling the village toward the river pass.

The wind from the south had stiffened its intent before the coming storm. The leaves shivered on frantic boughs, and many fled before the ominous breath, but the riders merely leaned forward in their saddles against it and gritted their teeth. After they had cleared a hundred yards or so, Terryll and many of the warriors stood up in their stirrups and waved their final salutes.

"God be with ye!" Brynwald called out with his magnificent thundering voice over the wind. The sound of it echoed high up into the hills surrounding Loch na Huric, then fell back upon the riders, a soft and comforting farewell.

"And with you also!" Terryll and the others returned.

Then, as soon as the column reached the river, Aeryck reined Sullie to a stop. Terryll and Gwyneth drew up on either side of him, curious.

"What's the matter?" Terryll asked jokingly. "Too much horse for you?"

"I'm going back," Aeryck replied.

"Going back? What do you mean you're going back? We didn't leave anything behind."

"I did."

"What're you talking about?"

Aeryck looked over at Gwyneth, who immediately took her cue—women being the quicker to see such things than men.

"I haven't had a chance to thank you properly for what you have done, Aeryck," she said. "I know that words cannot express my heart, but when you next come through Bowness, stop in and visit my papa and me. We'll treat you to a potful of the best venison stew you've ever tasted!"

Aeryck smiled. "I'd like that."

Gwyneth leaned over and gave him a kiss on his cheek, then spurred her horse forward and galloped away. "Farewell, my friend!"

"What's going on here?" Terryll objected. "He isn't serious!"

"Yes, I am," Aeryck countered. "Brynwald spent many months with my mother's family in Ireland, a family I never thought existed until last night. I don't expect for you to understand it, but I have to go back and—"

"You *are* serious, aren't you?" Terryll said, with his familiar edge.

Aeryck furrowed his brow. "Yes, so don't try to talk me out of it. You got me to come up here with you, but now that I'm here, I'm staying."

Terryll wore the desperate look of a barrister trying to salvage a crumbling defense. "What about my parents?" he argued. "They've grown quite attached to you, you know. My mother especially."

"I said, don't try to talk me out of it. I'm staying! At least through the winter."

And all at once it struck Terryll with prophetic clarity. As close as he'd come to Aeryck over the last several months, as intimate as they had become as friends, as adventurers, as watchers of rivers and clouds and the great movements of nature, as co-conspirators in a myriad boyish coups, he realized in that moment that he was beholding the face of a stranger. Looking into Aeryck's determined eyes, he felt as though they were miles apart, on different planes, as though an unseen rift had suddenly opened between them, which neither could span.

Terryll's heart swelled with a consummate ache, for it saddened him to think that he might never see his friend again. Letting go a heavy sigh, he said, "Well, I know you better than to argue with you once you've made your mind up on something."

"You're not upset?"

"Of course, I'm upset," Terryll retorted. "But I figured it might come to this."

"You did?"

"I could see it in your eyes last night while you were listening to Brynwald talking about Finn and the MacLlewald clan. I'd hoped I was wrong." Terryll glanced behind him to the village and found Brynwald and Tillie's smallish forms still standing by the gates. "I surely like those people. Strange, isn't it?"

"Very," Aeryck agreed, following his gaze. "I wonder if they'll have me back."

"Are you jesting? They want you for a son."

"What? What are you—"

"Yours weren't the only eyes I was watching last night."

A chilling gust strafed them with leaves and reminded each of his purpose. Presently Aeryck reached into his pocket and produced the little wooden carving of the cross and the lamb. "This belongs to someone back in Bowness," he said, offering it to Terryll. "Perhaps you can give it to Gwinnie. She'll know what to do with it."

Terryll looked down at the carving, arched a brow, then put it in his pocket. "All right."

"There's just one more thing I'd like for you to do for me," Aeryck said.

"Just one?" Terryll returned with a wry smile.

Aeryck hesitated for a moment. "Tell Dagmere that I'm sorry— that I'm sorry for having made fun of her freckles."

Terryll let out a laugh. "That, I'm sure she'll forgive you! But she's going to *kill* you for staying up here—and me for letting you!"

Aeryck thought briefly of Dagmere's beautiful blue eyes, how they sparkled so, her long waves of auburn hair rife with the shimmering hues of the sun, the exquisite delicacy of her hands, her pretty feet, and, yes, those wonderful freckles. This time there was no intrusion from the raven-haired beauty with the flashing green eyes. For a few moments Aeryck's face betrayed an inner struggle. He wavered once, and again. Then, stiffening with resolve, he looked into Terryll's eyes. "Just promise me that you'll tell her."

The young hunter smiled broadly. "I'll tell her. Don't worry."

Terryll presented his arm, and Aeryck took it with a firm clasp.

"I'm going to miss you," Terryll said, biting his lip.

"I'll miss you too. But remember, I'm coming home right after the winter!"

"You haven't even found your 'home' yet," Terryll said, "and I doubt you will until you've tasted Ireland."

The boys let go their grip and looked at each other awkwardly for several moments as Terryll's words found their place in each heart.

Then, with an abrupt salute and a broad and handsome smile, Terryll spurred Tempest into the wind and raced after the others. "God be with you, my friend!" he called back.

"And with you also!"

Aeryck watched until the last of the horses disappeared around the bend along the river.

Stamping her big feet and pulling at the reins, Sullie let out a whinny and snorted her complaints into the air. She didn't like the idea of being left behind, storm or no storm.

"I'll miss them too," Aeryck said, letting out a sigh.

He glanced at the storm front approaching on the horizon, looming nearer now than before, then turned Sullie back toward the village where Brynwald and Tillie stood looking on, bewildered.

"You said I was welcome back anytime!" Aeryck called out. "Is now too soon?"

The boy couldn't see their eyes from the distance, but if he could, he would know that Tillie's were watering over with an inexpressible joy, and not a few warm tears were trickling down Brynwald's cheeks as well.

32
A FAIR ROAD
TO TRAVEL

E very half mile or so Terryll looked back on their trail, hoping to see Aeryck galloping along on his ungainly horse, his face beaming through a wind-tousled mass of flaxen hair, having changed his mind. He hadn't.

By midafternoon the long column of riders turned south onto the Roman road at the stone ruins of Birrens, and, whether infected by Terryll's sullen mood or by the blackening skies overhead, a melancholy pall hung over the group like a deep oppression, dampening the mirthful purpose of the journey.

Dunnald, though fierce on the battlefield and never shying from trouble, was possessed of the sanguine humors. He came at life laughing. The stout warrior looked back upon the column of dour faces, chortled heartily, then, with a clarion voice, led out with a rousing song:

> "'Awake! Awake!' the heroes bade,
> The battle beckons all!
> Arise from beds of heather made,
> On yonder heath we fall!"

At once several men at the head of the column joined in the following stanzas, for it was a song familiar to the warriors of Loch na Huric and one sung often in their timbered hall. It bespoke tales of courage and honor and heroes slain in battles past and was of such infectious melody and verse that everyone, including the young hunter, was soon swept along in a grand air. Each sang with tremendous voice and with the childlike abandon of sailors. Even the horses, which had been walking with lowered heads and plodding gaits, perked up and quickened their steps into the southerly wind.

And though the lowering sky continued to threaten a downpour, it remained but a threat, doing little to thwart the now buoyant mood, and the company made fair passage along the road.

The roadway was straight and proud like the Romans who built it, and it climbed and dipped through forested tracts of rowans, sycamores, ashes, pines, and others, rolling out before the column of riders like gentle billows on a multicolored sea and charting a southeasterly course toward Hadrian's Wall and beyond.

During the latter half of the first century, the Romans (under Emperor Vespasian and the Roman governor of Britain, Gnaeus Julius Agricola) began to stretch a line of roads and forts across the length and breadth of the island—like some massive circulatory system that would course with the life flow of imperial Rome. And by the time of Emperor Hadrian some fifty years later, every corner of the island was easily accessible to the Roman legionaries—men who brought with them their Latin culture, coinage, religions, and system of law, forever changing the face of Britain.

The roads were built wide (forty to fifty feet on average) to accommodate columns of soldiers, chariots, and the great Roman war machines, having trenches dug along either side to allow for easy water drainage. They were founded below the surface with a thick bed of chalk, then covered with layers of flint, small stones, and gravel (each layer tamped solid using a mortar of chalk or clay) until the thickness of the road rose to a height of several feet. The Romans built their roads skillfully, proudly, expecting them to last—like the Empire itself—hundreds, into thousands, of years. Legends would grow in the centuries to come that giants had walked amid the lochs and heaths and ruled the mortals there, bequeathing to the land, in their passing, monstrous stone ruins, aqueducts, and of course the eternal roads themselves.

Here and there around the column of riders were pasturelands and harvested fields, now turned over for the winter months. Here and there were groves of oaks and yews, guaranteeing the blessings of the gods to the farmers. Occasionally a thin line of blue smoke was seen rising timorously from some farmer's cottage against the black, angry sky, only to be bent or swirled or flattened by the vagaries of the wind. But as the contrary air currents left in search of other mischief, the blue tendrils would snake again above the ridges, seeking the sky's cold escape.

Glancing over at the tree line two hundred yards to the west, Terryll remembered looking upon this very position from the cover of those trees, watching then a long column of Pictish warriors heading north with their plunder of packhorses and British women. Just ahead was the large knoll that forced a bend in the road, and rounding it they came upon the spot where Corrie had tripped and hurt herself.

Terryll looked down curiously as they passed and noticed a stone that had pushed two inches above the surface of this perfect road to blemish both it and the pride of the Roman road builders. *Who knows that, in the providence of time, the stone may have had a little help?* Terryll pondered the peculiar mercies of God, then looked back at the girl with the hurt ankle.

All he could see of her was a single eye amid a tangle of brown hair, staring anxiously over the shoulder of the girl in front of her—at what or whom, he had no idea. He smiled at her, then swung about and looked ahead on the road.

A rush of wind rustled through the treetops, shaking the boughs with its fury, and then was gone. Moments later a leaf fell spinning, twirling like some winged ballerina on an airy stage, and landed in Terryll's lap. And then another fell, also pirouetting, and then another. And then at once the air all about him was showered with whirling ballerinas dancing the *Autumnal Ballet.*

Terryll looked over at Gwyneth riding alongside him and beheld a lovely vision. He noted that, even in the scant, shadowless light, her hair pulled a radiant spectrum of reds from the sky as it unfurled its glory to the reckless currents. In that moment he discovered the meaning of color.

The boy marveled often and stupidly at how she had changed. This creature was no longer the little girl with the stringy red hair and teeth that stuck out a little too far, the one who constantly tugged on his sleeve and made ugly faces at him to get his attention. No, this creature was something totally other. All afternoon he stole glances at her, using any opportunity—feigned or otherwise—to look in her direction, daring each time to discover a graceful curve, a subtle line of beauty or feminine mannerism that lay hidden until his search. He was a wily thief and made off with prodigious booty.

Gwyneth could feel his eyes upon her, and she smiled inwardly. She had waited many years for such looks. It was as though a pent spring came bursting from some stony place and triumphed over the earth. For ever since their childhood days during her family's visits to Killwyn Eden, or when Terryll's family came to Bowness, she had loved him, had worshiped him. Fiercely.

He had been the singular inspiration behind a thousand passionate eulogies, songs, and poems, and these attended by a bounty of kisses, though his ears were none the wiser and his lips remained as beggars save in the fertile garden cloisters of the girl's romping imagination.

She knew that Terryll had always regarded her as a child, a little sister at best, though she was only one year his junior. But a year in the reckoning of a child is an insurmountable reach.

Looking away from his gaze, she spurred her horse forward with a subtle flex of her knees.

Terryll caught the movement and was puzzled by it. Stunned was a more fitting description. He didn't know if he was expected to follow or if she wanted to be left alone, for a queer aloofness had suddenly swept over her. His mind indicted him with accusations, as though he were guilty of committing some heinous offense. He fumbled clumsily with his thoughts as he gazed babelike at the ears of his horse.

Gwyneth slowed dutifully at her mark just ahead, having deftly exercised her part in the ancient drama. Moments later she heard the sound of Terryll's black, spirited horse drawing up on her left, and, as she turned lithely to the boy, he came trotting alongside as though to pass her by. His brow was arched ever so slightly as he displayed his own facade of detachment.

But her demure smile and "Windy day—isn't it?" ruined his unsophisticated schemes, and he slowed to a walk and resumed his wily thievery. Immediately an ovation of giggles twittered along the line of girls, and many applauded the scene with vicarious sighs.

An hour later Terryll moved up to the head of the column with Dunnald and five of his men. The other warriors had been posted as the rear guard to handle the packhorses and to watch for dangers along their flanks and back trail. The women rode two abreast in front of them.

Although he preferred the company of Gwyneth, Terryll felt a certain responsibility as his father's surrogate to take the forward position, even though Dunnald had matters well in hand. In so doing he also hoped to make a certain impression on the girl. He was a grand success.

Terryll conversed with the men on matters of Pictish history, culture, and religion. He learned that many of the people of Loch na Huric were descendants of the Scotti of Eire, who had long ago settled the northwestern coasts of Britain, immigrating, as they had, in many waves over hundreds of years. Some came to escape famine and hardships in Ireland; others sought the rich soils of Britain to farm and raise cattle and sheep.

The men talked freely of their new faith to Terryll's continual amazement, answering each of his probing questions with studied insight. He marveled that though they were Picts, intensely warlike, tattooed, and terrible to behold, they each possessed the understanding and speech of ones steeped in years in the faith. Patrick of Ireland had taught them well.

A movement caught Terryll's eyes along the timberline to the west, but it turned out to be only a small herd of wild boars rooting in a grove of scrub oaks. The noisy chattering of squirrels gathering nuts into their warm and cozy hiding places pulled his eyes to the vault of hickory boughs overhead.

The boy smiled and took a deep breath, taking in a sweeping scan of autumn's grand finale: leaves rustling in the trees, leaves on the wind; the air, crisp and chilling; a myriad hues of browns and oranges, yellows and reds. Soon the terrain would be laced white with the first flurries of winter's snow. It was good to be alive and going home to a warm hearth, venison stew, and mugs of piping hot cider.

Thoughts of Aeryck filled his mind, and he wondered how he fared. In his mind he caught a glimpse of Tillie's infectious smile and the look in Brynwald's fierce eyes as he talked of Ireland—Aeryck would do well. He would miss him.

Looking back on the road, he found Gwyneth's smiling green eyes gazing at him with a look that betrayed the sum of her heart. His own heart leaped within him, and he returned her smile, then looked at the road ahead, clucking his tongue as one receiving a great inheritance, ready to face any storm.

A deer bounded across a hillside about a mile down the road, as though spooked. The column was too far away—and downwind of the animal—to have caused its alarm. But something had spooked it, and Terryll said as much to Dunnald.

The stout warrior grunted. "Och—'tis probably a wolf or bear skulkin' about, stirrin' up a row." But though Dunnald was seemingly unimpressed, his keen eyes carefully raked the trees along the ridge from whence the deer had run.

Terryll didn't like the notion of wolves in the area, in light of the unusual wolf attacks of the summer, so he unshouldered his longbow and kept a wary eye on his surroundings.

As the column rounded a bend, a covey of twenty ptarmigans flushed violently from a cover of underbrush, clapping their wings furiously and careering every which way, startling both horses and riders.

Terryll's arrow took a hen in the breast, killing it instantly. The young hunter knew that there would be a second flush of birds moments later. There was. His second arrow caught a rooster through its neck and brought it flapping down fifty paces away.

Brynwald's men looked at one another and raised their eyebrows. One even let out a string of expletives. The boy had not just taken two birds from the air, he had taken them while astride a moving horse. They had heard tales at Loch na Huric of the boy's prowess with the bow, his coolness in battle, his lightning speed of delivery, his flawless aim, but until now they had thought the stories exaggerated. Each of Dunnald's men took a new measure of the lad.

The company of Picts and Britons continued along the road until the sun began to fall unseen behind a retreating palette of gray ridge lines. Then they spotted an old man and woman coming up the road in the distance, driving an ox cart mounted comically with hay under a large tarp.

They had seen only a few people that afternoon, mostly farmers out in the fields herding sheep and cattle into shelter before the storm broke, though every so often they had passed a lone traveler heading north.

As the man and woman approached, Dunnald called out a greeting to them and waved. But the old couple did not return the salutation. Instead, they looked straight ahead with nervous, giddy eyes, as though terror had gotten hold of them.

"Gang! Gang! Hyr-rup!" the old man shrieked, as he goaded the oxen with savage whips. *"Hyr-rup!"* And they rattled away, loosing bits of hay to the wind.

Suddenly on the treeless rise before them four horsemen appeared —Pictish warriors, fierce looking and fit for battle, cutting stark and menacing silhouettes against the cold, shale-hued sky. The warriors did not raise their hands in a friendly salute, neither did they hail a greeting of peace. Instead, they sat motionless upon the desolate ridge, bent in menacing postures as they peered intently at the long line of horses passing below them, betraying naught of their intentions.

Dunnald and his warriors eyed them guardedly, and an anxious murmuring cascaded down the column, attended by a wagging of heads. Rumors were conceived and given great authority.

Presently one of the four horsemen made a sweeping gesture with the point of his spear and grunted something inaudible, apparently indicating to the others either the length of the column or the placement of Dunnald's warriors within the column or the bounty of women therein.

It seemed a declaration of war.

33
THE HIDDEN
GLADE

The four Pictish horsemen were out of bowshot. Just. Even Terryll's longbow would be fair tested at such range, and in such a wind it would be a foolhardy attempt at best. Giving them chase would be equally foolish, for they might be lured into a trap, and dividing their forces would leave the women and cargo dangerously exposed. Who knew but that there might be a larger party of warriors just over the ridge? Or coming up on their rear to rush unexpectedly at the diminished forces.

Dunnald's fierce battle gaze belied his grave concern. There were many tribes in this barbaric land of the Picts and Scots that were not friendly to Brynwald, for he had made many enemies as his power and influence increased over the years. Many would consider the sacking of his column a great blessing from the gods.

The stout warrior had no fear of the four horsemen—he had no fear of mortal flesh for that matter. But news of a column laden with twenty packhorses of goods, as well as nine British women, would quickly spread and bring uninvited inquiry—and perhaps a bitter dispute. It was Dunnald's duty to see the women safely to their destination, and he regarded his task with singular ambition. He considered his options.

If they were attacked on their present course, the attackers would have all of the advantages. First, they had knowledge of Dunnald's strength of numbers, and his weaknesses; Dunnald had no such knowledge of their forces. Second, the attackers would pick the time most favorable for them to insure the element of surprise, and the place that offered to them the best cover and vantage point from which to execute an assault. The defenders would have to make do with whatever terrain was dealt to them. They were not good odds. Dunnald would have to change them.

Adding to his concern was the fact that he and Brynwald's warriors had been in Ireland for nigh unto seven months. Much can take place to change the political landscape in such time. Who were now Brynwald's friends? Who were now his enemies? Had some of his friends become enemies during his absence? In what villages would he be able to seek refuge? Certainly word would spread quickly concerning his conversion to Christianity—Sarteham would see to that. He would turn many against the chieftain of Loch na Huric; it was only a matter of time.

Sarteham. He was now a wounded serpent, dangerous, sure to strike when least expected. Dunnald had chided Brynwald for not killing him when he had the opportunity. Then he remembered, all too vividly, Brynwald's face as the chieftain turned to him. It was fierce, austere, typically Brynwald, yet tempered with the strangers of kindness and mercy.

"We must learn Christ," the chieftain had said to him. And though spoken without anger or rebuke, his words cut Dunnald deep into his soul. *The way of Christ is hard*, the stout warrior mused, *but such is the way of truth*.

Just as suddenly as the four intruders had appeared, they disappeared behind the ridge, whether to fetch reinforcements or to attend to other business, Dunnald could not know.

But he did know that it was time for him to act and to act quickly. Immediately he veered off the road and led the column along a less trodden path that snaked into the hills.

At dusk and miles later, the company made camp in a broad, tree-sheltered glade that abutted a rocky cliff. The campsite provided them with a decent windbreak and protection against the storm, as well as shielding them from the eyes of any raiding parties that might be wandering about. The clearing was ringed with all manner of trees, shrubbery, and outcroppings of rocks, offering them plenty of vantage points from which to make a satisfactory defense if need be. It was as if it were defined for their singular benefit.

They had found the place quite by accident, for even though Dunnald and his men had been along this path before, none of them had ever known of the glade.

Dunnald had earlier sent two of his men ahead to scout an area suitable for a campsite, and while one of them allowed his horse to drink from a small stream, he looked up by chance to espy a deer darting across the path into what seemed an impregnable tangle of brush and shrubbery. Curious, the warrior dismounted, found the labyrinthine track the deer had taken, and followed it to a wall of large boulders that seemed to forbid further passage. But the deer was nowhere in sight.

Further exploring, the warrior soon found a narrow gap in an outcropping of boulders, large enough to accommodate the passage of a horse. Through it he had spotted the clearing—beautiful, well-watered, inviting. Passing by, he would have missed it altogether.

A stream fell out of the cliffside in a series of small rushing water-falls (apparently fed by a subterranean spring, gushing from somewhere inside the mountain), then snaked its way through willows, sycamores, ancient yews, and oaks, cutting through the center of the glade. The air was rife with the tart smell of pines and firs and the musky, decaying smell of autumn leaves. Overhead, jagged cliffs raked the lowering sky, which was at once fearsome, wild, and exhilarating.

Sensing the immanency of the storm, the horses whickered nervously as they grazed amid the tall grasses growing along the gurgling stream banks, made sweet by the nourishing breasts of the rock-filtered water.

Dunnald had left the loads on the packhorses—not something he favored, but under the circumstances he had little choice. An attack would leave them with no time at all to deal with packhorses. He posted a few men among the rocks to watch for intruders. If the four horsemen had been scouts for a raiding party, they would undoubtedly be scouring the countryside for them even now, for the column was too great a plum to leave unplucked. Settling the women under a quiet awning of inter-twining yew boughs, the stout warrior stood up and looked about the glade. He wondered if anyone else knew about this place. And then he wondered if ever there was a man who had seen these sheltered grounds. It was one of those places that seemed caught in a rift of time and space—an ancient nook—well hidden from the ubiquitous sole of man's foot, lost somewhere in the peripheral vision of his ever-pioneering gaze.

It was a pleasant cradle of land, easily defended, well situated for camping overnight or for longer excursions. They should be safe, at least for the night, he mused.

Even so, his heart was beset with a feeling of dread, as though some sinister thing, or presence, had followed them into the glade and was somewhere skulking about in the gloaming shadows, unseen, watching them even now, studying their every move, hissing.

A shiver crawled up his spine as he gave thought to it, then immediately he shook it off with a rebuke. It had been a long journey back from Ireland with little rest to nourish him, and his body and mind were wracked with fatigue. Having made such an assessment, he left to check on his sentries.

Terryll took note that there were no signs of wildlife in the area—no squirrels chattering overhead in the trees, no birds in the air, no hint of game. Upon entering the clearing he had scouted the area for sign, especially along the stream banks where game would likely come, but there were no tracks whatsoever. It was queer. Such a sheltered place would be ideal to harbor animals during the cold winter months, as well as during the spring when they would mate and then raise their young.

Could it be that the glade had even escaped the notice of animalkind? That wasn't likely. After all, the deer had led them to this place.

The deer. The boy looked around for it. The glade was not so large that he wouldn't have been able to spot it somewhere among the trees or along the tangled hedge of shrubbery. But it was nowhere in sight. It had vanished. As he pondered the mystery, the back of his neck began to bristle of its own, as though it were a living thing. A little shudder of terror raced along his limbs, cackling.

Several cooking fires were going, for there was no shortage of fallen limbs and branches. Kindling was everywhere. Most of the smoke would be filtered by the latticework of tree leaves and branches overhead. Whatever escaped would be caught and swept by the wild currents of wind over the treetops and disseminated in every direction. There would be no way to trace its source.

The men broiled venison and pork, conversing in low tones as they quaffed goatskins full of warm ale and mead.

Though a few of them had helped to build the women's fire, the latter kept to themselves and cooked for themselves and chatted uneasily. Many were still wary of these fierce-looking men of Brynwald (though eased somewhat by their gregarious nature).

Corrie seemed wary of everyone. She sat a little off to one side, between the women and Terryll, nibbling at a crust of bread like a frightened mouse. Her eyes were quick and darting, appraising every nuance of activity in the camp as though it was a potential threat to her.

Terryll roasted the ptarmigans on a spit over a small fire, turning them slowly to a golden brown. He basted them in their own juices, which he collected in a small bark dish as they cooked. To the juices he added a sprinkling of salt and a mixture of herbs (basil, dill, mustard) and crushed nuts that he had gathered along the way, mixing them into a savory broth. The young hunter took pride in his culinary skills, and with Gwyneth's eyes upon him he wore the look of a prince in a grand court.

He had learned many of his skills from his father when he was a young boy and they had hunted together. However, since those early days, he had added many of his own touches to the woodland recipes. He knew what herbs, roots, and spices would soak up the gamey taste of the meat, yet at the same time bring out the rich, wild flavors of which he was so fond. He was particularly partial to making glazes from the juices of citrus fruits during the summer months, or from wild honey and various crushed berries. He also prepared sauces of diced chunks of apples and pears mixed with nuts during the offerings of autumn and winter.

He often experimented with the different herbs, mushrooms, and dried grasses that each area of the land provided. After all, Nature sets a grand table for those who are attentive. Most of the time he was pleased with his concoctions. But once he had discovered the telltale blue flowers and feathery leaves of the licorice root. He had heard it was used in the making of medicines, teas, and candy, so he decided to give it a try. He ground some of the dried root into a little bark bowl of wild honey, then spread the mixture over a broiled rabbit. It took several days before he was finally rid of the foul taste in his mouth. And from that day forward, he tended toward the recipes he knew and gave most candies a wide berth.

When Terryll was satisfied that the birds were turned to perfection, he handed one of them to Gwyneth, his fingers trembling slightly.

Noticing, she took it and thanked him with a generous smile. Having tasted his bird, the boy wished at once that he had had a little pepper to give it a more zesty flavor. And like a defendant anxiously surveying a returning jury, he watched her out of the corner of his eye as she bit into the meat, hoping she didn't notice the missing pepper also.

Immediately her eyes brightened. "Mmm!" she exclaimed, looking over at him. "Where did you learn how to cook like this?"

Terryll's heart about burst through his rib cage. "Oh . . . here and there." He chuckled with colossal nonchalance. "It's nothing—really."

"It's delicious!"

"If I had a better selection of herbs and spices, I could have—"

"Honestly, Terryll, it's perfect the way it is!"

"You don't think it needs a little pepper maybe?" he asked, with a dash of humility.

"I never use it—makes me sneeze."

That settled the matter at once. "Neither do I."

And so they ate their meal together, neither speaking another word. Each moment drew out an awkward silence between them. On occasion their eyes would wander into the other's; Terryll would sort of nod and grin stupidly, and Gwyneth would let out a little giggle and return to her meal.

With devoted fascination he observed the way she daintily bit into the meat with just her teeth, so as not to soil her lips. Never had he beheld such a pretty mouth. As he watched the light playing about her moist lips, his mind began to reel, and he was compelled to look away.

Finishing her meal, Gwyneth turned to Terryll, who was presently gazing at nothing along the tangle of shrubbery across the glade. "I have heard some of the men talking," she said softly.

"Really?" Terryll felt stupid for his reply and winced inwardly. He knew now the agonies that Aeryck must have suffered when he was around Dagmere, and he wished that he'd been kindlier to him.

"They say that you are a mighty archer and warrior," she continued. "The women say that you are handsome and would make a good provider." She averted her eyes from his and looked down at her fingers, which were busy attending to a fold in her dress. "Such talk pleases me."

Terryll stared at the side of her face dumbfounded. His cheeks flushed, then drained of blood, and though he searched his brain desperately for an appropriate response, words fled as cowards from his tongue. The ensuing silence mocked him. And then he remembered the little wooden carving that Aeryck had given him and retrieved it from his pocket. Perhaps it could provide some ease of conversation.

"Here, Gwinnie," he said, presenting the carving to the girl. "I want to give this to—"

"You made this for me?" She took it from his hand and eyed it gleefully. "How sweet of you!"

"Uh . . ."

She held the carving out in front of her, admiring it. "It's lovely!"

"But I didn't—"

"I will treasure it always," she added, clutching it against her bosom.

"It's . . . mine," a voice spoke haltingly.

Terryll and Gwyneth looked up, and looming over them was Corrie. Her eyes were tight at the corners, anxious, and framed by indignation.

"What do you mean, it's yours?" Gwyneth protested. "Terryll made it for me."

The girl stiffened, fidgeted about, then stretched forth a trembling hand. "It's mine," she reiterated, summoning an adamantine determination. Her eyes began to blink furiously. "They—they took it from me. I'll have it back now." She reinforced her boldness with yet another stretch of her hand.

Gwyneth looked at Terryll for help, but the boy only shrugged and forced a smile, pathetic though it was.

"I was trying to tell you that it—uh, belonged to someone from your village," he said, stammering. "But you . . . er . . . well . . ."

"What?"

"Aeryck found it on a dead Pict, and he asked me to give it to you—thinking that you might . . . uh . . . find its owner." These last three words died miserably.

Realizing her presumption, Gwyneth's face flushed as red as her hair. She jerked her eyes from his and looked down at the carving. Suddenly it had become a vile thing. She thrust it at the girl. "Here," she said, without looking at her. "I didn't know."

Quickly the girl took the carving and returned to her place with a pronounced limp.

Terryll watched as she gazed intently at the little shape, clutching it tightly in her hands. When he looked back at Gwyneth, she was staring proudly across the glade, trying not to look hurt. But her lower lip had pushed out a little, and it was quivering ever so slightly, betraying her.

A wisp of cool breeze brushed softly through Gwyneth's hair, lifting strands of it away from her face to reveal her striking features. Moments later this same breeze stiffened and tousled her fiery locks about her head, like some prankish schoolboy. She tossed her head back, once and then again, but it was of no use. The laughing breeze was all about her with its game.

Terryll looked on at the pitiful battle, champing under a supreme frustration. He wanted desperately to reach out and help her, but he knew that wouldn't do.

Finally she caught a vagrant tress and pulled it away from her face, pinning it neatly against her temple with her fingers.

Relieved, the boy sighed silently. Then another struggle began to tear at his brow, at his eyes, at the tips of his fingers. Clearing his throat, Terryll gazed upon her unyielding profile. "When I was younger, I remember how a little girl with red stringy hair used to follow me around everywhere I went," he said, at last loosing his tongue. "I used to point out long black sticks lying in the field and tell her they were mean snakes that liked to bite little girls. 'Nah,' she'd say, 'those are just sticks! You can't fool me!' But she'd always give them a hard look, just the same. 'Well, you best go home then—there's bugbears in the woods that love to eat little girls,' I'd say again. 'No such thing as bugbears!' she'd laugh. 'You're just trying to scare me!'

"Finally I'd get so angry that I'd just tell her to go home and quit pestering me. She'd stop and look up at me with her big green eyes, looking really hurt. Then her lower lip would push out a little and quiver some. She'd leave, pouting, telling me that I was mean. But it wouldn't take long before I'd look over my shoulder and there'd she be again—the little red stringy-haired girl, dragging on my heels and smiling big as ever."

Terryll paused to summon a tenuous courage. "Little did I know she'd grow up to be the most beautiful girl I've ever seen."

Gwyneth gave no indication that she had heard a word. During the whole of his anecdote, she gazed intently across the clearing, not moving a muscle, though the heroic wind struggled about her fingers, trying desperately to free her rebel captives.

A short span of silence followed his story, during which time Terryll fidgeted uncomfortably. As he gazed at her face, a little glint of light caught his attention. It was a tear beginning to form in the corner of her eye. Presently she released her prisoners to the wind and looked over at him, her big green eyes now peering through a rebellion of red hair, and upon her face there was a smile as big as ever.

At that moment a brilliant, jagged sword shattered the black sky into shards, illuminating the glade, followed instantly by a deafening report of thunder that shook the hills with its anger. The wind and sky had sent fair warning; still, it had taken everyone by surprise, and many were jolted to their feet.

From somewhere behind a tall screen of thicket at the base of the cliff, a man's voice called out. "Come here! I've found a cave that'll fit the lot of us!"

Terryll looked across the glade as cascading sheets of gray water came thundering across the landscape like a legion of dragoons, pummeling everything in their path. Jumping to his feet, he grabbed Gwyneth by the hand.

34
THE ANCIENT CAVE

The thick walls of the cave muted the raging tempest outside, allowing only the dull, incessant hiss of rain to penetrate its ancient bulwarks. Occasionally the lulling drone was interrupted by a flare of cool, whitish light that shone against the cave's mouth, followed by the imminent thunderclap. And though once terrible and fearsome, it was now muffled to a blunted rumbling that brought with it a measure of comfort to the hearts of man and beast inside.

The cave seemed a godsend, offering ample shelter to the entire company, including the mounts and packhorses. However, it was cold and damp and suffused with a blackness that might quickly drive one's mind to madness without the reprieve of light.

Upon entering the cave, Dunnald was immediately stricken with the feeling of dread that had troubled him outside. Immediately he had his men build a large fire with wood they had carried into the place before the rain had soaked it, and soon a friendly blaze was chasing the darkness into the shadowy nooks and clefts of the cave walls. The cold, however, was stubborn and clung tenaciously to the walls and floor and air, relinquishing only the immediate area around the fire.

It was an immense cave, like the towering nave of a Roman basilica. Its dome rose to nearly sixty feet at the center, and its length and breadth stretched several hundred feet. The air inside was clammy, foul, dead, as though it hadn't been breathed by human lungs in years, perhaps centuries, perhaps millenniums. There were no indications that man or beast had ever walked there before. Hanging all about its ceiling, like gnarled fingers bathed in the reddish glow of the firelight, were stalactites formed of limestone and calcite deposits; and here and there on the floor, stalagmites stretched their tips with infinite perseverance to touch them.

The effect was eerie. It was widely—though unvoicedly—assumed that evil things crouched hidden behind any one of the projections just beyond the firelight and were kept at bay there by the glowing pool.

Dunnald posted two men at the cave's entrance at once. The mouth was large enough to permit the passage of a single horse, forcing its rider, however, to bend low in the saddle to make entry or exit. The cave was virtually an impregnable fortress—or mausoleum. A single man positioned at the entryway might defend it against an entire army.

The stout warrior took an easy breath. They would be safe here for the night.

Presently one of his men called out from across the cavern. "Dunnald, over here! There's a passageway leadin' farther into the cave!" His voice resounded off the walls, such that it was difficult to pinpoint his position at first.

"And there's another one over here!" another called out somewhere opposite him.

Having secured the entrance, Dunnald sent others of his men with torches to explore the adjoining passageways. Perhaps there were other entrances into the cave. If there were, they too would need to be secured.

The rest of the men and women huddled around the fire, feeding its voracious appetite with endless offerings of wood. Some stretched out on their blankets to snatch a little sleep after the day's travel. Others talked in low voices. Others, still, sat quietly, staring pensively into the airy leaps of flame.

Soon a pot of water was boiling over the fire and mugs of piping hot tea were going around, taking the edge off the chill and lifting everyone's dampened spirits. Softly one of the men began singing a hymn he had learned in Ireland, one with a haunting, Gaelic lilt. Others joined in as it moved slowly along its course, until at last everyone around the fire was singing its soulful verses and bittersweet refrain.

> "Hark the call of Eire's bride,
> O coasts of darkened ruin;
> Receive the gift of ransom's side,
> The sum of heaven's boon.
> *"Rejoice in the flow of His crimson wounds.*

> "On gentle child of Mary's womb,
> The cross's shadow falls,
> Who once lay cold in borrowed tomb,
> With taste of bitter gall.
> *"Rejoice in the flow of His crimson wounds.*

> "Hark the verdant isle's refrain,
> Ye weak, ye lame and halt;

He rose to break death's dark domain,
Sin's captives to exalt.
"Rejoice in the flow of His crimson wounds."

As the hymn came to its reverent, soul-felt close, the refrain lingered in the cool air for several moments like a flutter of angels before a gentle draft of wind took it heavenward. No basilica of Rome was ever blessed with such sweet music as was heard in this ancient vault of stone.

Terryll looked around the circle of faces that shone out of the darkness like an orbit of yellow moons, many of which were baptized with the gift of precious tears. His eyes fell at last upon Corrie. She was rocking slowly back and forth, still humming the tender melody, still staring intently at the little wooden cross she clutched tightly in her hands.

Sensing his eyes, she turned her face to his. The firelight caught a thin glistening of tears wetting her cheeks and the faintest hint of a smile tugging mercifully at the corners of her mouth.

Terryll nodded to her and smiled.

But the horses were not so blissful. Robbed of their sweet river grasses, they whinnied and stamped their hooves in protest, pulling at their tethers and snorting their complaints at the men and women sitting around the fire.

Watching them, Gwyneth laughed, then took hold of Terryll's hand and pulled him to his feet.

"Come on!" she said, full of mischief. "Let's follow the men and see where those tunnels lead."

Terryll looked away from the inviting fire and shrugged his shoulders in surrender.

"Och! But a moment, lad," Dunnald countered from across the fire. "I'll not have ye gettin' lost—or worse. Ye'd best be waitin' till the men have returned with the 'all clear.' Caves can be full of treachery— aye! The playgrounds of deffils."

"It's all right," Terryll said, arching his brow. "I've found my way around a cave or two." Hefting the longbow, he added with a hint of pride, "And I have my bow to chase away any foul spirits that might be lurking about." He said this more for Gwyneth's benefit than for Dunnald's.

"I doubt your arrows would trouble any spirits," the stout warrior retorted. "'Tis the spirits that dwell in mortal flesh that concern me."

"We'll be careful," Terryll said.

"Yes," Gwyneth added.

Dunnald let out a grunt, then consented. "Aye. Dinna be gone lang, then, and be mindin' your feet."

"Don't worry."

Dunnald grunted again, then got up to check his sentries.

The boy quickly fashioned a couple of torches, wrapping twine around small bundles of hickory branches. Then the two of them took off after the others, Terryll holding one torch and Gwyneth the other.

The men were only a few minutes ahead of them, but there was neither sound nor light to betray their whereabouts. The darkness was thick, oppressive, not accustomed to being driven from its haunts, and stubbornly yielded only a few feet of sight to the torches.

Gwyneth clung tightly to Terryll's hand with feminine conviction.

Her little hand in his—a pretty thing, he knew—tightened its grip with every step, astounding the boy's fingers with its strength. It thrilled him no end.

Soon they came to a place in the passageway where three smaller tunnels led outward like the tines of a fork. Not knowing which direction the men had taken, they decided on the tine to the left. Presently the path fell before them with a gradual decline that offered no suggestion of leveling out.

Terryll was mindful of their feet (having explored many caves during his wanderings with Hauwka), knowing that the cave floor could suddenly present them with a hole or crevice that might fall away several hundred feet, taking the unwary explorer to his death. He listened intently to the brush of Gwyneth's slippers whispering over the stone floor, to her little gasps of breath, the occasional nervous cough and girlish giggle. He wore a heroic smile; the two of them were on a grand adventure, and he was her champion.

Glancing at her occasionally, as her face flickered in and out of the torchlight, he would catch her serious eyes scouring the ground, then they darted up to his, and she would smile. She was beautiful, even in the wan light. His heart rejoiced that God had made him male and made her female; and his soul congratulated His handiwork.

Suddenly he froze.

"Listen!" he said. "Do you hear it?"

"Hear what?" Gwyneth whispered, huddling just behind his ear.

"Water. There's some kind of underground stream or pool ahead."

"Ooh—let's go see!"

They continued along the tunnel, moving ever downward toward the soft gurgling sounds ahead. At length the passageway opened up into a grotto, one nearly as cavernous as the chamber they had come from, with a number of large stalagmites and stalactites here and about.

But as they entered, a remarkable phenomenon occurred. All at once the chamber lit up with a brilliant show of colorful lights. The effect was startling—blinding in fact—and they had to shield their eyes from the radiance. Once their eyes adjusted, Terryll looked around the grotto and was immediately awestruck. The walls and ceiling of the chamber were of a phosphorescent composition. They shimmered as the light from the torches reflected off crystalline surfaces, refracted through them like millions of tiny prisms, splitting into colors, magnifying the dazzling effect severalfold. It was as though tens of thousands of gemstones were embedded in them, evincing a comic opulence. Every eyeful appeared to be a king's ransom.

"What *is* this place!?" Gwyneth exclaimed.

"I don't know. I've never seen anything like it!"

"Isn't it *wonderful!*"

In the center of the grotto was a pool about fifty feet in width, fed by a small spring that fell like a thin blade of rainbow colors from a height of twenty feet. Handfuls of sparkling droplets were thrown into the air like watery jewels as the cascading arc splashed into the pool unceasingly. The downpour caused unbroken rings of glistening, multicolored ripples to push ever outward across its surface until they were finally spent against the pool's crystalline banks, lapping softly. The water at the surface was aquamarine but moved quickly through a spectrum of colors— azure blue, blue-violet, crimson, and then to black—the deeper it went.

Terryll wondered how deep the pool was, but as he was not able to see the bottom, there was no way to fathom it.

He had walked a few feet from Gwyneth, when something red and shiny on the ground caught his attention. He stooped to pick it up, and his eyes widened as he recognized the incredible treasure that he held in his hand—a ruby the size of a large walnut, which must have been worth a fortune. He blew out a silent whistle as he rotated the stone slowly between his thumb and index finger, peering astonished through its flawless blood-red center. Immediately he thought of Gwyneth and, smiling, he slipped the jewel into his pocket.

The girl was loitering off to one side of the entrance, smoothing her hand over the cave's shimmering surface. Her eyes were attending some detail on the wall.

Terryll looked across the chamber and noticed a shelf of rocks beetling over the pool at about the same height as the waterfall. Boulders ascended to it along the wall of the grotto. And leading out onto the shelf above was another passageway, hewn by the eternal patience of the subterranean stream. Where it might lead piqued the boy's imagination.

Then his eyes were drawn back to the ascending boulders, as though something in his subconscious mind was signaling his conscious mind with a flag. He stared at the boulders for several moments, not sure why he was suddenly intrigued by them. What was it? Then as his two minds drew together in focus, it struck him. He was looking at a staircase—a crude one, to be sure, but a staircase nonetheless, and with the realization came a shiver prickling along his nape.

"Look at this, Terryll," Gwyneth called excitedly, wedging her torch into a fissure in the wall. "It looks like some kind of design."

"Design?"

He walked over to the girl and laid his bow and arrow against the entrance, then wedged his own torch into the wall to free his hands.

He moved back a step, and his eyes opened full of wonder. It was a design, one fashioned of three sets of three unbroken rings, one within the other, each set of rings placed within a set larger—nine rings in all. Each was set with its own kind of jewel; one ring was made of aquamarine, another ring was of sapphire, another of topaz, another beryl, ruby, and so on down the rings toward the center one, which was made of the blackest jet stone.

Terryll's instincts bristled, and he looked around the grotto, at the staircase, at the shelf above, the passageway leading onto it, back to the design on the wall, his eyes moving like a hunter's now. *Men have been here,* he thought. *Why, and how long ago?* A sense of danger pervaded his thoughts, as though they had unwittingly stumbled into some sleeping animal's lair.

"Are these real gemstones?" Gwyneth wondered aloud.

"Perhaps," Terryll said, glancing at them warily.

"They're beautiful! Oh!" She started, noticing something. "One of the red ones has fallen out."

"Where?"

"Here—look," she said pointing to a gap in one of the rings.

Terryll looked at the place. There was a little scoop in the ring of rubies large enough to set a stone the size of a large walnut. He considered the one in his pocket.

Gwyneth's eyes swept around the rings of stones, her mind racing with inquiries. "Have you ever seen anything like it, Terryll?"

"A couple of times," he replied, thoughtfully. "Once when I was hunting near the plain of Stonehenge, I saw a design like it chiseled on the face of a dolmen. I saw it again on the side of a long-barrow a few miles away, near Sarum—only the rings were made with white stones and pressed into the earth."

"Does it mean anything, do you think?"

"I'm not sure," he replied. "I think it has something to do with an ancient Celtic religion—something to do with the stars." As he studied the rings, a thought flashed through the boy's mind. He glanced over at the pool and took note of its glistening ripples, like multicolored rings, moving lazily across its surface. Then he looked back and forth between the pool and the design.

"What is it?" Gwyneth asked.

Terryll grunted. "The ripples seem to have the same colors moving through them as the design—see?"

"You're right!" she exclaimed, then looked back at the design. A collage of colors flickered about her face. "Who do you think could have made it?"

"Druids, most likely. Long gone by now, I'm sure."

"Why do you say that?"

"I can't imagine anyone nowadays leaving here with this kind of wealth lying around," Terryll replied, scanning the dazzling lambency on the walls of the grotto. His sweep took him again up the crude stairway to the passage leading onto the overhanging shelf. "If we were to go and explore that tunnel up there, we might find some answers. Who knows— maybe there are more caves like this one."

"Shouldn't we tell Dunnald first?" Gwyneth asked, apprehensively.

"No, no. We won't be gone long," Terryll replied, with the superior air of his gender.

Suddenly a chilling draft blew through the chamber and swirled around their feet.

Gwyneth shuddered. "Terryll . . . it's *cold.*"

The boy looked at her awkwardly, not sure what she meant. He had heard her words clearly, but the way she said them unveiled in his mind a terrifying supposition. Did she mean that she was cold and wanted to go back to the fire to get warm? Or . . .

Looking into the emerald greenness of her eyes he found the answer. No blackness of tunnel, no treachery of cavern, could ever begin to accede the danger he beheld in them. He was reduced to a speechless stupor. His lips parted in awe.

Without mercy she came, inching closer as though to surround him, or so it seemed, and suddenly the grotto became quite claustrophobic. Terryll almost turned and fled in a wild panic. But his desire to hold her—to be held by her—constrained him, championed over his desire to flee. With the exhibition of lights frolicking in her hair and eyes, she had never looked more beautiful. Terryll put his arms around her waist affectionately and pulled her close. His eyes caressed her face, her hair, her eyes again, then fell at last upon her soft, full lips.

Gwyneth angled her head to one side and received his gentle kiss.

A moment passed. Then, looking into her eyes, Terryll pulled away with a silly smile screwing across his face. "I . . . I . . . er . . ." he stammered, searching for a profound tribute to dedicate the moment.

Gwyneth giggled.

"What's so funny?" Terryll asked.

"You are," she said. "You've never kissed anyone before, have you?"

"How'd—what!" Terryll was taken aback by her inquiry and flushed bright red. Then he started to pull away with terrific indignation. "Have *you?*"

Gwyneth stepped forward and took his hands. "No, silly." She smiled as she drew him back to her. Then, looking up into his eyes, she added demurely, "It was a lovely kiss—just like I dreamed it would be."

"It *was?*" Terryll asked incredulously.

But before she could reply, something *ker-ploink*ed behind them in the water. The boy jerked his head away and looked across the pool. "Did you hear that?"

Gwyneth smiled. "I hear the waterfall."

"No, something else—there—look!" He pointed at the surface. A whorl of ripples cut against the rings near the edge of the pool.

"So?"

"Fish—rising to feed," Terryll said.

"On what? I doubt there's a single bug or fly in here." Gwyneth lived on the firth and knew the business of fishing.

"Well, they must be feeding on something," Terryll reasoned. Stepping toward the pool, he added, "Maybe we can catch some for breakfast!"

But Gwyneth caught him by the arm. "Terryll!" she protested. "The fish can wait till breakfast." Then she rose onto her toes and kissed him again.

The surface of the water sounded with several more *ker-ploink*s, again drawing Terryll's attention. "There must be a whole school of them!" He turned to Gwyneth and smiled. "I just want to see what kind they are—maybe they're trout! You'd like the way I cook fresh trout! Lemon, butter—no pepper!" He pulled away.

Gwyneth folded her arms and frowned at the design on the wall. "I don't even like fish," she mumbled to herself. "Especially trout."

Terryll sneaked to the edge of the pool next to the waterfall, mindful that trout are easily spooked, and angled his head around a stalagmite to peer into the troubled water. But the surface was a violent turbulence of glaring lights, obscuring the waters below. The boy leaned over the edge farther to get a better look. "Funny . . . I can't see anything." A shadow grew over the surface. "Wait! There's one—"

Suddenly a leather noose was over his head and snapping taut around his throat, and before Terryll could react he was lifted off the ground, by whom or what he had no idea, for his eyes were clenched in pain. He tried to call out to Gwyneth, but his voice was cut off. Panicking, he flailed wildly at the leather thong that pulled him aloft, choking him, discharging his life in its merciless unyielding clasp, but to no avail. The noose bit deeply into his neck, and he couldn't pry his fingers beneath it.

The blood quickly drained from Terryll's head, leaving pinpoints of white light blinking frenetically in his brain. In vain he tried to free himself from the steely death grip, desperately tried to hold onto his ebbing strength, to breathe, desperately fought the swirling curtain of blackness that was drawing across his consciousness. Sounds lengthened to a pristine edge, cutting away the gurgling of the waterfall and the echo of a woman's scream, leaving only the pounding of his heart and the hissing. The hissing.

Silence came first.

And then the darkness.

Zzwip . . . tchank!

Terryll felt himself falling as though from a great height. An ear-splitting sound filled the cave with resonant thunder. He hit the ground hard. Light raced to dispel darkness. Consciousness rent the black curtain only to reveal weltering confusion. He blinked, and the chamber spun with kaleidoscopic effect—colors swirling, forms converging, then splitting, converging again.

Then through a blurred focus, he saw several vague shapes moving above him—huge, dangerous shapes.

He felt someone grab his arm and pull him away from the edge of the pool. His own legs aided him, scrambling independently of his mind, pushing his body clear of the water where death had caught hold of him. Sound returned in waves. He heard himself coughing, a hissing of water, then . . .

"Wake up, Terryll!"

The boy coughed again.

"Give me an arrow—*quick!*"

Again he coughed. Instincts returned, bristling with immediate danger, and terror rushed to envelop him. His heart began to pound furiously. At once Terryll's eyes glared open with cleared focus, and he took in the scene with a sweep.

Gwyneth was next to him, holding his longbow and reaching toward his quiver for another arrow. Glaring down at them menacingly from the ledge were several men of curious description, one of whom was clutching at a broken arrow-shaft sticking out of his shoulder.

The boy let out a gasp as he rolled away onto his feet, tearing the noose from his head.

"Thank God you're alive!" Gwyneth cried.

"Give me the bow!" Terryll yelled, grabbing at his quiver for an arrow. His heart raced with adrenaline as he gazed wide-eyed at the men now pouring out onto the overhanging ledge. Their numbers had swelled to fifteen or more, some of whom had made the stairway and were descending.

Terryll deftly fit an arrow to his bow. As he drew it, his focus narrowed to a single point in the center of the lead man's chest. The man jolted to a stop, then the boy's eyes swept the others to hold them at bay. They held, each with a fierce intensity of gaze narrowed on the weapon in Terryll's hands. He backed them up the stairs with it, gesturing with short upward jerks.

Gathering on the ledge, the men settled into a kind of restless savagery, flexing their hands over their spears and pole-axes. Others squatted down onto their haunches like ogres poised to leap, every one of them eyeing Terryll and Gwyneth with dark eyes that shone warily in the shimmering grotto.

Catching their breath, the boy and girl looked upon them with astonishment, for before them was a race of men of striking appearance. They were like none they had ever seen—indeed, could ever imagine—at once compelling their eyes and yet pervading their minds with fear.

They were silver-haired men, with features of exquisite turn and configuration. Their gleaming foreheads rose high over their brows and evinced a keenness through the wide-spaced eyes that were dark and luminous and penetrating. They wore their hair in many long and fine braids that encircled their heads like so many gossamer eels and were bound by headbands of bronze and pewter and what appeared to be beaten gold. Some were ringed with assorted gemstones, while others were fit with the antlers of stags, the tines clawing out and upward from their temples. Their arms and legs were bare and of perfect symmetry. However, their skin was of such pale color that it glimmered with a ghostly translucence. It seemed impossible the sun had ever touched it.

Even from a distance, Terryll could see the veins standing out purple over the pallid sheath of muscles and sinews, and around the eyes the skin was thin, membranous, of a red hue, and the red traced the finely formed nostrils and corners of the lips.

Gwyneth was awed by their appearance. "What manner of men are th—"

"Violent ones," Terryll interjected, his throat still burning with a salient reminder. His eyes narrowed on the stag antlers curving out from their headbands, on their cunning, simmering eyes glinting beneath. He grunted.

Shifting his gaze to the men at the head of the stairway, he marveled at the array of finely tooled armor that each wore, the battle accoutrements and furs, the swords of curious design hanging about their waists. The blades were broad and curved—heavy, wicked-looking things, seeming more fit for felling cattle than men—following the fashion of the Turkish scimitars, though longer and more ornate. It was clear from their workmanship that these were men highly skilled in metallurgy.

"Whoever they are, they're surely not Picts," Gwyneth whispered.

Terryll did not respond. His mind was working the passageway behind them, calculating a route of escape.

He looked to the side of the ledge where the stricken man was moaning pitifully. A few men huddled around him, it seemed with boyish fascination, for they were gaping at the broken shaft jutting from his shoulder as though observing a terrapin or a snake for the first time. A muttering of incredulity ebbed and flowed. Then seemingly careless of his suffering, one man took hold of the shaft and gave it a quick pull, and the stricken man howled lugubriously.

The bloodied bolt was passed from man to man, creating a boil of interest as each examined the deadly broadhead. Grunts of curiosity accompanied it. They seemed intrigued by the fact that such a small thing could have felled one of their kind with the effectiveness of a broadax. And when it had made the rounds, the luminous eyes narrowed darkly on the length of Terryll's longbow and along its feathered mate, bisecting the arch beneath his trained eye.

The thought struck Terryll that though the men appeared to be of an advanced civilization—be it Pict or Scot or Briton—they were ignorant of the bow and arrow and were no longer satisfied with their ignorance.

The man who had brutally jerked the shaft from his fellow stepped to the brink, and held his hand aloft in salutation. *"Bralnge ti wa loc l in!"* he said with authority.

"It's an ancient tongue, I think," Terryll said, searching his mind for translation.

"Tuatha Baalg!" the man said, slapping his fist against his chest. Then, gesturing to the others, he added sternly, *"Tiana Tuatha Baalg."*

"Tiana . . . Tuatha . . . Baalg?" Terryll repeated, isolating the words.

"Maybe it's his name," Gwyneth offered.

"Or tribe."

The man made a sweeping gesture with his hand, encompassing the environs of the grotto. *"Tuatha Baalg! Gwynthr tllur loc l in!"* he said, suddenly angry.

"We wish you no harm," Terryll enunciated carefully, not knowing if the man could understand him.

"T ir tr iwyl du, wyf wedá lynd!" the man bellowed. Then he drew his curved sword and brandished it threateningly with both hands, tracing great swaths of dazzling light through the air.

Terryll raised his tip to the man's throat, parrying the gesture. Then, keeping a wary eye on the man, he edged slowly back toward the entrance. "I think it's time for us to go now."

"Fine with me," Gwyneth said, smiling prettily.

A shadow grew quickly behind the cascading blade of water, followed by an explosion of a million watery jewels as one of the Tuatha Baalg burst through, bearing down on the boy and girl with a raised scimitar.

"Terryll!"

Hearing the swooshing cleft of air, Terryll instinctively whirled to one side, narrowly cheating the blade as it crashed against the floor. Turning, he loosed his arrow as the man came to a halt not three feet from his side. The broadhead passed through the man's neck, and he spun to the ground.

"Run!" Terryll yelled, pulling Gwyneth by the arm. Running himself, he fetched another arrow and fit it to his longbow. "Leave these to their mischief!"

Gwyneth screamed, "The torches!"

In his haste the boy had forgotten them. They were about twenty feet from the chamber exit, but as Terryll broke stride to collect them a scimitar scythed by his head and convinced him otherwise. He whirled about and loosed his arrow at the nearest man.

The man crumpled to the floor, while the others leaped behind stalagmites, uncertain of this strange weapon that could kill with the speed of thought.

Terryll shot a look at the torches, back at the men regrouping now with fevered vengeance. Then, grimacing, he pulled Gwyneth by the hand, and the two of them sprang into the blackness of the tunnel with the clatter of feet on their heels.

They hurried along the passage as best they could, panting, wide-eyed, grasping at the sightless space ahead that at any moment might present them with a wall or a boulder into which to crash. They were as helpless blind creatures, fleeing from an enemy that was undoubtedly familiar with every niche and turn of the tunnels. Terror lay behind them and before them, all about them, it seemed. Feeling their way along the rock sides, they moved haltingly, dipping, rising, turning back and forth around curves and over strewn rocks, climbing ever upward toward the adjoining passageway—however far ahead they had no idea—occasionally tripping over the broken path that offered only treachery in the darkness.

There was no sound of men in the passage behind then. However, an army of Baalgs might be advancing on their heels unseen, unheard, and at any moment one might reach out of the black and snatch him by the nape.

A brilliant flash of light exploded in Terryll's brain, followed by a sharp report of pain, and the boy fell sprawling to the ground. In the nigritude of the tunnel, he knew not whether he was conscious or unconscious, hoping it was the latter, hoping this was all some kind of horrible nightmare from which he would soon awaken.

"Terryll—are you all right?"

The boy let out a groan and sat up, feeling the side of his head gingerly. A lump was beginning to form, wet, warm, throbbing with pain.

"What happened?" Gwyneth pressed.

Terryll struggled to his feet groaning, mindful of the jutting rock over his head. He staggered backward but caught himself against the wall. "I hit my head against a rock," he grumbled.

"Do you need help?"

"No!" he returned sharply, mindful again of their imminent peril. "Now, go on ahead and warn Dunnald—I'll be along in a moment."

"I'm not leaving here without you!"

"I'll be right behind you. I just need to clear my head for a second."

"You *do* need help!"

"No, I don't. Now *go!*"

Gwyneth left reluctantly, mumbling something to herself about the stubbornness of men.

Terryll listened as her footsteps quickly faded, then he crouched in the silence and waited, peering into the tunnel, able to see nothing, listening now for any hint of the Tuatha Baalg. Hearing nothing. He leaned back against the cold wall to ease his legs and lay his bow across his lap, an arrow fitted and pointing down the passage. He flexed his fingers on the familiar grip of his longbow. Those of his other hand fiddled anxiously with the drawstring, the smooth nock of the arrow, testing the pull. His mind and body tensed with resolve. He knew that any moment they would be coming. He would slow them down, buy Gwyneth some time to reach safety.

A knife of pain stabbed his head, and Terryll spilled his arrow. Clasping his head with his right hand, he felt warm trickles of fluid inching through his fingers and down his neck, like warm snakes slithering into his collar. The shock of the wound had worn off, and the pain in his head—now intensifying with each chugging pulse—wracked his body with excruciating spasms. A wave of nausea swept over him, and he began to crumple. His back arched involuntarily into a wretched curve. Bracing himself against the wall with a tenuous hand, he lowered his head and spat twice on the ground to cleanse the acrid taste of bile from his mouth.

Not now, God. Please, not now. He groaned, fighting the convulsion. *Help me.*

He then fished around where he knew his feet to be, feeling for the arrow. Finding it, he refit his bow and steadied himself grimly against a lingering anarchy in his body, wincing with every sickening strike of his pulse. A minor revolt rumored, then rippled through his limbs, but was quickly subdued by the boy's tyrannical will. *Not now* was the edict.

He crouched at the ready, waiting, listening. But all that he could hear was the terrible whirring noise in his head, like a scourge of locusts taking wing. There were no reference points but the cold wall at his back, beneath his tread. It began to nibble at him. He raised his hand before his face, but was blind to it. His hands and feet and sight were remembered things, slipping quickly into a sucking void of black ink.

The blackness of the tunnel began to prey upon his mind. It was thick, smothering, like a living thing, a malignant evil thing that penetrated his mind with a little tremor of madness, tapping away at the inside of his skull until it was like a deafening clangor.

His senses began to cry for light, a glimmer, even a shadow. His mind reasoned with his members, staved off the unnerving assault of darkness.

But soon panic began to rise within him, a prickling sensation that came trundling up the back of his spine. What if the Baalgs weren't down the tunnel at all but had somehow gotten around him? Ahead of him? Another tunnel perhaps! Another thought rushed him with a horrible coldness that overwhelmed him. What if . . .

"Gwyneth!"

Terryll leaped to his feet, fighting off the knives of pain that ripped and stabbed his body. But as he lunged forward, at once he froze, as though stricken by an altogether new terror. Whirling about, he listened.

They were coming.

Somewhere down the tunnel their angry, guttural utterances echoed along the rocky corridor like distant breakers rolling and thundering, hissing, altogether alien and bent on violence.

He pulled back on his bow—the smooth arrow shaft brushing lightly against the length of yew like a friendly whisper. His pulse quickened, as did the pain in his wound, and he nearly faltered under it. He set his teeth and scowled. "Come on, you fiends. Come on. Let me see you."

But there was no sight of devils or of strange-looking men called Tuatha Baalg, only the sound as they came in a furious rush through the jet void of the tunnel. They were perhaps three hundred feet away, making a terrible row, shrieking and howling in their throaty language. The resonating din was unearthly, spellbinding, deadening to the senses.

Terryll's eyes widened into a deerlike trance, as his mind careered dangerously into an apathetic surrender.

Then suddenly there was nothing. Not a sound. It took a moment for the boy to gather in the silence, and, when he did, it startled him out of his stupor. What happened? Where'd they go? Did they take a side tunnel?

Horror reached up from his bowels and clutched his throat, gutting his breath. He could feel them! He could feel their dark, luminous eyes peering at him from the black, perhaps a hundred yards away, or fifty, or ten. Perhaps they were huddled around him now, grinning, close enough to reach out and flick his ear. He wouldn't know—he couldn't see an inch in front of his nose.

And then he shuddered. Could the Tuatha Baalg see him? Had they somehow adapted to a lightless world beneath the ground? Like bats? Or like blind men whose senses of smelling and hearing heighten to give them another kind of sight? Could they then "see" as well in the dark as he could in the light? Something stirred, he thought. He tensed, focused, craned his ears to the sound. Nothing. An impulse struck him to shoot blindly, to loose the tension, to have done with this cat-and-mouse nonsense. But there was no target, and his trained mind was repulsed by such foolishness. Fear was governing him.

Wait! There it was again. Yes. There was the faintest sound of scraping, like a boot brushing over the floor. There was a whisper of air, then something small and hard struck him on the cheek, stinging him.

Terryll winced and jerked his eyes against the wall of blackness. His mind lurched in terror. Nothing. Something pelted his leg, and then his arm, plinked around his feet. And then he realized that they were throwing pebbles at him, taunting him, testing his vision perhaps!

Aiming at nothing, Terryll stood and loosed his arrow into the blackness with a snapping twang of the bowstring. He heard the whistle of the shaft as it rifled through the air, then, moments later, the chink of stone and metal as the arrow skittered harmlessly along the tunnel floor. His heart sank.

And now that the arrow was spent, the Baalgs rushed.

Terrified, the boy grabbed hopelessly at another arrow and ran as well as he could to catch up with Gwyneth, praying that there were no walls, no jutting rocks, no . . . *"Oomph!"*

"Ouch!"

"Gwyneth!" he yelled, with terrific relief. But his relief was short-lived, felled by the immanency of death at his heels. "Come on!" He pulled her to her feet, mentally cursing the development, and they ran, stumbling, careening this way and that off walls and one another.

The invisible Tuatha Baalg were hard and fast upon them.

"I told you to go warn Dunnald!" he barked furiously.

"I didn't want to leave you!" she shouted back.

Presently the walls fell away on either side of the narrower tunnel into the broader corridor that led back to the main cavern. Terryll yanked Gwyneth around the corner, then jumped back to let fly another arrow down the blackened corridor.

Zzwiip . . . tchank!

Immediately a bloodcurdling howl resounded along the tunnel.

"There's more where that came from!" Terryll shouted. Then, feeling for Gwyneth, he hurried her along the passageway. "Come on. It's not much farther."

"I could move a lot easier if you weren't pulling on my arm!"

"What!"

"I can take care of myself!"

"This is no time for an argument!" he said, tightening his grip.

The Tuatha Baalg were not far behind—he could hear them muttering loudly—though they were making little effort to press their attack. *Why not?* Apparently his last kill had not only gained them a little distance but had curbed the creatures' appetite for the chase as well.

The tunnel was broader and leveled out quickly, affording them an easier go of it. But as they neared the main cavern, Terryll tripped over something lying across the path and hit the floor hard, losing his bow.

"This cursedness!" he cried.

"What happened?"

"There's a body on the ground," he said, clasping his pounding head with one hand, searching the ground frantically for his bow with the other.

"A body? Whose?"

"I think it's one of Dunnald's men—how should I know!? Now, get going! Go!"

"There's no need to yell. I'm staying."

"You are one stubborn girl," he said, still groping across the floor.

"And you've got the head of a bull!"

Terryll found the bowgrip. But too late! Out of the shadows something knocked him to the ground with brutal force, overpowering him at once. The Tuatha Baalg had taken him by surprise. They had tried a new tactic: while the others held back in the tunnel creating a diversion, one had moved stealthily along the wall under the cover of darkness and pounced upon the unsuspecting boy.

Terryll heard the cleft of wind over his head, a familiar whoosh that impelled his instincts to act. As he thrust his longbow upward with both hands to brace himself against the certain blow, the heavy edge of the man's scimitar severed it neatly in two with a sharp crack and crashed into the ground, peppering the side of Terryll's face with biting chips of stone.

Maddened by his thwarted blow, the man raised his sword to strike again.

Another whoosh cleft the air, followed by a sickening *thunk!* and a hellish scream that reverberated up and down the passageway. The man arched his back, twisting and yawing violently, then, heaving upon a furious swell, he pitched headlong beside the boy with a tremendous jolt, pinning him beneath his heavy arm.

"What's going on? What happened?" Terryll yelled, as he hefted the limb off him and scrambled to his feet.

"I told you I could take care of myself," Gwyneth said, pulling the slain warrior's broadsword out of the Baalg's chest.

"And me. That's twice today you've saved my life!" Terryll said, and without waiting for her approval he grabbed her hand and fled toward the main cavern.

Enraged, the waiting Tuatha Baalg resumed their furious pursuit. The sound of their language thundered and raced ahead of them through the corridor and enveloped the boy with terror.

35
THE TUATHA
BAALG

The Tuatha Baalg had come only moments before—without warning, scores of them, pouring into the cavern on the heels of Dunnald's scouts, screaming in their strange tongue, creating instant terror and confusion, scattering men, women, and horses into a panicked retreat.

Terrorized, the horses stamped and kicked, reeled and reared as they strained at flimsy tethers. Their eyes glared white with unstrung fear. One broke loose and immediately bolted for the entrance but was felled by a thrown ax, and, dying, it wedged sideways in the opening, trapping everyone inside.

At once there was a bottleneck of disorder, panic, and abject fear. Pandemonium reigned like an avenging tyrant. Every man and beast clambered to be free of the cave, which was once a sheltering comfort but now a womb of death.

Women screamed and shrieked as they fled for the cave's mouth, clawing the hostile air for the hope of life. The girl with the hurt ankle, however, sat next to the fire, still clutching tightly the little wooden carving, still swaying to the tempo of the hymn. Making no attempt to move, she just stared at the charging Tuatha Baalg without the slightest change of expression on her face, as if, like a rush of squealing children at play, spilling everywhere at once, they were no threat whatsoever. She would have surely been killed, but a mindful warrior whisked her off the ground in a heroic sweep and carried her back to the others.

Men shouted angrily over the cacophonous fray, some bellowing out commands to defend, others to flee the cave. All tried unsuccessfully to bridle the boiling swarm of trapped horses and women, while scrambling desperately for weapons, grabbing whatever blade or battle tool was nearest at hand, tripping over each other and the women as the shocking horror of the attack rent their once-quieted souls.

Several men tried in vain to drag the carcass of the horse out of the way so that the women and mounts could flee to safety, but in the turbulent crush of battle it was a near impossible task. The air was charged with a profound astonishment.

In the midst of the rolling terror, the battle-hardened and fearless Dunnald, though surprised by the onslaught of the Tuatha Baalg, was undaunted and kept his head. His commanding voice cut through the reasonless whorl like a herald of truth, and he quickly rallied his warriors to his side from every quarter. Had he not, everyone would have been killed in short order.

He and his men formed a hasty palisade of flesh, shields, and iron blades around the routed retreat of women and horses behind them, closing their ranks to present a meager front of determined resistance.

"Take heart, men! Take heart—lest we fall!" he trumpeted above the din, and his face shone like a prophet's. "Let us guard our charges with honor for the sake of Christ's holy Name—to the last man if need be! Aye! To the last of your mother's sons! Let us now fly into these deffils and give 'em a taste of our blades! Give 'em a fair show of it, lads!"

And, with such encouragement, his warriors took heart and let out the Pictish war cry as they closed with the Tuatha Baalg. A deafening clash of metal shook the ancient walls with explosions of white-hot sparks bursting along the battle line.

Immediately there were flashes of blades cleaving silver and crimson streaks through the air, clanging and ringing out a bloody herald. Battle-axes and maces rose and fell angrily, splintering and crushing and hammering bone and armor. The grim shapes of men, silhouetted and rim-lit by the frenzied dance of firelight, leaped out of the fray through the swirling smoke and cast violent shadows against the broken walls and around the gnarled and snarling limestone teeth of the cavern floor and ceiling, now resembling some infernal gullet. Their faces, caught for an instant in the flickers, could be seen twisted in grimaces of rage and horror and wonder as they gaped into it. Deafening outbursts ejaculated rhythmically along the battle line, roaring like the surf.

And then the ubiquitous flights of death, piloting the updrafts, began to fold their wings and knife into the surging demonstration. Here and there screams pierced the clamor as Picts and Baalgs fell to the others' prowess. And so the battle raged fierce and terrible, near overwhelming the souls of righteous men with its appalling ambience.

But Dunnald's men fought valiantly with holy fire in their breasts, giving little ground to the antlered men, inflicting instead a rack and ruin upon them with battle tactics unknown to the Tuatha Baalg. For though the Baalgs were fierce fighters, always on the offensive, it seemed they knew nothing of defensive maneuvers. It was a weakness that the Picts soon exploited. Unlike the Picts, the Baalgs had no shields, needing both hands to wield their heavy scimitars, and the Picts were able to thrust swiftly under their own shields into the exposed torsos of the Baalgs as they retrieved their weapons upward like sledgehammers. However, the Tuatha Baalg came in wave upon wave, outnumbering them four to one, relentlessly crashing against the tiny breakwater of Picts. Dunnald knew that unless his men were soon free of the cave, they would eventually be worn down by the Baalg's surging numbers and the punishment of their terrific blows. Even so, they would give a fair and stalwart show and spend the last of their strength and blood with honor.

Suddenly a savage battle cry cleft the din nearest the cave entrance, followed by the shouts and screams of desperate men and women.

Dunnald shot a look to the place to see what had happened, and immediately his heart sank. Several Baalgs had breached the Pict's human palisade, forcing the men tending the horse carcass to forsake it and defend themselves against their attack. The dead horse remained in place and sealed their doom.

"Close up the line! Close up the line!" Dunnald shouted to his defenders. "Or 'tis death to us all!"

The men did as best they could, but their defenses were crumbling. The situation proved abject. Horses whickered and screamed at the sight of the Tuatha Baalg pouring through the breach, and bucked and kicked and reared up to rain blows of sharp, iron hooves upon anything beneath or around them. The Pictish men and women knew well enough to avoid their hooves, but strangely the Baalgs did not.

In the moiling tangle of stabbing blades and flailing limbs at the breach, Terryll's black charger, Tempest, felled a Baalg with a downward crack of iron. Then, reeling in panic, the horse sideswiped another Baalg with its hindquarters, knocking the man to the ground.

And then the horses stampeded, breaking through Dunnald's flagging line into the crush of bewildered Baalgs, distracting them, scattering them into the waiting blades of the stout warrior and his men. Suddenly the violent maelstrom turned to advantage.

Terryll and Gwyneth ran out of the tunnel into the raging sea of battle just ahead of the Baalgs who had been pursuing them. They stopped cold in their tracks.

"God have mercy!" Terryll cried, scanning the grisly scene incredulously. At first glance it seemed the heads of men were floating over the tempestuous red swells of battle like little corks bobbing.

Behind them, the charging black shapes of the Tuatha Baalg took on burnished color as they drew near the cavern's fire, their antlered headbands glinting fiercely. There was nowhere for the boy and girl to turn—they were sandwiched between two hellish fronts.

"Terryll!" Gywneth screamed, pointing toward the battlefront. The ground shook, and the walls quaked with the thunder of hooves and

the blast of flaring nostrils. With Tempest in the lead, the stampede of horses blasted a clearing through the Baalgs, trampling many of the unwary, and was now heading directly at the boy and girl, an undulating storm of power and terror.

Grabbing Gwyneth's hand, Terryll yanked her to one side as the horses careered by in shuddering flight, charging blindly into the tunnel to escape the cavern. Immediately horrible cries shot out of the corridor as the Baalgs within met their startled end under a clapping tonnage of iron.

Terryll looked, but there was no sign of the charging men, only the sound of a distant clattering. The boy helped Gwyneth to her feet, then the two of them darted behind a large stalagmite and surveyed the battle.

"What can we do?" Gwyneth asked, gaping at the billowing wall of armored backs. "There are so many of them."

Spotting a sword on the ground nearby, Terryll answered grimly, "We can fight." Then looking at her, he smiled reassuringly. "Everything is going to be all right."

But she knew better.

Quickly he ran over to the sword and grabbed it, then thrust its gleaming tip at the broad, mailed flank of a towering Baalg warrior who had a wounded man pinned helplessly against the wall. But the blade had been administered with astounding ineptness and caromed to one side with a grazing blow, and the Baalg, more annoyed than injured, turned his fury on the boy.

Terryll looked down at his sword and scowled. "Worthless slab of metal." But, scuttling back and forth crablike, he brandished it pathetically at the man. "Come on! You want some of this? Come and get it."

Immediately the sword was struck from his hands by a lightning flash of the Baalg's scimitar, stinging his hand.

Terryll yelled.

The Baalg warrior chortled wickedly, then, hefting his blade, came at him.

Terryll looked around desperately for another weapon.

Rushing to his aid, Gwyneth threatened the man with her own sword. "Over here, handsome!" she taunted from his other flank. "Come on!"

As he shifted his dark, luminous eyes to the girl, a lascivious snarl twisted over his pallid features. Stepping toward her, the huge warrior swatted her blade aside as if it were a toy, tearing the hilt from her hands and sending the weapon clanging across the floor.

But such a diversion allowed Terryll to spot a stout bow and quiver of arrows abandoned near the cavern wall, and he made a Herculean dash for them.

The Baalg warrior hurled his scimitar at him like an ax. Running, Terryll caught the action in his peripheral vision and dove at the bow. Immediately the swooshing blade cartwheeled inches over his head, then shattered against the wall with a ringing explosion of sparks.

He hit the ground rolling to break his fall and came up with only his hunting knife in hand—all seven inches of it. The bow was several yards out of reach. Snatching up an abandoned ax, the Baalg sprang across the backfield of the battle and was upon him.

Terryll ducked as the man swung broadly at him and missed. Recoiling, the boy came up with his knife and plunged its length into a thick girth of armor.

Staggering to one side, however, the man was far from quitting the fight. Terryll's blade left little more than a flesh wound at his side, little more than a bee sting.

Pressing his attack, the enraged Baalg raised his ax to destroy the boy, who crouched before him like a bug with his little stinger.

But immediately his unattended flank was met by the upward thrust of Gwyneth's recovered blade.

The large warrior roared and spun around, flinging the girl across the ground like a rag doll into a stalagmite. Blinded with rage and bellowing out curses in his indiscernible tongue, the Baalg leaped at the dazed girl with his ax.

Zzwiip . . . tchonk! Terryll's arrow caught him in the side of his head.

Gwyneth rolled out of the way in time as his huge body crashed against the stalagmite, shaking the ground around them. Climbing to her feet, she retrieved her sword from his side.

Terryll grabbed an arrow from his quiver and smiled curiously at her. "Where'd you learn how to use that thing?"

Gwyneth wiped a tangle of hair from her face. "My father wanted a son. He got me."

"It's a good thing for me, isn't it?"

Gwyneth cocked her head and gave him a puzzled look.

An instant later Terryll's bowstring shuddered, and a black streak ripped across the cavern toward its mark. Immediately the broadhead plowed into the back of a Baalg warrior who was about to cleave a Pict's head with his scimitar.

The Baalgs on either flank paused to consider what had happened, so sudden had the little shaft appeared.

With equal suddenness, another Baalg lurched forward with a shaft of feathers sticking out of his chest and a bewildered look twisting over his face. And again, two more of their number reeled in quick succession.

Immediately a wave of confusion swept over the Tuatha Baalg in that quarter, for they knew nothing of these strange feathered darts that seemed to appear out of thin air and kill.

Dunnald could not see Terryll for the looming screen of Baalgs, neither did he understand the reason for their confusion, but he and his men took advantage of it and hacked away at their breaking offense.

Turning, Dunnald was aghast to see the warrior next to him pinned to the ground with a Baalg's knee in his back, his head yanked back, and the enemy warrior about to scalp him. But before he could fly to his aid, the Baalg lurched upright, then fell headlong at his feet. Dunnald recognized Terryll's feathery shaft and immediately made the connection.

From every quarter of the cavern, the screams of Baalgs ascended from the violent plot of stone, as Terryll's missiles of spruce and iron rifled from his tireless bowstring with rhythmic precision, every three seconds. The bow was not made with near the care or skill as any one of his father's longbows. It was stout, of either ash or lemon wood, with maybe half the range of his longbow—perhaps out of their reverence for the yew tree, the Pictish bowyers had not yet discovered its many secrets—but Terryll had little cause to complain. He held in his hands his weapon of choice, and in such close quarters the little bow served him well.

Whether or not the Tuatha Baalg knew terror, Terryll's deadly presence quickly drew the attention of many to his rearward position. But his arrows kept the bravest of them at bay, as they had done earlier in the pool cavern.

Reading the Baalgs' concern, Dunnald called out to those of his men who had bows to use them, for in their hasty defense they had had neither time nor opportunity for such. Terryll's diversion changed that. The Baalgs had fallen back somewhat, and soon the air was filled with dozens of black shafts, striking from every quarter, confusing their lines, thwarting their once-impending rout.

Slowly, the tide of battle ebbed. A cheer rang out from the men who witnessed the shift, and they hurled themselves against the faltering Baalgs with renewed zeal and abandon.

The sound of horses pulled Terryll's attention back to the tunnel entrance. With nowhere to go in the blinding darkness, the horses had filtered nervously back into the cavern, then bunched together near its opening as far from the battle as possible, their eyes starting with terror.

Tempest pranced anxiously back and forth, shaking his mane furiously, whipping his tail, and snorting his contempt into the air. The others stamped their hooves and whinnied, stricken with fear and desperate to be rid of the killing place.

Terryll and Gwyneth ran over to the horses, then slowed as they made their approach so as not to spook them.

Again a cheer rose up from a quarter of the battle, this time from the cave's entrance. The warriors had finally dragged the dead horse out of the way, at last freeing the narrow route of escape, and immediately the women began funneling out of the cave into the welcome fury of the thunderstorm.

However, the Tuatha Baalg were not given to retreat. They were given only to attack and were amazingly resilient and resourceful.

"Pior wk tiu, Tuatha! Parkuath tiu arká!" one of them bellowed.

Then, to the horror of Dunnald and his men, the Baalgs began using the bodies of the dead and wounded as shields against the Pict arrows and quickly amassed a terrible counterattack. They concentrated their efforts on the cave entrance with an overwhelming surge of force.

Dunnald's men were startled by their sudden turn of aggression, and being unable to answer it with their bows, they fell back. Their glimmer of hope was quickly snuffed under the smothering wave of Baalgs.

Dunnald, desperately holding a disintegrating line of defense, called those warriors at his side to shore up the line near the entrance. Suddenly his eyes caught a glint of movement above him, and immediately a heavy wedge of steel hammered down against his broadsword, severing his blade in two. His knees buckled under the force of the blow, and he nearly fell.

A Baalg loomed over him and let out a sneering hiss, the gleam of victory burning wickedly in his eyes. Presently the warriors on either side of him fell dead or wounded, he knew not which, but in that moment the stout warrior gave up the last of his hope. A prayer formed on his lips and flew.

However, before the Baalg could make good his advantage, the thunder of horses rocked the cavern walls and drew his attention hinder. Whether or not the Tuatha Baalg knew terror was answered at once in this one's eyes as he fought to reject a horrifying vision.

Storming into the midst of the battle with unbridled fury came the spirited Tempest—his nostrils blasting disdain at the antlered Baalgs, his iron hooves smiting the ancient slants of rock beneath him with sparks of lightning—followed by the thunderous stampede of horses, trampling those Baalgs who were too stunned to flee.

Atop the fiery charger sat Terryll with his little bow, chanting a feverish battle dirge, loosing arrow after arrow into the scattering Baalgs. Gwyneth sat behind him, a fierce battle maiden with a mass of fiery ringlets unfurled behind her, skillfully wielding her broadsword. They were a holy vision, a glorious apocalypse that rained judgment on the Tuatha

Baalg and inspired hope and courage in the hearts of the flagging Pict warriors.

Armed with only a jagged hilt, Dunnald hurled his stocky bulk into the distracted Baalg's midflanks and bowled the man over.

"By the Laird Christ and His reign upon the earth!" he shouted.

Reaching the battlefront quickly, Terryll looked down at Dunnald and his warriors. "How fares the battle?" he asked, with a cock of his head.

"*Och!* Well, lad—well!" Dunnald returned. "The boon of Christ upon you!"

"Then the day is ours!" And with that the boy turned his steed back into the panicked Baalgs.

Dunnald jumped up, grabbed a pole-axe from the wounded man next to him, then raised it above the line of warriors. "See how they tremble before the army of the Lord!" he shouted. "Let us send 'em flyin' back to the fiery gates!"

The men let out a deafening battle cry, then charged into the scrambling ranks of Baalgs, meting out great destruction.

It was clear that the Tuatha Baalg had lost their fighting spirit. Many could not focus on the warriors before them for fear of Terryll's darts and the terrible horses hinderward.

Suddenly a loud shout cleft the clamor of battle. *"Tuatha Baalg! Kiawawk tiu! Kiawawk tiu!"*

At once the Baalgs discarded their human shields, then turned and fled before the Picts into the adjoining passageways. Many still fell, however, beneath the iron hooves of the horses as the animals made a returning sweep through their midst.

The Pictish warriors pursued them as far as the tunnels, loosing volleys of arrows as they disappeared, bounding into the blackness.

Soon the last echoing sounds of the Baalgs' guttural gibberish trailed off into silence.

Dunnald's men stared into the dark corridor for several moments, panting for breath. Their faces were ashen and drawn from fatigue and the loss of blood, their fists clenched like steel vises around their hilts and ax-handles. Slowly they began looking about the littered field of battle. As many Baalgs had died during their retreat as during the whole of the fight.

Then all at once, as though a veil of astonishment were suddenly hoisted, the men shouted out a thunderous cry of victory. Dunnald raised his pole-ax and shouted over their cheers. "Quickly, men—there is not a moment to spare! Gather up our dead and wounded and let us be rid of this foul place—lessen these deffils return with greater numbers and catch us again unaware!"

Within minutes, the dead and wounded were set upon mounts, and all of them were filing out of the cave into the storm to join the women. They left nothing behind but the carcasses of four horses, a few scattered clothes and blankets, and a little carving of wood that reflected the smoldering remains of their once-warming fire. The Picts lost eleven of their twenty-six men (three of whom succumbed to their wounds outside the cave), and six more were severely wounded and needed immediate medical attention, lest they too perish. The rest had escaped with only a battery of cuts and bruises. One had broken an arm against a stalagmite. Of the women they lost none, though the majority of them sustained cuts and abrasions. All but four of the horses were saved. Two were killed in battle, and the other two were lost when the horses stampeded into the tunnel. That they did not all perish was a testimony to the unsearchable mercy of God.

The Tuatha Baalg lost seventy of their kind, and again as many lay wounded or dying across the ground of battle.

The storm had ceased throwing its jagged bolts across the sky, and the thunder had quit its stentorian outbursts, threatening now with only occasional distant rumbling. The rain, however, showed little sign of letting up.

The column of battle-spent and weary riders filed out of the hidden glade like a somber cortege, then traveled the rest of that night in the gloomy downpour, making its way southward once again along the main Roman road. It was doubtful that there would be any Pictish raiding parties out and about in such weather, plunder or no.

No one spoke. Those who knew how prayed silently as they sat in their saddles, hunched and shivering against the cold, slanting showers, each person lost in his own thoughts, each soul grateful for the tenuous breath of life. Eyes were downcast and gazed upon the slow-footed sweep of road. Appalling apparitions were conjured upon each face. There was a general glare of shock in the eyes. A brooding sullenness clung.

All that could be heard was the dreary spatter of raindrops through the soughing boughs overhead and against the puddled stone road below. A blustery, chilling wind sought them out through the trees, and the muffled shogging of horse hooves as they clomped out wearied tempos through the wet leaves plastered all about their feet. Occasionally a horse would shudder the water off its hide and complain with whinnies and snorts, but its objections were quickly deadened and dismissed by the dismal, smothering cloak of rain.

Terryll rode just behind Dunnald at the head of the column, with Gwyneth still sitting behind him, pressing against him, her arms folded firmly around his waist. There were other available mounts, but she liked it just where she was, and so did Terryll. Tempest didn't seem to mind either. However, he didn't care at all for his second position in line, and he let everyone know about it with snorts of supreme contempt. After all, he was the horse who had led a mighty charge in battle; his rightful place was out in front. Terryll had his hands full with the spirited charger.

At length, and of a sudden, the rain trailed off to a pestering drizzle. Terryll raked the mat of rain-soaked hair from his face and felt the lump on the side of his head. It had stopped bleeding, though it still smarted with pulsing jolts. He looked around at the black boles on either side of the road, cutting through the gathering swirls of fog, and took a deep breath, filling his lungs with the air's bracing freshness, then let it go with a rush.

Suddenly he felt Gwyneth straighten behind him, and moments later the soft brush of her face against his hair.

Speaking softly into his ear, she asked, "In the cave you said that it was a good thing for you my father had me instead of a son. What did you mean?" Terryll smiled and held his answer for a moment or two. But it was apparently for too long, for he soon felt a nudge against his ribs.

"Terryll?" It was a whisper.

The boy cocked his head back slightly and replied, "If your father had had a son, I doubt that I would be in love with him."

An inevitable span of silence ensued in which a dialogue of thoughts were exchanged. Presently Gwyneth kissed him on his back, then gave him a squeeze that worried his ribs some.

Terryll, however, smiled. He had not been looking for love; in fact he had shunned any suggestion of it. But he had found it—or it had found him—in the strangest of places and under the most harrowing of circumstances.

He thought of her tender kiss in the pool cavern, and, though there was scarce room on his face, his smile broadened. Suddenly he remembered the large ruby he had picked up from the bank, and a little panic scurried to his face. Fearful that he might have lost it in battle, he patted the outside of his pocket to see if it was still there. It was.

"Is there something wrong, Terryll?"

"No. Nothing at all. Not a thing."

At some point along the way, Gwyneth fell asleep against his back with her arms wrapped loosely about his waist. He could feel her warmth pressing against him affectionately, and occasionally, as the wind permitted, he heard a gentle sigh.

Terryll allowed Tempest to draw up next to Dunnald's mount, which liberty the horse took at once. The boy glanced over at the man, but the stout warrior did not appear to be aware of his presence. He was looking ahead like one caught in a trance.

Terryll wondered if he should interrupt the man's thoughts with a question, for the issue of the Tuatha Baalg weighed on his mind. He decided at last that his question could wait until a more opportune time, and he looked away into the sodden reaches of the fog.

"You've saved our lives, laddie," Dunnald said a moment later.

Terryll was startled by the voice.

"My men and I owe you a debt of gratitude—as do each of these lassies," Dunnald said, casting a smiling glance at Gwyneth, who was wrapped warmly around the boy. Looking back at Terryll, he added, "You're a fine warrior. Aye—like your father. 'Tis an honor to have fought at your side."

Terryll drew his lips into a tight smile and nodded appreciatively. It embarrassed him to hear such words of praise from this fierce-looking Pict. "You know of my father?" he asked.

Dunnald let out a hearty laugh, as Brynwald had done earlier that day. "*Och*, laddie! There are not too many warriors in the north country who dinna ken of Allyndaar. As for me—I was with Brynwald at the Wall when your father's longbowmen made a poor show of us." Dunnald laid his palm on the pommel of his sword and gave the boy a wink. Chortling, he added, "Aye. But we left our marks on a few of their hides as well."

Though it struck him odd at first, it pleased the boy that the man could laugh about it. Then, feeling the time appropriate, he changed the subject. "Who were those men back in the cave?"

"I've been tryin' to figure that out myself," Dunnald answered thoughtfully. "I have not seen the likes of 'em before nor heard tell of 'em in my heath." The man looked away down the road as his mind reached farther. "When we were in Eire, many there spake of a people once called the Tuatha de Danaam—'the Faerie folk,' as they are kenned today. The Irish claim them to be an ancient race of people that lang ago invaded their land. Accordin' to their legends, they now dwell in the belly of the underworld."

"Why?"

"To hear it told, they were sent flyin' by a scourge of Gaels kenned as the Sons of Mil—mighty men of old, hailin' from the Iberian Peninsula. In order to preserve unity of the land, the god Dagda gave rule of the underworld to the Tuatha de Danaam, and rule of the upper world to the Sons of Mil."

"Do you believe this?"

Dunnald scowled. "Hoot, mannie! Your askin' me iffen I believe a myth. Nay! I say to you—nay! Such tales concernin' the Faerie folk are the stuff of crafty bards and old women."

"But those men . . ."

The stout warrior gazed ahead for a few moments, shaking his head slowly. "'Tis a wonderment, laddie, of a surety. Aye—'tis got my mind in the mirligoes."

"One of the men said the words *Tuatha Baalg* as though it were his name," Terryll said, offering an insight. "Perhaps they're related somehow to the Tuatha de Danaam?"

"Perhaps, but I dinna ken," Dunnald replied. "But I'll wager they were spawned in the flamin' licks of hell. Aye, worshipers of Cernunnos, by their look."

"Cernunnos?"

"Aye, the antlered laird of animalkind, keeper of the gates of the underworld. Or so the druids say." Dunnald grunted contemptuously, then leaned over his horse and spat. "I say he is none other than the deffil himself."

Terryll was reminded of the design of jeweled rings on the wall of the grotto, and of similar designs he had seen on a barrow near Sarum and Stonehenge. "I know that the Romans drove the druids away from Britain when they came," he said, vocalizing his thoughts. "Killed many of them too. Perhaps the Tuatha Baalg are a race of ancient druids, driven underground to escape the Roman purge?"

"Who can say, lad?" Dunnald looked up at the sky, now casting the first gray hints of dawn, and sighed. "There are strange things afoot. I sense somethin' murksome—somethin' terribly evil at work in the air, and what it is I dinna ken. Nay, I dinna ken."

Terryll reacted to his words as though they had struck a chord. "'There is a darkness spreading across the land that will take greater weapons than those made of iron or even steel to fight,'" he mused aloud.

"What was that?"

"Oh—I was just remembering something that a Roman monk told Aeryck and me a few months back."

"Troth, and a wise monk he is, I'm sure." Dunnald paused, then, taking hold of his pommel, added grimly, "I shall return to that infernal cave with an army of warriors, and with the boon of th' Laird we'll rid the earth of their wickedness forever, ancient druids or not. By the oaks—I swear it!"

Three weeks later Dunnald attempted to do just that. With four hundred mounted men (Aeryck being among their number), armed with bows, javelins, and long pikes, he returned to the hidden glade to seek out the Tuatha Baalg. But once finding the glade, they found no trace of the cave's narrow opening, not the slightest fissure or hint of a crack to betray its whereabouts—nothing. It was as if the ancient cave had been swallowed by the mountain, or perhaps it had never existed at all. But eleven dead warriors bore testimony to the contrary.

36
ON TO BOWNESS

The day broke with a light mist hanging low and silvery over the well-featured landscape. The air was clear, crisp, full of the highlands, full of the hope of home. The storm had passed, leaving in its wake the sweet, musky fragrance of a wet autumn morning and the first taste of winter's chill. Steam rose from the backs of grazing animals and marked the breath of the living. Everywhere soggy leaves clung to feet and hooves, escaping the earth. Everywhere watery diamonds shimmered resplendently on blades of grass and dripped from trees.

The company of men and women had made camp in the Roman ruins about ten miles north of Netherby to eat a hasty meal and to catch a few hours sleep before continuing on to the Solway Firth, which they hoped to reach by sunset, barring any interruptions. It was a pause much needed and most refreshing.

The scouts that Dunnald had sent out earlier returned from their reconnoitering with welcome news. There were no signs of any raiding parties about. The news cheered the camp. Even Dunnald nodded his head and managed a smile, but his sanguine expression belied a nagging concern.

What had become of the four Pictish horsemen who had suddenly appeared the day before? Would they show up again with others? He and his men would be ill-equipped to undertake another fight. It gnawed at his mind. He would be relieved once the women and packhorses were safe below the Wall and his men and he were once again on their way back to their families in Loch na Huric.

The ruins were nothing more than a broken wall of stones encompassing a large foundation of flagstones. It had probably been built by the Romans to garrison a contingent of relief troops halfway between the larger forts of Netherby and Birrens, but it provided a decent break against the wind.

Dunnald left the wounded men inside against one of the higher walls with two warriors to guard and care for them until his return journey. Along another wall he carefully lined the dead in two rows, then covered their bodies with tarps. He looked at their stilled faces, once young and full of cheerful life, and it was a difficult moment for him.

Quickly everyone was saddled and ready to depart and, without further ado, the small company of men and women was again on its way.

The warming sun had burned away the light mist, leaving the sky the clearest blue, arching over the earthspun threads of browns and reds and yellows that colored the tapestry of the landscape. And such a fabric was filled high and low with the chirping of bird song and squirrel chatter and the songs and hymns offered along the heartened column of riders. The day's travel showed promise.

Tempest quickly found his place at the head of the column, just ahead of Dunnald's mount, followed by the sorrel mare that Gwyneth rode. She had already suffered much playful teasing from the other women, and it seemed best to her to sit her own mount. Terryll could have cared less about the teasing and told her so, but she persisted.

Dunnald leaned over and cautioned the boy to keep his eyes peeled for mischief. It was a needless caution. The young hunter spotted a small herd of red deer right off, grazing in a meadow to the west. Then not long afterward he spotted a fair-sized black bear rooting through a tangle of blackberry bushes that lined a creek not fifty yards away.

Undoubtedly, the bruin was doing some last-minute gorging before the long winter's hibernation, adding to his ample girth layers of fat that would nourish him through to the spring. The bear looked up from his feast, blackberry juice dripping from his snout, and eyed the column of riders curiously. Determining the humans to be of little consequence, he snorted a couple of times and went back to his feeding.

Terryll chuckled. But it made him think of Hauwka. He had not seen the great bear for many weeks now, and with winter coming on he might not see him again for many more. That troubled him. It was not like his old friend to stay away for so long a time. Thoughts began to ease into his mind like soft whispers, and he pondered each one in its turn. Perhaps Hauwka was roaming the dense woodlands to the east of the island, or the highlands and lochs to the north, looking as always for good hunting grounds. And then for all he knew Hauwka may have found a mate, someone of his own kind with whom to pass through the seasons. It was an odd thought, and the idea had never occurred to him until that moment. Hauwka had always been—well, Hauwka, the great mysterious bear, his companion in the wilds, the one who, like some angel sent to keep watch over him, seemed always to have been there when needed.

Then another thought crowded into his mind, one that did not whisper but yelled: the bear had not come to their aid in Loch na Huric! Why? Was he hurt? What if he was lying somewhere right now, incapacitated, and needed *him?* And then the boy was struck with a thought that made the blood drain from his head. What if he was . . .

That night they made camp near the easternmost shore of the Solway Firth. A dingle of maples, elms, and sycamores provided them with an ample screen from the road.

Dunnald decided at once to stay the night. Although he had delivered the women safely to the Solway Firth, thereby fulfilling his charge from Brynwald, he could not leave them alone in the night with the possibility of raiding parties here and about. He and his men would leave at first light.

Dunnald quickly posted two men, Oswald and Duncan, outside the camp to guard the horses and goods and to watch for trouble. He then assigned various duties to others to set the camp in order. Soon a fire was crackling, small but comfortable, with tendrils of blue smoke dissipating quickly into the bright gloaming through a canopy of falling yellow leaves.

The company ate a tasty meal of venison sausage and some fall berries and nuts that a few of the women had picked along the banks, washing them down with drafts of ale and cider. Afterward everyone sat around the fire refreshed and enjoying the clear starry evening (the women chatting at one end, and the men discussing the battle with the Tuatha Baalg at the other), each with the anticipation of returning home in the morning. An easy drift of wind rolled up from the firth, bringing with it the briny smell of the sea.

Suddenly Terryll stiffened. There had been scarce warning—only the faintest crush of wet leaves behind him betrayed the intruder's presence. But Terryll had heard it. Furtively, he reached for his bow.

"What is it?" Gwyneth asked, sensing his alarm.

"Shh! Take hold of your sword."

She did. And then Dunnald's head jerked up from across the fire and scanned the shadows behind Terryll and the women. Standing to his feet warily, he grabbed his sword.

"Is that you, Oswald? Duncan?" he asked.

"No," a voice spoke flatly. "But I am someone with an arrow pointed at your chest."

Terryll spun around, startled. *"Father!"*

"Yes, son. Are you all right?"

Terryll jumped to his feet, elated. "I'm fine! What are you doing here?"

"What do you *think* I'm doing here?" Allyndaar retorted. He was hidden behind a cover of trees, his shape obscured by their shadows. Only the tip of his broadhead could be seen penetrating the light to mark his presence, and occasionally the dull glint of his piercing blue eyes, now smoldering with rage. "Have these men harmed you?" he asked.

"No, Papa. They are friends."

"*Friends?* They are Picts! Or has that escaped your sight?"

"Picts or no, they are still friends."

Allyndaar emerged warily from his cover of trees—the shadows peeled slowly away from his cocked form—with his longbow drawn and his broadhead pointed at Dunnald's breastbone.

At once seeing his face, Dunnald's men whispered to one another. This was Allyndaar, the legendary archer, the one of whom they had heard songs sung in their halls. The men were not given to fear, but they were given to respect.

"I would hear more of this," Allyndaar said to his boy.

"But first, tell me what ye did to my sentries?" Dunnald said boldly, taking a step forward. "Did ye kill them, then?"

Allyndaar narrowed his eyes and said, "If you take another step, Pict, you will never know."

Dunnald halted abruptly and set himself square, facing the man. His men, however, fidgeted anxiously, looking at each other for cues. But with Allyndaar's arrow pointed at Dunnald's chest, there weren't a lot of options, so they held their seats. Dunnald merely grunted.

"Your men are sleeping," Allyndaar continued. "When they awaken, they will only have headaches."

"If that is all—then it'll serve 'em well for lettin' ye past them," Dunnald returned gruffly.

But as he spoke, there was a hint of relief rounding the gruffness in his voice, and his shoulders eased slightly, as did his brow. The shift was subtle, almost imperceptible, but Allyndaar obviously caught the stout warrior's paternal concern for his men, and it tempered his mood.

Still, Terryll wasn't sure at all how this was going to go. "These men saved my life, Papa," he quickly interceded.

"Saved your life?" Allyndaar said, shifting his eyes to his son.

Then easing the pull of his bow a mite, allowing the broadhead to fall just a span, he looked back at Dunnald and studied his face. It was the face of a Pict, fierce, warlike. Encircling his neck and arms were tattoos, grotesque, devilish, and Allyndaar was quickly reminded of the many friends and family that he had lost to the brutal savagery of the Picts. His own father, in fact, had been killed by them, and now Sophie.

Remembering, he quickened his pull and aim. "And what do these men have to say about the slaughter at Bowness?" he asked coolly.

"They weren't there—"

"Nay—but our people were," Dunnald said, interrupting the boy. "And for that we are contrite and at your mercy. Strike me doon, then, Briton, if it'll ease the blood-guilt of our deed."

"They are returning the goods that were taken, and more!" Terryll hastened to add. Then gesturing to Gwyneth and the others, he entreated, "And as you can see, Papa, Gwyneth and all of the women are here safe. Not a one is missing."

Allyndaar peered at Dunnald and his men curiously, trying to make sense of it all. He was moved by the stout warrior's penitent tone and character, aided as they were by Terryll's imploring defense. It was a bewildering turn of events.

"I do not understand the meaning of all this," he said, "but I will hear it out." Looking away from the Picts to Belfourt's daughter, he relaxed his longbow, then lowered it.

Terryll breathed easy; so did the warriors.

Allyndaar studied her face for the first time, and a broad smile took his expression. Like his son, neither did he recognize her.

"*Gwyneth?* No . . . this beautiful creature cannot be little Gwinnie. The Gwinnie I know is only this high," he said, holding his hand out at waist level.

Gwyneth ran over to him and gave him a big hug. "Yes, it's me, Papa Allyn!" She held onto him for several moments, then, at last, with tears streaming from her eyes, she looked up into his rugged face and carefully searched his eyes. "Does my father still live?"

Allyndaar again smiled broadly. "That old warhorse? My child, he will outlive us all!"

Gwyneth let his words take hold of her mind, then she buried her head into his chest and wept joyfully.

Suddenly Allyndaar jerked his eyes up from the girl and peered around the campsite. "Where is Aeryck?"

"He is safe," Terryll said. "By his own choice he remained behind in Loch na Huric with Brynwald."

"*Loch na Huric! Brynwald?*" Allyndaar was astounded. "Is it just my mind that is reeling, or has the whole world suddenly gone mad?"

"No, Papa. But those who were once our enemies are now our brothers in Christ."

Over the next few hours, Terryll told his father everything that had happened, from the time he and Aeryck had arrived at Bowness until the battle with the Tuatha Baalg. He related also the story of Brynwald and his men in Ireland and the marvelous things that had happened there.

Dunnald picked up the story at that point and told of their return to Loch na Huric, their confrontation with Sarteham, and how Aeryck had distinguished himself in battle against him. Each warrior in turn added his perspective to the events, polishing the details, of course, with only the slightest of embellishments. Even the women chimed in, bragging unabashedly of Terryll and Aeryck's brave rescue attempt, not wanting of course to be outdone by the men.

Allyndaar was amazed and kept shaking his head at all of the wondrous news. Throughout the evening Dunnald's men sat looking upon the chieftain of Killwyn Eden with awe. They were all younger than Dunnald and had not fought along the Wall as did Brynwald and he, but Allyndaar's feats were legendary even among his enemies, especially among his enemies. In their eyes he was a mighty man of valor—a hero of renown—and they gave him their unqualified respect. There would be stories to tell back at Loch na Huric.

At some point Oswald and Duncan staggered into the camp, each rubbing a new lump on the back of his head. Both looked at Allyndaar and wondered who he was and where he had come from. It didn't occur to either, until later, that he had been the one who had relieved them of their duty. They were young.

And so the evening passed under the witness of a host of stars. The fire burned low to a bed of black and reddish coals, during which time a bond was formed, and a pledge struck, between the people of Loch na Huric and the people of Killwyn Eden, between the chieftains Allyndaar and Brynwald, with Dunnald acting as mediator and surrogate for the latter.

No one got any sleep, so they were off to an early start. Long before sunup, Allyndaar and Terryll bade Dunnald and his men farewell and were soon following the southern banks of the Solway Firth toward Bowness.

They had made good friends. A visit would be in order, either to Loch na Huric or to Killwyn Eden to celebrate it—perhaps during the feast of Christ's Mass.

Allyndaar and Terryll split the packhorses into two strings and each took one. Gwyneth rode up front with them, while the women followed behind in pairs, each entertaining her own anxious thoughts privately. They could have taken the road on to Carlisle, which lay on the British side of the Wall, affording them an easier go of it. But that would have added hours to their journey, so it was ruled out at once. As it was, they had only to make one river ford, and the rest was a pleasant ride.

Daybreak found the column of horses entering the mile-castle just outside Bowness. They had made good time. Immediately there was a release of pent-up anxiety, and many of the women started laughing and chattering excitedly about anything. They were home again—Mother Britain.

Inside the mile-castle were two older guards (apparently all that Bowness could muster for a first line of defense) in place of the men killed by Sarteham's raid. One of the men opened the heavy oaken gates, while the other stood above on the parapets and waved them through. Each wore the once-fierce battle countenance that perhaps terrorized a forgotten enemy and stood proudly at his post. They smiled and waved cheerily as the riders passed through the wall, happy to welcome them home, happy to once again be of service.

The column was soon enveloped in the thick woods surrounding Bowness. Leaves were falling everywhere as a continual offering of the trees to the earth, and the dawn's light dappled the floor with cool shadows that rippled as though in adulation.

Terryll looked over at Gwyneth. She was beautiful, more beautiful than yesterday (or so it seemed to him), more so than the day before. He was possessed of a singular ambition.

She was staring straight ahead and didn't notice him. Her eyes were tight with apprehension, upon her countenance were inscribed uncertain epitaphs. A great sorrow encompassed her.

Terryll let her be. However, his eyes attended her closely. Presently, feeling the pull of his eyes, she darted a quick smile at him. Her eyes were wide and imploring as though poised on some tenuous brink. Then she looked ahead, composing herself.

Tempest, however, was quite upset and cared little for composure. He liked it not one bit that this new horse, who had come along late in the game, was upsetting the pecking order. Daktahr, on the other hand, couldn't have cared less. He knew his place well—in the lead—and he stayed there.

Tempest shook his mane and whinnied and blew out snorts. He pulled continuously against the reins to catch up to him, making for a miserable ride. Daktahr answered him by nonchalantly whipping his tail back and forth in his face and blowing great blasts of contempt himself.

As they cleared the trees, Bowness immediately rose into view atop its blunted promontory, and the laughter and chatter quickly died to a hush. Everyone felt it at once. Tears were soon falling from every eye, as the crush of reality and emotions met at last upon the salient brow before them.

Gwyneth let the whole of it go and sobbed. She covered her face, but her heaving shoulders betrayed her anguish. Sophie was gone. She would never see her smiling face again.

Terryll reached over and comforted her.

"Mama! Mama! Come quickly! It's Papa and Terryll! They're home!" Dagmere shouted excitedly, cupping her hands over her eyes to shield them from the morning light. "And there's a long line of women and horses with them!"

Dagmere stood at the gates of Bowness as the warming sun was just catching its wooden palisades. The column was a quarter mile away.

Moments later, Helena was at her side, straining her eyes to see. Then, finding the long line of horses threading out of the tree line, she burst into tears. "God be praised!" she cried.

Dagmere continued to scan along the line, counting each head as they emerged from the trees.

"Six . . . seven . . . there are eight—no, nine," she said happily, as the last of the women made the clearing. "That's all of them!"

Then she waited for another horse, *the* other horse. It didn't come. Surely it would. She waited. There were now several horse lengths between the last horse and the timberline. Dagmere stood on tiptoe suddenly as if to get a clearer view and watched anxiously. Nothing. Then her eyes shifted quickly along the line as if she had made a miscount, darting back and forth from head to head. Panic knitted across her brow. She hadn't made a miscount. There was one head missing.

"I don't see Aeryck, Mother."

"How can you be sure, Dagmere? They're so far away."

"He's not there! Something's happened!"

"But—"

Before Helena could say another word to the contrary, Dagmere was running.

The word quickly spread that a column of women and packhorses was heading toward the village, and soon people were pouring out of the gates. Presently Helena felt someone at her elbow, and, turning, she saw it was Belfourt, his great bulk propped against two crutches and still in his nightclothes.

"What are you doing out of bed?" Helena chided. "You will open your wounds!"

If Belfourt heard her, he didn't show it. He shielded his face from the advance of the sun, and his alert, little blue eyes quickly found a mane of flaming red color near the head of the column. He paused a moment to consider it, a smile eased its way tenderly across his lips, then haltingly he lowered his thick hand to reveal great rivulets of tears wetting his cheeks and bushy beard.

Immediately the village bell began to ring out peals of laughter and merriment, heralding to one and all the advent of a joyous celebration.

Terryll looked back on the bittersweet expressions of the women behind him. Every face was wet with tears of joy mixed with tears of grief. But now, at long last, the healing could begin. Just behind his string of packhorses was Corrie, sitting her own mount, clutching the reins loosely, and she was staring at him. He could tell that she wanted to say something, but there was a great struggle working across her face that informed him that she couldn't. Not today anyway. Maybe one day. She managed a healthy smile, and that was enough for now.

Looking ahead, Terryll laughed to see Dagmere racing down the escarpment toward them, waving her arms.

"Papa! Terryll! You're home!" she cried out in a burst of tears.

Terryll waved to her, as did Gwyneth.

Helena watched from the gates as Dagmere reached the column of horses. She could see her following alongside them at the lead, talking with Terryll and Allyndaar, first embracing their legs to welcome them, then making inquisitive gestures with her hands. They were now about two hundred yards away, so Helena could read their attitudes, if not their faces.

Suddenly Dagmere stopped and stared for a long moment at Terryll as if he had struck her. She paused for several moments, letting the horses move ahead of her, then looked behind her toward the Wall. Turning sharply, she ran to catch up to Terryll. However, once reaching him, she slowed her pace, as though she were suddenly stripped of her wind or suddenly struck with a new thought. Finally, as the last of the horses passed her by, she stopped, sat down in the grass, and buried her head in her arms. Helena shook her head and sighed a prayer.

Terryll looked back at his sister and grimaced.

"Is she going to be all right?" Gwyneth asked.

"I don't know. I guess so."

"Aeryck is all she's been talking about since you boys left," Allyndaar said. "She'll take this hard. You'd best be mindful of what you say around her."

"I will."

Suddenly the baleful howl of a wolf pierced the morning air. It had an ominous quality to its voice that was unnerving.

Turning in his saddle, Terryll was not prepared for the sight that awaited him. Just inside the tree line amidst the shadows, not far behind them, was the largest pack of wolves he had ever seen. By a quick rough count there were at least two hundred of the animals, perhaps even more deeper into the trees. He couldn't tell for sure.

Letting go his string rope, Terryll immediately galloped toward his sister, unshouldered his bow, and fit an arrow. Reaching her, he extended his arm.

"Come on, Dag—get up. It's time to go!"

Dagmere was sullen. "I don't want to."

"I said, let's go! *Now!*"

Without waiting for her, he leaned over, grabbed her arm, and pulled her to her feet.

She protested angrily and began to withdraw her arm—until she caught sight of the wolves. Then without hesitation she flew up behind Terryll in a bound.

Immediately Allyndaar was there. His longbow was drawn and pointed at the trees.

"Have you ever seen so many wolves at once, Papa?" Terryll asked.

"No, I haven't. Nothing like it."

The wolves were moving at a lope, heading northward over the earthen berm of the Wall. Wherever they were going, they seemed in a hurry to get there.

Suddenly one stopped and stared intently at the little group of riders, eyeing each carefully, holding its yellow-eyed gaze on Terryll the longest. It was a large wolf, around one hundred fifty pounds, with reddish-brown fur, grizzled tips, scars crisscrossing its snoot, and a torn ear. Two other wolves stopped briefly alongside it, cast quick glances at the three humans, then moved on. At length the first wolf bared its teeth with a snarl, threw its head back into a lupine arch, and howled. Then it took off with a dash and quickly reclaimed its place.

"The wolves are acting strange, Papa. I don't like it," Dagmere said, peering around Terryll's shoulder. "What's going on?"

"I don't know, Dag," Allyndaar answered reflectively. "I don't know." Allyndaar knew that wolves traveled in packs of eight to ten, like families. That there were so many in this group defied natural law. It was incredible. Then his thoughts recalled the night about a week before when he heard the wolves fighting in the mountains south of Killwyn Eden—and how it struck Helena that, even though they were mere animals, they seemed to be engaged in a terrible conflict between good and evil. It didn't make any earthly sense.

He shook his head, then turned Daktahr toward the gathering crowd outside the village gates, now receiving the women jubilantly, and put him into an easy lope.

Terryll lingered a moment and watched the last of the wolves disappear over the Wall, letting his thoughts shift anxiously between Hauwka and Aeryck.

A gust of wintry wind picked up and swirled around his head, sending shivers down his back. Winter was coming, was now sending its emissaries ahead over the countryside to warn. Soon the land would die and lie buried, quiet, beneath a shroud of ice and snow to await patiently spring's clarion call to life. Such was its hope. It had always been the natural order of the world.

Tempest whinnied and snorted and stamped his hooves, protesting the delay. The threat of the wolves had passed; there were no more glorious charges to lead; he now wanted only to race after the Arab stallion and pass him like the wind.

Then, with Dagmere clinging to his waist, Terryll reined the black charger toward the village and let him try.